Secrets of a Witch

by

Steph Ziders

Cover Art by *Lea Schizas*

The Wild Rose Press, Inc.
PO Box 708
Adams Basin, NY 14410-0708
Visit us at www.thewildrosepress.com

Publishing History
First Edition, 2025
Trade Paperback ISBN 978-1-5092-6174-1
Digital ISBN 978-1-5092-6175-8

Published in the United States of America

Dedication

This book is dedicated to all the people who have had their dreams change, and the support to pursue them.

Chapter 1

Praying to the Goddess, I rubbed my thumbs along my fingertips, itching for clarity. My second sight blurred and twitched like an old television trying to find reception. An unknown and unexpected energy disrupted the signal.

Focus, Shay.

"I see some water, maybe a river or a lake, surrounded by mountains. A man is walking beside you who's rocking a stylish mullet and mustache," I said to my eager customer sitting across from me when the mental images flickered.

"A mullet? Really?"

"They're coming back," I said. "He wears it well if that helps."

It was true—I saw it. Mother Goddess blessed me with the gift of premonitions. I could glimpse pieces of the future. With concentration, I could direct the visions to a person or a specific time.

"Are there any other details you could give me?" my customer, Cynthia, asked. Her freckled face bore an unmistakable look of anticipation as she swept some ginger hair away. "My family goes camping every year and there are always a few other families that go, too. Maybe my soulmate is one of them."

I reached for her hands, using the physical connection to dig deeper. Despite its psychic properties, my sapphire charm necklace wasn't doing enough. An invisible force tugged at my stomach, detaching my astral body and sending me through time and space until I stood beside her in the vision.

Pulsating orange auras outlined Cynthia and the mullet-wearing dude. They walked around a shimmering lake surrounded by a lush forest. She giggled at him, and he looked at her with lust in his eyes.

I pulled my astral body back to the present, smiling at her. "Your auras match. Proof the man in the vision is your soulmate."

Would they last? No clue, but I trusted my powers. The online ratings and testimonies The Wise Whitleys received solidified my confidence.

"Oh my god," she whispered. "How am I going to know? Will there be a neon sign that only I can see or something?"

"Not quite. I'll try to find more details."

The air whooshed past my ears again and felt the tell-tale tug at my navel. Only seeing fuzzy outlines of her and her soulmate, I breathed in, smelling grapefruit and jasmine wafting around me from the Virgo incense.

Vroom, vroom, vroom.

Inside her vision, my astral body turned to look behind me, expecting to see a motorcycle, but there was none.

Vroom, vroom, vroom.

I breathed in again, deeper, allowing the incense to calm my brain. The sweet smells permeated my nose and floated around me in the vision. Finally, a name appeared above the man's head, clear enough for me to make out the initials. I exhaled, opening my eyes, reorienting in the present.

"His name has the initials H. R." I dropped her hands, running mine over the cloth, ridding the moisture from my mental exertion.

"Oh wow. Wow," she said with wide eyes. "I usually hate camping with my family, but now I'm super excited. You can't offer me any more information?"

I smiled and stood, motioning for her to follow me through the store for payment.

"I can only see what the Fates allow me to see. It's best to not know too much about your future."

"I get it. Free will and all that," she said as she searched her purse.

I studied her for a moment, noting the paint speckles on her overalls and wild hair. Despite my judgements of her being a free-spirited, artist-type, she was insightful. Her conclusion was accurate. Humans were lesser beings than the celestial gods and goddesses who couldn't understand the strands of life choices that the Fates wove under the veil of "free will". Unless given the sight, like me.

"Thank you so much, Shay," Cynthia said, handing me money. "You truly are a talent. I will never forget this." She waved and left the store heading out into our small town of Ipswich, Massachusetts.

"That seemed like a struggle," a soothing but accusatory voice came from beside me at the register.

I turned toward my mother, Sandy Whitley. The pixie features of her nose and rounded cheeks were the same as mine. We were both petite and curvy. However, my lips were fuller and my eyes were blue, features inherited from my father.

Mom's hazel eyes zeroed in on me. She tucked a piece of her graying hair behind her ear, adjusting it back into her long-side braid. She was reading me, knowing that I was hiding something. My mom was an empath–a damn good one, too. Once she connected with a person, she felt their emotions no matter the distance. Imagine having a mom who felt your emotions when you started puberty. Not fun.

We came from a long line of witches, The Whitley Clan. Every female in my family was blessed with being a witch. The power of clairvoyance surged through our blood; it came in all shapes and sizes.

"I'm just distracted." I attempted to lie under her lasered scrutiny.

Mom leveled me with a look, silently calling me out on my bullshit. "Let's do a reading."

"Mom." I sighed her name like a child, although I wasn't a child. I was twenty-four. "I'll do one later. By myself."

She flicked her hand in a dismissal and walked back toward the cove where we conducted our readings. "How many times do we have to have this conversation? Magic works best when it's done together. Not alone. There're reasons why witches belong to a coven," she said.

I shuffled along the worn wooden floors of our family's mystical store, The Wise Whitleys, a Wiccan-centered store passed down through the generations. I plopped down in one of the plush purple chairs, still warm from Cynthia.

Mom sat beside me at the same time as she opened a burnt orange ornate box behind her on the bookshelf. She pulled out a hand-painted deck of tarot cards that she used for her readings. The cards had yellowed around the edges and some of the corners were ripped.

"I like things my way. Have you seen how beautiful the bookshelves look in rainbow and alphabetical order? Things can get messy when different personalities are involved," I said. "And I do stuff with the coven a lot."

Mom closed her eyes, indicating that she was done with my argument. When she opened her eyes, they held only seriousness. "It's okay to lean on someone now and then. You don't need to navigate the world alone." She slid the tarot cards across the table toward me.

I picked up the cards and shuffled them three times, choosing to ignore her statement. I've heard it before. I made three piles with the cards: the past, present, and future. I turned the top card from the past pile over–Judgement, upright. Judgement was depicted with an Archangel blowing a horn onto people praying to him.

I did the same with the second pile: the present.

Death, upright.

I scrunched my eyebrows, studying. The skeleton, dressed as a knight riding on his steed, stared at me.

I turned over the top card on the last pile: the future.

The Ace of Cups: upright.

I exhaled loud enough to be heard throughout the whole store. The overflowing chalice on the card held my attention, mocking and taunting me.

"Interesting," Mom said in a soothing tone. "What do they mean together?"

"Okay, well, Judgement is in the past," —I cleared

my throat.— "calling out the death of my normal life and the birth of my new witch life. Death is upright in the present position. A major transition or change is coming."

"Maybe the change is what's distracting you today," Mom added.

I shrugged but continued. "The Ace of Cups, in the future spot."

My mother's eyes popped open in surprise. A smile grew on her face. "A new romance, perhaps!"

I groaned. "The Ace of Cups doesn't necessarily mean romance. It could just mean emotional fulfillment. I don't have any romantic interests."

"What about Dean?" Mom asked with a gleam in her eye.

"Mom, you know he's just a friend."

I had known Dean Fellows all of my life. He was gorgeous in that All-American Boy way that made the locals swoon and the tourists drop their panties. He was also my oldest friend and a warlock.

Mom slid her long braid over her shoulder. "Fine, I'll drop it. What do the cards mean when you put them all together?"

"It means…" I paused. My eyes flitted along the cards, taking in all their meanings. I knew all the cards and their independent symbolism by heart. My mother taught me their meanings like other mothers taught their toddlers the alphabet.

"Death tells me that change is coming, as a bridge for my past and future. Possibly a change in my current life, like a new relationship that connects to my witch life. One that will fill me with happiness." My tone dripped with dramatic sarcasm.

"Agreed," Mom said, ignoring my theatrics. "I guess whatever is disrupting the energy today has something to do with the Ace of Cups." One finger pointed to the card in the last position. "Definitely a lover."

"Mom–" I started but was cut off by her bracelets banging against each other as she waved her hands. She stood, dropping a kiss on my head.

"Change is coming for you, Shay Moon Whitley. Will you be ready?" She left before I could respond, heading back into the store's main room.

I analyzed the three cards again. I hated change. I liked my world to be in order. Routines and plans were my bread and butter.

What were the Fates planning?

****

Later that night, I finished logging numbers in the store's electronic books and sighed, sitting back in my chair. The backroom was where we kept our files and inventory. I dug my hands through my long blonde hair, squeezing the sides of my head.

"Shit," I said to no one. "We lost money again this month."

I shook my head back and forth. We would be in trouble if the store continued down this financial path. After the computer turned off, I stood. My shirt brushed along some papers that were stacked. A few flittered down to the floor. I cursed, bending to pick them up.

Thanks for using my perfect filing system, Mom and Gram.

A bright orange envelope with the Ipswich Bank logo in the corner fell from the group.

Shit. Again.

I threw the other papers back on the table, swiped the orange envelope, and ripped it open.

Dear Sandy Whitley,

It has come to our attention that the current lease on your property located at 7 Main Street is in danger of non-renewal. Your lease will expire on November 30 unless the below amount is paid in full.

Amount due: $8,500

Sincerely,

Partners at Ipswich Federal Bank

The paper shook in my hands as I reread the notice. What the Hectate was this? How did something this important get forgotten? If Mom had used the filing system…

I rushed through the threshold that separated the backroom from the main room of our store. I snatched my purse from under the counter, rifling through it to find my phone.

I hit my mom's name.

Ring. Ring. Ring.

I knew she felt my rage, so she needed to pick up NOW.

No answer.

A heavy, long exhale escaped me, trying to calm the storm that raged inside me. I squeezed my hands into fists. If we lost our business—what would we do?

No rabbit hole jumping just yet. I needed to think. I needed to slow down and take in everything. I released my fists, spreading my fingers out wide. I needed to plan.

Step one, finish closing up the store.

Step two, repost the mail filing rules.

Step three, call my mother again on the way home.

Step four, brainstorm ways to get money and fast.

Preparing and executing a plan was a mechanism perfected over the years, more so when my powers started at sixteen. Being thrust into a vision with no warning was chaotic enough, add in a healthy dose of teenage horomones—disaster.

The tension in my shoulders eased with my focus on my nightly routine and the start of a plan. I straightened the merchandise, blew out anything that might be burning, turned out the lights, and locked the doors behind me.

While walking along the sidewalk, I breathed in the fall air. Autumn's crispness was in the air, causing me to pull my oversized sweater tighter around my body.

My phone buzzed. *Finally.*

Mom Calling.

"What the hell, Mom?" I questioned her without a greeting. "The lease is ending on our storefront."

She sighed on the other end.

"That's it?" I screeched, causing some birds to squawk from nearby trees. "We could lose the store and all you do is sigh?"

"Watch your tone, Shay. We've gotten these notices before and it hasn't stopped us."

"There have been OTHER notices!?"

"A few over the years, but The Wise Whitleys have been a staple in this town since the late 1600s, sweetie. We'll pull through. You know this story. Your ancestor, Alice Whitley started the store as a medicinal apothecary that she ran with her husband and daughter, Lucia. It grew into the Wiccan solace it is today. Don't you think she had struggles?"

My faux leather sneakers crunched on the early

fallen leaves that littered the sidewalk. I rolled my eyes toward the sky as it turned from a burnt orange to a deep red and purple while the sun set in the distance. The colors that exploded in the changing sky were intoxicating, drawing me in and soothing me at the same time. As a witch, I value color and the role it plays.

I prayed to the Mother Goddess for patience.

"I understand that, Mom. But, Alice and Lucia aren't running the store now. We are."

"That's true. And we will band together and pull through like we've always done. You, me, and Gram." Her words didn't soothe me.

"How can you be so confident in this? The notice said we had two months to pay the rent. We don't have that kind of cash."

"Shay. It's late." Mom sighed. "Your Gram has been talking to the spirits all evening and it's giving me a headache. I can feel her emotions, yours, and the spirits'." Her voice was laced with strain and exhaustion. I held my tongue as she continued. "We will talk about this tomorrow. We aren't losing the store tonight."

"Mom…"

"Everything will be fine. Love you, Moonbeam."

My lips shifted to the side. My resolve melted hearing her nickname for me. "Love you, too," I said, ending the call.

I stopped under a streetlight in front of the entrance to the Ipswich Cemetery. A crumbling stone wall separated me from the town's sacred grounds. Tall sculpted tombstones cast long dark shadows as the sun set behind them. Many of my ancestors were buried there, including Lucia. She was only a teenager when the Whitleys settled here. According to my mom, Lucia had the power of premonition, like me, and foresaw the Salem Witch Trials.

A cold breeze swept around me, freezing me in place. Goosebumps rose on my arms and up my neck. I scanned the streets, seeing nothing. Never before had my powers given me a complete pause. A tug at my navel flared to life and flung me into a different time and space. Fuzzy sepia-hued images flashed in my mind's eye.

I stood in the same spot in front of the iron gates to the cemetery entrance. Instead, it wasn't the cemetery it was in the present. It was just a field of open trees surrounded by a cobblestoned wall and a few gravestones.

Long dark hair flew in the wind behind me.

I looked down, noting my attire. A bodice and flowy skirt.

My head moved around as if looking for someone.

A rumble shook the ground below my worn leather boots.

Vroom. Vroom. Vroom.

I startled out of my vision, being thrust back to the present. My heart raced in my chest, swaying on my feet, struggling to reorient myself to my current surroundings.

Vroom. Vroom. Vroom.

I spun around, clutching my chest as the sound of a rumbling motorcycle careened toward me. A matte black machine roared to a stop beside me, causing me to step back. A man, wearing a leather jacket with sweatshirt sleeves, helmet, and white sneakers, stepped down on the ground as he straddled his motorcycle.

The man flipped up his helmet's visor, revealing his eyes. In the light from the streetlamp, his bright green eyes stood out in a deep contrast to the black of his helmet. The color of the mystery guy's eyes drew me in like a moth to a flame. They were the color of brand-new leaves shining in the morning light.

The cool air pocket I felt dissipated into a blazing heat. An electric current zapped in the atmosphere, keeping me on edge.

"Are you okay?" the man asked.

I blinked again and shook out my body from its rigid position. "Um. Yeah."

"I saw you from down the street. You looked like you were in pain or something."

"Totally fine," I lied.

His head tilted. "That's not what it looked like to me. What are you doing out here by yourself at night, anyway?"

I blinked in response to his question.

Who was this guy?

I crossed my arms over my chest. "Do you always approach women while they're walking by themselves in their town? A town that I was born and raised in."

Mystery Man laughed behind his helmet. "No. But, I do have a weakness for people in danger, and as I said before, you looked like you were hurt."

I snorted. "Thanks for the concern. I'm fine."

"I can see that," he said. His eyes raked over me, up and down. A strange jittery sensation flared to life, reaching down to my core.

"Okay. Well, bye," I snapped, wanting out of this conversation. I tried to move away, but my feet were still stuck in place. Fate's presence danced along my skin, keeping me here.

"Wait. Before you go," he called out as I tried once more to turn away. "I was hoping you could help me. I'm looking for Tree Top Apartments. GPS was working…"

"Cell service is spotty in this area."

The man pushed up his sleeves. My eyes flicked to a dark inked design on his entire forearm. I recognized it immediately. It was an elaborate black and gray depiction of the Capricorn symbol: a strong sea goat. The horns curled around the strong cords of his forearm and the tail swirled at his elbow. The image was stunning and seductive. The flutters in my stomach heightened.

"Um, the directions?" the man asked again.

"Sorry." I cleared my throat and the daydream. "Yeah, just keep going down this road, turn left at the town square, and it'll be right there. Ipswich is a really small town. You won't get lost."

"Any places where to get food?"

"The Witch's Brew is an old dive bar that has some really good food."

He nodded and hiked up on his toes to start the engine of his motorcycle. The loud ignition vibrated against my chest, shaking my bones.

"Thanks," he yelled over the rumbles. He flicked his visor back over his eyes and revved the engine. He drove off, leaving me staring at the fading red glow of his tail light.

A stronger tug pulled at my navel and brought my attention back. My body felt fuzzy as my power activated in my mind's eyes. My eyes squeezed shut, taking a deep breath.

AGAIN?

My astral body propelled me through space and time, showing a series of images.

Me.

Tents and booths were set up in the town square.

Many people chatted and smiled.

A man with a strong back and a confident stride carried boxes in his hand, helping two women.

A strong warmth swelled in my chest as he neared and planted a kiss on my cheek.

I stumbled backward, colliding with the cobblestone wall. Rubbing my fingers across my forehead, I regained my balance again.

What the fuck was happening right now?

Two unprompted visions in a matter of minutes. One in the future and one in the past. That was impossible. I had only seen the future before.

My world felt like it was spinning. There were too many unknowns. Too many questions without answers.

Chapter 2

An arm slapped down on my shoulders. I recognized the energy instantly. It soothed the storm that raged under my skin. My shoulders sagged, releasing the tension that had been holding them tight.

"Hi, Dean," Lackluster hung in my voice.

"Hey. What's wrong?" he asked, tuning into my energy as effectively as I did with his. Being a warlock, Dean had the ability to read and interpret energies. Being my friend, he learned to hone those interpretations.

"I can't even begin to tell you." Our footsteps were heavy as we walked along the sidewalk.

"Yes, you can. I'm all ears." Dean was persistent. That's one of the qualities that made his mayoral run impressive. "I'm the mayor, Shay. Tell me all your problems and maybe I can help you." He was also smug. A trait he had no doubt inherited from his family. The Fellows were as well known as the Whitleys. Fellows men held positions of power for many generations. Was it nepotism? Yes. Were they effective in their roles? Yes.

Dean was tall and bulky, with dirty blonde hair. He wore it clean and styled, cut close to his head with a swoop at the front. He took a lot of pride in his appearance. His teeth were perfect and his posture was regal. It came with the territory of being mayor.

Being a Scorpio and a traditional warlock, Dean spent a lot of time in the graveyard, and with his scientific tools, dabbling in Goddess knew what. We joked that he secretly hoped to be a necromancer. His mystical powers specialized in conjuring, or spell-casting. He was always mixing different elements to come up with various spells.

"I found a statement from the bank," I began. "The lease is ending on the store at the end of next month. And of course, Mom and Gram refuse to use the filing system I set up or else I would have seen the other notices."

"Oh, shit."

His body tensed as his brain backpedaled into its natural problem-solving mode. Dean liked to find solutions, weaving the scenarios with different variables into a simple web. He had an analytical mind. It was one of the qualities that we bonded over. I was street-smart, organized, and intuitive, and he was book-smart and a research lover.

"What are you going to do?" he asked.

"I don't have a fucking clue. Right now I'm just mad."

"That's understandable." He pulled me into a side hug.

I peeked up at him, finding his warm caramel eyes filled with sympathy as they met my gaze. His lips tipped up into a pity smile.

"Do you want to have a movie party? Pig out on all your favorite candy." He wiggled his eyebrows.

I laughed. "Honestly, I'm exhausted. Too much is happening right now. I just want to snuggle in my bed." I checked the time on my phone. "Plus, Mildred is probably dying of hunger."

"Ha. You're probably right there."

We came to a stop at the crossroads between our apartments.

"I appreciate it though," I said, removing myself from his embrace.

He smiled, tucking his hands into his khaki skinny pants. "I'll do—"

"Some research," we said at the same time before laughing. Dean shook his head.

"Yeah, I'll do that and see if there's anything that can be done. But, more than likely there isn't. Banks and mayors work separately," he said.

"I'll take anything at this point. This is my livelihood. My legacy." I swallowed past the lump forming in my throat. I was cruising at a high speed past anger toward worry.

Dean grabbed my upper arm, squeezing it.

"Shay. Take a few deep breaths. Do some tarot. Light a candle. Tomorrow's a new day."

I nodded, letting his words sink into my psyche. Doing some tarot sounded like a good idea. I could always rely on Fate to show me guidance.

"We're still on for the Halloween party at the end of the week, right?" Dean asked.

I smiled. "Duh. It's our annual tradition."

Dean's smile mirrored my own, his eyes sparkling with excitement.

"Good. I'll catch you later. Try to forget about all of this bad stuff. Just for tonight. Okay?"

"Okay," I conceded. With a wave, we went in our separate directions. I was thankful for his friendship. We both knew, though, all the shit that went down today wasn't going to be forgotten until there was a plan.

I scurried the rest of the way to my apartment and climbed the stairs. My legs felt like bags of wet cement under my ass. Electric currents continued to run under my skin and my brain felt like goo as it worked overtime to process.

My apartment was behind a colonial-styled bed & breakfast, The Sapphire Sisters, located a few blocks away from Main Street. Wilma and Agnes owned the bed & breakfast and my apartment. They were witches, too.

The two-bed/ two-bath space was perfect for me and my roommate, Harmony. It had an open kitchen that faced the living room. The furniture was either vintage from antique stores or hand-me-downs. Trinkets, Wiccan books, candles, crystals, and tarot cards lined the built-in bookshelves around the exterior walls of the living room. Several celestial tapestries and band posters hung on the walls.

My gray tabby cat, Mildred, greeted me with a poised meow. She perched on the counter, facing my direction, swishing her fluffy tail from side to side.

"What took you so long? I'm hungry," she spoke into my mind.

"Sorry, Your Majesty," I said, ignoring her attitude. "There's some kitty krispies or cat food in a can. Which one do you want?"

I flung my hair up into a messy top bun, using the threaded bracelet on my wrist as I waited for her answer. I toed my shoes off, shoving my feet into my seafoam-colored fuzzy slippers, and opened the cabinet where Mildred's food was.

"Mildred? Which one do you want?" I asked, turning to face her.

She stared at me with an impatient resting-bitch-face. Her pink tongue flicked out over her whiskers, clearly unhappy with the food choices.

"You could always go hunt for mice or something if you are that unhappy with the food selection."

Mildred hissed. Her muzzle curled. *"I would never stoop that low. Hunting is for animals."*

"You *are* an animal. You messed with dark magic, got caught, and punished to be a cat and my familiar. Now, listen, Ms. Priss. I had a really shitty day. The energy shifts. Two unprompted visions. Store problems. Cut me some slack."

Mildred jumped off the counter. She wrapped her body around my ankles, rubbing her warmth on me and purring.

"Sorry. I get bitchy when I'm hungry. Want to talk about it?"

I squatted down to scratch behind her ears before picking her up and holding her tightly in my arms. She purred loudly, snuggling her face underneath my neck.

"No. I don't want to talk about it."

A voice called out from the bedroom on the right. "Are you talking to me, yourself, or the cat?"

"The cat," I said.

Harmony emerged from her room with a towel wrapped around her slim body. Her hair was tied in a knot at the top of her head. Mildred jumped from my hold and sauntered over toward Harmony, perching on the counter again.

"I wish Mildred could talk to me in my head." She pouted. Her dark-painted nails scratched the top of

Mildred's head.

Harmony Silang was my best friend. She was a fiery, Filipina, punk-rock chick with long dark locks and dramatic winged eyeliner. She commanded the attention of everyone in the room, guys and girls alike. A textbook Leo and one of my few valued friendships. On the first day of first grade, Harmony sat down beside me at a table and bit a boy's arm, leaving teeth marks on his skin for calling me a "freak." She got in trouble, but the boy left me alone. I hadn't been able to get rid of her since.

"No, you really don't," I groaned. "She's super annoying and you're a Quaint."

Harmony pouted…again. "But, I *am* acquainted with the supernatural, so being a Quaint doesn't really apply to me, does it?"

"You're right, Harmony, but since you don't have any active powers…" We've had this conversation many times. Quaint was short for *unacquainted* or someone who had no clue about the supernatural. "You have a date?"

"Yes. With one of the guys on the force." She pretended to flick her hair, giving me a confident smile.

"Oh fun. Which one?"

Harmony looked at her nails, before looking at me smiling. "It's with Cute Cop. What's his real name?"

"Brad."

"Oh, Brad is sex on a stick," Mildred purred.

I gave Mildred a look and laughed. Harmony ignored our silent conversation. She was used to it.

"Brad. That's right," she said, lifting a shoulder. "Who knows? Maybe Brad is my soulmate." She wiggled her eyebrows.

"I can do your reading."

Harmony closed her eyes and shuddered. "No, thank you. I'm fine with *searching* for my soulmate by myself." A flirty gleam sparkled in her eyes. We laughed together before she left to get ready.

"Why don't you and Dean join her and Brad?" Mildred stared me down. *"They're friends, right?"*

"Yeah, they are. Go on a date with Dean? I don't know…That would be like dating my brother."

"It could be fun…if Dean wasn't a prick. You know he likes you, right?"

"Everyone in town knows, Mildred. Get some new gossip," I sassed, setting her food bowl in front of her. Mildred dove her snout into her food bowl.

"Dean is *just* a friend."

Mildred paused her eating and blinked at me.

"What? It's true. We've been friends since we were in diapers."

"Speaking of diapers…he's got a fine ass. You don't want to see what it looks like?"

"Oh, my Goddess. Stop. I don't want dating advice from you. I'd like to fall in love, not settle. I would have known if Dean and I were meant to be by now."

Mildred sidled up to me, stretching her body to rub her face along my jawline. *"The downfalls of your gift."*

"Isn't that the fuckin' truth. Who knows, I'm probably destined to be alone."

Mildred snorted. *"Well, if that's the case, we can grow old together and you can knit me ugly cat sweaters."*

I groaned, overcome with all the change. Mildred rubbed her face along my cheek and hairline.

"There's nothing wrong with change, Shay," she said, sensing my doubts. *"Some might even say it's good."*

"Change is scary," I whispered into her fur. "Change can lead to failure."

"Failure also leads to success. Maybe it's time to step out of your comfort zone."

Images of my visions swam together in my mind. The things I felt and saw in them were out of my comfort zone. I scratched Mildred's fur, letting her warm and simple courage seep into me.

"The store's lease is up in two months, which we don't have enough money for," I said, halting Mildred's purrs. "And I think I had a vision of the past."

Mildred smacked me. Her neon eyes were wide. *"What the...Shay?!"*

"Now, do you see why I might be a little resistant to love? There's too much other shit happening right now."

She twitched her head. *"Can Dean help?"*

I leaned back. "He's going to try. But for being the mayor, I'm sure there are laws about his direct involvement."

I cupped Mildred's face, bringing her tiny pink nose to mine. I gave her nose kisses. "Enough of this for now. I'll think of something. I always do. It's getting late."

"Thank God...sleep..." she yawned, stretching out her whole body.

"Don't you sleep all day?"

Mildred knocked her bowl off the counter with a loud clunk as she sauntered into my room.

"Ahh!" Harmony yelled from her room. "Mildred!

For fuck's sake. That dish better had been empty."

I laughed.

"Have fun on your date, Harm!" I called, following Mildred into my bedroom. Sleep was a powerful tool—restorative and purposeful. After the day I had, Mother Goddess knew I needed some of that.

****

I wrapped my deep green blanket around me as I scrolled through my phone. I peeked at the clock, grimacing: midnight. I stared at the darkened ceiling of my bedroom watching the shadows of the large oak tree flicker like long fingers. The only sounds in the apartment were Mildred's loud snores.

I expected sleep to happen quickly, but my mind had other plans. Thoughts of the store, tarot cards, my visions, and Mr. Motorcycle swirled in my head like a tornado, twisting and turning around each other in a complex dance.

I sighed, turning over in bed for what felt like the millionth time. My body was screaming for sleep, but my brain didn't care. I stared at the window, watching the breeze float through the tree. I don't know how much time passed, but eventually, my eyelids slid closed.

BANG!

Sweeping cold air blasted through my room, startling me. Mildred jumped four feet in the air with a snarl. The window had crashed open.

"What the...!" she screeched.

Chilly air blew through the room, knocking over candles and ruffling papers that were tacked to a corkboard. A few figurines and items fell to the floor.

"Shay! Get up and close the window. It's fucking

cold!" Mildred yelled in my head.

I shot from the bed, coming to my senses, and slammed the window shut. My chest heaved up and down, my body trembling as I pressed my hands against the window.

I opened my eyes and screamed, terror ripping through me. A ghastly sepia-toned silhouette of a woman stood behind me in the reflection. I whipped around, seeing nothing.

"What? Are you okay? Did you see something?" Mildred asked, her whiskers twitching as she sniffed the air. I ran a hand down my face as I stepped toward the bed.

"I have no idea. There was a woman behind me in the reflection of the window. She felt familiar…"

Mildred huffed and stretched her body, finding a cozy position. *"Maybe your powers are growing?"*

I flopped onto the bed, frowning. "Great. More change." I cuddled under the covers of my floral green blanket. My heart rate slowed and sleep pulled at my senses.

As my eyes drooped, a card sat in the middle of the floor. It must have fallen out of its resting place in the wind. I reached for it, turning it over: The Lovers.

"The fuck?" I whisper-yelled. My heart thumped against my rib cage as I stared at the two naked people standing together under a bright angel.

There are seventy-eight cards in a standard tarot deck, which meant there was a one-in-seventy-eight chance that this card would be the only one to be dislodged from the deck.

Another sign from Fate.

I shook out my hands, releasing the energy that

tingled there. I expected the Two or Seven of Pentacles, symbolizing wealth and finances, or even the Chariot, indicating a journey ahead.

What I didn't expect: the fucking Lovers.

I tried to take a calming breath through my seizing lungs. The Lovers didn't necessarily mean the obvious. It meant other things, like intuition with decisions, but in the back of my mind, I knew it meant love. A partnership. A relationship.

My eyes closed as I reeled that over in my mind. Who was Fate indicating? Love was tricky, unpredictable, and messy. Certainly, there wasn't any room for that in my comfortable world.

Chapter 3

The next day at The Wise Whitleys, I leaned on the counter, nursing a caffeine concoction and listening to my grandmother, Mom, Wilma, and Agnes' weekly gossip session. The older witches nestled in the vintage high-back chairs around a small round table used for crystal work.

"I think there's a newcomer," Wilma said. She was the older of the Sapphire Sisters, with short black hair, deep purple lipstick, and always smelled of lavender. She was an herbal witch, focusing on plants.

"You always think it's a newcomer and it turns out to just be a migrating flock of seagulls," Agnes said, tidying her long white hair that fell in waves down her back. She specialized in crystals. I owned many of her jewelry pieces. Wilma and Agnes were the embodiment of Yin and Yang. Total opposites but balanced.

"I do not," Wilma huffed.

"Yes, you do. You're just trying to make up for the fact that your power is in growing flowers, not premonitions," Agnes said. "I think it's the full moon. The air is always different when there's a full moon."

"Witch, *you* always think it's the moon."

"Will you two stop it?" Grandma Dotty pleaded, rubbing her temples. "I'll just ask around."

Grandma Dotty, or Gram, was the best kind of odd bird, with a constant bright shade of lipstick and painted nails to match. She spoke to the dead. Agnes and Wilma tsked together.

"The dead are hardly ever reliable," Wilma said.

"More reliable than you, old bat."

I laughed to myself as the old witches argued with each other. None of them had the power of premonition, so I didn't know why they even tried.

My mom stood beside me, holding the lease notice in her hand. "Did you lose sleep over this hogwash last night?"

"Maybe."

She rubbed her hand down my arm. "A little turmeric paste should clear up those dark circles."

"Have any thoughts about that?" I asked, pointing my head to the bank notice.

My mom shook her head. "You?"

"I've seen an uptick in online revenue since we launched the website last year, but it's not enough to cover the rent for another lease agreement. It's not a fast enough way to get money into the bank."

"I wonder if we could just buy the property," Mom suggested.

"That would solve our problems...if we had the money!" My pulse rose and pumped against my neck.

"We just need to work together to come up with ideas. We'll find a solution. We always do."

"This is why that filing system is in place, Mom. If you and Gram would just..." I threw my hands in the air. "Nevermind. I'll take care of it myself."

Mom stood to her full-petite height. "This isn't something you can deal with on your own."

"Yes, it is," I snapped, harsher than intended. "I'm the last living Whitley witch. If I fail, the Whitley line fails." A heavy weight fell on my shoulders threatening me to crush under its pressure.

Mom's eyes softened. She tucked a stray hair behind my ear, grazing her fingers down my face. Her love and care lessened my anger.

An infectious voice floated through the space, interrupting our conversation.

"Hello, my wicked witches!" Harmony announced. "Have I missed any juicy gossip?"

"Harmony!" the old witches crooned together.

"We were just talking about the rumblings in the town about a newcomer," Wilma started. "Hear anything?"

Harmony hung her black leather boho bag on the coat rack by the door, stopping at the bay window to pick up a Leo candle. She breathed it in deep.

"No," she said. "A tourist or a resident? Quaint or supernatural?"

"The spirits think he's going to be a permanent resident," Gram said.

Harmony's head perked up. "He?" She licked her ruby-red lips. Her pierced eyebrow cocked.

"It is a newcomer," I announced, deciding it was time to come clean. All eyes shifted to me. "He was kind of an over-protective jerk."

"You didn't think to tell us this when we first got here?" Wilma asked. I shrugged my shoulders.

"It was fun hearing you try to figure it out."

Agnes shook her bony finger at me. "I think you've forgotten the definition of gossip, missy."

"The cards were right. A new lover," my mom added.

"It was just a guy on a motorcycle. I didn't even

get his name," I argued. "And he scolded me for walking alone at night."

"Nothing wrong with a man checking on a woman alone. Very chivalrous," Agnes said.

"I call it alpha-asshole behavior," I said, getting a few chuckles.

"Regardless, I would have definitely gotten his name *and* number," Harmony crooned.

"That's because you're a little bit of a hussy, dear," Gram teased. Cackles reverberated through the store.

"OH! Starting strong this morning, I see," Harmony said. "Guess who I saw on my way over here?"

"Who?" Wilma and Agnes asked at the same time.

Harmony crossed one leathered leg over the other, setting the Leo candle down and pinning me with a look that spoke a thousand words. "Dean."

Oohs and aahs escaped everyone's mouths and a dreaminess clouded their gazes. Ever since Dean hit his twenties, he bulked up, lost his baby face, and attracted the attention of every female in town. Regardless of age.

"Dean's the mayor," I said. "It's his job to be around. Like an annoying insect."

"Insects are a very important part of our natural world. Many herbs and plants need insects," Wilma said. Silence descended on the space. I bit my lip to hide my laughter.

"Oh shut up, Wilma," Agnes groaned.

"Anyway…" Harmony said. "He asked about you. Said he was going to stop at the Brew later. We should have totally double-dated yesterday."

"Yesterday wasn't the best day, Harm," I said.

Harmony's face fell. "Oh?"

I took a few minutes to fill Harmony in on the day's events. Throughout the ordeal, her facial expression kept changing.

"Jeeeesus," she exhaled after I had finished. "That's a lot to deal with."

We all nodded, absorbed in our own thoughts.

Mom picked up the bank notice, scrunching her eyebrows.

"Shit," Harmony said as she stood, grabbing her bag. "Now, I hate that I have to leave. I want to hear the planning sesh."

"I'll bring you up to speed after our shifts," I said.

Harmony's lips tipped up, but only in the corners. "I did tell Dean you were working tonight. I bet he stayed up all night researching a solution."

"Probably. He *is* the master of research."

Harmony left with a wave, taking her effervescent energy with her. The air was thick and tense when she left. Silence filled the main room of my family's store again. Each of us grieving and reflecting on the potential of losing the store.

"We can't lose the store, Sandy," Gram said in a shaky voice, breaking the stuffy silence. "It's our legacy."

Mom's face fell, as she looked at Gram. "I know, Mom. Shay and I have already started thinking."

Gram's gray eyes were downcast, and she wrung her fingers together. A pit formed in my stomach. The weight on my shoulders grew heavier. I was confident I would buckle soon.

"Don't worry, Gram," I whispered. "I'm going to figure it out."

Gram's chin quivered as she swung her gaze to me. Her eyes were misty. "Our Whitley legacy is so important, Shay. The bloodline is precious and powerful. It needs to continue."

Wilma and Agnes bowed their heads with sorrowful grimaces.

Emotion clogged in my throat. What was I going to do? How was I going to save the store which ultimately saved the Whitley bloodline?

Gram's head snapped up and she gasped, drawing our attention. Her eyes widened. "The curse!"

Curse?!

Mom pinched the bridge of her nose. "How could I have been so blind?"

"Um, does someone want to fill me in? What curse?" I said, gazing around my coven.

Agnes and Wilma sat back in their chairs, shaking their heads. Their family was as old as the Whitley line. The looks on their faces told me they knew, too.

Gram cleared her throat, standing from her seat. She walked over to one of the walls that held old pictures of our family throughout the years. A pink-painted nail tapped on a picture of The Whitley Family that settled in Ipswich in the late 1600s.

I followed Gram. I had seen these portraits many times, but this was the first time they meant something more. My eyes zeroed in on Lucia Whitley, the daughter of Alice. She was petite, with a fierce face and determination in her eyes. Her long, dark hair flowed out behind her as she stared straight ahead. Her leather boots crossed at her ankles.

I scratched the back of my neck.

"As you know," Gram started, "Alice Whitley

started our store back during the beginning years of Ipswich. Back then, it was completely unheard of for a woman to own a business. Despite what the Ipswich council proclaimed, Alice found a loophole, using her husband, Samuel, as the 'on-paper' business owner. All the townsfolk knew it was Alice behind all the business deals. That, of course, made some of the men on the council angry."

"Wasn't one of the men on the council a Fellows?" Agnes asked.

My eyes widened. "A Fellows? Dean's family?"

Gram scratched her chin. "Agnes, you're right. He was about Lucia's age." She searched the pictures that hung on the wall until she found the right one. She pointed to an early painting of the Ipswich Council standing on the steps of city hall. "Here he is. Harrison Fellows."

I squinted my eyes, studying Harrison. There was nothing special about the way he looked, except his eyes. They reminded me of Dean's but with something hidden underneath.

"Okay. I'm sensing this story is more about Lucia than Alice. What happened?" I asked. Mom stepped next to me, placing her hand around my waist.

"The council found out that Lucia had actual magical powers, and although Alice had medical knowledge, Lucia was the one doing more," Mom said. "She was the one who helped get some of the witch families out of Salem during the trials. It was clear she was more powerful than most of the men on the council. They were probably jealous of Lucia's power. So, they cursed her. And our family."

"Dicks."

"Hear, hear," Wilma added. Agnes wore a sour look on her face.

"What does the curse have to do with the bank notice now?" I asked.

"I was told the curse focuses on Whitley women needing to have a man in their life and if they didn't have one, bad luck would fall upon them," Gram said.

The floor fell from under me, or so it seemed. The new information flooded my brain, adding more weight to our problems.

"Are you serious? That's fucking ridiculous."

"As much as I don't like your use of language," Mom scolded. "Yes, it is fucking ridiculous."

"Times were different back then," Wilma said. "Women couldn't do anything without a man. We were lesser, despite being the stronger of the two in the Wiccan culture. The men on the council had their egos bruised and did something about it."

"It makes sense," Agnes said. "Shay is about to be twenty-four, well past the right age for marriage, at least for back then. And she's the last in the Whitley line. The curse activated."

The curse activated.

The thought rattled around in my brain like an endless spin cycle.

I ran my thumbs along the pads of my fingers, trying to ground myself as I paced. This was massive and it changed everything.

It was all my responsibility.

Taking a deep breath, I said, "Are you implying that to protect the Whitley legacy, I need a man? In what way?"

They all nodded with confused looks on their faces,

offering no more information.

"That's totally barbaric and arcane. Mom. You didn't have a man in your life."

She played with the end of her graying braid. "I did," she whispered, her voice heavy with emotion. "And then your father came into the picture and I got pregnant with you. I suppose that was enough to pacify the curse. We don't know for sure. It's not like the curse is written down somewhere."

I threw my hands in the air. "Oh, great. So, all I need to do is get pregnant and I'll save both our store and our bloodline."

The only sound in the store was the tick of the dusty, ornate grandfather clock. With each second that ticked by, my body temperature rose. My cheeks flushed, and I began panting. Crumbling under the weight of the world.

Mom rushed to me, wrapping her arms around me.

"Shay, take deep breaths. You aren't alone in this." Her voice was soothing. She guided me to a chair and push my head between my legs. When I was younger, I got panic attacks. Over the years, I learned that planning, making lists, and organizing eased the attacks. They were also a clue that my power was emerging or growing.

With my head down, my body's center shifted, easing the pressure in my chest. Mom's hand ran up and down my back. Fresh oxygen flooded my lungs, bringing blood to my head. My heart rate slowed, and my mind cleared. Dean's face and goofy smile popped into my brain. A plan had formed.

Breathing slowly, I lifted my head, giving my coven a weak smile.

"I have an idea," I said. "What if I asked Dean to help?"

"Like as a business partner or something more?" Gram asked.

Mom swung her head in Gram's direction and then back at me. Her eyebrows furrowed and she toyed with her bracelets.

"He has that inheritance…" Agnes added.

"He's a pillar of our community…" Wilma said.

"He's pretty damn good-looking, too…" Gram chimed in.

All the women cast their eyes in my direction. Heat blossomed in my chest, drifting up my neck and flushing my cheeks. I hadn't thought that far…

Mom crouched in front of me, clutching my hands in hers. They were warm, and her grip was strong.

"Shay, what are you suggesting, exactly?"

"Dean has the means to help us with money and the stupid curse. Who better to have a partnership with than someone I've known my whole life?" I heard the hollowness of my voice. I wasn't fully on board with this solution, but I needed to save my family's namesake. For Mom. For Gram. For Lucia.

"What about love?" Mom's eyes locked onto mine as she asked the question.

I swallowed. My throat felt scratchy and tight. I wanted to look away from her stare, but couldn't.

"I can grow to love him." I heard the uncertainty in my voice, and I knew Mom felt it.

"Don't close off your heart, Shay," she said. "Love is worth fighting for." Her eyes misted with unshed tears and unknown secrets.

"He won't say no to her, Sandy. It's the perfect

solution," Gram said. Her voice was the most stern I've ever heard.

The alarm from my phone buzzed in my back pocket, indicating it was time for my second job. Mom's eyes held mine, locking me in. My heart broke under her gaze. She didn't like this plan. There was more she wanted to say, but we were out of time. I had to save the store and the legacy.

Dean was going to help me, no matter what my heart wanted.

Chapter 4

I hurried along the sidewalk toward The Witch's Brew, where I bartend a few times a week. My dark green Converse sneakers crunched on the early fallen leaves as I walked mindlessly down the street. So many thoughts swirled in my brain, I ran on auto-pilot.

"Shay..." a whispered moan sounded in my ear.

I stopped abruptly and looked around, only seeing the Ipswich Fire Department station. There was only one station in town. It was a traditional, colonial brick giant with bright red doors and signs indicating its services.

I hugged my arms around my body as chills ran up my spine. The smell of dirt, rot, and death wafted up my nose. I peered around, expecting to see a zombie or decaying body, but there was nothing. My feet were stuck to the ground, again. I couldn't move.

I was taken aback, caught off guard by the sudden rumble of deep voices coming out of one of the engine bays, just as two men exited. Chief Irons spoke animatedly. He was a large, stocky man with shoulder-length gray hair and a thick beard. He reminded me of a fisherman who had been lost out at sea for years. He was a fierce firefighter, an even stronger leader, and highly regarded in our community.

Familiarity drifted along my skin as I looked from Chief Irons to the other man. He had a large muscular back. Not bulky or wrestler-like build, but more muscular than most men. The cords of his arms and back were visible under his thin gray shirt. His sleeves were pushed up, revealing dark ink running down one of his forearms.

Was that a goat tattoo?

He stood with an easy confident stance with one hand in his pocket as he spoke with Chief Irons. My gaze drifted down his body, taking note of his thick thighs and tight ass. Flutters of nerves twisted in my gut as the atmosphere charged with attraction.

Like a lightning bolt, my brain sparked with recognition.

It was Mr. Motorcycle.

I blew out a resigned breath. Chief Irons saw me standing, stiff-legged in front of their three engine bays. He raised his hand in a wave.

"Evening, Shay, darlin'," Chief Irons called. "Tell your Mom I said hi, and that lotion worked wonders on my feet."

I flicked my hand up in a greeting. Mr. Motorcycle turned his body toward me. "Will do, Chief," I said, still plastered to the sidewalk.

Mr. Motorcycle had a strong, sharp jaw with stubble and a straight nose. He didn't turn all the way around, but I could tell from his profile he was handsome. Scratch that. He was fucking gorgeous. His eyes drifted down my body and back up as he smiled, before turning back around to continue his conversation with Chief Irons.

With their attention off of me, a strong breeze flew around me. It lifted the heaviness that held my feet to the ground. The unseen wall disappeared. I picked up a foot off the ground and moved down the sidewalk.

Wisps of charged air kissed my skin, and another invisible force tugged at my navel.

Not now...

I gripped my stomach and bent over slightly trying to gather control over my astral self. This was not the time or place for a freaking vision. After the days I've had, Fate was having a field day with me. Again, I was assaulted with a mirage of images as I fought against my power.

Me laying in bed.

A forearm clung to me from behind.

Feelings of warmth and safety.

The air around me whooshed as I jumped into a different time. I fell to my knees unaware that I teetered on the line of time between the present and the future.

Me in The Wise Whitleys alone.

A shadowy figure crowded me.

Coldness. Terror. Looking for an escape.

I clutched the sides of my head, curling into myself and resting my forehead against the cool, grassy earth. Soaking up the Earth Goddess's clarity, I breathed through the vision. I forced my astral self back to the present, smelling the dew on the grass, the leaves, and the dirt.

Feet scuffling sounded in my ears. I blinked my eyes several times as my premonitions faded.

"Shay? Are you okay?" A voice called out to me, sounding panicked.

I lifted my torso and sat back on my haunches, finding two sets of eyes on me. One familiar and brown, crouching on the ground. One intriguing and emerald green, looking down at me. Their stares shifted between me and each other.

"Dean," I said, facing him. My throat felt dry and scratchy. Dean held out his hand. He was dressed in his usual mayoral outfit: tight-fitting khaki pants, and a buttoned-up shirt, rolled at the sleeves. His shirt strained against the muscles of his biceps. His jaw was set and his eyes were light brown, like the color of a new tree bark.

I put my hand in his and he gently pulled me up. His eyes held mine. Concern was etched on his face. He cleared his throat, recognizing the signs of my distress.

"Low blood sugar again? How many times do I have to tell you to eat a better breakfast than cereal," he fake-scolded, covering for me in front of Mr. Motorcycle. I swiped at my blonde hair, removing a dead leaf from my loose waves.

"Sugar fuels my soul," I said, playing along with him. Though, I did really love sugar-filled cereals. Dean shook his head and rubbed my arm.

My eyes flicked to Mr. Motorcycle. More sparks zapped through me. The charge of the energy turned up to maximum levels. All the air in my lungs left. I coughed a few times, trying not to bring any more attention to my weirdness.

He was even more handsome up close without a helmet that covered his face. I blinked several times, fully absorbing the striking beauty of his face and his uniquely colored eyes.

Exactly how I remembered them from last night.

For a brief moment, my eyes unfocused and just stared, showing me Mr. Motorcycle's soft green and gray aura.

Mr. Motorcycle lifted one eyebrow in confusion.

"Aren't you the guy from last night?" I asked, blinking and trying to hide the awkwardness.

He smiled, which blinded me. "The guy you called an asshole? Yeah, that's me. Cade Thompson, the new firefighter."

I pulled on the sleeves of my jacket, covering my hands. "Shay Whitley. I thought I recognized your tattoo."

Cade looked down at his forearm, rubbing it with the other hand. "That was one hell of a sugar crash," he said as he tilted his head to the side, eyeing me.

"Cade, you said?" Dean spoke up, straightening his back. "It's nice to have a fresh face in our small town. I'm Dean Fellows, Ipswich Mayor." He held out his hand in a greeting with an overly fake smile.

Cade gripped Dean's hand, giving it a shake. They sized each other up. "Aren't you a little young to be mayor?"

"Yes, but don't worry. I've done my due diligence. I come from a long line of Fellows mayors."

"Oh, so nepotism is listed first on your CV?"

Dean laughed, although, his jaw ticked and his eyes hardened. Neither man made a good first impression and it was getting old. They puffed out their chests. The smell of testosterone permeated the air. I practically choked on their silent pissing contest.

"Okay…" I said. "Well, I need to get to work." I turned, facing Dean. "Harmony said you're coming to The Witch's Brew later, right?"

"Yeah," he said, keeping his eyes locked on Cade.

"Good. I need to talk to you about something important." I snuck a glance at Cade.

Dean's eyebrows dipped and he lowered his voice.

"About what just happened?"

"No. Something else."

Dean's eyes flicked back and forth between mine, reading me like he always did. He nodded.

"I'll be there," he said. Dean looked over my head at Cade. He cracked his neck as he relaxed the tension in his shoulders. He lifted his nose. "Cade, you have my hearty welcome to Ipswich. Not a whole lot of drama unless you get your gossip from the Grandmas." He winked, laying on his charm thick.

Cade squinted his eyes before giving Dean a small smile. He wasn't buying Dean's fake kindness. Frankly, I wasn't either. Dean smiled down at me and continued on his way.

I picked up my bag from the ground and turned toward the direction of The Witch's Brew. I needed to haul ass. I hated being late.

"Cade, a pleasure to meet you. Ipswich is a great town, but not very exciting for a firefighter, despite what the Gossiping Grandmas might tell you," I said, walking past him.

Cade smiled. A dimple punctured his cheek, making my knees weak. "I needed a change of pace compared to Boston." Cade ran up beside me. "Last night you mentioned a bar, Witch's Brew? And you just said it again now. I assume you know where it is."

"Um, yeah. That's where I'm going, actually," I pointed ahead of me. "I work there some nights."

"Perfect. I'll walk with you then. If you don't mind."

I pulled at my sleeves again. My palms grew moist. "It's a free country."

"We seem to have gotten off on the wrong foot last

night," Cade said, keeping my pace.

"Oh? You mean when you asserted your overprotectiveness on me. But, seeing as you're a firefighter, it makes a little more sense."

"You're a feisty one."

No comment.

"I apologize for making assumptions about you," he said, shocking me. "I am quickly learning that this is a small town and not a whole lot of crime. But, I will say this: women's safety is very important to me."

I cleared my throat, turning down my sass-o-meter. "Apology accepted." His candor was charming.

Jitters and electricity zapped my skin as we walked together. Over the years, cute tourists would drop into town. They were always fun little trysts, but nothing more. They were driven purely by arousal and lust.

The vibes with Cade were different. More serious. Unexpected. Troubling.

****

The Witch's Brew was *the* local bar in Ipswich, owned by Harmony's family. It was the definition of a dive bar. Your feet stuck to the floor, there were holes in the booth seats, and decór that littered the walls featured historical newspaper clippings of the witch trials and witch posters collected over decades. Dusty old frames filled in the rest of the wall space with photos of the locals' big fishing catches.

It was familiar and comforting, like The Wise Whitleys.

I pulled on the witch's broom handle, hearing the ding of the door's chime. A smell of grease, yeast, and liquor floated out the door.

"This is The Witch's Brew," I said to Cade. He

held the door with his hand above my hand, allowing me to go through the threshold first.

"I'm noticing a theme in this town," he said.

I chuckled, feeling more comfortable with him. "There's definitely a theme. Wait until you see the drink list."

"Man, dive bars are my kind of place," Cade said. "No lofty expectations."

I smiled to myself. It was my kind of place, too.

"Have a seat anywhere. I've got to get to prep before the evening rush comes in."

Cade smiled as he adjusted the ball cap on his head and replaced it. "Thanks for showing me the way, Shay."

With a small smile, I ducked behind the bar, setting my things down and clocking in. Wrapping a black apron around my waist, I started cutting up the garnishes for the tray. The entire time I was cutting and slicing, Cade's presence trickled along my skin from his seat at one end of the bar.

Harmony appeared from the back hallway, as I almost sliced my finger for the second time.

"Hey, girl," she greeted, staring at the knife and my fingers. She looked up at me. "Got everything you need for the night?"

"Um, yeah. I think so."

"You think so? You're missing the lemons," she quipped, staring into the large black garnish tray.

"Shit," I hissed. "This has been the second most fucked up day ever." I lowered my voice and faced her, blocking Cade. "There was a curse placed on my family."

"What?!"

"Yeah, the coven thinks it's the reason for The Wise Whitleys' hardships."

"No fucking way," she shook her head back and forth.

"And, I had two visions in the middle of the street earlier."

Her chocolatey eyes widened even more.

"Oh, I'm not done. The guy behind me–don't look–is the motorcycle guy. He saw my psychic freak-out."

Harmony's eyes bugged out of her head, almost literally. She flipped her hair over her shoulder, peeking behind me slyly. Her eyes went up and down and she licked her lips.

"Harmony!"

Her eyes flicked back to mine. "What? He's fucking hot."

"Not the point."

"I know. I know. Let's start with the least fucked up thing. What excuse did you use for hot stuff?"

"Low sugar. Dean came up with that one."

Harmony started laughing, bringing the attention of some of the early birds at the bar. I sent them pointed looks to mind their own business. Nosy bastards.

"I'm sorry for laughing, but it's damn funny. I doubt Dean took to the new guy too kindly. We both know how possessive he can get."

"There was some tension."

"Shit, the rush is starting and there's so much to talk about. Okay," she pointed a finger at me. "You and me. Girl sesh later after work. Got it?"

"Got it," I said with a smile. "With Mildred, of course."

"Duh!"

My smile grew. "Now, go away. I have work to do."

"Like slicing lemons," she snickered as she walked away, greeting some of the patrons.

I made quick work of the lemons, closing the lid on the tray. Tossing a pinch of salt over my left shoulder for luck, I grabbed a napkin and made my way toward Cade. I placed the napkin in front of him.

"Sorry I took so long to prep. I should have gotten you a drink first."

Cade grinned, showing off two dimples that punctured his rounded cheeks. My panties combusted. His eyes flicked down to my Bruins t-shirt and back to my face.

"No worries. It gave me time to take in all the stuff on the walls and the drink menu."

"So, you want the Poisoned Apple Martini?"

"Ha. Good one. No, I'll take an IPA on tap. You choose," he said. His voice was deep and assertive. Not like I noticed the way it sent ripples down to my core.

I nodded with a smile and turned on stiff legs to the beer tap. I lifted a tall glass to the spout and pulled the handle down, pouring to expert levels. Butterflies still fluttered in my stomach, when I set his drink down.

"Here you go. Our best local IPA and my personal favorite. Want me to keep a tab open?"

Cade looked away from the decorations on the wall. "Sure." He paused to take a drag from his beer. I watched his throat with a strange fascination. "That's a damn good beer. She likes beer and hockey," he said, nodding at my shirt.

I shrugged my shoulders with a small smile, failing

to ignore the way I felt at his observation.

"Is there anything better than game seven in a play-off series?" I pointed to his hat. "Glad to see you're a fan, too. Locals wouldn't like it if you were a Montreal fan."

He lifted his hat, and a few strands of dark hair flopped out before he placed it back on his head. "Not a Canadians fan."

"Thank Goddess. You'll fit right in with the men here at the bar. And most of the women."

"Like you?" He took another drag from his beer.

"I'm usually working on the games. I can get some big tips. So yeah, I guess, me too."

He smiled again with a nod. Those dimples punched me in the groin.

Damn.

Chapter 5

I moved away from Cade, leaving him to his drink as the bell on the door jingled several times while people poured in. A knock sounded on the counter, stealing my attention from the register. I peeked into the mirror where the liquor bottles sat on their shelves. Dean. I turned around, placing a napkin in front of him.

"Hey. Long time no see." My stomach churned thinking about the curse, how his family might be involved, but more importantly how I needed his help.

"Too long, love." Dean teased, taking a seat right at the center.

"Don't call me that," I spat, rolling my eyes playfully.

He grinned innocently. "I've gotta say, Shay. That felt right on my tongue."

"Ew."

"You know what I mean."

Heat tinged my cheeks.

"Want your usual?" I asked, ignoring what he said. "And thanks for earlier."

"A shot of whiskey." He looked to the side, pausing briefly where Cade sat. He leaned his torso over the bar, getting closer to my face. The top buttons of his shirt were undone, and the sleeves were rolled up. His dark, smokey tattoo on his forearm was visible now. "And no problem. You know I'm always here for you."

I poured his whiskey and slid it to him. I leaned forward and whispered, "My powers have been getting stronger lately. I haven't even had to call on them."

"That's weird." Dean's brow scrunched. "Does it have to do with what you need to talk to me about? I guess it's not something good."

"It's just more shit added on top of our money problems," I frowned, wiping my hands down my apron.

Dean reached across the bar again, grabbing my hand. "I'll be here when you're ready." He smiled as he walked away with a saunter.

I let go of a heavy sigh, raking a hand through my hair, feeling tingles up my spine. I turned my head. Cade stared at me. Did he hear? Noticing his glass was empty, I poured him another beer.

"Thanks, Shay," he said when I set his filled glass down. "Is the mayor your boyfriend?"

I blinked several times, taken aback by his assertiveness. "Um. No."

"Sure about that?" His leafy green eyes seared into me.

A snarky remark died on my tongue as our gazes locked on. The longer we stared, the more the rest of the bar faded away. It was like we were locked inside a powerful spell. The chemistry between us blazed with a distracting heat.

A roar of laughter broke away the haze.

"This town is really into the whole 'witch' thing, huh?" Cade asked, clearing his throat. "It's barely October and everything is decorated for Halloween." He lifted the plastic drink menu and read off a couple of the drinks. "The Black Cat, Poisoned Apple Martini, and the Rye Witch. Those all sound wicked." He laughed.

Our strange moment successfully ignored.

"I see what you did there," I teased. "Witches are real. And Ipswich always has Halloween decorations up."

Most Quaints believed in the idea of the supernatural, but when confronted with its reality, they were instantly skeptical. Quaints might watch and listen to ghost stories, believing what they say, but if they experience something unexplained, they brush it off.

Their blindness worked for the magical families here, though. We were able to exist hidden in plain sight. Quaints came to us if they needed healing, guidance, or comfort, but never admitted the truth.

"In this town, I guess witches *are* real. What's the story here, anyway?"

"Well, Ipswich was settled by Puritans in the mid-1600s. But, there's a theory that the population boomed a few years before the Salem Witch Trials because a psychic witch foretold it and fled to Ipswich. Some of the women that were accused of witchcraft were even imprisoned in the Ipswich Jailhouse."

"You said all that with such seriousness."

"Plus, the whole 'witch thing' is great for tourism," I added, trying to derail his perceptions.

"That makes a lot of sense. Good for small businesses, just like Salem has done. I guess I need to get a pumpkin or something for my apartment."

"Or black and white candles for protection. If you plan on staying, that is." As the words left my mouth, Cade's head ticked to the side. Hopefully, he thought I was still kidding.

"Whether I want to stay or not, I'm here for now." His voice was edged with a steely resolve.

My eyebrows knitted at his confession. "Sounds like a bigger story there."

He scoffed but didn't expand. "At least I know one person," he said, deflecting. A grin formed on his face as his dimples appeared.

"I could be your official Ipswich guide," I said without thinking, pointing to myself with both hands and smiling. "I mean, Ipswich isn't that hard to navigate, and being a firefighter, you'll get familiar pretty quickly. So, I didn't mean that, like exclusively." *Stop rambling.*

"Right," he said. His eyes twinkled with amusement. He tapped on his glass. "I'll take one more, though."

"Yup. You got it."

I turned on my heel and rushed away from him. I glanced at the ceiling, sending a silent prayer to the goddesses to banish my embarrassment. I've known this guy for two minutes and we were already chatting and teasing like we've known each other for decades. After dropping Cade's fresh beer at the bar without another word, I waited on other customers.

I was being neighborly. It didn't mean anything.

After a while, Harmony joined me behind the bar as the locals met up with friends after their work shifts. She mixed a Rye Witch while I filled pitchers at the tap.

"New guy keeps looking at you." She tipped her head in Cade's direction.

I peeked over at him. Sure enough, his eyes were on me, not the TV screen. Granted, the game was on

51

commercial. I looked back toward my task.

"Maybe he's looking at you."

Harmony shook the tumbler, winking at Brad who sat at the bar. "That is a big NO, girl."

I sighed. I didn't have any space or time for more men in my life. I had a suspicion Dean would be taking up enough of that space.

Harmony's hip bumped against mine, looking at a clock on the opposite wall. "Shay, go take your fifteen before the last period starts."

Dean heard Harmony and his face straightened. I wiped my hands on my apron and flicked my head to the side for him to follow. Awareness tapped on my shoulder as I reached the door. Looking back, Cade watched us while lifting the beer glass to his lips. His sharp green eyes flicked back to the TV, his face hardening.

Dean stood at the opened door. "You coming?"

I shook off Cade's glance and nodded. We walked through the alley to a row of benches. His muscular arm draped along the back, encircling my shoulders.

"Spill, Shay. What's going on?"

"Things are changing," I said. "Majorly. Did you know that your family put a curse on mine?"

Dean whipped his head in my direction. His eyes blazed. "The fuck? No."

I took the next five minutes to word-vomit everything. Puffs of air left my mouth when I finished. Dean rubbed his chin with his fingers as he thought and processed.

"That's…wow…a lot."

"Yeah."

The ambient noise from the bar filled the silence

around us. I fidgeted with my fingers while waiting for Dean to say something more. *Anything* more.

"I had no idea about a curse. For the time it makes sense," he said.

"What? How does condemning a whole bloodline make any sense?"

"Look," Dean said, twisting his body to face me. "I'm not saying what the council did was right. But, during that time, women were more or less property. It was the best they could come up with."

"Of course, you would say that. You're a man." My skin burned hot as anger coursed through me. Standing, I inwardly scolded myself and my emotions. I wasn't mad at Dean. He stood, gripping my shoulders and leveling his gaze with mine.

"What do you need me to do? How can I help?"

I held my tongue, arguing with myself. Gram and the coven thought asking Dean for help was a good idea. But, Mom's reaction haunted my brain. She wanted me to focus on finding love. She was a Pisces. Idealistic.

"Shay, please. Let me help." He wrapped his arms around me, snuggling me to his chest. "Whatever you need. Just ask."

I breathed in. "Can you find out more information about your family and their involvement? I know your grandpa's memory is failing, but maybe there are some records or something."

Dean laid his head on mine. "You got it, love…" I heard the teasing in his voice. "Anything else?"

His question hung in the air as we stayed embraced. Did he know that I was warring with myself? My heartbeat ticked up. I pulled back. He looked down at me with a sultry look in his eyes. If he bent his head, we'd kiss.

Kissing him never crossed my mind before. He was only ever a friend. He was caring, sweet, and ambitious. Being a warlock would also be helpful.

Was asking him–a man–the best thing? Would I be any better than the dipshits that made this curse?

We would forever be connected.

It would be a lifelong commitment.

I swallowed.

"Well…you have money from your inheritance and we've been friends for a super long time. What if we got into a relationship? Like an arranged marriage? That would certainly kill two birds with one stone."

I pulled out of his embrace when he didn't say anything. His face was serious and his brown eyes caught mine. I wrapped my arms around myself and laughed.

"That would tie us together forever," I backpedaled, rambling. "I'm not even sure that's the best option, especially if the store still failed and the bank took it away anyway. You'd lose a nice chunk of change."

"Hm…interesting," he said. The air sucked out of my lungs. He took a step closer, crowding me. He kept glancing between my eyes and lips. "Who knows, maybe the council created this curse to ensure our bloodlines *would* be connected forever."

My head snapped up. A shiver ran down my spine as a state of shock coated my body. My mind reeled as I added more variables to my plan. How did I not think this through? Dean smirked then planted a kiss on the top of my head.

"It's definitely something to think about," he said, walking back into the bar.

I stood statue-still on the sidewalk.

Well, this was a solution…

Chapter 6

The next day, I unlocked the front door of the Wise Whitleys and stepped inside. The lights flickered on. I breathed in, smelling the dust, candles, herbs, and wood. The smells of home. My family's store. *My* store.

Like faded photographs, memories dotted every corner of the store. I remembered sitting in the vintage chairs practicing building crystal patterns with Gram. When I got tall enough to reach the Wiccan books to learn new spells. My first customer, an older lady looking for a second chance at love. Emotion clogged in my throat.

I had to save this place. This was the Whitley legacy.

A burst of chilly air whirled around me, spouting goosebumps along my skin. I looked behind me. Nothing.

BANG! BANG! BANG!

I whipped my head around and yelped.

"The fuck!?"

My eyes widened as the large, regal bookshelves thumped against the wall. Books shook and a few fell to the floor. My heart raced as I stepped toward the quaking bookshelf. It stopped as soon as I stood in front of it.

It was confirmed. I was being haunted.

I rushed to the counter, shuffling through the various candles, oil diffusers, and incense. I shoved them aside, finding a bundle of twigs. Sage. I palmed the sage, lit it, and ran back over to the bookshelf. I waved the smoking sage around the bookshelf. There was probably an incantation I should say, but I had no clue what I was doing.

Ghosts were Gram's thing.

"Stop with the theatrics. Show me what you need me to see," I said out loud. There had to be other ways for this spirit to get my attention besides scaring the shit out of me.

A few more seconds passed and nothing happened. I cleaned up the books, returning them to their spots, when a worn, yellowed piece of paper fell out from one of the books: *A History of Ipswich.*

I picked up the piece of paper and read it.

The 200th Annual Ipswich Autumn Solstice Festival

1834

Come One! Come All to Ipswich.

Tents! Arts! Bobbing for Apples! Fortune-Teller!

The flier shook in my hand. Ipswich used to have an annual festival. How had I never known this? Then again, the curse was news to me, too.

As if the fog cleared in my head, an idea formed. With the books in my possession placed on a small table, I slammed the flier onto the counter. A smile pulled at my cheeks.

I would bring back the festival. Bring tourists back. All the small businesses would benefit. Wins all around. It could even be a fundraiser for our beloved store.

Lately, my tarot card readings implicated change and celebration. This had to be the change that Fate needed me to follow. When everyone had extra profit from this festival, we would celebrate like the Ace of Cups foretold.

My chest filled with joy. With this idea, I wouldn't have to lock myself in a marriage—er, loan agreement with Dean. I wouldn't need his help– at all.

The door's bells jingled, causing my fingers to flinch.

Dean sauntered in, holding a bouquet of deep red roses. A sultry smile on his lips. He was dressed in simple skinny blue jeans and a tight black t-shirt. His white sneakers were in stark contrast to his jeans.

"Dean? Roses?"

"I thought about your suggestion." He walked further into the store.

I grabbed the flowers from him, smelling their sickly sweet scent. I *hated* roses. My thumb brushed the velvety petal. I hated *red* roses even more.

Even Quaints knew what the color red symbolized: Anger. Passion. Love.

I knew Dean very well. He meant to pick red roses. If he wanted to highlight our friendship he would have gifted white roses or lilies of the valley.

"Dean, you didn't have to get me roses, especially red rose–"

"You know I care about you," Dean said, cutting off my words. "About your family. So, let's do it."

Silence clung in the air. My lungs tightened as the weight of his agreement settled over me. I blinked several times. Though it was my plan, now that it was in motion, doubt crept in. I shook my head.

The legacy needs this.

Dean took a step closer, backing me up against the counter.

"We'd make a great pair. It's always been inevitable we'd be together. And now, this is our chance."

"Are you sure this is what you really want?" I asked, my voice betraying me with a faint tremble.

"I like you, Shay. I have for a long time. You're a witch. I'm a warlock. Our bloodlines are powerful. It makes a lot of sense. I can save you from this."

Dean smiled, placing each of his hands on either side of me on the counter, caging me. The air whooshed out of my lungs. Blood rushed to my head, pounding in my ears. Dean looked down at me with hope in his eyes.

Fuck.

This was too much. I needed space to think. Why did I open my big mouth without all the information finalized? I didn't make rash decisions like this.

Looking down, the top of my head grazed against his chest.

"How about this?" Dean said, tipping my chin up with his finger. "We go out to dinner tomorrow. That will give you some time to think. Make sure this is the plan you want to go with." His brown eyes shimmered in the morning sun, highlighting the specks of green, which reminded me of Cade's eyes.

I took in a sharp breath, trying to refocus on Dean. My brain moved at a million miles, second-guessing. Before I could say anything, my head nodded in agreement. Dean smiled.

"This is going to be great." He leaned forward,

planting a tiny peck on my cheek. "You can stop stressing. We're going to save your store and the Whitley bloodline…together."

His kiss pulled me from my mental stupor. It was sloppy and felt wrong. He stepped away from me, walking backward out of the store. His smile was smug, and he winked before leaving.

I sunk against the counter, feeling pain erupt behind my eyes. Too many variables clashed and collided with each other. I didn't expect Dean to agree to this so quickly. I didn't expect to ask him without thinking it all the way through.

This was the best choice, right?

Even if it wasn't. There was no turning back now. I had to save my family's livelihood, no matter how I felt.

Chapter 7

"Sorry, I'm late." I exhaled, shoving into the booth at Sinful Delights, a tiny cafe located in the heart of Ipswich. I closed The Wise Whitleys for lunch, even though I had no appetite to eat. The juices in my stomach kept rolling over.

"No worries, honey," Mom said, "Lydia insisted you have a chamomile tea with a dash of cardamom."

Lydia owned Sinful Delights and was another witch residing in Ipswich. She was an empath like my mother and brewed caffeinated "potions" to help soothe emotions. You never argued with what she made you.

I wrapped my fingers around the small cauldron-shaped mug and took a greedy sip. The sweet, floral taste exploded on my tongue, instantly melting the tension away from my shoulders.

Mom surveyed me as I enjoyed the last peaceful sips of my tea before the questions started.

"You're very...chaotic today," Mom said.

"Wouldn't you be after everything that's happened?"

She frowned, sipping from her steaming mug.

"Oh, don't worry your pretty little head, Shay. We are," Gram added with her squeaky voice.

"There's something more underneath your panic. What happened?" Mom asked.

"Last night I asked Dean to be in a relationship to

save the store." I paused. "Then today he showed up at the store with *red roses*, saying yes."

Both witches' eyes widened.

Silence.

"You did what?" Mom screeched loud enough that other patrons took notice. "You don't love him. How could you risk your chance at finding love?" Her face flushed with disbelief. My head ticked back at her reaction. I didn't understand her resistance.

"Why are you so upset, Sandy? Dean is so hunky," Gram said with an eyebrow wiggle. "And this solves both our money and curse troubles. Sounds like a win-win to me." Her eyes were unfocused. A sign she was communicating with the dead. She swished her hand in the air. "Ronny, you'll always be my number one," she spoke to the air.

Mom shook her head, her eyes lowering to the swirling steam rising from her mug. A haunted expression crossed her face. I reached across the table, gripping her fingers.

"Mom, this is what needs to happen. Dean is a close friend, knows most of my secrets, and has the means to help us."

She swallowed hard. "I don't want you making the same mistakes as I did."

"What mistakes?"

Mom pulled her hand from my grip and swished it. "Nothing."

"I like Dean, I do."

"It's obvious Dean likes you," Gram said. "Love can grow from that."

"I know love is important, Mom," I said. "It's also complicated and messy. It's out of control and unpredictable. At least with Dean, I know what to expect. It'll be just like our friendship."

Mom tsked but kept quiet. The emotions she felt suffocated the air around us. You didn't have to be an empath to know she didn't like this idea. Being the last in line meant it was my responsibility.

"What do the cards say?" Gram asked.

I shrugged. Usually, when there's a big problem in my life, I resort to Fate's guidance.

Why didn't I this time?

"You might want to start there, hon," Mom suggested. "Let Fate show you the way or at the very least give you some guidance before things go too far."

That triggered my memory. I sat up straight. "Something strange did happen to me at the store today," I said, sharing the details about the festival flier and setting it out on the table.

"You're being haunted?" Gram asked when I finished.

I swiped some fallen hair out of my face, taking another sip of my perfect tea. "I guess. My window flew open by itself, felt cold spots, and heard voices."

"That's a ghost, baby," she said.

"Do you know who it is, Mom?" Mom asked Gram.

Gram folded her fingers together on top of the table and closed her eyes. Her eyes shifted from side-to-side under her eyelids. With her eyes still closed, she said, "The spirit is blocking me from seeing who they are. But they feel familiar." She paused. "Jerry, I'm not trying to channel you, creep. Go away."

My mom and I exchanged glances. Watching Gram work was always entertaining. She channeled old townspeople, old lovers, and sometimes family members. One time, she stayed up all night talking to Ipswich's most famous fisherman, River Jones. He gave her his secret clam chowder recipe.

"They don't want to reveal themselves, yet. The other spirits say it's a guardian," Gram said, finally opening her eyes.

Mom and Gram studied the flier closer.

"I think doing this festival is a better idea than being tied to Dean," Mom said.

I wrung my hands together, running my thumbs across the pads, thinking.

"What harm can it do, bringing it back? It'll be good, not just for The Wise Whitleys, but for the town. A time to get back to our roots," Mom said.

"The festival wouldn't satisfy the curse, Sandy," Gram said.

A tingle in the back of my mind ignited. The festival sounded like a fun idea and would involve the whole town. But what would I do about the curse? A relationship with Dean still solved that problem. My shoulders slumped. More variables. My phone vibrated in my purse, breaking my thoughts.

"I've got to go reopen the store," I said, standing from the booth, gathering my things, and giving them each a kiss. "We can talk more about this later. Love you both."

"Love you, too, Moonbeam," Mom said. "Remember, we're here to help you. But, I seriously suggest consulting Fate when it comes to Dean. Love might feel messy to you, but it's worth it. Trust me."

"Good luck with your ghost, too!" Gram called out. A few customers turned to look at her.

I shook my head and continued walking through the bakery, emerging into the town square. The bright fall sunlight enveloped me, and I blinked several times, adjusting to its brightness. I breathed deeply, smelling the dirt, leaves, and nature that the Mother Earth Goddess provided, soothing the chaos.

The town square was coated with lush green grass and planters along paved walkways. Townies milled about, greeting or sitting with each other. Businesses lined the perimeter, making the town square cozy and inviting.

In my imagination, tents and booths were set up. Locals and tourists browsed the offerings, laughing and enjoying the lore behind the town. A smile formed on my face as I folded up the flier. It would be amazing to bring back the festival.

I lifted my head, seeing Cade walk toward me. His hands were tucked in his pockets and he walked with a confident stride. He looked even better than the last time I saw him. He was dressed in a tight navy blue t-shirt that was tucked into his blue pants. His shirt donned the Ipswich Fire Department logo.

He ran a hand through the dark brown hair, moving the longer strands into their place. In the sunlight, the longer strands had hints of blonde. The rest of his hair was shaved close to his head on the sides.

I swallowed roughly, feeling my heart leap into my throat. Damn, he looked good.

"Hey, Shay," he said. His voice sent shivers down my spine.

"Hi," I croaked before clearing my throat. "First day on the job?"

He smoothed a hand down his chest, accentuating

his muscles. "Yup, out on a lunch run. Whatcha got there?" he asked, pointing to the flier still in my hands.

I unfolded it and held it open. He took a step closer to see what it was. My skin sparked with electricity, something I realized only happened around Cade. His smell wafted in my nose, making my eyes blink slower than normal.

"It's an old flier I found in the store."

"Store?"

"The Wise Whitleys. It's my family's store. You've probably seen it. It's across the street from the fire station."

"Oh yeah. I've seen that place. It's like a candle store?" Cade asked.

I nodded. "We sell more than that. A lot of crystals and tarot cards. Things like that. It used to be an apothecary when it was first opened in the late 1600s."

"Huh. Another witchy thing," Cade said, reading the flier. "What is it with this town? Everyone knows witches are fake, right?"

"Ha. Fake, right." Inside, I felt the sting of his skepticism. I wasn't shocked that he didn't believe. He was a Quaint, but now he was just a pretty face and nothing more.

Figures.

"Though, a festival would be lots of fun."

"Yeah, I was thinking about petitioning to have it again. My family's store needs the money."

Cade ran his hand through his hair. "Shit. Really?"

"The bank's not renewing the lease." I folded the flier and put it carefully back into my bag.

"Fucking bureaucrats."

I laughed. "You work for the government, don't

you?"

Cade shrugged. "Only at the city and county level. Most stations are public sector organizations. But, here in Ipswich, I guess we're a government agency. Either way, FD is better than PD."

"But cops keep the peace. Right?"

Cade's face hardened. He crossed his arms, making his biceps bulge. "Who're the ones going out saving people?"

It was natural for him to have resentment toward cops, but this felt heavier, bigger.

An invisible tug pulled at my stomach as the air whooshed past my ears.

A beautiful young woman.

Cade cradling her as they walked into a police station.

An apathetic cop sitting at the front desk.

Cade's anger visually rippled through my vision, sending sparks of red through it.

I coughed and blinked my eyes, coming back to the present.

"Shay? Where'd you go there?" Cade asked. His leafy green eyes searched my face. Some of the hardness in his face softened.

"Uh...I space out sometimes."

"Right..." Cade said, squinting his eyes in my direction. "So, do you even know where to start with planning a festival?"

"Not really," I said, thankful Cade decided to drop the interrogation of my weirdness. "The town square would be the perfect place for it."

Cade turned, eyeing the quad. "Yeah, that's badass." He turned back. "My best friend, Aaron, in

Boston, is a part-time EMT and part-time party planner."

"Interesting combo."

"It suits him. He's a one-of-a-kind guy." Cade smiled. "Anyway, I could ask him about this sort of thing. Get him up here to help with the planning and such."

My thoughts froze in my head. I pulled on my sleeves, covering my hands. I was stunned by how easily Cade was offering to help. What were his motivations? If I went through with the festival, I wouldn't be in debt to Dean. He could use his inheritance for something else.

"Why would you do that?"

"Why not? It's always good to have help. Especially with something this big." He dipped his head down, bringing our eyes level. I shifted on my feet, beginning to get lost in the color of his eyes.

"Well, I'm still deciding, but thanks for the offer," I said, clearing my throat and thinking of Dean.

"Of course. I mean, we barely know each other. But, my word's good for it," he said, pulling out his phone from his front pocket. "Let me give you my number for when you decide. You can just text me."

Heat tingled along my neck and up my cheeks. "Okay." I pulled my phone from my purse and handed it to him.

The invisible cord that connected us thickened and pulsed in my mind's eye. I tried to ignore it as it sparkled with swirls of silver and green. Cade handed my phone back to me with an easy grin.

"Working at the Brew tonight?" he asked, bringing my focus to this plane of the universe.

"No, thank Goddess. I have the night off. I just plan on spending it inside. Goddess knows I need it."

"That sounds magical," he teased. "Obviously, you know I'm on shift."

I laughed at his choice of words. "That sounds boring," I said, echoing his tone. Cade's wide smile highlighted his dimples and eyes.

"I can't believe how many candle fires happen around here. There have been two already today."

I choked on my laughter, biting hard on my lower lip.

"I didn't realize a person could have so many candles," he continued, laughing along with me.

"You have no idea."

We stood for a few lingering moments in silence. Not awkward, just heavy, as if there was more that needed to be said.

Secrets. That hung on the tip of my tongue. I wanted to spill all my secrets with Cade and I barely knew him. He was just easy to talk to. Easier than Harmony or Dean.

"Well, I've got to get back to the store," I said.

Cade looked at his phone and pocketed it. "Yeah, I've got to get back to the station. I just wanted a drink from the bakery. I don't know what she puts in her stuff, but they are amazing."

I rubbed my lips together.

Another unordinary thing he noticed.

I hoped he wasn't keeping a list.

Chapter 8

I shoved through the front door of my apartment with an epic sigh. My body dragged with exhaustion deep down into my bones. My tossed keys landed into the pentacle-shaped bowl on the hallway table. My hands rubbed my temples in circular motions.

"Mildred? Harmony? I'm home," I called into the living room, flinging my stuff, including the roses, onto the kitchen counter. No one responded.

I shuffled into my bedroom, my limbs moving like useless lumps of jelly. I flopped back on the bed while a storm brewed in my mind. Too many people relied on me. The more I learned about my family's past and the curse, the more it seemed like I wasn't going to be able to solve this by myself.

I felt pulled in too many directions, and all the solutions and problems swirled in my head like a dangerous tornado.

I turned my head toward my en-suite bathroom, eyeing the bronze claw-footed tub. My lips tipped up. I jumped off the bed with a new purpose and walked into the living room, toward the large wall-to-ceiling shelves that housed all of my witchcraft ingredients. My hand glided along the mass of different labeled jars. All my herbs, crystals, and candles were carefully organized and color-coded.

I found the jar with a yellow lid labeled

Lemongrass to clarify the mind. Next, I opened a jar with a green lid labeled Nettle for protection during recharge. My lips pursed to the side as I rubbed my fingers along my chin, thinking. Last, I lifted the lid of a black swirled box, pulling out black tourmaline. It tingled in my palm. The rough, jagged edges of the shiny black stone would help rid my body of negative thoughts.

In the kitchen, I used my worn black and purple mortar and pestle, grinding the herbs together and smelling the citrusy sweet and earthy scent. I breathed in. My energy started to relax. I scooped the herbs into a small mesh bag and tied it.

As I walked out of my kitchen with my spell's ingredients, the roses suddenly caught my attention. Instinctively, I plucked one rose out of the bunch and returned to the bathroom.

After lighting a few white candles, I tossed the herb bag into the tub while it filled. The natural oils seeped a light green into the hot water. The black tourmaline went in next, followed by some powdered coconut milk. A girl needed to have smooth skin, too.

I held the rose in my hand, cradling the petals in my palm, sprinkling them into the water, too. Once submerged, my muscles unwound and loosened. I placed the black tourmaline crystal over my heart, focusing on positive thoughts and solutions.

"Mother Goddess, I open the circle of meditation," I prayed. "I ask you for your ultimate guidance and to help me untangle the mess in my head. I need to figure out how to save my family's legacy. Am I making the right choices?"

A cool breeze blew through the bathroom,

conflicting with my warm skin and sprouting goosebumps. I breathed in deeply, feeling Mother Goddess's energy. I soaked in the essence of the herbs, crystal, and candles.

My brain went blank for a few moments, lost in the rhythm of my own breathing. After several minutes, I opened my eyes, ready to tackle my problem. I reached over the side of the tub and grabbed a spare tarot deck. Naturally, there were decks stashed all over the apartment.

I shuffled the deck three times, turning over the first card: Queen of Wands, upright.

The Queen of Wands depicted a matron manager. A woman who invoked teamwork, delegation, and leadership. Once again, the Fates reminded me of my strengths to tackle any roadblocks. This was how I worked. I organized, planned, and executed.

The water in the tub sloshed as I sat back. The Queen of Wands reminded me I was the leader on this task and had to make a decision: Dean's money or the festival.

Dean would offer his money without hesitation. That's the type of person he was. Open and giving. It was a reason he worked well as the mayor. But, I would be indebted to him. Mom's face sprung in my mind. She was against my plan with Dean. Vehemently. She wanted me to fall in love. I didn't have time for that. I had to save the store above all else and Dean had the means to help.

Then, there was the festival. A long-lost tradition that celebrated the town's rich Wiccan history and culture. As fun as it would be to plan and pull off, it wouldn't solve the curse problem. Standing in the quad earlier today with Cade, my imagination and creativity sparked. I imagined the townspeople enjoying each other, pitching in to save the Wise Whitleys. It could become an annual tradition again.

A smile pulled on my lips. The more I thought of the festival, the more I fell in love with its idea.

I was going to plan a festival and raise money for the store.

Confidence filled my body as I shuffled the cards again. Now, I needed to reflect on the curse. I couldn't have success with the business without that piece of the puzzle. Dean was the obvious choice, but Mom's reaction to my idea was so visceral, it gave me pause.

I redirected my thinking as I shuffled: *what about the curse?*

Dean was familiar and reliable. We cared about each other and have known one another for decades. He was the obvious choice. Love was complex. I could grow to love him. In the back of my mind, I knew trying to love him satisfied the curse, but not the desires of my heart. If I didn't love him by now, would I ever? Did that matter?

I let my melancholy thoughts swim in my brain as I turned over the first tarot card: Ace of Swords - reversed.

Shit.

The Ace of Swords, a hand holding a sword through a crown, reversed symbolized my confusion. It warned against making hasty decisions without thinking about the long-term consequences. I had to take a step back, focus on self-reflection, and seek others' perspectives before choosing the path forward.

I ran my warm, wet hands down my face, closing

my eyes. Damnit Fate. I thought propositioning Dean was the best choice. The cards told me something different. Deep down, I hoped there was a different choice.

I was confused. I had no clue how to satisfy the curse. Was I destined to be in a loveless relationship or did I have a chance at love?

Mom was convinced. Even my powers told me there was someone else out there. Despite knowing Dean for a long time, nothing about him sparked arousal or passion. I didn't feel tingles when I was around him. Never did. He didn't make me lose my breath.

Cade's handsome face popped into my mind. My heart rate pulsed against my neck.

Shit. Again.

The couple of times that we've interacted, he made my blood boil. Not only was he seriously attractive, but I also realized he was caring, helpful and, at times, overprotective. He was a firefighter, so that made sense. He was the opposite of selfish.

Did he have the potential to break the curse?

I barely knew him. Although I liked what I saw on the outside, there was more to a person than their insane hotness. He was a Quaint. A non-believer. A skeptic. I refused to open that can of worms.

What would Cade think of the secrets of Ipswich?

A hollow laugh left my throat, echoing in my tiny bathroom. There was no way he'd believe. He was logical and perceptive. Although, he had begun to notice some of the strangeness around town, there was no guarantee he wouldn't have me committed if he knew the truth. Or worse, reject me.

I frowned. I could never be in a relationship with someone who didn't believe me.

I ran my hands along the surface of the water. My body grew more restless while my mind ping-ponged back and forth between my options.

How would I break the curse?

Dean? Cade? Lose it all?

Cade entered my mind again. Honestly, maybe he never left. Those intense green eyes gleamed mischievously. I had never felt so raw and exposed around a person. As if all my secrets were written on my skin.

My body flushed under the hot water as my mind wandered. I dreamed about his lips on mine. It was as if I could feel them. I squeezed my thighs together, feeling the silky smoothness of the milk powder.

My hands glided along my arms as I wrapped them across my chest. I imagined my hands were Cade's. His face became clearer in my imagination. A confident smirk pulled at his imaginary lips. My hands traveled down my stomach to the tops of my thighs.

My fingertips traced up the sides of my body, leaving a trail of goosebumps along my skin. The prickled coldness stung against the warmth of the water. I ran my hands around the swells of my breasts, and my breath quickened. I licked my lips, savoring the sensation. The hot water enveloped me in a steamy embrace between my thighs.

My fingers grazed back down to my thighs and connected with my clit. I rubbed my finger in lazy circles, igniting the fire I boiled just beneath the surface.

I fantasized about Cade's nimble fingers working

my spot, speeding up my torture. My breathing increased with each second that passed. Soon, prickles along the base of my neck sparked my orgasm. My release spasmed, exploding the tension out of my body.

My arms flopped back into the water with a splash. Heat bloomed on my cheeks as my breathing came out in small puffs. I blinked slowly, savoring the moment. My skin was on fire and felt smooth to my touch.

I needed that.

I exhaled a deep sigh as my body sunk further into the water's embrace. I was fully relaxed now and ran my thumbs along my fingertips. I wasn't leaving this bath until I made a decision.

"Okay," I said out loud to myself. "I'm going to give Dean a chance and plan the festival with Cade."

I frowned, knowing asking for help wasn't my strong suit. Growing up in an uncontrolled Wiccan world, I learned quickly to control the things that I could. My bedroom was always clean and my spell-casting ingredients were always uber-organized.

Now, I was going to ask for help from two polar opposites.

A whooshing sound vibrated against my ears and a tug pulled at my stomach. I closed my eyes, letting my astral self take me to a different time.

Me in The Wise Whitleys alone.

A shadowy figure crowding me.

Me. Looking for an escape. Terror. Confusion. Betrayal.

The figure stepped closer with a twisted smile. His face was familiar but cruel. Tainted.

My astral self slammed back into my body, causing me to slip down into the water, sploshing water over the side of the tub. Sourness clung to my tongue so thick I started coughing. My body quaked in the vision's aftermath.

What the fuck was that?

It was clearly a warning, but for what?

****

After closing the spell circle, giving my thanks to Mother Goddess, I pulled the plug from the drain and wrapped myself in a green towel, rising from the now luke-warm water. I cleaned up the bath, threw the herb bag away, and tucked the crystal into my hand. I padded back through my apartment to return the tourmaline to its spot in the black-decorated box on the shelf.

A cool breeze blew through the apartment. I wrapped the towel tighter around my body. The large living room window caught my attention. It was wide open. The photo frames of Harmony and I were toppled over and scattered.

I rolled my eyes. Mildred probably knocked all that over in protest of something.

I tip-toed over, leaned on the ledge, and stuck my head out the window. A tall, old maple tree loomed above my roof. Muted green leaves in transition to bright orange shook on the upper branches. A few of the leaves fell to the ground. I followed their path up the tree.

Mildred was napping on one of the highest branches.

"What the fuck are you doing out there!?"

My yell startled her, causing her back to go rigid in surprise. A loud hiss escaped her mouth.

"It's about time you noticed I was gone," she

sassed. *"Good bath?"*

Heat flared my cheeks at her assumption. I gritted my teeth as her tail flicked back and forth.

"It was heaven," I spat. "Now, get down."

Mildred's pink tongue peeked out as she licked her whiskers. *"I can't."*

"What do you mean you can't? Cats always land on their feet, Mildred."

"Well, I'm not a typical cat, Shay," she hissed. *"I seem to be afraid of heights."*

"Are you kidding me? You were just sleeping!"

Mildred tilted her head to the side.

"Just jump."

She hissed at me again, sitting awkwardly, like she was in pain. My eyes took inventory of her body. Her back paw hung off the branch.

"You're hurt?" My voice softened. My poor kitty.

"When I jumped out here, my paw scraped along a stray branch. So, maybe I don't want to risk jumping down. Plus, I didn't realize how high this stupid tree was from the ground."

Some of my anger eased, taking in her pathetic state.

"Why did you go out here in the first place?"

"I saw a raven."

My eyelids closed. Ravens were a warning. An omen. Images of my most recent vision sprung in my mind.

"I see your motivation, but chase them on the ground, Mildred."

"I was protecting you."

"You stubborn pussy." I threw my arms up in the air. My towel dropped to the floor, giving Mildred a full frontal. Mildred yowled and dipped her head to hide under her paw. Her body shook with laughter. I snapped the towel off the floor, fixing it to my body.

"Oh, shut up. You've seen me naked plenty of times."

My body vibrated as I stomped to get my phone from my bag.

"Don't forget to put clothes on before someone comes to help."

I bit hard on my bottom lip as I stared daggers through the window. After a painfully embarrassing conversation, help was on the way.

"I hope you're happy. The fire department is on its way."

Mildred stretched her body along the branch, staring at me with a blank expression. I rolled my eyes and headed toward my bedroom.

Chapter 9

I wiggled my toes into the fuzzy cushion of my bright seafoam-colored slippers as I sat on the last step leading up to my apartment door. My gaze drifted to the back of my nosy neighbor's business. The Sapphires' Bed and Breakfast had a large wrap-around porch with outdoor seating so patrons could enjoy the surrounding forest at the back of the property.

My shoulders relaxed. No one out there.

Flashing lights brought my attention back to the end of my driveway. Dean's truck rolled to a stop, followed by one of the fire engines.

As soon as the door to Dean's SUV closed and the engine stopped, two older faces appeared in the bay window of the bed and breakfast. I narrowed my eyes at them and flicked my hand in their direction. Of course, they ignored my nonverbal brush-off.

"Twice in one day, Shay? Can't get enough of me?" Dean quipped with a stupid grin on his face that I wanted to smack off.

"Your favorite animal got stuck in a tree. Hardly a creative enough tactic to get your attention," I sassed. "Plus, I called the fire department, not the mayor."

Dean laughed as he raked a hand through his hair.

"It's a slow day at the office." He leaned around me, looking at the tree. "Heard your address on the scanner and thought I'd come to see if you've decided.

Too much curiousity, too."

I swallowed, knowing my decision, but this wasn't the time to talk about it.

"How did Mildred get up there and not figure out how to get down?" Dean asked when I didn't answer him.

"She saw a raven and chased after it."

Dean surveyed the tree. "A warning?"

I wrapped my arms tighter around my middle. "I guess so. I've been having some weird and terrifying visions. With all the stuff going on, it makes sense a raven would be around."

Dean spotted Mildred up in the tree and continued looking around the branches. He looked over his shoulder at me. "Hopefully, that will all stop now that we're together."

My heart dropped. We haven't even had a date yet and he already decided that we were a couple.

"Dean…" I began.

"Shay," Chief Irons greeted me, hopping down from the driver's side of the fire truck, interrupting us. "Have a little cat-in-tree problem?"

Two other firefighters jumped from the engine, moving toward the ladder attached to the side. One of them caught my eye. Sparks erupted on my skin. His red suspenders were visible on his muscled navy t-shirt holding up his heavy fire pants. He smiled.

Cade.

Shit.

My cheeks burst into flames.

"Yes," I stuttered, answering Chief Irons. "I think she hurt her paw which is why she can't get down. Sorry. This isn't exactly an emergency."

Chief Irons stepped beside me. He towered over me, patting my back too hard. "No worries, kiddo. It's the perfect situation for our newest recruit to earn some experience points."

"Thompson!" Chief Irons yelled, turning his head to the firefighters. "Simpson! Hustle up with that ladder."

His loud voice reverberated through my body, causing me to jump. My eyes followed his gaze and landed on Cade.

Cade's heavy firefighter pants hung from his slender hips, accentuating his broad shoulders. His t-shirt stretched across his chest and curled above his biceps. Images of his fingers doing nasty things to my most sensitive part exploded in my brain. Now, here he stood.

The flush that burned my cheeks traveled down my neck.

"Bring it to the tree," Chief Irons boomed. "The little kitty seems to be about two, maybe three stories up."

Simpson, a much burlier man with a flattened nose, grabbed hold of the ladder at the front, hoisting it under his arm. Cade grabbed the back of the ladder, mirroring the hold. They walked together toward the tree.

"Funny how the first non-candle call we get in the station is for a cat," Cade said as he passed me. A hint of humor painted his tone.

"Not just any cat," I defended, and quickened my steps to walk beside him. "*My* cat. Even if she's annoying."

They set the ladder down. "We'll take good care of her, Miss," Cade teased with a smirk on his full, kissable lips.

A loud yowl screeched from the tree. My head whipped up to where Mildred perched. Her body was arched and her muzzle pointed in Dean's direction.

"I don't want him to save me. I want the sexy one," Mildred hissed.

I shook my head, trying to hide my laughter.

Dean held his hands up in surrender, stepping back away from the tree. He pushed his shirt sleeves up. When he turned, his eyes trained on Cade, who still stood next to me.

"I didn't even do anything," Dean spoke. His eyes flicked to Cade.

"Don't take it too personally. She's a little emotional right now," I said to pacify him, but deep down I questioned it. Mildred wasn't a hugely friendly cat, but she never showed animosity toward Dean in all the years we've been friends.

"Simpson, steady the ladder at the bottom. Thompson, climb up there to get the cat," Chief Irons commanded, regaining control of the scene.

A look of disappointment flashed across Simpson's face as he leaned the ladder against the tree.

"He must have wanted to be the one to rescue the cat," Cade whispered against my ear, sending goosebumps down my neck. The heat from his body permeated my bubble. I breathed in deeply, smelling his fresh, woodsy scent mixed with his sweat.

"I have four kitties at home," Simpson said. An odd picture formed in my mind of this big gruff guy snuggling small cats with his beefy hands.

I laughed.

"Okay, bro," Cade chuckled. "Let's save this cat."

Dean's boots crunched under the fallen leaves as he stood on my other side. Anger radiated off him like a space heater. His eyes threw daggers at the firefighters as they worked, more specifically Cade. His jaw was tight. My fingertips touched his tattooed forearm.

"You okay?"

"I can't believe Chief Irons let that delinquent work in our town."

My eyebrows scrunched at the viciousness in his voice.

"You know how gossip runs in this town. Don't be so quick to judge. I haven't gotten any weird vibes from him."

Dean's head snapped in my direction, causing me to take a step back. His mood change was sudden. My forehead tingled. My mind's eye ignited while I unfocused my gaze, reading Dean's aura. His usual deep maroon aura had faded spots of black intertwining. I tucked my sleeves around my hands, covering them completely, bringing my focus back.

That's odd.

"After we met him yesterday, I did some digging," he said in a hushed voice. "He's involved in an assault charge—on a cop. And here he is saving your cat from a tree instead of being punished."

Cade's muscles flexed while he lifted his body up the ladder with confidence and ease. Simpson held the ladder steady and Chief Irons supervised. Because of my vision, Cade had a strong resentment toward cops. I felt his rage. However, Cade's energy now felt anything but sinister.

"I think you're overreacting. I doubt there's some big mystery surrounding Cade's appearance in our town. Instead, why don't you tell me what potion you've taken?" I hissed. Dean's eyes flicked to mine.

"It's just a pick-me-up potion. Like an energy drink. Nothing I haven't taken before. Why?"

"Your aura has black spots."

"Why did you read my aura?" he chided.

"You just seem angrier than earlier." I grabbed his hand, squeezing it. His face softened at my touch.

"I swear I'm fine. It's no different than the nettle and lemongrass I smell on your skin." His voice was smooth.

I pursed my lips, giving him a small shoulder shove. "All right, show-off."

He smirked. "As far as Thompson goes, just be careful."

"I can take care of myself. You aren't my brother, you know."

Dean's lips grew into a wider smile. "I definitely don't want to be your brother. I thought we decided that this morning."

Blush graced my cheeks at his insinuation, but my stomach twisted uncomfortably. The Ace of Swords flashed in my brain.

"I did some meditating. I think we should go on a date first before we jump into anything too serious," I told him.

Dean's caramel eyes darkened, as if he were struggling to control his emotions. "Why the sudden change?"

"Just reflection and some guidance…" I said, letting him fill in the blanks. "I don't want to rush into anything. You know you cornered me this morning." I played with the cuffs of my sleeves, hiding my fingers.

His cheeks flushed with guiltiness.

"Shay, do you see his muscles? I want to curl up in those biceps. Oh..." Mildred interrupted, bringing my attention to her. *"His energy is intoxicating. I feel drunk off of him."*

Cade had reached the branch where my sex-crazed feline perched. Cade held his hands out. "Here kitty, kitty," he coaxed. The words had barely left his mouth when Mildred leapt into his arms. Cade steadied himself on the ladder, adjusting for the extra weight. Mildred hissed.

"Ow...his meaty muscles are crushing my paw," she whined. *"I don't mind too much, though."*

"Cade, careful," I called to him. "Her back paw is hurt."

Cade repositioned Mildred in his hold. "Sorry, pretty girl," he said as he stepped down the ladder, watching his footing. Once on the ground, we all gathered around him. Simpson smiled warmly before scratching the top of Mildred's head. Mildred twitched and growled deep from her belly heart at his touch. Simpson lifted her paw, despite her protest, inspecting it.

"Looks like just a scratch, Shay," he said. "I don't think she needs a vet, just some bandages."

"I'm not going to the fucking vet. She has no clue how cold her hands are." I hid my laughter with my hand. *"I'm staying right here."*

Mildred's purrs echoed around us.

"Great job, boys," Chief Irons praised, clapping Cade on the back. "Simpson, help me carry the ladder back." The two men picked up the ladder and carried it in tandem back to the engine. Cade stepped closer

86

toward me, his face triumphant.

"That's odd," Dean mentioned.

"What?" Cade asked as he scratched behind Mildred's ears.

"I've known Mildred most of my life. And she's never let me hold her," Dean said.

My gaze darted between the men on opposing sides. The energy surrounding us was stifling, a blend of confusion, competition, and dominance.

"That's not entirely true," I lied. Dean's head turned in my direction.

"Maybe she just has good instincts. She can tell who the good ones are," Cade said, making his hidden meaning crystal clear. He let Mildred nuzzle her face on his chest.

Dean's posture shifted as he puffed out his chest and squared his shoulders. Cade continued to pet Mildred as if nothing happened.

"Have something to say, Thompson?" Dean spat, his anger erupting again. Mildred picked her head up and bared her teeth at Dean. Cade's stance stayed relaxed and unfazed by Dean's show of manly stupidity.

"Not yet," Cade said, the words heavy with unspoken meaning as his eyes finally locked with Dean's. "Just making observations."

The testosterone-filled haze clung to the air like honey to a spoon.

"Thompson," Chief Irons yelled from the truck. "Let's go!"

Dean cleared his throat, keeping his stance rigid. "I'm glad you're down, Mildred." He turned me, stepping in front of Cade. His face had switched back to his easy-going grin. "So, Shay, what time can I pick you up for our date?"

"Um, after work tomorrow," I answered through clenched teeth. Dean gave me a confident smile. Funny how he was now on board with my plan to go slow.

"Sounds perfect. I looked into my inheritance and there's plenty of money to help with the bank."

Cade lifted his head from the pets he still gave Mildred. "I thought you were going to go with the festival idea. You seemed pretty set on it this afternoon."

They both focused on me. The pissing-contest was in full stream now.

"Um, yeah," I said to Dean. "I am going to do the festival instead of taking away from your inheritance. I don't want to take advantage of you and our friendship."

Dean's legs widened, and he crossed his arms over his chest. "So, you want to date me for my good looks and charm and not just for my money?" He teased with a cocky smirk.

Mildred snorted.

"Uh…" I didn't know how to get out of this one. Dean wanted me to express my romantic interest in him in front of Cade. I wasn't even sure I had romantic feelings for either of them. Dean had all the Wiccan information and familial connections to help with the curse. I couldn't say any of that in front of Cade. "Dean, don't you have to go back to work or something?"

"In fact, I do, love. I'll see you tomorrow." He grinned. After giving Cade the once-over, he strode to his SUV and drove away.

I exhaled, tugging on the sleeves of my oversized hoodie.

"For what it's worth," Cade said, "I think you're doing the right thing with the festival. You don't want to be eternally indebted to someone like Dean."

"Someone like Dean? What does that mean?"

Cade narrowed his eyes, growing serious. "Something feels off about him. Trust me."

"I don't know you enough to trust you." My fists clenched under my sleeves.

"There's an easy solution to that. Let me help with the festival. We can get to know each other through planning. I'm a man of many talents. And one of my talents is reading people. And I don't like what I see with Dean."

My throat dried and my brow scrunched. Dean's mood was weird, and I needed Cade's connection to his party-planner friend.

"Thompson!" Chief Iron's yelled.

"Coming, sir," Cade called back to the truck. "I talked to Aaron and he's totally on board to help with the festival. If you want, I'd love to help, too. It'll be a great way for me to get to know more of the townspeople."

My face tightened at Cade's interest. He was speaking to all the pros of the festival, which continued to solidify the idea, bringing confidence to my decision regarding the festival.

"Okay," I said. "I'd love to have your help. And Aaron's."

Cade smiled. Two dimples pierced his cheeks, sending zaps of energy through my body. I smiled, too.

"Here's your cat, Shay." Cade went to hand

Mildred over when she caterwauled a throaty yelp, digging her claws into his shirt.

I gently pulled at Mildred, but she didn't budge. Her paws flexed, ready to dig them further into his chest. Carefully, I increased the pressure, entering a careful dance with her. Too much pressure and she would gouge him.

"Mildred, come on."

"I love him. Leave me alone."

"I don't care if you love him," I gritted out in a whisper. "Let go."

Cade's eyes shifted back and forth between Mildred and me. One of his eyebrows cocked up. I smiled as if he didn't just hear me arguing with my cat.

Finally, Mildred leapt to the ground, giving me a hiss. She rubbed her body along Cade's ankles before sashaying away from us, tenderly stepping on her injured paw.

The horn of the fire truck honked. "Thompson! Get your ass on this truck now or you're stuck with muck duty the rest of the week," Chief Irons yelled. Cade grimaced.

"Yes, sir. Mildred wouldn't let go," he said. He set his gaze on me. "Seriously, though, Shay, be careful with Dean."

I snorted. "He said the exact same thing about you."

Cade's face hardened. "Of course he would. He's threatened by me. That much is obvious."

"He said you were involved in an assault on an officer."

Cade crossed his arms over his chest. His ears tinted pink, and he swallowed hard. "He doesn't know the full story," he clipped out. "Doubt he even cares to hear it."

"I want to hear it. Whenever you want to share.".

"Gotta go," Cade said, giving me a lingering look, then backed away. "I'll share if you do, too. I get the feeling you have a lot of secrets. As does this town."

My jaw dropped briefly before I recovered. "Thanks for the rescue...or something," I said, pointing my thumb in Mildred's direction.

"It's my job," Cade said and half-jogged over to the truck. He hoisted himself onto the back with ease. With a loud honk, the engine backed out of the driveway.

My shoulders slumped forward as my head lolled back.

The sky had turned from a dim blue to a darkened purple as the sun set behind the trees. The tall pines and oaks cast a silhouette against the pastel sky. Purple symbolized spiritual enlightenment and emotional turmoil.

Fuck. Cade was incredibly perceptive, which was sexy as hell but a huge problem.

I peered over at the Sapphires, startling. Wilma and Agnes still had their wrinkled faces plastered against the window. Agnes's lips curled up into a smile and she wiggled her eyebrows. Wilma whispered something in Agnes's ear and the two ladies cackled behind floral curtains.

Whatever just happened between Cade, Dean, and me was going to be front-page news on the Gossiping Grandma's Gazette in the morning.

Chapter 10

Later that evening, Mildred and I snuggled on the couch after all the drama died down. Her paw was wrapped in a thick gauze and she munched on catnip.

"You're making a huge mess, Mildred."

She licked her whiskers and tilted her head up to stare at me.

"Fine. I'll let it go for tonight." I scratched the top of her head. "You've had such a rough night," I teased, turning my attention back to my book: *Reading the Omens.*

Being a witch, omens were a daily occurrence in nature. A sign in the clouds. Colors or rings around the moon. A dang acorn falling. Not everything meant something bad, but you shouldn't ignore them when you saw them. Everything was ambiguous. The Fates offered guidance but only in ways that you had to interpret. Nothing was ever straightforward.

Mildred saw a raven. According to this book, ravens meant a several things. A loss, a warning, or a transition. Either way, it was another puzzle I had to figure out.

The door to the apartment burst open, startling Mildred and me. Harmony rushed through the space. She knelt in front of Mildred, smushing the sides of her head in her hands.

"My poor kitty. What happened to you?" She

kissed Mildred's face, then lifted her wrapped paw, giving it a tender kiss.

I laughed. "Harmony, chill. Mildred will be fine."

She stood and squished herself between Mildred and me. "Tell me what happened."

I told Harmony about the entire day, starting with finding the festival flier and ending with Mildred's incident. It wasn't until the apartment grew much darker in the night's shade that I realized how much actually happened to me in one day. A part of me longed for the days when all I did was give Lovers Readings.

Harmony was quiet while she chewed on one of her nails, processing. "So, how did Dean react when you told him that you'd go on a date?"

"He was happy, of course."

"Are you only going on a date with him because of the curse?"

"Do you actually like him?" Mildred asked, as well.

I repeated her words to Harmony and winced. "I don't know. Doesn't it make sense to partner up with him?"

Harmony shrugged her shoulders, toeing off her shoes and stuffing her feet under her. "Maybe. He's a warlock. Knows most of the secrets that surround this town. So, yeah. It does make sense."

"He's a convenience, of course, but what about love?" Mildred asked. *"You've known Dean for a long time and have never felt anything more than friends for him. Why would that change now? I'm on Sandy's team with this one, Shay."*

Love was important when getting involved with

someone, but it wasn't a luxury I had right now. The Whitley legacy was in danger and I already had a solid foundation with Dean. I frowned.

"I don't have time to fall in love."

Harmony studied me, petting lazy circles on Mildred's body. "What about love at first sight?"

"I don't believe in that. You have to get to know someone first. An instant connection with someone is beyond rare."

Images of Cade and his presence flooded my brain. We had an instant connection that was hard to ignore. The atmosphere that surrounded us every time we were together was suffocating.

"What about Cade?" Mildred suggested as if she were reading my mind. *"The chemistry between you two is beyond palpable."*

Harmony smirked. "Millie's right there, Shay," she said, when I repeated. "Anyone who has eyes can see there's something brewing between you and Cade. And it's much stronger than between you and Dean. You should date Cade."

I sighed, flopping my head on the back of the couch. "He's a skeptic. It would never work. Dean's my best option."

Harmony wrapped her arm around me, pulling me toward her and Mildred. "You are such a downer. Love is exciting and fun. It's electric when it's with the right person."

"It's unpredictable," I grumbled. "I have to save the Whitley bloodline. I can't focus on myself. The family is more important."

Mildred snorted, whacking me with a paw. Harmony pinched me playfully under my arm, causing me to shriek.

"Hey!"

"Will you just fucking let go and live a little?!" Harmony shouted. "Stop trying to do everything on your own. You're a freaking witch with an amazing power, an infectious personality, and you're beautiful inside and out. There are people around you that just want you to be happy."

"I am happy," I argued.

"That's such bullshit and you know it! Don't you think Sandy and Dotty would only want you to be happy, even if that meant losing the store? Don't you think you're more important than some dumb curse?"

Mildred hopped onto my lap, rubbing her face along my chin. *We only want what's best for you, Shay. Are you sure Dean is what's best for you?*

I ran my hands along her face and body, hearing her purrs. "I hear you both." I sighed.

Harmony wrapped her arms around both of us, squishing the three of us together until we were laughing. "I love you, gals," she said.

"I love you, too."

"Me too," Mildred added. *"As long as you keep feeding me and bringing Cade around,"* she purred long and sultry.

"Mildred!" I laughed. "You're as man-crazy as Harmony."

We all laughed together, settling onto the couch. Harmony flipped through the channels on the TV.

My mind swirled with all the things that they said. How could I think about myself when the Whitley legacy was in such trouble? Once the curse was satisfied then I would think about myself.

Frustration bubbled up in my gut. This curse was fucking stupid.

"What do you guys think Lucia did to earn the wrath of the council?" I said after a few minutes. "I just don't understand. And needing a man? That's so barbaric."

Harmony and Mildred stared at me.

"Why don't you try to trigger a past vision?" Mildred said. *"Focus on Lucia and see if she communes with you."*

"I'm not a medium. And my powers have been acting up," I argued.

"You're in control of your powers, Shay. Use them to guide you, like they're meant to do."

My lips tipped down. "Fine." An exasperated sigh escaped my lips. "I'll try."

Harmony clicked off the TV, sitting up straighter. "I love it when you use your powers."

"Harmony, can you light a purple candle?"

Harmony jumped up. "For psychic clarity, right?"

"She's been brushing up on her Wiccan knowledge," Mildred meowed.

"Right," I answered, smiling at her. Harmony placed the purple candle in front of me on the coffee table and lit it. I stared into the candle's flame, unfocusing my eyes and letting the world around me dissolve. I ran my thumbs over my fingertips, imagining Lucia in my mind's eye. I breathed in deeply, letting go of the control I had on my body.

A tug pulled on my stomach.

"It's working," I said, doubling down on my concentration.

I floated through time and space, morphing with

Lucia's essence. I merged with her, seeing through her eyes. I smelled the fresh nature that she smelled and heard the chatter of the townspeople as she did.

Lucia walked along the cobbled stone road. The sun was high in the sky, bringing warmth to her face. There was a stack of books in her arms.

A man stood on the opposite side of the road, causing Lucia to halt. He strode with a smug confidence as he took long steps to reach her. His face was familiar and his eyes were a deep dark brown, almost black.

Chills ran down Lucia's back and mine.

"Miss Whitley," the man spoke.

"Mr. Fellows," Lucia said, rolling her shoulders back. It was Harrison Fellows, Dean's ancestor.

"You are looking quite beautiful today," he said, smiling.

Lucia swallowed. "Thank you, sir. You are too kind." Her answers were clipped. Lucia unfocused her eyes, reading his aura. It was an inky black swirl with lightning bolts of red.

Terror coated her body, bringing sweat to her brow.

Harrison took a step closer to Lucia, reaching out his hand to grab hers. She stepped back out of his reach.

"Sir, it was lovely to see you, but I must make haste. My father needs these books on the vegetation around the rivers."

Harrison tilted his head to the side like a predator. "Right. Your father *needs those books." He stepped closer, bringing his face next to her ear. "Be careful not to practice in public. Men don't like to be upstaged by a woman. Especially an unbetrothed, childless woman."*

Lucia ground her teeth together, working hard to hold her tongue. Rebellion surged through her body. She wanted to argue but knew better.

"I could protect you, Lucia. If we married." He stepped back with a sly grin.

Lucia's heart raced and she tilted her head away from his proximity. "I'm sure there are many willing ladies in our town who would swoon at your hand in marriage."

"There's only one young lady I've got my eyes set on," he said, making his intention clear. Harrison stepped back and tipped his hat to Lucia. "Good day, Miss Whitley."

He walked away, leaving Lucia in shock on the road.

As I snapped back to the present, I collapsed against the couch, the remnants of my vision dissolved. I wiped away the sheen of sweat that had gathered on my forehead. My heart thumped in my chest. For the first time in several days, I felt in control. A full vision had materialized, not just snippets left for interpretation.

"What did you see?" Harmony asked, sharing a look of concern that Mildred held.

"Lucia had very strong negative reactions to Harrison Fellows, especially when he practically proposed to her on the street. She read his aura and it was a color I've never seen on a human before."

"What was Lucia trying to show you?"

"I have no idea. But I do know that Harrison Fellows was a creepy dude. I just hoped Harrison's issue isn't hereditary."

****

I ran my oiled fingers through my hair, trying to tame the wayward strands of blonde hair that refused to stay down. I turned around, checking out the back of my hair in the mirror. There was a slight fluttering in my stomach as I straightened my casual long-sleeved green dress. I shouldn't be this jittery to go out on a date with Dean.

"Why are you nervous, Shay?" Mildred asked from where she perched on my bed. Her tail swished back and forth lazily. I heard her smugness.

"I have no idea." I slipped my feet into black flats.

"I do."

I sighed. Dean would be here any minute. After a strenuous day of researching permits for community events and party rental places, I didn't want to have another drawn-out conversation about how controlling I was or what I was doing was wrong.

"Please, tell me what you think."

"You are afraid that you'll never feel anything more for Dean and that the curse will still be intact," Mildred spoke with confidence. *"Then all your hard work on the festival will go to waste."*

I swallowed. Is that what my problem was? Was I wishing that this date would open romantic feelings for Dean? That would be the easiest. In the back of my mind, yes, I was afraid. Afraid to have feelings for Dean and afraid not to.

Mildred rolled over onto her back, nipping at my fingers. I scratched her belly.

"See, I'm right. I can sense it."

A knock sounded on my door.

Mildred bounced off my bed, scurrying through the apartment. Before following her, I grazed my fingertips along the necklace stand full of jewelry Agnes made for me over the years. Each piece had a different crystal or stone. I grabbed the long chain with a bloodstone.

The greenish stone with specks of orange and red warmed against my skin as it settled over my chest. Bloodstone helped ground the body, invoked courage, and dispelled confusion. It was perfect for tonight.

I walked toward the door. Mildred was at attention beside me.

Here goes nothing.

I opened the door with a smile on my face. Dean stood on the other side, grinning. My eyes racked him up and down. He was dressed in a black button-down shirt, rolled up at the sleeves, and fitting jeans. I'd be lying to myself if I didn't think he looked handsome.

"Hey, Shay. You look beautiful as ever."

Blush heated my cheeks as I swiped a piece of hair off my face. "Thanks, Dean. You look…great, too."

He chuckled. "Now that the weird first interactions are out of the way, are you ready to go?"

I nodded. "Yes." I turned toward Mildred. "Be good," I told her with a stern voice. Closing the door behind me, I locked it and followed him down the front steps. "Where are we off to?"

Dean was a few steps ahead of me so he could open the door to his black truck. The heady scents of bergamot and rose, with hints of citrus from his cologne, assaulted my nose, causing it to crinkle on instinct.

"The Mystic Grove," Dean told me, bringing my attention back to him instead of his overpowering cologne.

"I love their food," I said, climbing into his car.

The whole cab of his truck smelled like his cologne. I sneezed.

"Bless you," he said as he started up the truck with a rev. "Coming down with a cold?"

"Thanks. No." I rubbed my nose. "Are you wearing cologne?"

Dean peeked over at me as he drove toward our destination. "Yeah. I always wear some when I'm on a date."

"Oh.".

"Shit. Is it making you sneeze?" he asked, looking at me with sympathetic eyes.

"Yeah. It's strong. And it kind of smells bad. You've never worn it around me before."

"Fuck," he frowned. "I'm sorry. I just... I don't know I was nervous or something. I won't wear it again." He reached across the center console, laying his hand on my thigh and squeezing it.

I looked down at his hand. It felt heavy and odd. No tingles. I moved my legs slightly, causing Dean's hand to fall out of reach.

"So," I started, breaking the silence in the cab as Dean drove us to The Mystic Grove. It wasn't uncomfortable, except that my nose kept itching. "I'm being haunted."

Dean glanced at me for a brief second. "Really? That's not your territory. Do you know who it is?"

I fidgeted with my necklace. "I think it's Lucia Whitley, one of my ancestors." I watched as Dean's throat bobbed with his thick swallow.

"What makes you say that?"

I rubbed my thumbs across my fingertips, watching the trees and buildings of Ipswich pass us by. "Weird poltergeist things keep happening to me. I've heard my name called and I saw a reflection of her in my window. I've had a couple of visions with her, too. Clearly about the past."

"Why is it happening to you and not your grandmother?" he said, gripping the steering wheel. My eyebrows knit together. The air in the car unmistakably shifted. Why was he getting defensive? Weird shit happened all the time in the Wiccan culture.

"I'm actually not sure. You know my powers have been changing. There's some parallel. Everything I've encountered with her has felt like a warning. I just don't know what she's warning me against."

Dean scoffed as he ran a hand over his buzzed head a few times. "Wow." He shook his head. "That's just perfect." His jaw tightened.

"Why are you mad?" I snapped.

"I'm not mad."

"You look mad." I poked his face. "Your jaw is tight."

Dean breathed out, slapping my hand away. He stretched his fingers out on the steering wheel. "Your powers are growing and getting stronger. It's kind of unfair."

He sounded like a spoiled brat, but I understood. Some witches and warlocks didn't have active powers. All of our powers were heredity and some were more passive, like an insane ability to grow plants or perfect success in spell-casting. I bet that would be frustrating to see another witch be more powerful.

I reached across the middle console, touching his

forearm. His skin was slick and clammy, causing me to flinch at its strangeness.

"I didn't ask for my powers to change," I told him with a small pout. I didn't want him to be mad. This was our first date. It would be a Magic-8 ball for the rest of our relationship. "In fact, it's getting in the way. Like when I had *two* random visions on the sidewalk in front of the fire station the other day, remember? In front of two Quaints."

His lips thinned and he shrugged his shoulders, cracking his neck. "That's true. I guess I'm still better at hiding than you."

Silence filled the car's cab again. Dean was competitive, always wanting a better body, a nicer car, a higher ranked job, but this was the first time I'd seen him jealous of me. Jealous of my gifts.

I stared out the window, fiddling with my sleeves. If I asked about our romantic potential, the Magic-8 ball would say: very doubtful.

Chapter 11

The tires of Dean's truck crunched on the gravel as he pulled into Mystic Grove's parking lot. It was a diner-style restaurant that sold a variety of American food, from burgers and pancakes, to fish sandwiches and a salad bar. It was the opposite of a fancy restaurant. It was comfort.

The diner's neon lights reflected off the rain puddles, creating miniature rainbows. Dean pulled into a spot and hopped out of the car. He rounded the front of the car and opened my door, shocking me with his chivalry. He held out his hand with a smile.

"Sorry, Shay. I didn't mean to snap at you. That's not the way I wanted to start this night. I…I actually don't know what my problem was. Anger just bubbled up."

I returned his smile, slipping my hand into his and hopping out of the car. He kept hold of my hand, tucking into the crook of his elbow.

"You've never been jealous of my powers before," I said.

"I know and I'm not."

"If we are going to be together for this curse thing, then we need to be able to talk to each other about stuff. Like partners."

Dean nodded his head and opened the door for me. "Right. Partners," he grumbled.

We got seated in a booth in the corner. The young waitress kept her eyes on Dean for a little longer than usual as she handed out our menus and left.

"I'm glad you agreed to this date," Dean said. "It's been a long time coming." He flashed me a charming smile. I offered one of my own before distracting myself with the food on the menu.

"I'm grateful you're willing to help out the family. Did your grandfather have any ideas?" My chest thumped as my heart beat rose. In the back of my mind, this date was essential for solving the curse placed on my family. My heart, however, wasn't feeling it. It hadn't since the moment he coorced me in front of Cade.

Dean set his menu down, clasping his hands together. "Shay?"

I looked above the menu to see him staring me down with a smoldering gaze. "Y-yeah?"

"Agreeing to date you isn't because I want to only help out the Whitleys."

I set the menu down, swallowing. His caramel eyes darkened as he held my gaze, making my heart beat faster.

"I agreed because I want you. I always have. I'm so happy that you finally can see me other than a friend. Being friends first is a great way to become romantic, too."

I tucked a piece of my hair behind my ear, squirming under his gaze. He was sending me primal, lust-filled signals. With all the emotions and hesitation, panic rose in my throat. Dean was ready to jump head first into my proposition while I was sinking fast, drowning under my hasty decisions. Fate had warned me and I didn't listen.

"O-oh. Well, that's nice to hear."

The waitress came over, delivering our drinks. She took our orders and shimmied away. Silence stretched between us. My body fidgeted in the awkwardness, knowing that my motives were the complete opposite of Dean's. My lack of feelings wasn't fair to Dean and his heart. Not to mention being a shitty friend.

"Did you find anything out about the curse?" I repeated.

Dean sat back, rolling his shoulders. "Not really. Gramps's memory is just not there. Thank god for Sara." Sara was their live-in nurse. She was as sweet as they came and extraordinarly compassionate. Plus, she wasn't opposed to the holistic healing supplies my family's store sold.

I wrung my hands together under the table. "I'm sorry."

"It's fine. But, I did find something interesting in the basement." He smirked.

"Oh? About the curse?" I took a sip of my drink.

He leaned forward. "I found an old journal of my ancestor's, Harrison."

My drink slid down the wrong pipe, triggering a fit of coughing. "What?! What was in there? Anything about Lucia?"

"No." He shook his head. "There were some pretty cool spells, though. He was a traditional warlock, like me, and a borderline necromancer."

My eyes widened, as haunting shivers ran down my spine. "A necromancer?"

Necromancy, used by dark magic users, teetered on the line between communing with the dead and using the dead. In ancient times, necromancers conjured the dead as protectors or spiritual guides, but now light witches associated it with demon-conjuring.

"I know. It was a little scary reading some of the stuff he was researching," Dean admitted. "But fascinating. It's a side of magic we don't really talk about. Some of his ideas were radical."

"Did he do any summoning?"

Dean stared at me, tilting his head to the side. "Why do you ask?" His eyes bore into mine as his voice hardened. Taken back by his question, I leaned away from him. His eyes darkened. Suspicion swirled in their depths.

"I had a vision yesterday. It was of Lucia and Harrison. I got major creep vibes from him. Something about him felt wrong. You need to be careful."

"Awe. That's sweet that you care." Dean laughed, breaking his stare. "Don't worry about me, Shay. I can take care of myself. I'm a warlock, remember?"

He was still laughing when the waitress brought our food. I'm sure to her it looked like we were having a good time, but Dean was laughing at me, not with me. We ate in silence. It was loud and stifling. The energy around us had shifted again, doing another one-eighty turn since this date had started. It was dizzying.

"So, I've been doing a lot of research on the permits I would need for the festival. The town square will be a perfect central spot," I said, trying to fill the silence.

"You still want to do that?"

"Yeah. It'll be great for all the businesses, not just The Wise Whitleys. I just need to get those permits and rally the community."

Dean scoffed. "Why can't you just let me give you the money? Then you wouldn't even have to worry about all the planning, setup, and cleanup."

I absentmindedly played with the bloodstone around my neck. Dean's gaze followed the movement, his eyes lingering to where the necklace sat between my breasts. He licked his lips.

"Confused about something?"

I lifted a shoulder, dropping the necklace from my fingers. The way he looked at me made me feel uncomfortable, like he wanted to eat me instead of his food. His moods were giving me whiplash. First, he was apologetic, then mad and jealous, now aroused.

"I'm not confused," I said, finding my courage. "I'm doing the festival."

Dean sat back, scowling. "Why? I have all this money from my parents' inheritance. Let me take care of you. That's my job as the man in the relationship."

My stomach dropped to my feet. *His job?* What century was he living in? We weren't in Puritan times like Lucia and Harrison. Women had the same rights as their male counterparts, despite what some might want to shun. I refused to be one of those women who *needed* a man in her life. I was my own person. Capable of anything a man could do. In the Wiccan culture, I was more powerful *because* I was a woman.

I ground my teeth together, overcompensating for the angry words that burned my tongue. The waitress interrupted our heated conversation, placing the check on the table, and giving Dean one last longing look.

"I *want* to do it, Dean. It was an Ipswich tradition and I'm bringing it back," I said when she left. "I like planning, you know this. Plus, Cade has a friend in

Boston who's a party-planner—"

Dean held up a hand in my face, interrupting me. Fury was evident on his face. "You'll accept a convict's help over mine? Someone you don't know over me?"

My gut soured even more. "Cade is *not* a convict. So, knock it the fuck off. You just think I can't do it myself. That I need a man to solve all my problems. Why can't you support me? If you can't, then this…" I pointed my finger between the two of us. "…will *never* work."

Dean laughed hollowly, shaking his head from side to side. He pulled a credit card from his wallet and slapped it on the check.

"Trust me," he started, his voice low and lethal. "I support you. I've been by your side since we were kids. Hoping. Waiting for you to get your head out of your ass. So, here I am jumping on the chance to offer my *support* through money and whatever else you need. I'm willing to do the work. I'm willing to fucking wait for you. But you're throwing it all away for some newcomer Quaint."

I gathered my hair and pulled it over to one side, playing with the tips. My hands needed to do something with all the energy thrumming through my body. My fight-or-flight instincts ignited. I wanted to punch him in his smug face. Gouge his eyes out. Run away.

A heated, stifling silence stretched between us as we puffed out breaths. We had fought before, smaller and more insignificant.

Gram's sullen face entered my mind, dousing my anger and refocusing my motivations. I had forgotten what was on the line: the Whitley Legacy.

Desite my anger for Dean's stupidity, another

bigger part of my fury was toward myself. Harmony and Mildred had it wrong. I didn't need to be selfish, I already was. I was only thinking about myself. I wasn't thinking about everything my grandmother and mother worked for. I wasn't even thinking about Dean's feelings in all this.

The truth was I needed him for the dumb curse. Right now, there were no other options. I had to save the store.

"Dean." I reached across the table, grabbing his hand, ignoring its clamminess and the lack of sparks. "Look at me." He lifted his eyes to meet mine. They were back to their light caramel color.

"I'm sorry. I'm being an asshole."

Dean's lips tipped up on one side. "You said it. Not me."

I laughed, feeling a little lighter. "I know you've been by my side for a long time, which is why I want your support for this festival. I don't want you to use your inheritance on me or my family. Your parents left it for you."

He stayed frozen for a moment. He brought my hand to his lips, planting a soft kiss. Again, no tingles. He breathed in as he cracked his neck again.

"I'll support you. But know that if it doesn't work out, my offer is still on the table."

I smiled, pulling my hand from his grasp. "You got it."

"I still don't like Thompson," he said with a huff as he stood from the booth.

"He doesn't like you either."

Dean frowned, but let it go.

Note to self: stop bringing up Cade around Dean.

"You'll need to get approval from the city council. Luckily, I know someone who can help," he said with a cheeky smile as we walked toward his truck. "And a permit to hold an event in the space. Oh, you'll need approval from the police department to have security."

"Okay. That's a lot."

He glanced down, looking at me. "You've got this." He opened the door for me. "Do you want to get a couple of drinks from the Brew? The Bruins are playing."

I looked up at him. He towered over me as he held the door. His eyes shifted in color again, growing darker, almost black.

"What's wrong with your eyes?"

Dean's gaze dropped to my lips and he shrugged a shoulder. "Maybe you bring out the beast in me."

I fake-laughed, slapping him in the chest. He caught my hand, holding it there. Beneath my palm, I felt the pulse of his heartbeat. The air around us grew thick. My own heartbeat ticked up, preparing for us to cross the line from friends to something more.

His gaze flickered to my lips. Then he closed the space between us and kissed me. I stood there, frozen. His lips felt foreign, wrong. I felt absolutely nothing.

No sparks. No excitement. No passion.

His lips moved against mine, creating spit on my mouth. I opened my eyes and pulled away. My back hit the truck. It was as if he couldn't find the right amount of pressure to apply. His cheeks lifted in a dopey smile.

"I've wanted to do that for so long," he breathed. He swiped his fingers across my forehead, tucking a piece of blonde hair behind my ear.

"How 'bout that drink?" I asked, turning my back

on him and settling into the passenger seat.

"You got it, love." He closed the door and walked to the driver's side.

I bowed my head, licking my lips, feeling too much moisture. The kiss wasn't horrible, but I should have felt something. Anything.

****

Dean pulled into a spot in front of The Witch's Brew. We got out of the car. I halted on the curb, causing Dean to pause and look over his shoulder. The hairs on the back of my neck stood up.

"Something wrong?" he asked.

A chilly blast of air swirled around me.

"Shaaay," a feminine whisper sounded behind me.

I turned around, gasping at a white, misty silhouette of a woman in olden clothes. Her dark hair blew around her face under her bonnet.

Lucia?

"Don't trust him," she moaned, holding a hand out to me.

Dean gripped my arms, spinning me around. "Shay? What is it?" His voice was calm, with a hint of concern. Taking a deep breath, I rubbed my forehead before looking back over my shoulder. Lucia was gone.

"N-nothing. I-I just saw a ghost."

Dean's eyes peeked behind me. "What?! Are you sure? Was it Lucia?"

"Yeah."

His eyebrow cocked. "Did she say anything?"

My instincts screamed at me not to tell him. "No," I lied. Dean squinted at me for a moment, then he wrapped his arm around my shoulders, pulling me toward him.

"Let's go get some drinks. You can solve this mystery tomorrow," he said, giving me a once-over and leading me toward The Witch's Brew.

As predicted, the place was packed full of people, cheering and drinking. Harmony was behind the bar. Her hand was propped on her hip as she flirted with Brad. Dean let go of my shoulders as we walked toward the bar, weaving through the crowd. His mayoral mask slipped into place as he smiled at locals who stopped him.

The energy around me charged with recognition. My heart skipped a beat as I spotted Cade sitting at the bar with a few of the town's firefighters.

"Brad," Dean greeted. "How's the game?" He wrapped an arm around my shoulders, bringing me to a halt directly behind Cade.

His sweet, dewy, woodsy smell wafted up to my nose, sending shivers down my spine. Through the reflection of the mirror behind the bar, Cade's beautiful green eyes drifted up and down my body. He lifted a corner of his mouth in a smirk.

"Shay," he greeted, turning in his seat. His dimples were on full display.

"Cade," I returned his greeting, licking my lips. It was painfully obvious that my body enjoyed his attention much more than Dean's. He said one word to me and my panties practically melted off.

"Shay?" Dean asked. "Shay, what do you want to drink?"

I snapped my head in his direction. My eyes flicked to Harmony. "Oh, um, a Poisoned Apple Martini."

She winked. "I knew you were going to say that."

"How's the date going?" Cade asked. His deep voice startled me. Dean turned, pulling me toward him. I faltered on my feet at his force. An intensity sharpened behind Cade's eyes as he caught the movement.

"It's going awesome, Thompson," Dean answered over my shoulder. He peeked down at me. "Right, Shay? We just came over for the end of the game after eating at The Mystic Grove."

"Classy," Cade answered, his eyes shifting between the two of us.

"Here's your drink, Shay," Harmony chimed in, setting the drink as far away from me as she could. She scanned the men and me with humor in her eyes as if she were watching a soap opera. She lived for this kind of drama.

I gently eased out of Dean's heavy arm, squeezing between him and Cade. The heat from Cade's body seared my skin through my clothes, boiling me from the inside. The sparks of attraction and arousal fueled an imaginary fire in my gut. I'd felt none of these things all night with Dean. This was bad.

"Thanks, Harm," I said, trying to hide the breathlessness in my voice.

"Shay! Do a shot with me," Dean said. He knocked a shoulder into me, pushing me into Cade. Dean threw back one shot before I had a chance to answer. That was the second time he didn't let me talk. Not like I kept score.

Cade's hand captured my waist, stopping me from falling. His fingers dug into my hip. I peeked over my shoulder at him. Our faces were inches apart from each other. Our breathing intertwined. My eyes flicked down to his lips and back up to his eyes. It would be so easy to kiss him.

"Dickhead better slow down if he plans to take you home later," he whispered.

His eyes pierced mine. My throat dried at his intense protectiveness. It felt oddly energizing to have someone looking out for me. Even if it was unsolicited. Again. I stood upright, moving out of Cade's hold. I took a long drag of my drink, tasting the fake-sour apple flavors. Dean was talking animatedly with Brad. He threw back two more shots.

I gripped the bloodstone. The kiss we shared spun in my mind. Playing on repeat. My breathing increased watching Dean's demeanor change. My fight or flight instincts were still activated and with Lucia's warning, dread settled in my gut.

Shaking it off, I tapped Dean's shoulder. "Come on. Let's go sit down."

Dean flopped his arm back around my shoulders, giving me a goofy smile. We walked toward an empty table and sat. I sipped my drink and Dean glued his eyes to the TV. They were glassy and sweat had gathered on his forehead. How many shots did he have? He handled his liquor better than this.

"Dean, are you okay?"

"Fuck! That was a cheap call, ref," he yelled at the TV. His face turned red. "Yeah, I'm fine. Did you see that call? That was bullshit."

His anger jolted me, but turned to watch the game's replay. It was a clear slashing penalty on one of our guys. The opponent's stick broke.

"It looks like a legit penalty to me."

"Whatever," he growled. His voice was deep. "You

must not be watching the same game as me."

I scoffed and drank another sip. The Bruins were on a penalty kill, down one player on the ice. The other team scored. Dean slammed his hands down and shoved away from the table, yelling obscenities at the screen. The table shook under his movements, tipping my drink, spilling onto the table.

I recoiled. "Dean!" He paused his yelling and looked over at me.

"Shit. Sorry." He grabbed some napkins and leaned over to help me clean up the mess. The Witch's Brew had crappy napkins, so all he did was push more of the sticky liquid onto my crotch.

"Dean. Stop," I hissed, wiping my hands at my dress. "You aren't helping."

He moved around the table closer to me and started wiping at my crotch with the napkins. I jumped further back, bumping into the wall that was between the booths. Pain radiated up my back. Sourness churned in my stomach as I slapped his hands away.

"Stop touching me."

"I'm just trying to help, Shay. Fuck. What's your problem?"

"I could ask you the same thing. You've had like three shots and you're acting like a total drunk," I said, lowering my voice so we wouldn't draw attention. "Stop touching me."

"If we're going to satisfy the curse, Shay, I'm going to have to touch you," he snarled, his dark eyes scanning me from head to toe. I shrank back against the wall and squirmed uncomfortably under his gaze. My hands shook as he stared at me like I was the tastiest thing he'd ever seen. Dean blinked his eyes a few times and shook his head. He ran his hands over his head, slapping them down at his sides.

"Gods! Shay, I'm sorry." He sat back down in his seat. His whole demeanor changed, deflated and defeated. "I was just trying to help."

I exhaled and sat as well, ignoring the stiffness in my shoulders. "Well, maybe you need to chill on the alcohol. You're being erratic."

He gave me a sloppy frown. "Yes, Mom," he mocked. Sweat dripped down his forehead.

My brow furrowed as the headache in my temple grew. This night had become all sorts of fucked up. With his strange behavior, his mood swings at The Mystic Grove, and his eyes changing color, something was amiss with Dean.

When the game ended, I touched Dean's arm, getting his attention. He had barely spoken to me. He turned, staring at me. The expression on his face changed immediately to seductive. His eyes drifted up and down my body.

"Have I told you how beautiful you look tonight?" he said through slurred words.

I swallowed. "Um, yeah. Earlier. But, I think I'm—"

"You are deliciously tasty-looking," he said, cutting me off, again. His eyes darkened to a burnt caramel. Flush crept up my neck under his perusal. He scooted his chair closer to mine. Our knees touched. I turned my legs away. He leaned in. "I can't stop thinking about our kiss." His breath stank of alcohol.

"Oh."

His arms caged me. One on the back of my chair and the other across the table. His fingers gripped the sides of my back, holding me in place. Dean wedged me between him, the table, and the wall. Trapped.

I looked around the bar. Most of the patrons were involved with their own conversations, except one. Cade. He sat sideways in his chair, facing his firefighter buddies, but his attention was on me. His jaw ticked as he watched.

"How about it, babe?" Dean spoke.

I flicked my gaze to him. He was even closer, crowding my space. "What?" I hadn't heard a word he said.

"Want to go back to my place?" His voice, thick with need, and his fingers dug into my skin. "We could get a head start on breaking your family's curse."

I ran my tongue over my lips, trying to wet my drying mouth. "No."

Dean blinked a few times, shocked. "The fuck?"

My body tensed. "I'm really tired. I just want to go home." As I reached for my purse, Dean gripped my arms with his hands, freezing me in place.

"I thought we were having fun," he spat. His eyes turned completely black. Empty. Soulless.

I grimaced. He'd never manhandled me like this. I placed my hands on his chest and pushed.

"Let me go, Dean. Something is wrong with you and I don't have the energy to deal with it. The date was kind of fun at first, but now it's not. I think I made a mistake asking you for help. Fate warned me and I didn't listen."

"Fucking typical, Shay." Dean shook his head as he gripped my wrist, pulling me toward him. "Too fucking scared to let someone in." He opened his mouth to say more when a hand landed on his shoulder with a thud.

"Everything okay over here?" Cade asked, pulling at Dean's shoulder to put more space between us. Cade stood beside Dean, with the two other firefighters behind him. They all stood tall with their shoulders straight.

I exhaled a heavy breath. I didn't need saving from Dean, but was grateful for Cade's savior complex.

Dean let go of my wrist and backed away. He turned on Cade, standing from his chair. "Just having a private conversation with my girl, Thompson. One that you aren't welcome in."

I balked. *His girl? Nope.*

The fingers of Cade's hand flexed as he gripped Dean's shoulder. "Well, when someone gets in the face of a woman, I have to get involved. Even if they don't like it," he added, sending a sharp glance in my direction.

Danger lingered in the air. Dean was already on edge. Cade's protectiveness added fuel to the fire. I grabbed my purse from the chair and stood, ready to walk away.

Dean slapped Cade's arm, knocking his hand off his shoulder. His hands fisted at his side, causing his shoulders and biceps to flex. He was primed for a fight. I had never seen Dean get into a fistfight with anyone.

"'Someone like me?'" Dean scoffed. "As I said, this is a *private* conversation."

Cade looked at me, ignoring Dean. "You okay?"

"Peachy," I snapped. This night was all done for me. Dean was acting strangely. I felt zero romantic feelings for him, and although Cade had better intentions, he was acting all caveman. I was over all of

119

it. "I'm taking off."

"I can drive you home," Dean said.

I stared at him, sending him daggers with my eyes. Dean had been traveling down a dark road all night. Whatever his issue was, I was over it and he wasn't taking me with him. I didn't want to think about what he would have done if Cade hadn't come over when he did.

"Ha! No thanks. I'll walk."

Dean snubbed my suggestion with a snort. "Bullshit. It's dark. I'll drive you."

"I. Said. No."

"Shay, I'm the Mayor. I know my limits and I'm totally fine. Besides, you don't live that far away."

"Exactly. I don't live that far away. Enough. You don't make decisions for me." I stepped out from the circle of testosterone, giving Dean a hardened look. I silently dared him to keep pushing, especially with an audience around.

Dean squinted his eyes at me but stayed put.

The first smart thing he's done all night.

I walked past the bar, connecting gazes with Harmony. "See you at home."

"You got it, girl," she said, while her eyes held worry. I gave her a reassuring smile. I had made the right choice to end this disastrous mind-fuck of a date.

I sensed Cade's eyes tracking me as I walked out of the bar.

I exhaled when I finally exited The Witch's Brew. The fresh air cooled my heated skin. I inhaled a deep breath through my nose and started walking down the street.

I yelped when someone grabbed my elbow, pulling

me to a stop.

Dean.

"Shay, wait. I don't want you to leave this way." He gripped my elbow a little tighter, trying to pull me toward him. I held strong.

I sighed, tilting my head to the side and looking up into his light caramel eyes. They held an insecurity that was all too familiar. Some of my anger drifted away.

"Something is going on with you, Dean. And I don't like it."

Dean hung his head for a brief moment before he lifted it again. "I'm sorry, Shay, I really am. I don't know what's wrong with me. I don't feel like myself. Maybe I was just really nervous about finally getting my chance with you, and I took it too far."

"You called me 'your girl'."

He smirked. "It felt right to say."

I looked to the heavens before leveling him with a pointed look. "I'm not your girl."

Tentatively, he wrapped his arms around me, pulling me into a hug. I let him.

"I know. I know. We'll take it slow, okay?"

"Dean…"

"Just give me a second chance. I can do better by you," he begged into the crook of my neck. I had never heard Dean beg for anything before. It wasn't him. I pulled away from the hug. My body still tense, but I smiled.

"I'm sorry, but no. This isn't going to work. I'm going home. You should do the same."

Dean tucked his hands into his pockets and gave me a boyish heartbroken frown. For the first time tonight, I got a glimpse of my old friend. In this moment, he was the Dean I knew. He was my friend. And would *only* be my friend.

"Bye, Dean," I said as I turned and walked in the direction of my apartment.

"I'm not giving up, Shay," he called after me.

I ignored him and sped toward my apartment just below the speed of running.

My head spun after the events of the night. Between Lucia's warning and Dean's mercurial behavior, I was ready to cuddle deep in my bed's blankets.

I turned the corner onto my street when crunching and footsteps sounded behind me. I shrieked, turning and holding my bag up as a shield.

"Whoa, it's just me," a voice said, holding their hands up with slight humor in their tone. The person stepped under a streetlight. Cade's muscular build came into view.

"Cade! You scared the shit out of me. What are you doing following a woman at night?"

"Sorry. I wanted to make sure you were actually all right. Things looked pretty intense back there. And he left after you."

"That's very chivalrous of you." I rolled my eyes.

"Yeah, well, I don't really care how you feel about that." He ran a hand through his hair and took a step closer to me.

I pulled my sleeves over my hands, trying to suppress the wave of energy his admission sent down my spine. There was no doubt he was confident and a rule breaker, but all of his motivations came from a place of kindness. Those qualities made him more appealing. My heartbeat slowed, knowing I wasn't in any danger.

"Care to walk me the rest of the way?" I asked, surprising myself.

"I was going to whether you asked or not," Cade said with a smile as he stepped up beside me. "This way my following you won't be as creepy."

"Classic hero," I teased, feeling at ease that he was here. We walked together the short distance to my apartment.

"So, do you want Aaron's number?" Cade asked. I looked up at him as we walked in tandem, thankful for the safe topic.

"Oh, yeah, that'd be great. Thanks."

"Sure. Aaron's been itching to come up here anyway. He goes to Salem all the time, but he didn't know Ipswich was equally as…spirited."

I laughed. "Hopefully, this festival will change that."

"Your boyfriend didn't seem too happy about your decision."

"He's not my boyfriend," I snapped, hating that everyone assumed we were a couple. We went on one freaking disaster date. This stupid curse. "Especially after tonight."

Cade peered down at me. "Why do you say that?"

"Nevermind. Dean is only a friend and will always be. Tonight confirmed that."

"Does he know that? You guys seemed cozy when you first came in. Not a good date? Is he a bad kisser?"

"You're very nosy, you know that?"

Cade laughed. "I'm just interested. Small town, big gossip, you know?"

"I don't kiss and tell, Cade. Sorry."

"That means it was a horrible kiss," he said with a cocky humor in his voice.

"What?" A blush crept up my neck. "I never said that."

"You are such a bad liar. I've got a pretty good bullshit-radar, Shay." His arm brushed against mine, sending tingles up my arm. What it would feel like to hold his hand or share a kiss with him? It felt so natural walking and talking with him. Effortless. I liked that. Instinctively, my thumbs ran across my fingertips.

"You're slowly becoming an all-around hero, aren't you?" I teased.

"I didn't become a firefighter just to play with fire all day."

"You don't know me well enough to know if I'm bullshitting you or not."

"You're easy to read." Cade snorted again. "You have secrets. Big ones. I know it."

I swallowed over the thickness in my throat. His confidence was borderline arrogant. Maybe I wasn't starting to like him…

"I'm not some puzzle for you to piece together because you're bored."

Cade shrugged his shoulders. "Am I trying to figure you out? Yes. But, because I know you're hiding something. Most of the people are in this town. I'm intrigued."

"Isn't there some cliché idiom about a cat and its curiosity?" I eyed him, watching his reaction. He smirked. "You aren't going to leave me alone, are you?"

"Probably not. I like your snarky attitude. And I *do not* like Dean. He has his sights set on you. And that does not sit well with me."

Swirls of satisfaction and anxiety bubbled in my stomach. It was nice to have someone looking out for me, whether I asked for it or not. Cade proved his prime skill of observation. There *was* something going on with Dean, but I knew it was a supernatural issue, not a Quaint problem. If Dean's problem grew, Cade could be caught in the crosshairs. I clamped my mouth shut, choosing not to respond. Luckily, I was saved by my apartment coming into view.

"This is me," I said, pointing a thumb back toward my apartment. "Which you know 'cause you were just here a couple of days ago."

Cade peered behind me. "Speaking of which, how's the cat?"

"Mildred. She's good. Dramatic. But her paw is healing fine."

"That's good. She seems like a feisty one."

I laughed. "You have no idea."

Cade eyed me as he nodded.

"Thanks, Cade. For walking me home…and for earlier at the bar." As much grief I was giving him, I was thankful he was there. His lips curled into a tight smile. His attentiveness to my safety didn't go unnoticed.

"Wow. An actual 'thank you'?"

"Don't get used to it," I teased, slapping his shoulder with my hand. A tiny spark ignited under my skin at our touch. I pulled my hand away.

"Give Millie a pet for me," he said, ticking his head toward my front window.

I turned, seeing a feline silhouette in the window. I chuckled, turning back toward Cade. "I will."

I unlocked and opened the door. Before stepping through the threshold, I peered over the railing to my driveway down below. Cade still stood, waiting for me to get into my apartment. He lifted a hand in a salute and walked down my driveway and out of sight.

I closed the door behind me and banged my forehead against it. My heart was thumping wildly under my chest and my skin had sparks running along it.

"Okay, so Cade is the one dropping you off after your date with Dean. Give me the T, now," Mildred yowled at me from the window sill.

I laughed into the door before turning and filling her in on the night's details.

Chapter 12

I hiked my bag up on my shoulder, pulling my heavy poncho closer to my body. The chill of the early October air whipped around me. Goosebumps pricked my skin. The sun would be rising soon, clearing the darkness from the night. I always enjoyed the in-between moments of a day: when night turned to day or day to night. Transition times were perfect for declaring clear intentions.

The large ironed gates of the Ipswich Cemetery loomed above me. Their spiked tendrils scratched against the sky. My feet were unsteady on the cracked sidewalk, indicating the landmark's age. I pushed through the gates, making a rusty creak as they moved.

The only things awake this early were birds, fishermen, and me. A dewy fog stuck to my skin as I walked through the cemetery, passing by faded tombstones and thick trees. The rocky path crunched beneath my feet while traipsing under some willowy trees, finding our family's plot toward the center of the cemetery. We didn't have a mausoleum, but we did have a large section of the land. Different tombstones littered the area, all in various stages of decay.

I found Lucia's in the back. Her tombstone a simple cross.

Lucia Whitley
1672—1733

Devoted daughter, wife, and mother.
"Until we meet again in the next plane."

Pulling a large quilt from my tote, I laid it out on the damp grass above her grave. I sat down, facing the tombstone and pulled out candles in different colors: purple, psychic clarity; black, protection; and brown, decision-making. I lit them, taking a minute to set my intention for each.

Next, I grabbed my baggie of herbs and dried flowers to make a circle around me for my spell. I scattered nutmeg, violets, bay leaves, and cinnamon—each carefully chosen for their power to boost positive thinking, spiritual development, and decision clarity. I sprinkled some parsley for communing with the dead, too.

With my legs now crossed, I placed my hands palm up on my knees, and closed my eyes. I focused on using my senses to begin my spell. The freshness of the woody cemetery surrounded me. I heard the chirping of the early birds, and felt the chilly fog licking my skin.

"Mother Earth," I whispered, "I want to set my intention for this spell. I ask for clarity and protection." I stopped talking, letting the words take hold in the atmosphere around me, giving the Mother Goddess a chance to hear them.

"I open my mind, body, and powers to Lucia Whitley. I need information about the curse in order to preserve our family's bloodline and legacy since it all falls on my shoulders." I took a deep breath, trying to calm the annoyance rising in my body. "I know it's you, Lucia, who's giving me warnings. Please use me and my powers of premonition to show me what you want me to see."

A chilly burst of air flew through my hair. I swallowed. My throat grew thick as something from another realm joined me. Leaves flew around me in a circle as the breeze picked up. The familiar tug pulled at my stomach, while the air whooshed past my ears. I closed my eyes, surrendering to my powers. My astral body tore from me, sending me flying through time.

"Good morning, Lucia," Goody Sapphire greeted me. Her white-blonde hair was tied in braids down her back under her bonnet.

"Good day, Sally. How are you this clear morning?" I lifted my skirts as we walked down the gravel road toward the town square.

"Did you hear Harrison Fellows is looking to ask for your hand in marriage? I heard he's set an appointment with your father this afternoon." Sally spoke excitedly, but it was all for show. We were walking in the middle of town with too many prying ears.

"Why, no," I said, hearing the hiccup in my voice. "I didn't. I will try to act surprised."

My family's store came into view: The Wise Whitleys. My father, Samuel, was the local physician, and my mother, Alice, aided him using her knowledge of medicinal herbs and empathy to help him with their patients. What my father didn't know was that my mother and I had supernatural talents.

Sally and I shuffled through the door of the store, knocking the dirt off our tied boots.

"Mother," I called, setting the basket of flowers, herbs, and plants on the wooden counter. "I'm back with supplies from the market."

My mother came out from the side cove, wiping her

hands down her apron. *"Wonderful. Your father has an appointment with Goody Jessop this afternoon. She's feeling very nauseous."* She rummaged through the basket, finding the peppermint and chamomile. She pulled them out, smelling them. *"These are perfect,"* she said, cupping my face with her hand. Her soft blue eyes held all the love in the world for me.

I smiled. *"Goody Jessop is with child."*

My mother's face slackened. Her eyes shifted around. *"You saw it?"*

I nodded. My long dark hair moved with my head under my bonnet. *"She will give birth to two babes under a crescent moon. It will be a tough delivery. You and Father need to be prepared."*

Mother straightened, clasping her hands in front of her. *"Thank you, child. Your gifts are truly magnificent."* She smiled before returning to the side room where she kept her medicines.

Sally pursed her lips. *"You shouldn't use your gifts that openly, Lucy."*

I shrugged my shoulders, moving around the counter. *"I can't help it. They are a part of me that I trust fully."*

"You already knew that Harrison was going to ask for your hand."

I bowed my head. *"No. I knew that he was going to ask for someone's hand, I didn't know it would be mine."* I frowned.

"You are not happy about that?"

"Harrison is not a gentleman. There is a darkness to him. I'm not sure I could love someone who is not a white witch."

Sally leaned forward. Her eyes blazed as she spoke

in hushed tones. "You can not deny his hand."

I rolled my shoulders. "I will not marry him. I have had visions of him forcing himself upon other women. He is not virtuous."

"What a man does does not matter like it does for us. I'll warn you again. You can not deny him."

"We shall see about that," I said with a nod.

My body shot backward, knocking me onto the soft quilt. I blinked my eyes, scanning the brightening clouds in the sunrise. My heart beat rapidly against my chest.

I sat up, tucking my hair behind my ears. A cold hand pressed down on my shoulder. I shrieked, snapping my head up behind me. A wispy, ghostly image of Lucia stood behind me.

"*Don't trust the Fellows boy,*" she whispered, her mouth barely moving.

Chills ran down my spine as my body shook. "W-why?"

Lucia shook her head sorrowfully. "*He holds the same darkness that Harrison did.*"

"W-what about the c-curse?"

"*There is another…*" she whispered, being interrupted. Her misty body flickered and faded. I held out my hand, moving to kneel.

"Wait! There's another what? Way to break the curse?"

"*Trust your instincts…*" she finished as she faded from sight.

I blew out all the breath I was holding, making puffs of vapor in the chilly air. My hand fell with a thud against the blanket as I stared at the absence where she stood.

My body shook. Not only did I summon Lucia, but she showed me another past vision. I rubbed my thumbs along the pads of my fingers. I felt my power there just under the surface. If one thing was most true, my powers were growing stronger.

I reflected on Lucia's words and actions in my vision. Harrison Fellows wanted to marry Lucia, but she clearly didn't. What happened to the two of them? How was the curse formed?

She had told me to trust my instincts, warning me about Dean's darkness and confirming my suspicions.

I blew a raspberry past my lips and turned toward Lucia's tombstone. "Thank you for showing me clarity, Lucia. Thank you, Mother Goddess, for enhancing my gifts, allowing me to find some answers." I bowed forward in prayer. "I want to close this circle."

I rose, blowing out the candles. A rustling of leaves sounded beside me. I whipped my head to the side and froze in place, holding a candle in my hand. A dark silhouette rounded the corner of the path. A man was running, dressed in a dark hoodie and pants. Sparks of recognition zapped my skin.

Cade.

He pulled the hood off his head when he saw me. He slowed his pace and ticked his head to the side. He walked up to me, breathing heavily. He plucked an earbud out of his ear and bent down.

"Morning," he greeted. I watched as his eyes flicked around all my herbs, candles, and blanket. "Um, whatcha doin'?"

What lie could I possibly tell this time?

"You didn't have those candles lit out here, did you?" he asked, still puffing.

"Yes…"

He stood to full height, lifting one of his legs behind him to stretch his thigh. "Come on, now, do I really have to remind you about forest fires? Do I look like Smokey the Bear to you?" He laughed. His joke broke the tension that I felt. I shook my head, shoving the candles back into my satchel.

"I was careful, Smokey."

His eyes squinted as I shoved the rest of my spell ingredients into my bag. I gathered my blanket, draped it over my arm, and stood up.

"So, what are you doing here?" he asked again.

"I could ask you the same thing."

He smiled as he ran a hand through his messy and damp hair. I watched the motion, noting how his muscles bunched and how much I wanted to run my hand through his hair. I bet it was soft.

"Is that not obvious?" he snarked. "I have to stay in shape for my job. But, seeing as you were sitting on the ground, at dawn, with all your weird shit on a grave, I am very curious to hear what *you* were doing."

"Would you believe that I was, um, reading?" I quipped. Cade laughed. The sound sent tingles down my skin.

"Fuck no. Try again."

I scanned around me and spied the tombstone. I gestured to it. "This is one of my ancestor's graves, Lucia Whitley. I'm paying my respects." I smiled, looking him directly in the eye. Cade's gaze bounced between my eyes and the tombstone.

"With lit candles?"

"Yup. Many cultures use candles to pay homage. Ever heard of *Dia De Las Muertos*?"

He crossed his arms over his chest. "Of course. I'm still not buying your shit, though."

I mimicked his stance. "I don't care."

I turned and started down the hill toward the path that led back to my apartment. The sun had fully risen, illuminating the morning dew on the trees and grass. Splashes of fall color had begun to bloom. The gravel crunched behind me as Cade followed.

"I talked with Aaron," Cade said. "He said you contacted him. He's going to come soon to scope out the town square."

"I reached out to him when my eyes crossed from researching all the different permits and rentals that I would need. He said he'll take care of all that. He only wanted my 'mood board' for the theme. Which, naturally, I already had set up," I said. "There's a lot to do."

"How can I help?"

Warmth built in my chest. "I bet I need approval from the fire department or something."

Cade chuckled. "I'll put in a good word for ya."

"Thanks."

We walked through the rest of the cemetery in a comfortable silence. My mind replayed the vision and conversation I had with Lucia. She kept showing me memories of her and Harrison. The parallels between Lucia and Harrison and Dean and me were clear. There was no love between Lucia and Harrison, similar to me and Dean. So, what was I supposed to learn? How did this new information help me with the curse?

A sourness drifted up my throat thinking about being romantic with Dean. As if I got punched in the stomach, I realized I wasn't listening to my instincts, like Lucia warned.

I peeked up at Cade. Could Cade even be an option to help with the curse? He was handsome and genuine, annoying and sexy, but he didn't believe. The friendship we were building felt uncomplicated...except for the massive secrets I kept. Deep down I knew he wouldn't handle the news of "real witches" well. But, maybe I wanted to try with him. Being around Cade felt right, for whatever reason.

When we got to the sidewalk, knowing he was going in the opposite direction as me, I grabbed his arm, turning him toward me. I felt the tingles in my fingers.

"Cade."

He looked down at my hand before looking at me with a soft smile.

"I want you to know that I do have a lot of big secrets. You were right about that."

He ticked his head to the side. "Okay."

I took a deep breath. "I can't tell you them...yet. One thing I can tell you, Dean will never be my boyfriend." I chewed on my lip as I lifted my head. "I don't want anything romantic with him."

Cade's green eyes smoldered to a darker green as he stared into my eyes. Arousal swirled around us as we stood on the sidewalk.

"Why are you telling me this?"

"I felt like I needed to tell you."

Cade's lips curled into a sexy smirk. My heart skipped a beat. "Noted."

I took in a deep breath, suddenly feeling like a weight was lifted from my chest. "Well...I've got to get ready to open the store," I said.

"Same. But for my work. Not yours."

"Got it." I laughed.

"I bet you a million bucks, I'll see you later," he teased with a smile.

"That's a bet I'm not going to take because it's inevitable."

He waved as he turned in his direction, taking off at a jog. I watched him go until I couldn't see him anymore. My cheeks hurt from smiling. For the first time in several dramatic days, I felt confident with my actions.

Chapter 13

Bang. Bang. Bang.

I groaned, rubbing my face against my pillow. "Goddamn it," I said into the fluffy fabric.

Bang. Bang. Bang.

"What the Hecate?"

I flipped my phone over from my nightstand. I popped straight out of bed, noticing several texts from Cade and a couple of missed calls from him, too. I rubbed my hand down my face, wiping the sleep off. I unlocked my phone to read the notifications when the banging happened again. It came from the front door.

"Shay," a voice called. "I have your cat."

I furrowed my eyebrows in confusion as I swiped up on my phone, seeing the first few messages from Cade.

Cade:—Somehow your cat made her way into my apartment.—

Cade:—Can I drop her off? Or should I keep her here? She's hogging my bed and I need sleep.—

An hour later, there was another text.

Cade:—I can't take it anymore. I'll be there in ten to drop her off.—

"Oh, shit," I exhaled.

I flung the covers off my body feeling goosebumps pierce my skin. Turning on my bedroom light, I checked the time on the clock.

4:00 a.m.

I grabbed my hoodie off the floor and flung it over my head. I put on my teal-framed glasses, my feet in my slippers, and made my way toward the door, stealing a peek at Harmony's open door. Her room was empty.

I opened the front door, ignoring the shiver that caressed my bare legs.

"Cade." I frowned. The air crackled around us. "I'm so sorry. I didn't hear my phone."

"Surprise," Mildred said in my head without hesitation. My eyes flicked down to her gray furry body lying on Cade's chest, her head tucked in his neck like a cradled baby.

"Mildred..." I growled, lifting my eyes to meet Cade's. "I'm so sorry. Sometimes I sleep like the dead."

"Even more so now that your powers are changing," Mildred added her two cents.

His eyebrows dipped with concern. "It's no problem. I wish I didn't have to wake you up. I couldn't go back to sleep with her in my bed."

An image of Cade trying to snuggle with Mildred the Pillow Hog formed in my mind. His strong muscled body in contrast with her furry body made me smile. Mildred's head popped up and she leveled me with a look. Her whiskers twitched.

"He was so warm, soft, and manly," she purred.

I tilted my head to the side and narrowed my eyes at her. I held my sleeved-covered hands in front of my face, blocking the chill from the night breeze.

"I had no idea she'd gotten out. She never does this. She's not really an 'outdoor' cat," I said, using air quotes. Heat pricked my cheeks. "You didn't have to come over here."

Cade shrugged his shoulders, an easy smile on his lips. "Of course I did. I didn't want you to worry and…" He paused, stepping closer to me. "…it was an excuse to see you again."

Warmth spread through my belly at his lame line. It had been a couple of days since I admitted I had feelings for Cade. I was glad to see he picked up on the clues.

"That was really lame," I deadpanned.

"Okay… maybe Millie made herself at home in my apartment," he added. "Getting fur all over my sheets."

"So safe and cozy. I loooove him."

I rolled my eyes and covered a laugh with a fake cough. The energy between us ticked up a few degrees as I felt my walls wobble against his kindness. I adjusted my glasses and stepped back, opening the door wider.

"Please, come inside. It's cold."

Mildred lifted her head to look at me. A look of disdain was evident on her face. A low growl came from her throat.

"I'm not leaving his arms, Shay."

"I'm sure you need to get back to bed, Cade," I spoke to Mildred while looking at him.

Mildred snuggled further into his arms, nuzzling his cheek with hers. Cade's eyebrows dipped with humor.

"I'm pretty awake right now, but I wouldn't mind getting out of the cold."

"Are you sure? It's the middle of the night."

He nodded, scratching Mildred under her jaw. I shook my head. I couldn't decide if I was angry or embarrassed, but Mildred was going to get an earful later. The wind whipped around us. I crossed my arms over my chest, holding on tightly. The cool air tickled the exposed skin of my legs. Cade's eyes traveled down the length of my body, smoldering my skin as they lingered on my legs. Giddiness erupted in my chest under his gaze. I tucked a piece of my fallen hair behind my ear while he tracked my motions, causing the fire to burn hotter beneath my skin. Cade swallowed.

"Come on in." I cleared my throat and stepped out of the way, allowing Cade to walk over the threshold. I watched as his long fingers scratched her head. She purred. Mildred nuzzled her head toward his hand and licked his fingers. I cocked an eyebrow. I had *never* seen her give kisses to anyone besides me and Harmony.

"Are you okay?" Cade asked, scratching Mildred, standing at the entry of my apartment.

"Uh, yeah," I sputtered, completely taken aback by Mildred's show of affection. "Make yourself at home."

His body heat and aroma overwhelmed me, sending shivers through my body. Cade walked into my space confidently, moving toward the bookshelves that stood on either side of the TV stand. Mildred was stuck in his arms like glue. He perused the contents of the bookshelves while petting Mildred. His head ticked back every few seconds as he no doubt formed opinions about the displayed Wiccan paraphernalia.

My heart raced and my hands shook as I grabbed Mildred's treats from the cabinet, turning my back on Cade. My apartment was my safest space. It was a mix of my and Harmony's things. The different decór didn't match, but it was our home. I had weird goddess statues, palm-reading hand statues, and a highly organized arrangement of herbs, crystals, and candles. Harmony had glittery goth, rock band shit, and a few traditional Filipina trinkets.

As I turned back around, Cade shook his head as he looked at my Mother Goddess of the Four Wicca Elements statues. I suppressed a shudder at his reaction to the strange baby-looking statues with symbols of the four elements etched on their bellies.

"Can I get you something to drink?" I asked, needing to break the tension.

I shoved a random deck of tarot cards to the side and fished out a couple of kitty treats in hopes of detaching Mildred. Cade looked toward me, working hard to school his expression. He smiled as he sat down at my worn blue wooden bar stools. He shifted his weight as he settled, still holding the She-Devil. Her pink tongue snuck out reaching for a treat, barely lifting her head. Cade obliged her. She was going to get spoiled...furry brat.

"Sure. What do you have?"

"I have tea, water, whiskey, and maybe a green smoothie." I placed a filled kettle on the stove. "I'm going to have tea."

He scratched at his cheek, the sound echoed through the apartment. "I'll have a cup, too; but add a little whiskey to mine."

"Perfect," I said, smiling. Having Cade in my safe space was disrupting my Virgo-ness. I needed to chill the fuck out. I grabbed the basket of bagged and loose tea containers from atop the refrigerator, setting them on the counter.

"Your roses are dying."

My eyes swung to the darkening ugly roses sitting at the end of my counter and frowned.

"Finally," I sighed. "Roses aren't my thing. Though they are very useful for many things, I just don't think they're pretty."

"They are so cliché," Mildred added, her mouth full of catnip treats.

"What do you like, then?"

My eyes spied a naked Earth Goddess vase that held the chrysanthemums my grandmother got me. I touched the buds.

"Chrysanthemums. Their colors are vibrant and bold. And they bloom in the fall. One of my favorite times of the year." The chrysanthemums were layered with a gradient of purple, pink, and orange.

"Let me guess," —he pointed to the roses— "those are from Dean."

A small laugh escaped my lips. "Caring, protective, and smart. You're an enigma of a guy, Cade Thompson."

As soon as the words were out of my mouth, heat seared my cheeks. I had just complimented him. It was so easy to tell him things. I turned away to hide my face.

I gathered two of my favorite mugs from a hanging rack attached to the wall. One mug was a speckled green with swirls of gray, and a moon printed on it. The other mug was black with a silver star surrounded by a circle. Rifling through the small glass canisters, I picked one and popped out the cork. Leafy green tea leaves fell into the mortar. Green tea paired well with whiskey. I ground the leaves up with my well-worn pestle.

"You take your tea-making seriously," Cade pointed out as he rifled through the different tea bags.

I gave him a sheepish smile while stuffing the tea leaves into a metal eye-shaped steeper, followed by hot water that sat in a pot on the counter.

"Tea has a lot of health benefits and mystic ones, too."

"Like snake oil science? Aaron is all about the homeopathic healing."

I brushed off what he said. It was just another example of his skepticism. Despite my growing feelings for him, I needed to be reminded that he would never fit in my world. I frowned, watching him. He picked up a packet of berry tea, examining the bag.

"Wow, I haven't seen this type of tea in a long time. My grandma, back in Scotland, had a berry patch outside her house. She used to make her own tea from those bushes. Similarly to you, actually." His cheeks rounded as he smiled.

I studied him as my tea steeped into my mug, turning the black mug to white revealing the hidden phrase: *My Morning Potion*. Cade's eyes had a faraway gaze as he dipped the tea bag into the empty green mug and added his water.

"You must be a Capricorn," I said.

"You mean like the thirteen astronomy signs?"

I chortled. "The *twelve astrological* signs. The Zodiac. Yeah, those."

Cade shrugged his shoulders. I reached into the cabinet above the sink for a bottle of scotch, setting it down between the two of us. Cade reached for it first, adding a little over a shot's worth to his tea. I did the same.

"So, I'm right? You're a Capricorn?"

Cade nodded while lifting the mug to his lips. I watched in fascination as his throat swallowed the steaming elixir.

"Yeah. Not like I know what that means. My sister told me once," he said. "How did you figure that out? I never told you my birthday is at the end of the year."

I lifted a shoulder and leaned forward on the counter. I wrapped my sleeve-covered hands around my mug, blowing on the steam. "Let's just say I know a lot about new-agey things."

"Very subtle," Mildred snorted, before hopping from Cade's lap.

I lifted my gaze to meet his.

"Obviously, you work at a witch store...that your family owns," he said with humor in his voice. I laughed. "You have many weird things in your apartment and you're always wearing a crystal somewhere."

I blinked at his observations. *He noticed those things?*

"True," I said, shaking my head. "There are other things I picked up on, too. Capricorns are loyal, ambitious, and headstrong. Not necessarily stingy, but they spend their money wisely. Usually in a profession that requires something physical and heroism. And..." I continued as if I was reading all the information from a book, "Capricorns are basically lie-detectors and extremely self-confident to the point that it could get them in trouble."

I took a sip of my tea. The scotch burned its way down my throat, heating my body as it went. The air grew stifling as we silently assessed the other. When he didn't respond, I peeked up. His face was a stoic mask, causing me to stand straighter.

"Did I say something wrong?"

Cade's jaw ticked as he stared at his mug. With a small shake of his head, he lifted his eyes to meet mine. A haunted look swept across his eyes that struck me with sadness and insecurity.

On instinct, I reached across the counter, gripping his hand with mine. When our skin made contact, an electric current ran up my arm, making my hair stand on edge. I gasped and tried to pull my hand away, but Cade turned his over, capturing my hand in his. He cleared his throat.

"You didn't say anything wrong, Shay. You scarily hit the nail on the head. My fucking stubbornness landed me here."

I lowered my head, keeping my eyes on our joined hands. His calloused thumb glided along my palm slowly. As his thumbs made their circles, my skin lit up with tingles of arousal. Remembering that he just told me something important, I spoke.

"Shit. I'm sorry."

"Yeah. It's not something I'm proud of. So, I don't really like talking about it."

"Everyone makes wrong decisions when their emotions are overwhelming," I offered. "I'm a good listener if you ever want to talk about it more." Cade nodded before rolling his shoulders back and sitting up tall. He flashed me a blinding smile.

"What sign are you?" he asked. "Not like I'd know what it meant or anything."

"Ha. I'm a Virgo. I like things neat and organized. I'm a planner and live for nature."

"Yeah. I had no idea. Does this mean we're friends? Now that we've both asked the 'what sign are you' question?" he asked with a wink. My lips tipped up in a smile, mirroring him.

"I suppose it does." I pulled my hand out of his grip. Although, I wanted to hold onto it forever. I stood up straight, adjusting my glasses. "It's getting late or early. I should try to get more sleep."

Cade took another sip of his tea before standing from the stool. He looked at the large crescent moon clock on the wall. "Shit. I didn't realize the time. I've got to get a workout in before my shift."

I watched as he stretched his body out from sitting on my old stools. He certainly was dedicated to keeping his body in shape by the way his joggers fit his legs and hugged his hips. Cade walked toward Mildred where she was sprawled out on the couch. Her hind legs out flat behind her. He bent down to pet the top of her head. Even in her sleep, she purred at his touch.

Watching him with Mildred and in my space, my heart filled with emotions I wasn't used to. There was no doubt. I was starting to actually fall for him. Genuine attraction beyond his looks.

Electricity sparked between us as our chemistry came to the surface. An invisible tether attached to us, pulling me closer. With my mind's eyes, I saw the tether sparkle with gray and green.

I met him in the small hallway in front of my door. I adjusted my glasses again as we stood in front of each other. The heat radiated from his body as we crowded each other. The hallway felt much smaller.

His eyes flicked down to my lips and back up to my eyes. My skin blazed under his gaze and my heartbeat raced. A bubble began to form around us as everything else faded away. I licked my lips in anticipation as he closed the distance between us.

I couldn't pull away from him, no matter how much I might have needed to. I wanted him to kiss me like we were the only two people on Earth. The attraction I felt for him was unbearable. I no longer wanted to resist it. His true colors were brighter than anything else in my world.

Just one kiss and I would be satisfied.

I moved closer, erasing the space between us. Cade tracked my every movement with steady eagerness. Taking in a sharp inhale, his hand traced along my jawline, fingers sliding into the hair behind my ears. Shivers ran down my spine at the tingles his fingers left in their trail. I peeked up at him through my eyelashes, noticing how his normally bright green eyes now blazed with need.

I took a deep breath as I pressed myself against him, my braless chest meeting his strong pec muscles. Giving into temptation, I pressed my lips to his. Fireworks and electricity burst at our contact. Cade dug his fingers into my hair, pulling me closer, if that was even possible.

Our lips moved seamlessly, as if they were made to mold together. My breath hitched in my chest. The rest of the world drifted away.

His lips moved with mine in a sensual dance. As my body melted under his touch, a warm surge coursed through my stomach. Wisps of charged air danced along my skin as an invisible force tugged at my stomach.

I abruptly broke the kiss, throwing myself back

against the opposite wall. I squeezed my eyes shut. My hands flew to my stomach. Cade's hands gripped my upper arms, steadying my wobbly feet. Fuzziness blurred my sight around the edges of my mind's eye.

"Shay? What's wrong?" Cade asked, concern lacing his voice.

"You're having a vision? Right now?" Mildred questioned.

With my heart hammering against my chest, my astral body flew through time and space as a vision formed behind my closed eyes.

"Shay, seriously, are you okay? Are you a diabetic?" Cade asked.

His voice sounded far away as I struggled to stay in the present time. I pushed against the vision, working to keep myself in the here and now. Sweat broke out along my neck as I clutched onto Cade's forearms for support. Mildred's body rubbed along my legs and she yowled.

He couldn't know this secret.

"Focus on me, Shay. You do not need to have this vision if you don't want to. You are in control." Her authoritative and calm voice spoke.

Continuing to keep my eyes closed, I concentrated on Mildred's body weaving in and out of my legs and her mantras inside my head. After several deep breaths, my astral body cemented itself back to mine. My breathing was rapid when I opened my eyes to face Cade. He bent down to my eye level.

"What the fuck, Shay? What happened?" Fear and confusion swirled on his perfect face.

I pulled on my sweatshirt's sleeves, bringing them over my fists. Cade's hands ran up and down my arms in a calming motion. When I was sure I stayed in the current realm, my body relaxed in his touch. My limbs felt like bags of rocks as they hung from my body.

"Sorry if I scared you. Maybe I put too much Scotch in my tea," I lied.

Cade narrowed his eyes. "That's another fucking lie. Another secret, Shay. Stop insulting my intelligence."

I swallowed hard. "Yeah, it was a lie. I told you I had secrets. I'm not ready to tell you and you aren't ready to hear them."

"If you're going to keep having 'dizzy spells', I think I need to know."

He brushed a piece of my hair off my face and shoved his hands in his hoodie pocket.

"I can't..." I whispered. My chest physically hurt from not telling him the truth. Bringing him into my world wasn't an option. He was a wrecking ball to my heart's fortress. Cade squinted his eyes as he looked around my face. I felt him searching for something.

"It's killing me not knowing, Shay," he said as he cupped my face.

"You're going to have to deal with it."

He pursed his lips with a small smile. "Fine. But, I'm not a very patient person."

"Ha!" I scoffed, leaning away from him. "I don't really give a fuck. Be impulsive and see what happens."

He grinned. "So snarky." He looked at the wall behind me where a monthly calendar hung. "The 115th Annual Ipswich Halloween Party?"

I turned, noting the date of the town's annual extravaganza in city hall. Heavy emphasis on "extra".

"Yup. The biggest event of the year. Everyone goes."

Cade smiled. "Including you?"

"Of course. I've had my costume planned since summer."

"So, you're saying that I should make an appearance, too?"

"If you want to be a part of the community, yeah. Or if you want to be talked about behind your back, then I guess don't go."

I searched his face for a moment.

"We could go together."

My chest expanded at his invitation, filling me with anticipation and excitement.

"We can't match costumes," I stuttered. "I already–"

"Have your costume planned, I know," he said. "What do you say?"

My resolve crumbled and I smiled. I blamed it on the early morning hours, the scotch, or the lack of sleep, but most definitely on the pantie-melting kiss.

"I'm going with Harmony and Brad. You can meet me here and we'll meet up with them there," I conceded.

Cade raised his lips in a smoldering smirk.

"You better have a good costume," I teased, wrapping my arms around my body to control its vibration.

"Oh, don't worry about that." He smirked, highlighting his dimples. He stepped toward the door. "I will definitely have a costume."

"Let me guess…" I tapped my finger on my chin. "A sexy firefighter?"

Cade laughed. "You think I'm sexy, huh?"

My eyes widened at my admission, and heat crept

up my neck. "You know you are," I sassed. "Now, please leave."

I opened the door and started to shove Cade out. Halfway through, he turned back toward me.

"You're sure you're okay?"

"Yeah." I nodded with a smile. "Thanks for bringing Her Royal Highness back."

"Anytime." His eyes flicked to my lips before looking back up at me. He gave one last blinding smile then bounded down the front steps.

I closed the door and walked toward my bedroom. The early morning sun peeked through my green, leafy print blinds, casting a soft hazy glow on my bed. My body shook with adrenaline from my vision and the kiss Cade and I shared. I touched my fingers to my lips. They felt swollen.

Cade's kiss will forever be seared into my brain as the best first kiss of my life.

Better than Dean's.

My eyes drifted closed as I thought of two things.

One: I wanted more kisses from Cade.

Two: If I wasn't careful, he was going to shatter my carefully, controlled world.

Chapter 14

My lips twisted in concentration as I brushed the pale purple nail polish on my nails. Soulful music blasted through our apartment. Harmony scrolled through her phone, reading the latest celebrity gossip, while Mildred sat on her lap, reading along.

The annual Halloween party was at the end of the week and I had to decide on the right color of nail polish to match my costume. Out of all the shit I had lost control over, the completion of my Halloween costume was the easiest thing in my control.

When finished, I held my hand out in front of me. The purple shimmered in the afternoon sunlight shining through the living room windows. My other hand was painted with bright sea green.

My lips tipped down in a frown as I turned my hand in different directions, admiring my handy work. Pun intended.

"I think I'm going to go with the purple," I said.

Harmony lifted her head. Her dark hair bobbed in its high messy bun on the top of her head. "Let me see," she said. I turned my hands around. "Oh, the purple for sure. It's so sparkly."

"Definitely the purple. The color of psychics," Mildred added, rubbing her head along Harmony's chin.

Usually green plays a bigger role in my life being a

Virgo, but I was thankful for my powers. Highlighting purple would be my way to thank the Goddess for my sixth sense.

"I'm so excited to see what the boys dress like," Harmony gushed.

"I wish I could go." Mildred snorted. She had been pouting for the past week, complaining about pets not being allowed to attend.

I scratched her behind her ears.

"Sorry, kitty, but we go through this every year."

"I know. And every year until I've lived out my sentence I'm going to bitch about it."

"Any news on the Lucia/curse front?" Harmony asked.

"Not really. Things have been pretty quiet."

"Except for Millie playing matchmaker in the middle of the night," she said.

We both swung our gazes toward the furball in question. After telling Harmony all about Cade's late night visit and kiss, she was all over the love drama happening in my life. I wasn't complaining. The memory of our kiss would forever be burned in my brain.

Mildred blinked her neon green eyes at us, completely unfazed by her deeds.

Shaking my head, I said, "I talked with Florence at the library. There were a bunch of records that I got a chance to look at. They confirmed that Lucia never did marry Harrison."

"Well that's good," Harmony said. "To confirm that the kiss you shared with Dean was only gross because of the lack of passion."

"Thank Goddess. Zero chemistry is just that."

My phone buzzed beside me. Mom.

"Hey, Mom. What's up?"

"Hey, Moonbeam. I'm calling to let you know that I've been talking with some of the other business owners. They want to help with the festival and are ready to have their own tents. Lots of locals feel really excited about bringing back this tradition."

I smiled. "That's great. I'm still waiting to hear back from Dean and Aaron about permits or whatever. But, I don't think it should be a problem, especially if all the other business owners are involved."

My chest filled with warmth, looking over at Harmony and Mildred. Harmony had a large smile that lit up her face. Mildred's eyes were big and she was smiling in a way a cat would smile.

"I'm starting to feel like we can actually do this, Mom. That we could buy out the lease."

"Have you thought more about the curse, though? I'm worried that this is only a bandaid from something much larger."

I pulled on my sleeves, sliding more under the blanket. "Harm, Mildred, and I were just talking about that."

"I know. I felt it," she admitted.

"Based on what Lucia told and showed me, I think Harrison Fellows enacted the curse himself," I said.

"Because of his jealousy? Anger? You said Lucia turned down his proposal," she added.

"That's what I assume. We obviously know that Lucia didn't marry Harrison, but now we know his intentions. All motives to create the curse."

Mom sighed on the other end of the line. "And how are things going with Dean?" Her voice was tentative as if she didn't want to breach the subject.

"Mom. You know already."

She exhaled. The regret ever thinking I could have a romantic relationship with Dean. Mom was too kind-hearted to ever say "I told you so."

"I do. You shouldn't feel shameful for following your heart," she said. I looked down at my nails, controlling the emotions swirling within.

"If Harrison meant for a Whitley and a Fellows to be together, how do we know that isn't the way to break the curse?" she asked.

I ground my teeth together. The thought had crossed my mind, too. I didn't want to be tied up in a loveless relationship with Dean. Our date was totally weird and that's not including his erratic behavior.

Mildred hissed beside me, hopping up on my lap and staring at me. Her face was fierce.

"Glad Mildred and I are on the same page," Mom said.

Mildred licked her muzzle with a nod.

"Anyway," Mom continued. "What are we going to do about the curse now that Dean is out of the picture? I feel like we're missing something. I didn't have a strong romantic relationship with your father and there wasn't any evidence of the curse. That's why I forgot about it."

Harmony's eyebrows scrunched and she chewed on the tip of her red nail. "Has Dotty been able to get any more info from the spirits?" she asked.

"No," Mom answered through the speaker. "Something is blocking her. She can feel the spirit's essence, but it doesn't want to make contact. Like the connection isn't strong enough."

I ran my hands down my face. How was I supposed to learn more about the curse? It would have been easier if Harrison had written down his reasons in his journal. But, none of this situation was easy.

"Shay," Mom said, bringing my attention back to the conversation. "Does Dean know that you've definitely taken back your offer?"

"I told him after our date, but I'm not sure he heard me or took it to heart," I said.

Harmony made a disgusted face and shook her head.

"Don't waste time on this, Moonbeam. His emotions are very strong. Overpowering almost."

"Mom, I get it," I said, my voice harsher than intended. "There're more important things going on. It's not my problem he decided to get drunk in multiple ways and didn't hear me. He was definitely abusing his potions again."

"You can't just ignore him," Mom scolded.

I didn't understand her persistence in telling Dean, but trusted her intentions. The curse and saving the store were absolutely more important than Dean's feelings. I felt my phone buzz on my cheek with a notification.

"Mom, I've got to go. I promise I'll talk to Dean...again." I hung up before she had a chance to say anything else.

I opened my messages, finding a couple from Cade.

Cade:—I've got my costume ready.—
Cade:—Prepare to be dazzled.—
I smiled.
—Me: Can't wait.—

He replied right away.

Cade:—I can't get our kiss out of my head. Please tell me it's the same with you.—

Blush crept up my face. Harmony and Mildred snorted, trying to hide their laughter. My thumbs floated across my fingertips. His words were intoxicating. Honestly, everything about him drew me in. His looks. His smell. His essence. His charm and attentiveness were becoming harder and harder to ignore.

I sighed. If we kept going down this road, he would find out my secrets. I had no doubt about that. Would he reject me? He was logical. Logical and magical didn't blend. They were like oil and water.

What would happen if he found out the truth? Could I even keep my secrets from him for too much longer?

Taking a deep breath, I typed out my response using my heart instead of my head.

Me:—Me neither.—

"You have to tell Dean," Harmony said, breaking my flirty bubble. "I saw him yesterday at the bakery. He looked like he was on cloud nine." She chewed on one of her nails. "He did not hear you."

"He's not going to take it well, Shay. You need to be prepared," Mildred said, stretching out on my lap.

"Fuck!" I exhaled, throwing my head back against the couch. "I'll tell him at the Halloween party. He's been so busy with the preparations, I haven't been able to see him."

"More like you're avoiding him," Harmony said.

I frowned. She caught me. I was avoiding Dean for the obvious reasons. Yet, living in a small town, I couldn't dodge him forever.

"I promise. I'll tell him tomorrow at the party. We all know he'll be there."

"Just be careful," Mildred said into my mind.

"What do you mean be careful? It's Dean," I said, shrugging off her serious vibes.

"If Lucia was warned about Harrison and she warned you about Dean, then you need to listen to her and take it seriously. His energy has started to feel unpredictable. There has to be a connection that we're missing. I just can't put my paw on it."

I relayed the message to Harmony. Crossing my arms over my chest, I wrapped the blanket tighter around me.

"Do you remember that time he stole all the frogs from the science lab?" Harmony asked.

"Yeah. He was freeing them."

"No, he wasn't. I saw him later on that day. He was dropping them from a tree branch in the cemetery. And he wasn't on the first branch. He was at the top of the tree."

The knot in my stomach grew more intense with each passing second. Dean experimented with magic and spent a lot of his youth in the cemetery and woods. I thought it was because he wanted to get away from his parents fighting. But now, was there a darker reason?

I blew a breath from my lips. My skin crawled as we talked about Dean, remembering his weird mood swings on our date.

"Was that Cade?" Harmony asked, ticking her head in the direction of my phone. I pulled the hood up over my head to hide the blush and goofy grin that pulled at my lips.

"Yeah. Just telling me he has a costume for the party. He's going to meet me here. Then, we'll meet up with you."

Harmony clapped her hands. "This is going to be so much fun. A double date!"

Mildred yowled. Harmony gripped her and pulled her furry body close to her chest.

"I'm so sorry, Millie."

Mildred snorted and went limp in Harmony's hold like the drama queen she was.

"Okay, the Halloween Party…is your costume all set?" Harmony asked.

I gave her a "duh" look.

"Good. Now, what do you think Brad is going to go as? Sexy cop? Sexy farmer? Sexy doctor?"

My phone buzzed with a text from Dean, as if he knew we were talking about him.

Dean:—Ready for the PARTY??—

Me:—Yup. Same as every year. Please tell me you're wearing a different costume than "Mr. Mayor."—

Dean:—HA! Yes, totally different one this year. It'll be a total surprise. See you there, sexy.—

I frowned, reading Harmony and Mildred the texts.

"Yeah, you need to tell him," Mildred concluded, snapping her jaw at my phone.

Harmony nodded, snuggling further onto the couch. Her face frowned with worry. Mildred rubbed her face along my hood.

"You can do this."

"I know. I just don't want to. It's going to be messy. I don't like messy."

"Suck it up and grow some ovaries."

****

I stood in front of my bedroom's tall mirror, putting the last few touches on my Halloween costume. Tonight was the Annual Ipswich Halloween Party. All of the townspeople pitched in to make this the biggest event of the year. In the back of my mind, I hoped for the festival to be of the same caliber as the Halloween party someday. Aaron and I had been texting daily, getting to know each other, and talking about festival themes. He planned on coming to visit soon to check out the town square.

I blew a breath passed my lips. Soon, I'd be knee-deep in festival planning and saving my family's livelihood, but tonight, was about a fun tradition. Harmony insisted I take tonight for myself. Let my hair down.

I brushed some glitter from beneath my eyes, my hands trembling and scattering it to fall from my fingers. Glancing to the heavens, the fluttering in my stomach grew with each minute that passed.

Cade would be showing up here to take me to the Halloween party. My body teemed with jitters. I've only ever gone to the party with Dean or Harmony. Never a date. This was new. To say I was nervous would be a major understatement. Not to mention the conversation I needed to have with Dean. What would he think seeing me with Cade?

Nope. Not going there.

I didn't his approval. He lost that priviledge when our date imploded.

Mildred rolled along the floor next to me playing with her favorite cat toy. I watched her for a few minutes. The moments where she acted completely feline and not human gave me pause. I bent down and gave her some ear scratches.

"Leave me alone," she said, swatting my hand away. *"I'm trying to distract myself from the fact that I don't get to go to the party. Fucking unfair."*

I shook my head, not hiding my smile.

"Maybe you shouldn't have been a dark witch and messed around with dark magic."

"Hm, thanks, Shay. It's not like I don't spend every day thinking about not casting that spell," she growled in my direction, pinning me with a look of disgust. She hissed at me for an extra dramatic flair and stalked away.

"Sorry," I called after her while dabbing more purple shimmery eyeshadow on my lids. It wasn't her fault that I got bitchy when nervous.

"Yeah, yeah. You look sexy, by the way."

I stood a little taller, looking at my reflection in the mirror. Blonde tendrils fell along the sides of my face and down my neck from the curly bun on the top of my head. My full lips were shiny. My cheeks were glittered and rosy. I even put some glitz onto the tip of my pixie nose.

My phone buzzed with an incoming video chat: Harmony.

I pressed to accept, holding the phone out so Harmony could see my costume.

Her shocked face was heavily made up with black and red hearts.

"Oh, my god. Cade is going to jizz in his pants when he sees you, girl."

"That wasn't my intention."

"Brad said your intentions don't matter." Her red

lips, smiling like she knew something I didn't.

"And how trustworthy is Brad?"

Her lips curled in a sultry smile. "Enough for me to have a drawer and space in his closet." She giggled.

"Really!? He gave you some of your own space? That's awesome. He must really like you."

A genuine smile made her dark-stained eyes crinkle at the corners. "The feeling goes both ways."

I mirrored her smile. I was happy for her. It was time she found someone who liked her for her—if only I would be so lucky.

"As long as you're happy, I'm happy."

"Plus, who knows? Maybe Cade will be spending more time there. Three's a crowd, you know."

My face heated. "Harm…"

"Four's more fun!" Brad called from the background, causing Harmony to slap him on the arm.

"Gross," I teased. "I'm leaving in a few. Meet you there. Nice costume, by the way, Brad."

"Thanks, Shay!" He laughed. He was a sexy construction worker with a shirtless chest, suspenders, and a hard hat. A costume that Harmony never ended up guessing.

"You look amazing," Harmony cooed. "I, of course, look amazing. I'll see you there!"

Confidence swelled in my stomach as I touched my face in the phone camera. She gave me an air kiss and ended the call. I tossed my phone next to my shoes on my bed and turned back toward the mirror.

A classy but sexy purple fairy stared back at me.

Excitement grew in my belly as I slipped on my gladiator sandals, clasping the straps up my calves. I fluffed out the sheer skirt, feeling the silky material on my bare legs. I straightened the amethyst crystal necklace that hung at the base of my neck in a lacey choker. Amethysts were used for their calming positivity. Both things needed in my life right now. Plus, the deep purple gem matched my fairy costume.

"Mildred, I'm leaving."

An angry meow came from somewhere in the apartment. I pocketed my phone into the pouch my Gram sewed into my costume without replying and stepped up toward the door, exiting and locking the apartment.

It was now or never.

I made it two steps before halting, my eyes widening. Cade leaned against the railing at the bottom of the steps. He looked up at me, grinning. His full black outfit and black feather wings on his back gave him a commanding presence that was impossible to ignore.

The air swirled with electricity. My gaze hungrily scanned him from head to toe. His tight leather, sleeveless shirt hugged him in all the right places. His skinny jeans were just as tight, with chained leather straps hanging down, leaving nothing to the imagination. I sucked in a breath when my eyes reached his face. It was smudged with black streaks and thick dark eyeliner outlined his green eyes causing the color to pop in contrast.

My panties soaked instantly.

"Um, hi." My voice sounded breathless, which I was.

"Don't worry. I'm not here to end your life."

"It would be a perfect way to go, though."

"You look…" He paused, looking at me with a

predatory stare. "…fucking hot." Heat seared my cheeks. "Are you going to come down the rest of the stairs?"

I swallowed. "Yeah. My foot got stuck or something."

"Or something." Cade chuckled.

I descended the rest of the stairs. He didn't move when I reached the bottom of the stairs, putting us in very close proximity. Cade's eyes darkened with need and his breath hitched. By some miracle, I tore my eyes away and stepped around him, finding my wits.

"Come on, Angel. Let's get to the party."

Chapter 15

Cade smiled and linked his hand with mine.

"I almost brought my bike. You know, to complete the whole shit-kicker Death Angel vibe."

"I've never been on a motorcycle."

Cade grinned as he looked down at me. "We're going to have to change that."

"Who did your makeup?"

A hint of pink tinted his cheeks. "Me."

I giggled. "You are a man of many talents, Cade."

"My sister needed someone to practice on when she was learning. Who better than her younger brother."

"That's so cute. What a great little brother you were."

"How about you? Do you have any siblings?"

"No," I said, swallowing over the lump in my throat. Being an only child boosted the need to control my world. I never had people push my boundaries or wake me up in the middle of the night with their nightmares. But, that meant all the burdens and tribulations fell solely on my shoulders.

Cade pulled me under his arm. His feathers bonked me in the head, making us laugh. The negative thoughts evaporated from my brain.

Shay...we're having fun tonight, remember?

"Oh, man. At least having no other siblings meant all the toys were yours," he said.

"That's true. Something tells me you were never a good sharer, even with siblings."

Cade lowered his head and laughed. "Got me there." He stopped, twisting me to face him. His bright eyes drank me in as he pulled me closer. My lips parted. Waiting. He leaned in closer, a dangerous smile tugging at the corners of his lips. "I don't share."

Why did I even bother wearing underwear tonight?

I licked my lips, tasting the fruity stickiness of my lip gloss. A soft breath escaped my throat. Suddenly, a loud laugh erupted nearby as a group of costumed teenagers ran by, breaking our chemistry spell.

The sights and sounds of the Halloween party appeared around us. The loud vibrations from the music buzzed as we took in the scene. The Ipswich Town Hall was a colonial-style building up on a small hill. It had large stone columns in front dawned with twisting orange and black ribbons. The exterior lights were changed to black ultraviolet lights, casting a bright purple glow on the front entrance.

"Wow. Town Hall looks wicked," Cade exclaimed, taking in the extravagance.

"Yeah, it does. Wait until you see the inside."

Cade gestured for me to lead the way. We walked up the hill and through the entrance, where the black lights lit up his face. My purple dress and glitter illuminated against my skin. Cade swallowed hard, then shook his head with a grin as we took in each other's appearance. My heart raced as his eyes lingered on my face and the curves of my body.

Following the music, toward the ballroom, we weaved through the townspeople. Many people greeted us equally. Stealing a glance at Cade as he said hello to

Lydia. I realized that Cade was making himself a part of our Ipswich community.

"Come on," I said, nodding to Lydia with a smile. "The bar's this way." I hooked my arm in Cade's, pulling him.

A sea of doctors, bloody brides, superheroes, zombies, and of course, witches occupied the main dance area in the center. Decorated tables of black and orange were placed along the perimeter of the room, in front of fake skeletons and cobwebs that hung on the walls. The music vibrated under my feet. The main lights were off, but there were black and colored lights that flickered in motion with the music.

"Wow. It feels like the whole town is here," Cade said in my ear. His voice sent tingles along my neck as he breathed near a sensitive spot under my ear.

"They are. Remember—social leper if you don't attend."

Cade gripped my shoulder. "I see some guys from the station over there." He pointed to a group of men who were dressed as firefighters. "I'm gonna go say hi real quick. Be right back."

"They're really creative." I laughed.

Cade's shoulders shook with laughter as he moved toward them.

"Shay!" I heard someone call my name from the side. "Honey, over here!"

I turned, finding the voice at a table along the wall. A large smile grew on my face when I recognized a hippie, a sea witch, a wood nymph, and a classic witch.

"Hey, ladies! Your costumes look wonderful as usual."

Mom, the hippie, stood to hug me. "You make a

beautiful fairy, darling."

"Seems like Wilma and I had the same idea," I said, speaking around my mom to Wilma who dressed as the wood nymph.

"Well, plants are my life and I wasn't going to go for some cockamamie costume like this one over here," Wilma spoke, pointing a thumb in her sister's direction. Agnes had her long hair tinted with black hairspray giving her sea witch a dark vibe.

"Oh shut up, Wilma. I wanted to do something different. I can't help it I'm still trying to stay young, you old hag," Agnes said, lifting her orange cup in the air toward me before chugging the whole thing.

"Have you guys been here long?" I asked, not bothering to hide my smile. This was one of the reasons I loved this party. Everyone, Quaint and Witch, lowered their barriers and differences to enjoy a childish tradition. Mom fiddled with her crocheted vest that she probably borrowed from Gram.

"I'm only one drink in," she said. "But those ones…" —waving her hand in Wilma, Agnes, and Gram's direction— "started earlier in the day."

"Oh boy."

"Maybe some old coot will ask me to dance," Gram said from her seat.

"Going with an old classic, again, Gram?"

"Of course." Her black lips grinned. "Gotta keep my streak going."

Grandma Dolly had been dressing up in a simple lace witch costume for as long as I can remember. Her costume was complete with an ancient Whitley witch's hat that only came out of its box for this event.

Gram leaned forward pointing a black nail in my

direction. "The spirits say you came to the party with a certain firefighter."

Agnes cackled.

"Oh, witch. You're caught," Wilma accused, joining the laughter. My mother gave me a knowing smile as she sat back down next to Gram.

"We came as friends. He showed up at my apartment all dressed up. I wasn't going to just ignore him."

"And what about that amethyst around your neck?" Agnes asked. "Are you having trouble with your physic powers that you need protecting?"

Instinctively, I touched the crystal at the base of my neck, choosing not to respond.

"Have you guys seen Dean yet?" I asked, knowing that he was lurking around here somewhere.

"Not yet," Wilma said. "But, you know he wouldn't miss this."

"I feel him," Mom said. Her eyes looked off into the distance, unfocused. "He's happy and searching. Probably looking for you."

I took a deep breath, steeling myself for the inevitable conversation. It was important for him to understand that I wasn't pursuing a relationship with him. I wasn't excited about telling him, but he deserved to know.

"The dead think you're getting lucky tonight," Gram said, changing the subject. All three sets of eyes drilled into me. A range of cackles sounded.

"Gram!" Heat prickled at my back at their overt comments.

"Witch, are you always this horny?" Agnes asked Gram.

"Must be the alcohol." Wilma giggled. "Either way, Shay don't waste your sexiness on that stick up your butt. Let loose," she said, pointing her cup in my direction.

"Leave her alone, you old witches," Mom said, patting my shoulder. "And be nice."

A warm hand landed on the small of my back, causing me to startle.

"Did I hear the words, 'the dead think'?" Cade asked. "And 'sexy butt'. Are you ladies getting into trouble tonight?"

My coven zeroed in on Cade when he spoke. Heat broke out on my cheeks as the black and orange ribbon hanging from the ceiling suddenly became very appealing.

"Oh," Mom started, "you must be Cade. You're the new firefighter we've seen around town." She held out her hand in a greeting, ignoring his question. "Hi. I'm Sandy Whitley. Shay's mother."

Cade threw a smile at me, signaling that he knew this was killing me as he shook her hand. "Hi. Cade Thompson."

Resigning to my fate, I introduced Wilma and Agnes, who were still over the moon with Cade saying "sexy" in a sentence.

"Wilma and Agnes own Sapphires & Sailors and I rent my apartment from them. And, this is my Grandma Dolly."

Cade bent down low to greet my grandmother. "Pleasure to meet you, Dolly." He brought her hand to his lips with a small kiss. "Your witch costume suits you. I can tell."

Gram blushed, "Oh, what a debonair you are."

Wilma and Agnes melted in their seats with Cade kissing both of their hands, too.

"About the dead…" Cade said, standing.

Their eyes flitted between each other, before landing on me. I cleared my throat, giving Cade a large grin.

"They're just playing along with the whole Halloween vibe," I lied. "And they're all drunk."

Cade smiled with his charm shining through. "I like the commitment, ladies," he said. He swung his mesmerizing gaze my way. I almost crumbled under his attention, falling to my feet with his lips catching my fall or spilling all my secrets that tasted toxic on my tongue.

"Oookay," I drawled, coming to my senses and pulling on Cade's arm. "I need a strong drink now." I widened my eyes in my mom's direction. She bit on her lower lip, hiding her laughter, and gave us a wave.

"Stop by the store anytime, Cade! I'll give you a free Tarot Reading," she said.

"Nice to meet you all," Cade said behind him hesitantly, as I dragged him toward the bar. "Interesting group."

"That's one word for it."

At some point, Cade had ditched his leather jacket, but kept his wings on, adding more width to his already broad shoulders. My eyes could not move away from the intricate ink that slithered up his flexed, muscled arm, wrapping around his shoulder and disappearing under his shirt. The design of the strong sea-goat, Capricorn's symbol on his forearm, held my gaze.

I swallowed and licked my lips. He looked like sex on a stick. I shook the thoughts from my head and

171

squared my shoulders. A thin arm landed around my shoulders, saving me from answering Cade's question.

"Finally, you're here," Harmony spoke. "And you came with the sexiest dark angel I've ever seen."

"Hey," Brad whined.

Harmony snuggled next to Brad. "I specified angel, babe. You're still the sexiest *construction* guy."

"Well that's good," Brad grumbled. "Considering the only other construction worker here is the old pediatrician, Dr. Roberts."

"Good thing he kept his shirt on," Cade teased, causing Brad's chest to puff with pride.

"Let's get some more alcohol!" Harmony announced. Her mostly naked Queen of Hearts costume caused many heads to turn as she pushed her way to the bar. It was fun to watch the other guys glaze over with lust before Brad cleared his throat in a warning. Soon, Harmony returned with eight syringes of jello shots. She handed two to each of us.

"I got these on the house, by the way," she winked. "So, next round is on you guys. Gotta support the Ipswich Parks and Rec."

I put the syringe in my mouth, pushed on the plunger, and sucked up the green goo. The tang of strong alcohol burned my throat. My eyes peeked at Cade. He looked at the syringe, turning it around.

"What is this thing?"

"Jello shot, man," Brad answered. "You suck it up and enjoy the dedication to the theme."

Cade laughed. "How can I say no to that?" He put the syringe in his mouth and sucked up the goop with a slurp. "Damn. That's strong."

We all laughed. I sucked up my second syringe,

before tossing them in the recycle bin next to the bar.

"Ipswich knows how to throw a party," I said to Cade. "They have 'blood bags' filled with a red alcoholic goo if you're interested, too."

"I wasn't expecting them to be so strong," He coughed. "It's a wicked idea." He turned to our group. "Blood bags are on me next round."

"Let's go dance," Harmony said, pulling on my hand.

"I don't know, Harm…" I hesitated.

"Stop being such a downer! You've had your two obligatory jello shots. Now, you dance. Enjoy this one night before you're consumed by planning and prepping." She tugged on me again, causing me to smile. I resigned and followed her into a sea of people, glancing in Cade's direction. His eyes scanned me from head to toe. He stayed rooted in place with a thumb hooked in his pocket. The colored lights flashed along the chains of his costume, illuminating them like stars against a night sky.

As we moved more into the center of the crowd, the music thumping through my body, the throngs of the bodies, and the alcohol pushed the need for control further away. This was the only time of the year that I drank in public. I had no problem drinking locked in my apartment, but in public was different.

The crowd's body heat radiated around me, instantly bringing a sheen of sweat to my forehead. I looked around, satisfied at the wide range of ages that swayed to the beat of the music. The older party-goers danced more tastefully than some of the younger ones, but no one cared either way.

The hypnotic bass reverberated through my chest

causing my heart to beat in its rhythm. Harmony and I twisted and shook our hips in tandem, oblivious to the world around us as we heard, felt, and tasted the music, as we got lost in the atmosphere and community. My eyes were closed as I swayed to the rhythm. I lifted my hands above my head for a few beats before trailing my fingers down the sides of my face, rib cage, and legs. I lost track of time and responsiblity as a numbness washed over me, lowering my inhibitions further. Tingly electricity exploded at my back at the same time as someone gripped my hips, yanking me against their body.

"I tried to just watch, but couldn't stop myself from needing to touch you," Cade said in my ear. "The way you move is hypnotic."

Our bodies were flush against each other, his front to my back. His muscular chest rippled with every move. The parts of his skin that were exposed as part of his costume seared my bare back and arms. Cade flexed his fingers on my hips, moving both of us in the rhythm of the music.

The man had moves.

His breath huffed out along my neck and ear while we ground our bodies together. I wiggled my fingers over his head.

"Maybe I put a spell on you," I whispered in his ear.

****

"I Put a Spell On You" blasted its haunting notes through the speakers. The colored lights swirled above, mixing with the smoke from a fog machine. We were in our own little bubble in the middle of everyone.

Only me and him.

Even in a crowd of masked party-goers, my bones relaxed within his protection.

Cade spun me around to face him, holding me close. His dark eyeliner started to run as sweat peppered his face. The streaks of make-up gave his face an even more devilish look against the brightness of his eyes. I tried to break away from him, but his strong hands on my hips kept me in place.

"Can I tell you a secret?" he asked.

He gripped my chin, forcing me to look at him. The lights danced in his eyes. I nodded, swallowing hard.

"I want you. So badly sometimes it's suffocating."

I blinked a couple of times and arousal flooded my veins.

Before I could respond, Harmony and Brad wiggled their way next to us. There wasn't a millimeter of space between them either.

"I scored some blood bags!" Brad yelled.

Cade's hands let go of my hips, allowing me to take a step away from him. With the space between us, I was able to take in a cleansing breath as I touched the amethyst around my neck. I had already done my two shots, but to hell with the emotions that swirled in my body and brain, why not? I snatched the blood bag from Brad and slurped it down in one go.

"Wooo! Go, girl!" Harmony cheered, raising her hands in the air before wrapping them around Brad's neck. "It's about damn time you let go and just live."

Cade shook his head in refusal of the blood bag. "No, I'm good." His eyes continued to watch me with such intensity that my breath caught in my throat.

"Your loss," Brad said as he drank some. He

passed it to Harmony, who drank some, and I finished it off. Brad and Harmony smiled at each other before they locked lips.

I stole a glance at Cade as we stood still in the middle of writhing bodies. For the first time since I met him, there was a haunting vulnerability to him. His shoulders were hunched as he rubbed one of his wrists, watching me, waiting, and showing me he doesn't admit these feelings often.

A fogginess entered my brain as I soaked him in from head to toe.

An insatiable hunger rolled in my stomach.

Maybe it was his secret or the alcohol, but at that moment I decided to throw caution to the wind. Starting something with Cade was the last thing I should be worrying about. Relationships were messy and frustrating, but I didn't fucking care.

Everyone in my life was right. I needed to lose control a little bit. I stepped up to him, locking my eyes with his. My heart pounded as I licked my lips in response to my sexual hunger.

"I want you, too," I admitted.

It was the ultimate truth. I couldn't get him out of my head since the first time I met him when he rode in on his motorcycle.

Maybe it was *him* that put a spell on *me*.

Cade's eyes flicked down to my lips watching the motion, darkening with his own yearning. Slowly, one of his hands ghosted up my body, wrapping his fingers around the back of my neck. Goosebumps trailed after his fingers along my skin. His thumb stroked my jaw before he closed the distance between us, planting his lips on mine with a greedy sigh.

I moaned in response to his soft lips against mine. All I heard was the intoxicating music and all I felt was Cade. His strength. His desire. His literal energy. He pulled away and looked deeply into my eyes, questioning.

I grabbed hold of his face, dug my fingers into the hair at the base of his neck, and kissed him again. His fingers flexed on my neck as he deepened the kiss, pulling us closer together. His tongue flicked against my lips, asking for permission. I opened my mouth to let him in.

The kiss combusted.

Electricity sparked along my skin and desire burned in my veins as our tongues collided. Once again, it was only him and me at that moment.

One of his hands drifted down my back to squeeze my ass, eliminating the last bit of space between our bodies. I felt a growing pressure against my most sensitive spot as our hips moved against each other with a dizzying sensation.

A loud throat clearing behind us broke our kiss. I pulled back, watching Cade's eyes shift. The arousal morphed into something else. Something that matched his costume's persona. Staying in our embrace, I turned to see who interrupted us.

A man stood behind us, wearing a dark ripped t-shirt under a black hooded sweatshirt. Anger rolled off of him, suffocating me. He had black eyeshadow and eyeliner smudged around his eyes, which gave him a deeply sinister vibe under the shadow of his hood. The blade of the sickle he held shined in the dancing lights.

Dean.

Chapter 16

My breath hitched, my throat tightened, and a chilling sensation flooded my veins.

"What the fuck is this?" Dean asked. His voice was deathly low. Cade's muscles tensed behind me and his fingers flexed against my hips.

"Mayor Fellows," he said, unfazed, despite what his body told me. I blinked, getting blinded by the lights, sounds, and energy that flowed between the polar opposite men.

Dean's jaw ticked as he swung his glare up to meet Cade's. His knuckles were white as he gripped the handle of his sickle.

I pushed out of Cade's hold, laying a hand on Dean's chest. His heart thrashed against his ribcage at otherworldly speeds. I scanned his pained face. Sweat beaded on his brow, trickling down the side of his face. His light brown eyes were darkened, like burnt sugar.

"Dean," I started, giving his chest a little push, "we need to talk."

His eyes flicked from Cade's to mine. A growl came from his throat. "I thought we had something—"

"Outside. Now." I didn't want Cade to hear this conversation. Anything I said would raise Cade's suspicions higher.

Was it possible to have one night without drama?

Dean turned, stiff-legged. He left the dance floor. It

seemed as though the crowd separated for him. I moved to follow when Cade grabbed my arm.

"You can't seriously be thinking about going anywhere with him," he pleaded.

"I need to talk to him about things. He thinks we're are still a couple."

Cade's eyes blazed. "You said he wasn't your boyfriend."

"He's not. I told him as much after our date but maybe I wasn't clear enough. I'll be right back." I left Cade behind. Anything he might have said was swallowed by the music and partygoers.

The cool air bit at my cheeks exiting Town Hall. I wrapped my arms around my center, scanning the people milling about. Walking along the cobbled path that led to the side of the colonial brick building, Dean was nowhere to be found.

"Dean?" I called out, peeking around the corner. The area beside the town hall was darkened and filled with bushes and trees.

A surge of energy startled me from behind. I yelped as I turned to find Dean standing there.

We stood in silence. I suppressed shivers that his Grim Reaper costume sent down my spine. My brain struggled to separate Dean from his costume. His features appeared to melt with his costume.

Stupid alcohol…

"Dean—"

"Are you fucking him?"

I swallowed my words. My head ticked back. "Excuse me?"

"You heard me," he said. His hood covered most of his face, but saw how dark his eyes were. My pulse

179

quickened as a fiery heat coursed through me.

"As if it's any of your business, no. I'm not fucking him."

Dean threw his hands in the air. "What about us? What happened to us getting together to solve your fucking curse problem?" His voice quivered.

"I'm sorry, Dean," I mumbled. "I should have told you sooner but I didn't want to hurt your feelings. After our date, I tried telling you that we won't work." I clasped my hands tight around my body. "I guess I wasn't clear enough."

"You knew we wouldn't 'work'?" He mocked loudly. "We've been friends our whole lives and I know all of your secrets. One second you're begging to date me and then next your tongue is deep down someone else's throat."

"I didn't beg you. You willingly wanted to help me."

"Tell me why we shouldn't date?"

"There's no chemistry. No passion. No heat," I snapped. "I just don't feel those things with you, Dean. Our auras don't match and never did. We aren't soulmates. I don't want a loveless relationship."

"Fuck your powers, Shay." He took a large step toward me, backing me against the brick wall of the town hall. "You don't always have to listen to them." Some of his spit sprinkled my face. "Breaking away from your tight-ass controlling world would probably do you some good, anyway. And we aren't soulmates? How many fucking people are in this world? You really think you're going to find your soulmate by staying here? I'm the best choice you've got."

I shoved him back with both of my hands. "Get out

of my face, Dean." My push didn't move him at all. "I know you're hurt. And I'm sorry for that. Being with me was something you've always dreamed about. But, it's just not going to happen." I exhaled, feeling my own anger rise to the surface. "You don't have to be so mean."

Dean laughed. The sound of his snickers pierced my ears, sending more shivers down my spine. "I'm being mean? You're fucking stringing me along. All I've ever done is be your friend."

"I did not string you along. I asked one of my best friends for help. You were the best choice at the time. Now you're not. Which you keep proving, by the way."

"Is it going to happen with that firefighter? Do you guys have 'passion'? Is he your best choice?"

"That's none of your business."

"It's never going to work out with him, either."

I stayed quiet, knowing my words were falling on deaf ears. Dean crossed his arms, staring down at me, using his size to intimidate me.

"Have you told him you're a witch?"

"No."

"I'll be waiting for you when he rejects you for being a witch." Dean snorted and shook his head. "You'll be fucking crawling back to me when that curse crushes your precious store and legacy." His face was smug and his eyes were so dark I couldn't see the whites in them anymore. I ground my teeth together so tightly they probably cracked.

"Not a fucking chance..." I whispered. "Especially not now with you being a huge asshat and all."

Dean took a large step forward, forcing me back against the wall completely. He gripped my neck the same way Cade had earlier. Only this time, I felt cold terror with his hurtful grip. Dean's fingers dug into the back of my head, holding me in place. I tried to turn my face away, but his hold tightened. He leaned in, his black eyes never wavering from my face.

"We'll fucking see about that, *love*," Dean taunted. His eyes dipped to my lips. He planted a hard kiss on them. I froze.

I tried to pull away, but he pushed me harder against the wall. My hands pressed against his chest, which felt like a boulder. He had me trapped. My body felt sluggish from the alcohol, but I knew I had to get out of this situation and fast.

Changing tactics, I bit down hard on his bottom lip, channeling every ounce of hatred and anger he stirred within me. He yelled as he flew back, holding his lip. Blood poured down his chin and between his fingers. I swiped at my chin, feeling the warm residue. I shoved from the wall as he shouted curses at me.

"Don't ever fucking kiss me again."

I spun in my heel and ran toward the party. Toward safety. Toward Cade.

****

My legs wobbled unsteadily as I pushed through the front entrance of town hall. I bumped into a couple of people along the way, muttering a weak apology. The black lights distorted my vision. The sights, the music, the fog, and the teetering between times were all disorienting. I slunk into a darkened corner of the lobby, away from everyone.

The sticky liquid remained on my lips. I probably looked like a freakin' vampire fairy, not that anyone would notice it was real blood.

I was in shock. My oldest friend had just turned on me so fast when I was only trying to be truthful. And he tried to kiss me against my will!

That asshole.

Trembling, I hugged myself tightly. Bravely, tears were kept at bay. I would not cry over him, despite the cracking inside my chest from his betrayal. I licked my lips, a metallic taste on my tongue. My stomach lurched.

Alcohol flowed through my veins, mixing with the emotional rollercoaster I rode. I wanted all the feelings to float away. I closed my eyes and ran my thumbs across my finger pads. I meditated, thinking of nature and the Earth Goddess, praying for her to give me strength.

An icy chill brushed across my face. My eyes snapped open, looking around for the source of cold air. Adrenaline and alcohol surged again. Lucia's ghostly figure stood in front of me. She stared at me, smiling before misting away.

What the—?

"Shay," a deep voice spoke beside me. Tingles broke out along my skin, recognizing the voice. I whipped my head to the side and lunged into Cade's chest, hiding my face in his ripped black t-shirt. I shouldn't be using him as a comfort, but I needed it. Cade's arms wrapped around my shaking body. He laid his chin on top of my head.

"Shh. I got you," he whispered. I gripped his shirt until my knuckles turned white. After a few minutes, my body relaxed, melting in Cade's comfort.

"What happened?" he asked.

"I had to tell him there wasn't going to ever be a

me and him."

"Oh."

"He didn't take it well," I said after a few moments of silence.

"What did he say?"

"A lot of mean things. He also kissed me."

"Without your consent?" Cade's chest rumbled under my ear.

I nodded, turning my face to lay my cheek against his chest. The steady beat of his heart pounded in my ear like a metronome, calming my senses.

"I bit his lip."

Cade breathed out in a soft laugh. He pulled away from our embrace, tipping my face up with his finger. His eyes blazed a deep green as his gaze flickered across my face. He swiped a finger along my chin where Dean's blood had stained.

"That's my girl."

My eyebrows hiked up my forehead. "Your girl?"

Cade lifted a shoulder. His eyes looked me up and down, darkening with each second. His words were enticing but shocking. Fire scorched through my veins. I could listen to him tell me sweet things all night long. I giggled at my thoughts. The effects of the shots and blood bag still held my inhibitions captive.

"Want to get out of here?" he asked, staring at me. Sweat had trickled down his face, smearing his dark eye makeup even more. He looked sexy as sin. A true dark angel.

Jitteriness settled into my muscles, causing my body to shake. Was I in shock? Probably. Was I excited to go home with Cade? Fuck yes.

"Yes, please. Take me home, Cade."

Chapter 17

Me:—Heading home early.—

Me:—with Cade!—

Harmony:—Get it, girl!—

Me:—P.S. Dean is a dick.—

Harmony:—He kinda always was. Tell me all about it later. Xoxo—

Cade stood up straight, let go of my arms, and tangled his long fingers through one of my hands. He tugged on me and together we walked in silence toward my apartment, leaving the party behind. Our walk was quiet and quick. As we climbed the stairs to my front door, I felt his eyes trailing down my bare legs.

"Are you checking out my ass?"

"Of course. If it's in my view, I'm looking at it. Just facts."

I fiddled with my costume pouch to get my keys. My hands were shaking and the pain behind my eyes grew as the adrenaline, or alcohol, took their toll on my body. Cade stepped up close to me and wrapped his hands around mine.

"Let me."

I dropped my hands. His long fingers deftly opened the pouch and pulled out my keys. He stared into my eyes as he crowded me, leaning in close to unlock my door. I swallowed hard and stepped through the threshold. Cade followed, closing the door behind him.

I dashed into the kitchen, splashing water onto my face. I rubbed at the spot where I knew Dean's blood was stained. Cade stepped up behind me.

"Here," he said. "I'll help."

I faced him. He put his hands under my arms and lifted me onto the counter as if I weighed nothing. A giggle escaped my throat. Now that I was home, I felt lighter. Although Dean crossed a line, that issue was resolved. He finally knew that we would never be a thing.

Cade reached around me, pulling on a paper towel. His energy wrapped around me like a cozy blanket. My head fell back and I released a deep sigh.

After wetting the towel, he leaned forward, placing one hand on the counter beside me and the other dabbed the towel to my chin. His face scrunched with concentration while cleaning me.

On instinct, my tongue licked my lips, tasting one of his fingers. His leafy eyes flicked to mine. Then, they fell to my lips. The world melted away around us. All I saw was him. "You know, I haven't been able to get our kisses out of my mind."

My throat dried. I couldn't look away from his intoxicating eyes even if I wanted to. His words trapped me. His lips called to me. His very essence sang to me.

"Same," I whispered, surprising myself how easily that truth left my mouth.

Cade set the towel down and leaned forward. His strong arms caged around me. I sat straighter, bringing our faces in line. The air crackled with attraction and our energies hummed. He cupped the side of my face, eliminating the space between us.

"Is this okay?" he asked. His voice was thick and

strained. "Please don't say no."

My eyes bounced between his. "Yes. This is perfect."

Cade pressed his lips to mine as soon as the words left my mouth. I melted into him, wrapping my arms around his neck. His lips moved against mine, sparking the fire that bloomed in my gut for only him. His hand tightened around the back of my neck before flexing into my hair. His other hand slid down my back, arching it, and landed on my ass. He pressed me flush against his body. I moaned, wrapping my legs around his waist. I felt his excitement through the sheer material of my costume, instantly flooding my pussy.

This kiss was everything. It was more passionate because I dreamed about it happening again. I pressed my lips further into his. My boobs smashed against his hard chest and felt him hardening through his jeans. I pushed my tongue past his lips, which he accepted willingly. The kiss deepened, as if it even could. I felt it in my toes, at the top of my head. In my most sensitive spots. Everywhere. It felt so right.

"Where's Mildred?" he asked.

I shrugged my shoulders. "Off pouting somewhere."

Cade's eyebrows scrunched. My eyes widened at my error.

"She's the biggest drama queen," I deflected. "Can I get you some water or something?"

"How about we do something fun?" Cade asked. "Want to play a game?"

"What kind of game?" I asked, brushing some hair off his forehead and taking in his features.

"How about truth or dare? More like truth or

Steph Ziders

truth." The corner of his mouth tipped up into a mischievous grin. I squinted my eyes, matching his smile with my own playful one.

"Sure. But I think we'll need some liquor to go with this."

I planted a quick kiss on his lips before hopping down from the counter. I grabbed two oddly painted glasses that I bought from the antique store in the next town. I held them between my fingers, picked up the bottle of whiskey, and moved into the living room to sit on the couch.

Cade followed me. He sat beside me on the couch. His body heat instantly enveloped me, filling me with a sense of contentment in his presence. Something that I felt with family and Harmony. I never felt this comfortable in Dean's presence. The contrast was so obvious.

I poured a decent amount of whiskey into the glasses, handing one to him. I sat back against the couch, peering down at my body, tugging at the corset that wrapped around my stomach. My finger pulled at my top that rested along the swell of my breasts.

"Why do you want to play a game?"

He took a sip of his drink. "Oh, that's smooth," he said, licking his lips. "I want to know more about you, and I'm sure you want to know more about me. Plus, it'll be fun."

"Is this the obligatory 'get to know you' section of our friendship so you won't feel guilty when you take me to bed?"

Cade coughed on his whiskey, sitting forward. He swung his head in my direction. "Wow, Whitley. That was blunt."

I took a greedy gulp of my whiskey, easing the flutters that buzzed in my body. Him being in my space was intoxicating, making all the to-dos and dramatics that swam in my head go away.

"Sorry."

Cade laughed. "No need to apologize. This is just me wanting to know more about you."

"Why?"

"I like puzzles, and I can't quite figure you out."

"I'm an open book," I said, taking another drink.

Cade leaned back and crossed his leg over his knee. He tipped his head to the side then pointed a finger at me. "See, that's where you're wrong. You are not an open book, Shay. You're hiding things from me."

I shrugged a shoulder, trying to hide my nerves. He has continued to prove that he was inquisitive, observant, and intelligent. His bullshit-radar was impressive. I said nothing.

"I'm right," he said with a smirk. "So, let's play. A secret for a secret."

"Can't we just drink?"

"No. I'll even go first. I didn't think you were such a scaredy-cat."

I shifted on the couch to face him, crossing my legs, and straightened my back, staring him in the eyes. "I am not a scaredy-cat."

Cade smirked, angling his body to face mine. "There she is."

With arched eyebrows, I looked at him expectantly, waiting for his first secret.

"I thought I would hate leaving Boston. The whole big, bustling city life. Do I miss the rush of real emergencies? Yes. But, I'm really starting to like Ipswich more than I thought I would," Cade said.

"Is that because of me?" I asked, feeling confident. My mind started to cloud over, so I wasn't too sure about my inferences.

Yay, alcohol!

His cheeks rounded in a smile. "I can't answer that until you share a secret."

"Fine," I huffed. "Um…I realized that I wouldn't be able to pull off the festival without your and Aaron's help. It's not easy for me to ask for help."

"That's not really a secret," Cade countered, drinking his whiskey.

I slapped his leg. "Yes it is. It might be assumed, but it's not often I admit that out loud."

Cade laughed. "Okay, okay. Aaron is super excited. He texted me the other day saying that he's coming up soon."

"I know. We've been texting too."

Cade laughed. "Obviously. My turn, again," he said, pressing a finger to his chin, thinking. "I don't like being deceived."

"Does anyone?" I quipped.

Cade shook his head. "I would hope not. I have a knack for smelling bullshit and I'm pretty stubborn when it comes to figuring out a mystery."

My whiskey threatened to come back up at his confession. I knew he suspected I was lying. Hearing his words out loud, solidified it.

"People are allowed to have secrets, Cade," I said. "Especially if that person has a hard time trusting others. Could you imagine a world where everyone said the whole truth all the time?"

Cade shook his head with laughter. "That would be insane. And I'm not talking about all secrets. Just the big ones. The ones that define who a person is."

I played with the tips of my hair, watching the glitter from my costume float down. "Sometimes there are secrets because the other person wants to protect you."

"That's a cop-out."

"If you say so."

"My sister, Leyla, kept secrets from me. 'For my protection'. I knew there was something more going on. And her secret got us both in trouble."

"Oh. You said something about that before." I cleared my throat. "What happened?" I intertwined our fingers, feeling the warmth surge through this simple act. Cade looked down at our hands and thinned his lips.

"She was dating someone on the police force in our suburb of Boston. He was much older than her. She got pulled into his charm, good looks, status, and all that shit. One day, she came home with a black eye. She lied about how she got it."

I flinched.

"It wasn't long after that I got a phone call from her, crying, saying that she needed me to pick her up from his house. I drove my bike over there as fast as I could. She was sitting on the step outside in the cold, shivering. Her face was bleeding and her clothes were ripped. I took her to the police station to file a report, and who do you think was there on duty?"

"Oh, no…"

Cade nodded. "I saw red. I didn't even think. I fucking punched him in the face, knocking him out. I spent a few nights in jail. And as part of my 'rehabilitation', I was transferred here. Leyla never filed a police report because she didn't want to be the laughingstock of the town. Now she's a shell of the person she was before. He ruined her life. I still don't even know what exactly happened. Did he rape her? Just beat her up? I have no idea and it kills me that I don't know."

"Fuck. I'm so sorry, Cade. That's horrible."

I squeezed his hand and snuggled beside him. His body cocooned mine. My head nestled on his shoulder, resting my hand on his chest. Beneath my fingers, his heart beat fast.

"It's fucking ridiculous that he had zero accountability for his actions and my sister can't even function without drugs."

"Is that why you care about my safety so much?"

I felt his sharp inhale. "Yes. Though, you've proven several times you can hold your own."

"Is being away from Boston helpful? Is that why you like Ipswich? The escape from it all?"

He huffed a laugh, making my body move with his. "Yeah. It's refreshing not having to worry about all that drama."

"What about me?" I asked, feeling the whiskey loosen my lips and filter. "Do I have anything to do with you liking Ipswich?"

"Give me another secret and I'll tell you." His voice was husky and deep, sending vibrations along my skin.

"Fine." I smiled against his shoulder. "I'm really glad you came to Ispwich."

Cade laughed again, before kissing the top of my

head. "You have a lot to do with me liking Ipswich."

My smile grew as we snuggled together on the couch. My limbs loosened with each tick of the clock. The constant list-making in my head quieted. My fingers skimmed over his chest.

"Now you know why I really don't like Dean," Cade said, breaking the comfortable silence.

"Does he remind you of that other guy?"

"Yeah. I can see the same aggro-ness to him that the cop in Boston had. There's something off about Dean. I can't put my finger on it though."

I leaned forward, downing the rest of my whiskey. I scoffed, feeling my disgust for him travel up my throat. The sting of his words and actions tonight were still fresh. My oldest friendship…just over.

"He's a jealous asshole who comes from a line of asshole warlocks with a god-complexes. Add in his conjuring skills, he's basically a walking time bomb." I blew past my lips, feeling a weight lifted from my chest, getting my honest feelings about Dean out in the open. "I mean, we shared one gross kiss that has *zero chemistry* and he acts like we're meant to be together. As if we're soulmates. I would have known if we were soulmates by now given my gifts. I do give people Lovers Readings on a daily basis."

Silence.

Oh. Shit.

"Oh. Shit," I said out loud, turning to look at Cade. His eye were wide. It wasn't just disgust I felt in my throat. It was word vomit. His jaw ticked once, then twice as he swallowed.

"Did you say warlock?"

"Uh…" I hiccupped, then swiped at my brow and

blinked. Cade put his glass down on the coffee table with a sturdy clank.

"Are you saying Dean Fellows is an actual witch with real powers? Like a real spell-casting wizard?" His voice shook. I couldn't tell if he was mad or teetering on hysteria.

Stupid whiskey.

I swallowed, looking down at my hands. This was an unplanned turn of events.

"Shay. Answer me." He stood from the couch, towering over me. I licked my lips as I raised my head. Cade's authoritative voice called to me in more ways than one.

"Technically, he's a warlock. That's the word for a male witch."

Cade's hands fisted. "What the fuck does that mean? He has powers or something?"

My shoulders caved in. "Yeah. He has a knack for making potions and conjuring."

"Like drugs or demons?" Cade's voice was hard and his breathing came out as heavy puffs. "I can tell you're saying the truth, but this goes beyond my scope of understanding."

"No demons. At least I don't think so. Lydia, at Sinful Delights, also makes potions but puts her magic into her drinks and food. That's why all of her stuff tastes soooo good," I slurred, wishing I was eating one of her donuts right now. "And helps with your mood."

Fuck. Why did I say that?

Cade ran his hands through his hair, making it stick out in all directions. He paced the living room.

"I'm sorry. I just spewed all that on you. Like a secret bomb. You know for the game that we were playing." I chuckled and hiccuped at the same time. I swallowed, trying to gain some control of the situation. "How are you feeling?"

"I don't know what to feel, Shay. You're sitting there, looking all fucking adorable in your sexy fairy costume, telling me that witches are real. After I just shared some pretty serious stuff with you about my sister and my opinion of cops."

"Awe, you think I look adorable?" Heat flowed through my body at his compliment.

"Shay…"

I shifted on the couch, tucking my hair behind my ears. "I'm sorry, but this is serious stuff for me, too. I feel much better now that the cat's out of the bag." I giggled.

Cade stopped pacing. His head dipped and his gaze turned toward me in slow motion. His piercing green eyes blazed as he stared at me. My eyes widened and I leaned back further into the couch.

"Serious to you?" Cade asked. "You're a witch, too?" His voice was stiff, but not angry. Cold. Calculating.

I frowned. The warmth from the whiskey froze under his gaze. This night had taken a complete one-eighty from the sizzling kiss we shared in the kitchen. I opened my mouth to lie. Maybe if I kept my secret in its tidy box, he wouldn't judge me and my structured world could stay together. Cade's eyes narrowed. His jaw set.

"The truth, Shay. Now."

I took in a sharp breath and stood from the couch. Approaching him, my head lifted, and I stared into his hypnotizing leaf-green eyes. This truth needed to come out sooner than later. The real truth, however, was that I was terrified of his judgment and rejection.

"I am the last in a long line of Whitley witches. I can see the future and sometimes the past, now, too."

Chapter 18

"Are you fucking serious?!" Cade laugh-shouted. My face scrunched into a wince. Mildred ran out of Harmony's room. The fur on her face was matted down.

"What the hell is happening?"

"You're a real fucking witch?" Cade asked. He fisted his hands into his hair. He looked crazed.

"Oh. You told him…" Mildred concluded, perching on the couch. *"This should be good."* I snuck a peek at her, sending her a mental message to shut up. This was what I was afraid of, but I couldn't deny how light and airy my chest felt. Cade needed to know.

"Yes, I am."

A hollow laugh escaped Cade's lips, and he started pacing again. "This is fucking crazy. Witches are real. But, then again, you work in a Wiccan store for fuck's sake and you're bringing back the Ipwsich Annual Wiccan Fesitval. How could I have been so thick-headed?" Cade rambled.

"He's losing it, Shay. Do something."

Cade continued talking incoherently to himself, pointing at the random witch things around my apartment and gesturing to me. I stepped into his path, blocking him. My movement surprised him. I gripped his shoulders and lunged forward, pressing my lips to his. He froze. His lips didn't move, despite the sparks that ignited on my lips. He pulled away from me.

"Don't."

"I didn't know how to stop your mental breakdown." My head bowed and took a step back, feeling the space grow between us.

"I'm not having a psychotic break, Shay. I'm having a fairy-tale crisis." His voice was icy. "I was raised Catholic. I don't practice or even believe in God now, but I sure as fuck didn't believe in witches, either."

I flinched. "Don't worry, vampire and werewolves aren't real, if that helps."

Cade's head whipped toward me. His eyes narrowed. "Not fucking funny."

"I'm sorry!" I shouted at him, surrendering my hands up in the air. "Clearly, I'm tipsy, which is how that secret spilled out, anyway. But, come on. What's the big deal? I have psychic talents. I'm still the same Shay." I wiped my hands down my face, ignoring the makeup that probably smeared. "Or at least I'm trying to still be the same. I recently found out that there's some crazy curse placed on my family by Dean's ancestors—" Mildred coughed on a hairball.

"You're pushing it, Shay. You must be closer to drunk than tipsy."

"Haha. You're right," I said, looking at Mildred. "I think I'm drunk." I laughed, feeling the giggles bubbling in my throat. I flopped down on the couch behind me.

"Shay," Cade said, crouching in front of me.

I lifted my gaze to his, losing myself in the depths of their color. A smile played on my lips as I leaned forward, cupping his face.

"You are so sweet, protective, and muscular. I'm so glad you came to Ipswich even if you are a skeptical Quaint," I slurred. Mildred snorted a laugh. She always enjoyed it when I got drunk. "I've been struggling with telling you my secret. But, now that it's out, I feel much better." I gave him a sloppy smile. "I'm glad you now know the real truth. The real me."

Cade gripped my wrists, pulling them away from his face. They fell to my legs with a slap. "What's a Quaint?" he asked. I opened my mouth to respond when his eyes closed and he held up a hand. "Nevermind, I don't want to know."

I frowned.

"I need to go," he said in a strained whisper.

"Why?" I whined. Cade sighed, rubbing a hand down his face.

"Because your secret just exploded my whole world and I don't know how to deal with it." He stood, going toward the door, and putting his shoes back on.

The fog from the whiskey cleared as I processed his words. He was leaving. I told him my secret and he was leaving.

Dean was right.

"Cade. Wait." I jumped up from the couch, tripping over my feet. "This is what I was afraid of!" My words stopped him. "This is why I didn't tell you! I tell you something personal and something that I can't change. I don't want to change. I love being a witch. And you're running away from who I am."

Cade's shoulders lifted and fell as he took in a breath. "I'm sorry, Shay."

He left.

I stood there staring at the closed door.

Silent tears fell down my cheeks. His rejection hurt harder than anything I've felt before.

"Come on, Shay. Let's get you to bed," Mildred said as she nuzzled her face against my leg.

Like a zombie, I walked to my bedroom, shutting the door behind me. The echo rumbled the apartment. I flopped down on my bed, sniffling. A warm, fuzzy body jumped on my back and nestled her head on my shoulder. Mildred's weight added the right amount of pressure to my back as I soaked up her strength.

"How were you expecting him to react?"

"I don't know," I murmured. "I wasn't expecting to tell him anything! It slipped out that Dean was a warlock and Cade's smart. He made the connections. I couldn't lie anymore. Honestly, I didn't want to."

Mildred rubbed her face along mine. Her whiskers tickled.

I grabbed a pillow from the top of my bed and shoved it under my head for more support. I didn't move from the horizontal position. Although it should drive me crazy, I didn't even care that I would get glitter and makeup from my costume everywhere.

"He'll come around."

"You don't know that."

"It's obvious how he feels about you. Everyone knows it. Including Dean. We can call Sandy for confirmation, but I don't think we need to. Just give him time to come to terms with the fact that his world is no longer black and white."

"I don't know why I'm so upset," I said into my pillow, tasting the salty tears.

"Yes, you do. You were starting to open your heart to him, whether your brain wanted to or not."

The lump in my throat grew, and more tears welled behind my closed eyes. "Yeah."

Mildred licked at the tears that fell down my cheeks, pawing at my hair like a mother would to a child.

"Rejection hurts, hon. It's part of life. Give him time."

"You're so confident."

"And you are so controlling, you always think before you speak. I bet all my catnip that you've been wanting to tell him about your abilities for a long time. You were just waiting for the right moment."

"I almost slipped a few times. It's effortless with him. Even though I feel hurt, it feels like a weight has lifted from my shoulders now that he knows."

"I'm sure he feels that, too. So, I'll say again. Give him time."

I snorted. "Just because you want him around more doesn't mean *he* wants to."

"I refuse to think that. But, if you guys don't make up soon, I'm going to leave you for him."

A laugh escaped past my lips and my tears began to dry. Mildred snuggled under my chin. I gave her a few ear scratches. Mildred nestled beside me.

My phone buzzed on my nightstand. My heartbeat kicked up as I reached for it. Maybe Cade was texting me.

I frowned when I saw the text.

Mom:—Are you OK? I feel your sadness.—

Me:—No. I accidentally told Cade that we're witches. He didn't take it well.—

Mom:—Oh, honey. I'm sorry. Why don't you do a tarot reading? It might help you sleep. Or I can tap into his emotions…—

    Me:—Thanks, Mom.—

    Me:—NO! Leave his emotions alone.—

    Mom:—It's a standing offer.—

    "See. Sandy knows."

    "Oh my Goddess. Stop."

I kicked the covers off me. Mildred yelped as the blankets covered her face. Doing tarot was the perfect suggestion. It always calmed me during rough times. And this was rough times. I left the warmth of my bedroom and tiptoed into the kitchen, finding my tarot cards. I paused, looking at the two whiskey glasses sitting on the coffee table. Abandoned. The lump clogged my throat as I looked toward the door and sighed. Back in my bedroom, I sat cross-legged on the floor, and lit three candles: a blue for healing, purple for spirituality, and red for courage.

I shuffled my tarot cards three times, reflecting on Cade and wondering what was going to happen next. The cards were spread out on the floor in a semicircle. With eyes closed, I ran my fingers along the cards. I touched them, feeling for the one that called out to me.

A card stuck to my finger. I turned it over, opening my eyes: Page of Swords—reversed.

The Page of Swords showed a young boy holding a sword, symbolizing a thirst for knowledge. He tackled any challenge that was put in his path. But, the card was reversed, warning me from being too critical or judgemental of others. I needed to take a step back and reassess my priorities.

I breathed out.

"Well, that card makes a lot of sense," Mildred said, adding her two cents.

"Yeah."

"Even Fate is telling you not to be so quick to jump to conclusions. You have no idea how Cade will deal with this new information. He might surprise you."

"Stop being so encouraging. It's not your normal diposition. It's distracting." I cleaned up my cards and blew out the candles. Before climbing back into bed, I ditched my fairy costume and pulled the pins from my hair. Laying my head on my pillow, I snuggled close with Mildred's body.

"Oh, don't worry. The bitch is still in me. I was completely serious that I will go live with Cade if you don't fix this."

Chapter 19

The wood floor creaked and groaned as footfalls fell beside my bed. I held my eyes closed, hoping the person would think I was sleeping and go away.

"I know you're awake." Harmony's sharp voice pierced through my cocoon of silence and despair. "Get up."

"No," I groaned into my pillow. "I'm going to stay here forever."

"I've never known you to hide from your problems."

"Maybe I want to start now." My tongue felt thick inside my mouth.

"Shay, get your ass up. I brought you a hangover drink from Lydia. She says it has dandelion root and ginger."

I rolled over, cracking one eye open. Harmony stood beside my bed, holding a to-go cup. The steam rolled from the small hole in the top. The earthy, bittersweet scents wafted into the air. I sat up and grunted, gripping my head.

Were construction workers jackhammering in my brain?

I reached out for the cup, bringing it to my lips and taking a sip. I closed my eyes again, invoking the herbs' healing powers, and sent a silent prayer to Saint Bibiana, the patron saint of hangovers, for extra support.

"Thanks. That tastes amazing."

"Do you want to tell me why you're still in bed? It's one in the afternoon." Her hand was propped on one hip as she leveled me with her eyes.

"I'm tired. Duh."

"You never sleep this late. Now, spill. Even if I could hear Mildred in my head, I still wouldn't ask her. I want to hear it from you."

I sat up further, pulling my legs into a criss-cross, giving Harmony space to sit on the bed. "Sit down. Let me tell you all about last night."

After telling Harmony about last night with Cade, she sat frozen with her jaw on the floor.

"You…I…You told him you're a witch? And that Dean's one and Lydia?" She stuttered.

"I literally just said all that."

She blinked her fake eyelashes. "I know. I'm just…I can't believe it. And Cade just left?"

I nodded, wincing. Lydia's drink had worked wonders for my headache and overall ickiness, but there wasn't any potion to cure the sting of rejection.

"What a dickhead."

"He's not a dickhead," I countered. "He's a Quaint who's realizing that some lores are real."

Harmony tsked. "It didn't take me long to get over it."

"You took about two seconds when I first told you. But we were sixteen and you were going through your witch phase anyway. You would have believed me if I said vampires were real too."

Harmony swung her eyes to me. "They still aren't, are they?" she asked, changing the topics seamlessly as she moved into the kitchen. I rolled out of bed, careful not to spill Lydia's concoction, following her.

"No."

Her shoulders slumped. "Bummer." She gripped my hand in hers, giving it a squeeze. "Things are going to turn out just fine. Concentrate on the things you can control. You can't control how Cade feels, as much as you might want to."

I frowned.

After a few hours of much-needed girl talk and greasy bacon, I realized something was missing. I looked behind me, scanning the apartment.

"Harm, have you seen Mildred?"

She turned in the stool. Her gaze bounced around the space. "No."

I stood, feeling the frustration bubble in my stomach. "Mildred? Where are you?" I scurried through the apartment, searching her usual hiding spots.

Nothing.

"Where do you think she is?" Harmony asked.

My stomach dropped as a single dreadful thought popped into my head. "I'll give you one guess."

I walked into my bedroom. Harmony followed close behind. I felt around a pile of blankets, evidence of my restless sleep, searching for my phone. Pulling it from the depth of my blanket fort, I saw that the screen showed a missed call and a couple of texts.

Cade:—I have Mildred. She was outside my door when I left for my shift. Come by the station and get her when you can.—

"That bitch." Harmony laughed. "She did that on purpose."

"She told me to give him space and then the very

next morning, she's setting us up," I grumbled, pressing my fingers to my temple.

Harmony pursed her lips together trying to hide a smile. "Better get cute, girl."

"Stop it. He doesn't want to see me. He just wants Mildred out of his hair."

"You don't know that. Seems like this is the perfect time to test the waters on his feelings. He could have woken up completely okay with it."

"Ugh." I pushed past her into my bathroom. "Stop being so positive," I said as I threw the door shut, hearing her cackles over the running water of the shower.

****

As I walked through the town square toward the fire station, I brushed at the makeup under my eyes, feeling my high ponytail bob. The chilly breeze pricked at my exposed skin. I preferred the bite to the constant burning blush on my skin.

The town was quiet, despite its late afternoon hour. It was usually dead the day after the Halloween party, for obvious reasons. This year I was grateful I didn't have to talk to anyone. To say I was nervous to see Cade would be a serious understatement. I had fallen asleep last night and resigned to giving him space. I understood that I had dropped major truth-bombs on him and he asked for space. The Fates even told me so by showing me the Page of Swords, reversed.

I took a deep breath, fidgeting with my sleeves. I was going to listen to Fate, taking this situation slowly.

A shadow crossed in front of my path, causing me to almost bump into the townsperson.

"Oh, my bad," I started to apologize, looking up to

find the last person I wanted to see. A sneer formed on my lips, registering his stupid face and stupid button-up shirt. I took an instinctive step back. Dean held a brown paper bag in his hand.

"Hi," he greeted. His voice was level, tentative even.

I stared at him, zeroing in on the faded scab on his lip. My teeth ground together as I exhaled audibly through my nose. It was naïve to think I would never run into him again, but I didn't think it'd be so soon.

"I, uh, bought your favorite pastry from the bakery." He held out the bag. "I saw you from the window while I was in there and thought you might like one."

I ignored the bag, keeping my eyes trained on him. His light brown eyes were soft and apologetic, despite the dark circles under them. In fact, his whole face and demeanor screamed exhaustion.

Not like I cared...

"I don't want your half-assed apology danish, Dean." He looked down at the ground, shuffling his boot on the sidewalk.

"Shit, I know I messed up. It was the first Halloween party we didn't go to together and have pancakes after. I missed you."

I worked to keep my face neutral, despite the fact that I wanted to curl my lips. It was easy to hold on to the anger, even if there was a gleam of forgiveness swimming in my veins.

"I was clear about how I felt last night, Dean." I tipped my head toward his lip where I bit him.

His tongue poked out, licking along the cut. "I... miss my friend."

"You said that." I crossed my arms over my body.

I wanted out of this conversation. The fresh memories of him kissing me without permission still stung. Being near him for this long was making my skin crawl.

Dean swallowed hard and moved the brown bag to his other hand. He raked the free hand through his hair, which had started to grow out. He lifted his eyes to meet mine. Regret, hurt, and something darker swam in his caramel depths. My heart was too shattered by his choices that his puppy-dog pout wasn't going to work this time.

"Please, I'm sorry. I realize that I pushed you too far." Awkwardness clung to the air between us for several moments.

"I don't forgive you."

As if a trigger switched, Dean's jaw ticked and he swallowed hard. A dangerous vibe washed over him.

"I won't be ignored for too much longer, Shay. You and I are destined. Our ancestors made sure of that."

"Oh? Your ancestor *Harrison*, put a curse on my entire family because Lucia turned him down. Are you really going to stoop to his loser level? Follow in his footsteps? Grow up and accept the fact that there will *never* be anything between us," I spat. "And don't threaten me."

Dean sucked in a sharp breath. His shoulders straightened and he white-knuckled the pastry bag. His jaw was equally as tight.

"I can't believe I didn't see your true colors until now," I scoffed. "Have you just playing me this whole time?"

Have I been so focused on control that I was blind to the dangers that stood before me?

"I'll say it again," I said, cutting him off from answering my rhetorical question. "Stay away from me."

I turned my back on him when I bounced off a strong wall of muscle. My body tensed and sizzled at the same time. Cade reached a tattooed forearm around me, snatching the brown bag out of Dean's hand. He opened the bag and peered inside.

"Awe, Dean. You got me a cheese danish. Thanks, man." He lifted out the pastry and took a large bite.

"That wasn't for you, asshole," Dean said, widening his stance even more.

"Oh, my bad." He held the half-eaten treat to me. "You want some?"

Cade's tired eyes pierced mine. Dark circles lined his eyes and his hair was unkempt. There was a playful but controlled look on his face.

My eyes drifted down his body, noting his delicious muscles bunching under his red IFD t-shirt and navy slacks. My body heated, watching his mouth chew on the pastry, his eyes not leaving mine. All of my secrets that I shared swirled between us like a giant dark cloud of words left unsaid.

My head gave a small shake. Cade shoved the rest of the danish in his mouth in one bite.

"Looks like I was too hungry to share," Cade said with a cheeky smile. "There you have it." He addressed Dean in a carefree stance. "Shay doesn't want anything you have to offer. So maybe, Mayor Fellows, fuck off, before things actually get physical between me and you. I've been patient so far."

Dean rolled his shoulders back and stepped up to Cade, forcing me to the side. "Watch yourself, Thompson. I could have you arrested for threatening me. How does a night in a cell sound? Your empty promises don't scare me." Dean's hands fisted at his side.

Cade shrugged his shoulders and stuffed his hands in the pockets of his IFD slacks, unaffected by Dean's pomp and circumstance.

"Or…" Cade ticked his head in my direction. His voice was deathly serious. "Shay could still press charges against you for sexual assault. Don't think that'd look good on your record. Especially if you're up for reelection. We all know how politicians and sexual assault go hand-in-hand."

I waited for regret or shame to flood my senses at Cade's threats, but none came.

A low growl came from Dean's throat.

Cade stepped in front of me on the sidewalk. He was alert and still willing to protect me, despite the truths he knew.

That had to mean something…right?

Dean squinted his eyes at Cade, calculating. With a frown in my direction, he took a step back, away from Cade. A mask of fake kindess fell over his face, similar to the one that Cade had also perfected.

"I'll be seeing you, Shay. We live in a small town. I bet we'll run into each other again," Dean said. His threat hung in the air like a suffocating cloud. He smiled again, showing his teeth. It was anything but warm. He backed away before turning and strolling through the town square.

"Why did you egg him on like that?" I asked Cade,

211

turning to face him. His face fell, showing how tired he looked.

"He needed to know where I stand as far as him and you," he said, holding my stare.

"You don't know what he's capable of."

"Like with his magic? I'm not afraid of him."

I blinked, wrapping my arms around my center. A shiver ran down my spine. Silence descended upon us. It was heavy, stifling, and loud. I ran my thumbs over my fingertips.

"Mildred?" I asked, avoiding the millions of things I wanted to say to him.

"She was outside my door this morning when I left for my shift."

"Why didn't you just drop her off?"

"I was already running late. I didn't sleep at all last night," he said.

"Oh." I cleared my throat. "All the witch stuff—"

Cade held up his hand and closed his eyes with a sigh, cutting off my words. "Shay…"

"Cade, please," I whispered. "I just wanted to tell you that I understand that was a lot to hear. And I get it if you don't want anything to do with me anymore. I'm basically a freak of nature. Something that you thought never existed."

Cade sighed again, more mournfully than the last one.

"You aren't a freak of nature," he said. His voice softened. "I asked for time to process."

"Right. Well, lead the way to Mildred so I can get out of your hair."

"All the guys will be happy to get rid of her," he said with a spark of humor.

We walked side-by-side. My body screamed at me to grab onto him, to pull him into an embrace, but I held my arms tight.

"She doesn't really like anyone."

"She's given her fair share of scratches. To everyone except me, of course." He grinned down at me.

"She must actually like you."

"Does she like Dean?"

"Hell no," I said, quickly. "She despises him." Cade turned his head to look at me as we walked. His stare burned a hole in the side of my face.

"How many more examples do you need that Dean is a bad guy?"

"There's still a lot you don't know about our families. And as you just said, you aren't ready to talk about it yet. Maybe stop with the hero-complex. You can't be one foot in, one foot out and expect me to blindly listen to you."

There was heat behind my words. A small part of me liked having Cade's support when it came to Dean. He threatened me, again. Someone with his power both mystically and societally was dangerous. I didn't know what to do about it. Only, I didn't like being a damsel in distress in Cade's eyes.

And my words were the absolute truth. He needed to accept all of me. All of my world if he wanted to keep giving me unsolicited advice.

"It's not a hero-complex," Cade huffed.

"Yes, it is. You feel like you couldn't save your sister and now you're trying to with me."

Cade halted on the sidewalk. He gripped my arm, twisting me around to face him. His eyes blazed and his nostrils flared. "That's part of it. But, you are worth so much more. If I'm not there to save you, and he does something, that would ruin me. I wouldn't be able to come back from that guilt. I feel much different things for you than I do for my sister, Shay."

"What are you saying, Cade?" I asked. My voice was barely above a whisper. My brain swirled with questions. One second he's telling me to leave him alone and now he's telling me something more.

"I care about you more than I think I should," he said, flicking his eyes between my lips and eyes.

My stomach jumped into my throat. His confession wrapped around me like a cozy blanket. His hands seared into the skin on my arms. We stood for a few moments, gazing at each other. I saw into his soul, behind his bravado. There was a battle within himself. Fantasy vs. reality. His brain and heart were at war, much like mine. Witches are aren't supposed to be real, but one was standing before him with her heart on her sleeve.

A familiar tug pulled at my stomach. The air whooshed past my ears. My eyes unfocused as my powers activated.

Someone was kissing me as they held themselves over me.

A man. A familiar man with strong arms.

My body tingled all over as his lips moved down my body.

I arched my naked back into his caresses.

I felt safe, warm, loved, content.

My hands dove into the person's hair as his lips tasted my body's most sensitive spot.

Green and sliver bursts of colors erupted from

around the man.

"Shay?" Cade's panicked voice broke through my vision.

I blinked, seeing his face, which was poised in my line of sight. Heat crept up my neck. The arousal from my vision flowed through my veins. The man in the vision knew what he was doing. I swallowed, taking in a deep breath through my nose.

"What just happened?"

"A vision," I said, moving out of his grip. If he continued holding me, I was going to explode.

"A what?" he asked, standing to his full height.

"A vision…my witch powers. You haven't given me a chance to explain."

"Oh."

"I'll spare you the details. Let's go get Mildred." I beelined for the station as the remnants of the vision ebbed. The last thing I wanted was for Cade to ask what it was about. He caught up to me.

"How often does that happen?"

"Whenever I call on it. Lately, it's been happening on its own. Like Fate is trying to show me something."

Cade shoved his hands in his pant pockets. Thankfully, the fire station came into view, cutting off anymore of this discussion. The big red doors of the firehouse were wide open. Some of the other firefighters were washing the engine.

"Is that Shay Whitley?" Chief Irons boomed from the doorway, leading into the firehouse.

"Yes. You have something that belongs to me. How many scratches did she give you?" I teased.

"Only one. He was smart enough to stay away after that." Mildred's confident voice sounded in my

head. She slithered out of the door behind Chief Irons before it closed. Mildred sauntered toward Cade, rubbing her body along his ankles and between his legs. Cade sat on his haunches and scratched her ears, rubbing his hands along her lithe body, making it arch.

"She gave me one before I learned to leave her alone," Chief replied, putting his hands on his hips. "She's a feisty one."

"Well, thanks for letting her hang with you guys. She slipped from my apartment at some point."

"How's your mother?" Chief asked. He looked behind me toward my family's store.

"She's good. Living the life."

The chief's cheeks reddened as he looked down at the ground for a brief second. "Well, tell her hi for me and that she should stop by the station sometime. I guess I could also make a visit across the street."

My lips tipped up in a smile. For a split second, I unfocused my eyes to read his aura. It sparkled with an aqua-blue color with swirls of yellow.

It was unique and familiar, but I couldn't place it.

"Did you see her at the Halloween party? She was there."

"Yes. Yes. We chatted for a bit," he said, running a hand through his thick gray hair. "We're all looking forward to the festival."

"There certainly is a lot of buzz around the festival. I hope it's a success and we can save the store."

"Don't worry your pretty little head, darlin'," Chief Irons said as his face lit up. "The town's not letting an iconic pillar of Ipswich go that easily despite what those bureaucrats at the bank think."

"Thanks, Chief."

"Mildred's been well fed and Cade's been very attentive to her. He's the only one she likes," he said.

I peeked down at Cade, who played with Mildred on the floor, swishing his hand around her face. She meowed as she swatted at his fingers.

"Well, thanks so much, guys. I'll grab Mildred and give you a chance to tend to your wounds."

I heard a groan and a few cheers from the surrounding firefighters that had come to see Mildred off.

"I don't want to go," Mildred whined. Ignoring her, I scooped her into my arms, which she protested until I got her in a secure hold. Then her body went slack, resigning to her fate.

"What happened to giving him space?" I whispered in her ear, pretending I was telling her cute things.

"I changed my mind after hearing you snort and cry in your sleep," Mildred replied with a meow. *"You were interrupting MY beauty sleep."*

I poked her belly, giving a small smile when she meowed.

"Ow. Bitch. You're lucky my claws never come out for you."

With a nod to the guys, I walked down the long driveway of the fire station. Cade fell instep beside me. There was so much I wanted to say. So much I wanted him to say, but instead we walked. The breeze blew around us, wafting some fallen dead leaves up.

The jackhammering started again in my brain...and heart.

"Well, I'll see you around," I mumbled to him. "Thanks again for looking after Mildred."

Cade's face was slack and unreadable. His gaze

seared into my skin until I rounded the corner out of sight. My heart sank when he didn't call out to me.

Chapter 20

Harmony and I cuddled in blankets on the couch, watching reruns of our favorite teenage witch show. Mildred sat between us, finally content with her strict house arrest. It had been a couple of days since I last saw Cade or Dean. Not that I was counting. I saw Cade once in passing. We were cordial, but nothing more. He didn't scour or throw daggers my way. He only looked pained and confused. It tested my control to not ask him every three seconds if he was okay.

"Do you ever wish you had more active powers like that?" Harmony asked, taking a sip from her steaming mug. Her hair was up in a bun, she wore zero make-up, and her feet were in red lip-shaped slippers. I was dressed as equally comfy. It was a lazy morning since both of us worked at The Witch's Brew later. A tiny, little, miniscule part of me hoped Cade would show up.

"No. I like the powers that I have," I answered truthfully.

"It's been giving you problems lately. I still can't believe you had a conversation with Lucia in the cemetery the other day."

"Yeah. That's kind of crazy," Mildred added in my head.

"I know. But she's been all quiet since I bit Dean's lip. And it's kind of making me anxious. I have so many questions and none of them are getting answered."

Harmony squeezed my shoulder across the back of the couch. "It's definitely frustrating. But the festival is coming up. That's a good distraction, right?"

I nodded.

"I'm excited. Aaron has a lot more connections in Boston than I thought he would. He's been sending me all sorts of different vendors. We're going to go with a medieval mystic theme. I'm glad I asked for his help. For the first time, I feel like I might be able to pull this off."

"I'm sure Sandy and Dotty are happy to hear about that."

"They are. Though, Mom's been more hung up on the whole Dean thing."

"Why?" Harmony's eyebrows dipped. "She was against your arrangement from the start."

My phone buzzed on the counter.

"Speaking of Sandy…" I answered, putting the call on speaker. "Hi, Mom."

"I felt something else from Dean today," Mom said without a greeting.

Harmony and Mildred kept their eyes on me, listening.

"What did you feel?" I asked with a sigh. She has been sending me daily texts about Dean's feelings for the past week. I was done hearing about him. Childishly, I went out of my way to avoid him in town. A hefty task. He crossed a line and broke my trust.

"Anger. Jealousy. Hurt," she said.

"Of course he is, Mom. I crushed his hopes and bit his lip."

"He fuckin' attacked her, Sandy," Harmony piped up. "Why are you so focused on *his* emotions?"

Mom swallowed over the line. "Something feels more sinister than just a typical breakup. I'm worried. Which is why I called."

A little of my annoyance ebbed. "I get that, Mom. I do. I'm trying to move on. There are more important things."

"I know, sweetheart." A tense silence lingered over the phone before she spoke again. "Just be careful. I can feel him planning something. There's been some strange things, too. Sometimes I can feel his emotions and other times I can't. As if he's disappeared from the Earth's plane."

"I can handle him."

Mildred snuffed.

"I know you can," Mom said. "Have you had any more past visions?"

"No. Everything's been pretty quiet on the psychic front. I wonder if Lucia is done telling me what I need to know."

A silence settled over the phone and in my apartment as we each contemplated our own thoughts.

"I wouldn't be too sure about that, Shay," Gram's squeaky voice added. "The curse isn't satisfied. Especially now that your only suitor messed up."

Reality doused on top of me. I frowned.

"You forgot about the curse?" Mom asked.

"A little bit. With everything going on, my head feels like it's spinning. I can only prioritize so much." I looked at Harmony. She was biting on her long red nail, deep in thought.

"What are the exact perimeters of the curse,

221

anyway?" she asked.

"I'm not getting much luck with the spirits," Gram said. "They've been pretty tight-lipped, which is odd cause they're usually a real chatty bunch. They're all hinting at the same thing. Harrison is involved with the curse. He probably created it out of spite. That prick."

"Okay…" I said, feeling the panic rise in my throat. I took a deep breath, creating a list in my head. "First things first, I need to finish planning the festival. Now that the Halloween party is over, I need to focus on that. I got a text from Aaron the other day saying he's going to be stopping by this weekend to scope out the town square.

"And… then I'll deal with the angry mayor with a hidden agenda, an unsolvable curse, and a skeptical firefighter that won't give me the time of day."

My last words stung. My throat tightened, fighting against the tears. I had started opening up to Cade before I dropped the "witch-bomb," and now there was just silence. His rejection hurt…a lot. Despite that, he still occupied my thoughts and dreams.

I missed him. I missed our friendship…and our scorching kisses.

"That's a lot," Harmony said. "Is Cade a contender to resolve the curse?"

"If you and Cade got together," Mom said, "that might satisfy the curse."

"He's a skeptic," I said quickly. I had considered this already. Each time it swirled in my head, I countered it. I couldn't be with someone who didn't value *all* of me. I promised myself I would tell him no more lies. I wanted him to know all my secrets; and keeping them hidden was no way to be in a relationship. It wouldn't be fair to either of us.

"I doubt that matters to the curse," Mom said. "Your dad was a skeptic at first, too."

"I don't think I could be with a man just because of a curse, Mom."

"Even if it's Cade?" Mildred added. *"I mean, I could definitely sacrifice my independence for him."*

I booped Mildred's nose, moving my hand behind her ears to scratch her head. "Very funny. There's more to a relationship than just sex, Mildred."

"Who said anything about sex?" She purred. *"You're the one that went there."*

"Mildred, you dirty pussy." Harmony laughed after I told the ladies what she said. "But she's right."

"Guys," I whined. "One disaster at a time. Love can wait."

"The curse won't wait for long," Mom said.

"Do we even know what will happen if Shay doesn't satisfy the curse?" Harmony asked.

Silence.

"Add that to the list, I guess," I mumbled. "We have to find out those perimeters. Maybe Lucia will offer more information."

A knock sounded at the door, interrupting our conversation. Mildred hopped off the couch, running to the door. Using her paw, she pushed the curtain away from the window next to the door.

"It's Cade," she purred, flicking her tail back and forth, mewing.

"Just a second," I yelled to the door. My voice cracked.

What was he doing here?

"I've got to go," I said to the phone, hearing the

223

excitement in my voice.

"Okay, honey. We'll talk later," Mom said.

"Bye." I pressed the red button before they could say anything else. I stood from the couch, looking down at my comfy clothes.

"He's not going to care about your leggings and old baggy sweatshirt, Shay. That's what he gets for coming over unannounced," Harmony said, standing from the couch. She winked before she went into her bedroom, closing the door.

I tucked a few tendrils that fell from my ponytail behind my ears. My heart raced in my chest as I pulled the door open.

Cade wore jeans and a t-shirt that molded to his chest under a zip-up hoodie. A knit beanie, matching the forest green of his eyes, covered his head. The sky behind him was darkening as the sun set. Deep purples and pinks surrounded him. He looked like a divine, dangerous god. I swallowed. Memories of him, me, and kissing flooded my brain.

"Hey," I croaked, shaking away the memories. "What are you doing here?"

"I brought you the permits for the festival," he said, his jaw set. His eyes raked me up and down. Heat bloomed on my cheeks, squirming under his gaze.

"You didn't have to come all the way here," I said. "You could have just dropped them in my mailbox or something."

Cade shifted on his feet, glancing at the ground. His shoulders bunched as he tucked his hands into his hoodie pocket. When he lifted his head, his face relaxed.

"Maybe I wanted to see you again."

"Oh." My stomach jumped into my throat.

The air sizzled around us as we stood in the open doorway. My breathing quickened as I got sucked into his essence. Mildred meowed, breaking our attention. She pushed past my legs, wrapping her body around his ankles. Cade crouched to pet her, greeting her in a coo.

"Invite him in, dummy," Mildred snapped. *"He clearly wants to."*

"Want to come in?"

Cade stood up, flashing me a small smile. "Sure."

His smile made my knees weak. I breathed in deeply, smelling the woods and fresh dew as he brushed past me. He smelled fresh and clean. Mildred bounced after him, hot on his heels. He reached into his back pocket and placed several folded envelopes on the counter.

"Here you go. Everything you need to have a festival in the town square. Do you feel like you're ready for it?"

"No," I said truthfully, following him into the kitchen. "I'm really putting all of my faith in Aaron, but he's been very thorough. So, I don't really know why I'm still worried about it."

"'Cause you're a control-freak," Cade teased as he sat at the counter. Dean said something similar, but it didn't sound mean from Cade as it did from Dean. I shrugged.

"I can't really help it. I've always been organized and meticulous. It's my happy place."

"It's not a bad thing. Lord knows I could use more organization in my life. I mean you should see my apartment. You'd hate it."

"Oh no. You're a slob?" I cringed.

"Not entirely, but close. My mom hates it, especially the way I fold towels." He laughed.

I leaned forward on the counter, placing my head in my hands, covering my face. "Please tell me you tri-fold the towels." My voice was muffled.

"Nope. Just in half and half again."

"Ugh," I groaned. "That's not how you do it."

"The tri-fold takes too much time," he continued, laughing at my discomfort.

"I don't think we can keep seeing each other unless you fix the way you fold your towels."

The energy shifted in the kitchen. I had forgotten we weren't in a good place. He was a skeptic and rejected that portion of me that made me who I was. He stopped laughing and cleared his throat.

"Sorry," I muttered, squeezing my eyes shut. "I didn't mean anything–"

"It's fine," Cade said, cutting off my words. He licked his lips. "I actually wanted to talk to you about–"

The door to Harmony's room opened.

"Oh shit. Sorry," she squeaked. Cade sat straighter, turning toward Harmony. The energy thickened so much with her interruption you tasted it.

"Hi, Harmony," he said.

"Hi, Cade." Harmony's lips were painted red and pulled up in a smile.

"Going out with Brad?" I asked, fidgeting with the cuffs of my sleeves.

Harmony smushed her lips against each other as she gave me a sultry look. "Yeah. It feels a little too tense here for my liking."

Heat flushed through my body. I swung my eyes to the ceiling, praying for patience. Nothing like having a roommate who called it like she saw it.

Cade said nothing, but stared at an invisible spot on the counter. Harmony raised an eyebrow and winked at me as she moved through the apartment, gathering her bag and keys.

"Look, kids," Harmony started as she pulled on her leather jacket. "Play nice. Shay, see you at the Brew later."

The heat on my face ticked up several degrees. Or a hundred.

"Bye, Harmony," Cade said.

"Bye, Cade." She blew me a kiss and gave Mildred a pet as she left the apartment. Mildred flicked her gaze toward me.

"I'm gonna go sleep in Harmony's room. She's right. It's uncomfortable here."

She sauntered past the kitchen into Harmony's room, pausing at the threshold to look at me before leaving us alone.

"Is Harmony a witch too?" Cade asked once the apartment was silent.

"No. Although she's about as close as a Quaint could be."

Cade flicked his intense eyes all over my face and body. "What's a Quaint?"

I pulled on my sleeves, hiding my hands. "You really want to learn about some of the Wiccan culture here in Ipswich?"

He nodded, not taking his eyes off mine.

"A Quaint is a person who doesn't have any magical powers."

Silence. I squirmed.

"Cade. Why are you here?" I asked when I

227

couldn't take it anymore. I didn't have to be psychic to know that he wasn't here just for the permits.

"I've done some thinking…" he said. "I don't care that you're a witch."

He stood from the stool and walked into the living room, leaving me in the kitchen with my mouth open. He sat on the couch, crossing one leg over the other and stretched an arm across the back.

Wait… what?

Chapter 21

"What did you just say?" I asked.

He patted the seat beside him. Without any hesitation, I moved into the living room and sat beside him. His body heat encased mine. His arm curled. His fingers centimeters away from touching me. The zaps of our connection tickled along my skin.

"I don't care that you're a witch." His gaze drilled into mine with a sincere intensity.

"What changed?" I asked, swallowing as if my throat forgot how to work.

"I went on three calls this past week after you told me the truth. All three calls were to houses dripping in Wiccan paraphernalia. Candles, crystals, weird statues, all the stuff that you sell in your store and have in your apartment. Then, I went to Sinful Delights. Lydia didn't even ask me for my order. She handed me a drink and said, 'For clarity and answers you're looking for.'"

Beautiful Lydia.

"Did the drink help?"

Cade smiled, making my thighs squeeze together. "I had the best night's sleep of my life, and when I woke up, I could see all the pieces to the puzzle."

"So, you believe me?"

"That you're a real witch with real powers?" he asked, dipping his head so our eyes lined up.

I nodded, getting caught in his gaze. My skin

sparked with the electricity of our energies intertwining. He tucked a piece of my hair behind my ear, leaving his hand on my neck.

"I believe you, but I need more proof. Like I said, I was raised believing that witches were not real or Satan worshippers."

I lowered my head, hiding the blush that ramped up on my face. Was I ready to bring him into my world fully? I didn't know. But if he was willing to try, then I would, too. Besides my family and Harmony, he was the first outsider whose opinion held weight in my eyes.

I trusted him.

As we sat together, I realized how attuned I was to him. I always sensed his presence, effortlessly distinguishing his energy from all the others and noticed his little quirks and nuances. Unable to control myself, I leaned on him, resting my shoulder against his. The heat of our contact encased in my bones. Closing my eyes, I drank in his touch. His arm curled around me.

He wasn't running away. He was pulling me closer. In fact, it felt like no amount of time had passed since we last were affectionate.

"Let's continue our game," Cade said.

"Our secret game? Wasn't the last secret traumatic enough?"

Cade laughed. "I want to know more about you. It's okay if you're just too stubborn to admit defeat."

"Smartass," I murmured, sighing. "Let the secrets fly."

Zaps of electricity sparked my skin as his long fingers drew circles on the back of my neck. It felt so good, I almost purred.

"I'll go first," he said. "I haven't slept with anyone since my sister's assault."

"Is that supposed to be impressive? You were sent here for your punishment and I know for a fact the selection of single ladies in this town are slim."

"I was on probation in Boston for a while before the sentencing."

"Why are you telling me this? I really couldn't care less if you've had sex with anyone or not. Maybe, Harmony." I poked him with my finger. "No sex with her."

Cade chuckled, snatching my hand and planting a kiss on my index finger. I breathed in his touch. "Just thinking about the shit Leyla went through made me feel so disgusted. I didn't want any woman to feel that way because of me, so I distanced myself from them."

My eyes drifted along his body and face. Was he always this charming?

"Cade, no woman would ever think that about you. You're a firefighter, for Goddess' sakes. What are the statistics of cops and domestic violence? Probably a lot higher than firefighters. Have you seen those calendars of firefighters posing with cuddly animals? No way could any of those guys harm their partners."

He shook his head, playing with the tips of my fingers. A sense of grounding flowed through my body. "You never know."

"I know you."

"Just barely."

"We can change that." My lips turned into a seductive smile.

Cade stared at me. The color of his eyes smoldered the longer he held my gaze, filling me with confidence.

"My turn for a secret."

Cade stayed quiet, watching.

"I've never wanted to have a serious relationship–ever. They take a lot of work, and can be hard to navigate. I know I'm not the easiest person to be around. I'm bossy. I like things done in a specific way. I don't ask for help. But since you rode into my life on your metal steed, I finally feel ready to try."

His eyes seared into me while his lips curved up.

"Plus, I saw you before you arrived," I admitted.

"What?" His eyebrows dipped.

"I saw a vision of a stranger riding into town with this tattoo on their arm." I skimmed my fingers along his Capricorn tattoo.

He took a deep breath. "How? How do your powers work?"

"I first got them at sixteen–"

"Sounds familiar."

I snorted a laugh. "Media gets it right sometimes. Makes me think there are more witches out there. But I feel a tug in my stomach and I guess it's my soul that gets transported into the future."

"How does your soul know when to go?"

"I usually have to meditate or ask a spiritually pointed question. Just like I do when I'm doing a tarot card reading."

I rubbed my lips together, suppressing a smile. Warmth flowed through my body at his interest and our constant physical contact. It was natural, comforting, and easy.

"What about the Lovers Readers you offer?"

I lifted an eyebrow. "You did some research?"

He shrugged. "When I told you I needed space, I

had time to learn."

Cade pressed the pads of each of my fingers to his lips, giving them tiny kisses. I scooched closer not wanting him to stop. The kisses on my fingers sent me into a tizzy. My brain felt empty of my worries. The hair on top of my head suddenly felt too constricting on my scalp. I pulled out the hair tie, letting the blonde waves fall down my back. I wiggled my fingers in it, releasing some of the tension, and flipped my hair back.

"Over time, I've learned how to read people's auras. When I do Lovers Readings, I focus on them, sending myself into the time and place where they meet their soulmate. If the Fates are willing, they'll show me the person's soulmate with matching auras."

Cade sat there, watching me and playing with my fingers.

"Are you ever wrong?" He planted kisses on my palm, filling me with a deep desire.

"I haven't been yet," I said, closing the distance between us on the couch. My voice breathy and eager. Our knees touched. "I've done a lot of practice, tarot card readings, and conjuring to enhance my power. Sometimes the matches aren't lovers but deeply connected friends."

Cade pulled me all the way to him. I leaned into his touch as he bent his head into my neck. He placed tiny kisses up and down my neck, sending chills along my arms.

"Do you know who your soulmate is?" He whispered between kisses.

"No," I breathed out, letting my head fall back. "I'm too scared they won't be the right match."

"Didn't you say Fate chooses the soulmates?" Cade

dragged his lips up my neck, kissing below my earlobe. "Why would they be wrong?"

I gripped his shoulders, shuddering under his attention.

"They do. But what if that person doesn't want *me*? What if I don't like them? The future is never set in stone. I don't want my soulmate vision to be the first one I get wrong."

Thankfully, Cade's kisses blocked my ability to think straight or to dwell on my depressing thoughts. One of his hands skimmed up my leg, hip, and ribcage, leaving sparks in its wake. I moaned, melting under his touch. The energy around me swirled and flickered with lust.

"I have another secret," he whispered into my ear.

I pulled back to look into his eyes. They had darkened to the color of pine tree needles against hills of white snow.

"Tell me." My face was millimeters away from his.

"I want you," he said. "I want to stay with you tonight."

"I want that, too," I admitted, smiling up at him.

The weight I had been carrying on my shoulders around him had lifted after revealing more of my secrets. It felt right to tell him. Felt right to bring him into my structured Wiccan world. My brain had quieted enough that I was able to feel. I wanted to feel Cade's hands on parts of my body that hadn't been touched in a while. I *needed* to feel his lips, his muscles, all of him. In an instant, our lips collided in a feverish combustion. Our hands roamed over each other as we held onto each other as if our lives depended upon it. Cade's hands wrapped around my hips and he pulled me on top of his lap without breaking our scorched kiss.

I gripped his neck, trying to pull him closer, feeling the lines of his hard body parts pressed against my soft curves. Tingles ran along my spine as he slid his fingers up and down my back.

"Tell me if it gets to be too much," he said between kisses.

I nodded, twisting on Cade's lap to lift my sweatshirt over my head. Cade's grip on my thighs tightened as I threw it behind me, exposing myself. His eyes drifted down my neck and settled on my breasts. His throat bobbed as he swallowed.

His eyes closed as he drew me closer, his lips pressing soft kisses on the tops of my breasts. With gentle squeezes, he popped a nipple in his mouth, savoring it with teasing laps. I arched my back and moaned. He kissed along one breast to the other, nibbling on the other nipple.

Sparks of arousal shot down to my clit. Moisture gathered in my underwear as I wiggled on his lap, creating a delicious friction. Goosebumps dotted my skin. Cade kissed his way up my sternum toward my neck and jaw, sending me into a frenzy. Hungry for more of his touch and only his touch.

"I can't get enough of you," he murmured.

I gripped the top of his shoulders, puffing out heavy breaths. I pulled away from his torture, cupping his face and kissing his nose. He licked his red and swollen lips in anticipation. I climbed off his lap and couch to stand in front of him. I shimmied out of my leggings and underwear. Rolling my shoulders, I gave him a sexy smile, watching as his eyes drift up and down my exposed body. He took in a sharp inhale when he finally met my eyes with his.

I grabbed his hand and pulled him off the couch. With some strength, I pushed him to the ground, forcing him to kneel. His green eyes sparkled with excitement as he looked up at me. I tucked a piece of hair behind my ear.

"You are so beautiful, Shay. Are you sure you want this? I'm ready," he said, adjusting his hard length. "But you're in charge here, babe."

Lust and arousal crashed against my chest as I looked down at him. He was in the most submissive position. My strong, brave hero. The complete opposite of Dean.

"I'm sure. Kiss me."

He bit his lip with a devilish grin. His hands traveled up my legs. His fingertip brushed the soft skin above my underwear, igniting a fire that sent shivers everywhere. Leaning forward on his haunches, he planted kisses up my legs. I grabbed his head for support, yanking his beanie off and digging my fingers into his messy strands. I moaned as he landed a big kiss right on my clit through my underwear.

"Ahh." Curling inward, I dropped my head to look down at him. A playful smirk played on his lips as he kissed me again.

His hands held onto my ass, holding me upright.

I was done. I needed a release. *Now*.

I slipped my fingers under the band of my panties and thrust them down. Here I was, naked, with a hot man on his knees for me. I didn't give a fucking damn. Cade's smile grew as he stood to full height. He planted another burning kiss on my lips as he gripped my shoulders. He turned me around and pushed me to the couch, taking control of the situation.

I flopped on my back, my legs spread open for him, not caring about him seeing me fully exposed. I was too far gone to be shy.

Crouching down to the floor, he grazed his fingertips up my legs, causing the hair on my skin to stand. He licked his lips with a blazing gaze. He lifted my legs over his shoulders, his gaze unwavering and intense. I propped myself up on my elbows, my heart pounding as I met his smoldering gaze. He buried himself between my thighs, his tongue lavishing my clit.

"Oh my Goddess. Please don't stop."

Cade chuckled against my sensitive skin as he continued his expert assault. The wetness from his tongue added to my own juices as he worked my clit, pushing me closer and closer to an orgasm. My body tensed as he showed off his impressive oral skills.

"Mmm," he moaned. "You taste as sweet as sin."

My fingers wound around the edge of the couch, arching against the back, unable to hold myself up anymore. My breathing came out in puffs and my eyes closed tightly. All my nerve endings were firing at once.

Cade pushed one finger inside me. "Oh, yes…"

The muscles of my vagina clenched around his finger as he tickled the inside, giving me exactly what I needed. His tongue continued flicking against my clit, sending zaps of electricity through my body.

"Fuck, Shay. This is even better than I imagined."

"Use more," I pleaded, needing to be filled more to get that sweet, sweet release.

"Yes, ma'am." He plunged another finger inside

me slowly, with no problem.

"Ahh," I moaned as my body filled deliciously.

Cade growled against my clit, moving his fingers in and out, making sure to hit that perfect spot. He licked up my wetness and swirled his tongue around my clit. He continued his torture, bringing me closer to my orgasm. He hummed, vibrating the already sensitive area.

"Yessss!" I shouted. Light burst behind my eyes as my whole body quivered against his face. Wave after wave hit me deep inside and below as I rode my orgasm.

I sunk into the cushion and let my legs fall open.

Cade wiped the back of his hand along his face as he leaned on his elbows above me. He was careful not to crush me. The hardness of his dick pressing against my throbbing bud. My eyes flicked around his face, noting the glistening on his chin and lips.

"Feel good?" he asked with a smile on his face.

"Um, yes, smartass," I breathed out, feeling no tension in my body as I planted a firm kiss on his lips. He tasted salty and sweet at the same time, sending floods of arousal in my blood again.

"It was my pleasure." He nipped at my lips. I wrapped my arms around his neck, bringing him on top of me, and pressing my lips against his. I was a woman obsessed and I wanted more.

A buzz sounded from somewhere in the apartment. I groaned, flopping my head back against the couch.

"It's my alarm for work."

Cade chuckled in the crook of my neck, sending shivers down my spine.

"Well, that's perfect," he said.

I pouted, bringing his face up to meet mine. "No. It's not. I want to take this game into the bedroom."

Cade laughed. "Aaron is arriving tonight and we were going to swing by the Brew." He cocked an eyebrow. "I thought you'd be excited to meet him."

My eyes widened and I slapped Cade's shoulder. "He's coming tonight?!"

Cade nodded, smiling wide. I pushed him off me and sprung from the couch, unfazed that I was still naked.

"I can't wait to meet him. I want to show him the town square and get his opinion on a few things. Oh, and I need to tell him how much money we can spend," I rambled, running into the bedroom to get dressed for work.

Cade's laughter rang through the apartment.

Chapter 22

The Witch's Brew was busy like every other Friday night. The local regulars drank their glasses of beer while some of the other younger clientele drank the special drinks. The atmosphere was chill.

I played with the tip of my side braid. Cade and I had gone our separate ways because of work. He needed to get Aaron and would be meeting me here later. I felt calm and carefree. Maybe even a little distracted. Cade's kisses were burned into my memories and his skills with his tongue…

Shaking my daydreams away, I pulled on the tap, pouring four glasses of beer. Harmony worked beside me, chatting away with the patrons and Brad, who sat in front of her. Zaps of electricity ran up my arms when I handed off the beers to the guy in front of me, holding all four glasses between my fingers.

Cade was here.

"That's a pretty special skill you got there, girly," the man in front of me said. His aging beer-belly hung over his pants and his shirt was too small, showing off a line of gut and hair.

"All the years working here, man," I replied, showing him a fake smile. He leaned on his elbow, getting closer to me from across the bar.

"Whatcha doin' later, beautiful?"

"Not you, bro," Cade said, slapping a strong hand

on the guy's shoulder. Cade's voice was stern and friendly. The patron stood up straight. He looked Cade up and down, then to the larger black man standing behind Cade. He visibly swallowed.

"Got it," he said. "Message received." He grabbed his beer glasses and returned to his group of friends at the back of the bar. I cocked an eyebrow, one hand on my hip.

"I had it handled."

Cade smiled as he tucked his hands into his tight jean pockets, making his biceps bulge in his long-sleeved shirt. He had ditched his hoodie and beanie. His sexy astrological tattoo called to be touched.

"I know. And I don't care," he said.

I rolled my eyes, trying to hide my smile.

"Dude, you said she was beautiful, but that word doesn't do Ms. Shay justice," the large black guy said. I felt my cheeks heat at his words.

Cade knocked into his friend's shoulder. "No, it doesn't."

"Aaron?!" I concluded, taking the attention off me.

Aaron smiled wide. He was a very bulky, not obese, guy, like a well-groomed grizzly bear. Large arms, big hands, and the poise of a swan.

"That's me, sweetheart. It's a pleasure to finally meet you." His smile was as big as he was. I felt my cheeks pulling up in a smile to match his. So far, we've only had a texting relationship. It was nice to put a face to the name.

"I'm so happy you're here. What can I get you guys to drink?"

Cade smiled, showcasing his dimple as Aaron picked up the drink special menu.

"I'll take my usual," he said, leaning over the bar. I followed suit, being pulled in by his energy. I breathed in through my nose, smelling the forest. My soul instantly soothed. Cade gripped my chin between his finger and thumb. My heartbeat ramped up, hearing it pulse in my ears.

"It's been too long since we've seen each other," Cade whispered. My surroundings drifted away as I got pulled into his bright green eyes.

"Cade," I whispered. "It's been like two hours."

The side of his lips tipped up into a smile. I zeroed in on his full lips, remembering what they tasted and felt like. I swallowed.

"Too long."

The bell above the door jingled and the door slammed shut, startling me. It must have been slammed hard to be heard over the crowd. Cade and I turned to find Dean glaring at us. I felt the color drain from my face. I ripped out of Cade's hold, backing away from him. Cade wore a smug grin on his face.

"So, you want the IPA?" I asked, trying to control the shudder in my throat. Cade and I were new, but the last time Dean saw us we were cold to each other. Cade nodded, keeping the grin on his face as he settled onto the bar stool in front of me.

"A-and you, Aaron?" My eyes kept shifting between Cade and Dean, who hadn't moved from his spot by the door. His stare was so icy it sliced through my skin.

"Girl, give me a Poisoned Apple Martini," Aaron said as he sat beside Cade.

His drink order gave me pause and I stared at him.

"I *hate* beer," he clarified with a smile that shifted

into a serious face. "Almost as much as I hate dicks."

My eyebrows furrowed.

"Like that douchebag over there," Aaron clarified, thumbing toward Dean. Dean had turned away from us, chatting with a group of younger men that he fished with. "I can just tell that guy's a prick. But, I actually really, really love the other kind of dicks."

I paused in making Aaron's drink. He started laughing a loud, hearty chuckle.

"The look on your face is priceless."

"Bro…" Cade said, taking a swig of his drink. "I can't take you anywhere."

I set Aaron's bright green drink down on a napkin. Aaron smiled before taking a sip and sighing. "Damn. That's good. At least you aren't stunned anymore about that guy who just walked in."

"You're right. I had forgotten about him for a hot minute."

"Oh, look. He's coming over here. I can feel the drama that he's bringing," Aaron said, causing Cade to sit a little taller in his seat. Cade kept his eyes on me. I cleaned up the bar from Aaron's drink and wiped my clammy hands down my apron. Dean stalked toward me.

"He does not look happy," Harmony said, joining the party.

"No shit, Harm," I deadpanned.

Cade made introductions, distracting Harmony as I watched Dean weave his way through the patrons.

"I love your style, Harmony." I heard Aaron say as he and Harmony talked about nail polish colors.

Dean slapped his hand on the bar top. "Shay," he hissed, his voice low and tight. His body was just as tight as his voice, like he was priming for a fight.

"Mayor," I said, trying to keep my voice even. The sting of his betrayal burned in my stomach, but I ignored it. Right now, he was only a patron in the bar. "Can I get you a drink?"

"Whiskey."

I kept my gaze down, concentrating on filling a glass with the whiskey he liked. The energy around him was stifling and hostile. I slid the glass toward him, lifting my eyes.

His normal caramel eyes were as dark as night, like at the Halloween party. His skin was ashen and his hair was dirty. He didn't look like the kempt gentleman that I called a friend. He was a different person. Guilt and confusion swam in my gut.

"Are you okay?" I asked.

He snatched the glass, downing the amber liquid in one go. His eyes bore into mine, causing me to squirm.

"Another."

Cade shifted in his seat. I shot him a look, telling him to stay out of it. I poured Dean another shot. He knocked it back, slamming the glass back on the bar.

"Are you going to pay for those, Mayor?" Harmony asked. Her voice was sweet and venomous at the same time. It was obvious that everyone around us, including Aaron and Brad, were picking up on Dean's animosity. We all were waiting. Waiting for him to do something drastic. It was the vibe he was projecting: unpredictable.

Dean turned his face toward Harmony, a fake smile pulling at his lip. "Of course. I would never take advantage of my status in our small town." He slapped his card on the bar, leveling me with his gaze. "Close it up, please."

I did as he asked, turning my back on him to ring him up on the register. I took a deep breath, now that I wasn't caught in his menacing gaze, but I felt his eyes on me. It took all my energy not to look at him in the mirror behind the liquor bottles.

I turned, handing him his slip. He grabbed it and left without another word, getting lost in the sea of bar-goers. Everyone visibly relaxed as the energy shifted to normal. The sights and sounds of the busy bar came back into focus.

"What's that guy's problem?" Aaron asked.

"Not now, bro," Cade answered. "Shay. You okay?" His eyes scanned my face.

I swallowed hard while nodding. My voice refused to work. My stomach clenched. I didn't realize how much my rejection would affect Dean. I ran my thumbs over my fingers, needing to feel grounded.

Suddenly, wisps of air soared past my ears and a telltale tug gripped my stomach. I slapped a hand on my stomach, urging my astral body to stay put. I've never had a vision while at work. The sensation in my stomach grew, signaling that this vision was going to be strong.

"Shay?" I heard someone ask. A tiny hand gripped my arm.

I blinked a few times, trying to reorientate myself in the present. Behind my eyes, I felt pulled in two different directions. The sea of bodies and sounds around me blurred into a gray mist. Cade was the only clear thing in my line of vision. His eyes were wide as he stood from his stool.

"What's happening?" he asked.

Harmony whispered something beside me. Her voice was strained and her words were rushed. The foggy mist swirled as new colors and shapes formed, projecting me into a different time and space. My mind's eye was taking over my regular sight.

I took a step back. "S-Sorry, guys. I-I need to get some air."

"Go out back," Harmony said. "Take your break." I felt her hands shoving me toward the bar's back door.

"Do you need me to come with you?" Cade asked, standing beside me.

"No. I just need to get some air. Please."

He opened his mouth to say something, but I didn't hear it over the deafening panic that rose in my throat and ears as I rushed away.

I stumbled out of the back door into the alley between the bar and the next business. The alley was dark and dingy, littered with bits of trash and papers. Large metal trash containers sat against the brick wall of the Brew.

The cool air stung my heated cheeks, but I welcomed it. I pressed my back against the brick wall and slid down into a crouch, holding my head in between my hands. After a couple of deep breaths, I controlled the sensation of the sudden vision and let go. My astral self took over, sending me into another dimension.

My long cotton skirt swished between my legs as I walked down the cobbled path. The evening sky was turning to night. I had lost track of time out in the woods beside the town's cemetery. Dark purple clouds coated the sky and hoots from owls sounded. My basket filled with flowers, herbs, and mushrooms tapped my hip.

Crunching gravel came from behind me. My heartbeat picked up and the hairs on the nape of my neck stood at attention.

"Harrison," I said, speaking to the air in front of me. "It's impolite to follow a woman without announcing yourself." I turned, clutching my basket in front of me like a shield.

Harrison stood behind me in his fancy three-piece suit, a cap on his head, and an undone necktie. His dark eyes seared into mine.

"It's uncouth for a woman to be walking alone at night. Something ungodly could happen to you," he said, his tone dark and grave. "I'll escort you."

I swallowed, rolling my shoulders and lifting my chin.

"Is there something you need, Harrison? I don't need your help to find my home."

He took a slow, calculated step toward me. I didn't dare back up. I didn't want to show him any weakness.

"It's not so much what I need, more like what I want."

"And what is that? Some flowers that I picked?" I sassed. Mother always told me to hold my tongue, but she also knew I had a problem with authority.

"On the contrary," he said, stepping closer to me. We were within an arm's length. He reached out, grasping a strand of my hair in his fingers. I tilted my head back. The smell of alcohol drifted into my nose.

"I already said no to your marriage proposal." My voice quaked. "You reek of strong libations, Harrison. Perhaps you should retire for the night."

"You don't get to tell me what to do, Lucia,"

Harrison hissed before smiling. His devilish grin made my blood freeze.

"And you certainly don't get to, Harrison Fellows, no."

I swallowed and took a step back. My foot twisted on an uneven brick, causing my balance to falter. Harrison's reflexes were quick as he gripped my arm tightly. He pulled me toward him so we were chest to chest. This amount of body contact was inappropriate for an unmarried couple with or without an escort.

I turned my face to the side, pushing him away. It felt like moving a heavy stone. "Touching me without permission is not how you get me to change my mind," I pleaded, continuing to struggle against him.

"My dear, Lucia..." Harrison laughed. The sound sent chills down my spine. "I will make sure that no other man will ever want you again. You are mine."

My eyes widened. His face was unrecognizable, twisted into a devil's glare. My stomach dropped as my heart pounded violently against my ribcage. He pulled the necktie from his collar and wrapped it around my wrists. My basket fell to the ground.

"Harrison, please, no." My chin quivered as I tugged against his efforts.

"Silence, Lucia. I will have you." He pulled on my bound arms through the gates of the Ipswich cemetery.

"Help!" I yelled. "Anyone!"

Harrison smacked my face with the back of his hand, whipping my face to the side. Pain exploded on my cheek and behind my eye. My eyes blinked and tears fell down my face. He pushed me to the ground. My backside slammed onto the hard ground.

Harrison climbed on top of me, holding my hands

above my head. I cried harder than I thought I ever could.

"Quiet, Lucia, or I'll knock you out and still have you."

I sobbed and choked on blood and tears as he shoved my skirt and pettiskirt up my thighs. The cool air hit my bare thighs, causing my teeth to chatter.

Harrison's hand slid up my thighs and his knees dug into my legs to keep them open. "Lucia," he cooed as if he were with a willing lover. "This will all be worth it. It'll be good for both of us. I promise. This will connect our families for the end of time."

"Harrison, please, don't."

I squeezed my eyes tighter as my virtue shattered. Harrison muttered words as he debased and degraded my womanhood. I tried to focus on his words. It sounded like he was chanting, a spell perhaps, but my brain struggled to function.

Soon, it turned off entirely.

I gasped and my body fell back against the wall as I returned to the present. I brought my hands to my face, feeling the wetness from mine or Lucia's tears. My body quaked and rocked back and forth. I was in shock from what Fate had shown me.

Harrison raped Lucia.

I was startled when the crunch of boots sounded in the once silent alleyway. The chatter and laughter of the bar wafted back into my ears. My eyebrows dipped on my forehead.

"Were you in a vision?" Dean asked.

I popped up straight, turning toward him.

"What are you doing here?" I growled.

My brain focused on Dean, morphing him with

Harrison. He was the last person I wanted to be around right now. Was it fair to unload my post-vision feelings on him? No. But I did not fucking care. Whatever guilt I felt about him from the bar earlier was long gone now.

"What do you want?" I asked him again. My voice grated in my throat. Exhaustion, confusion, and rage seeped into my bones. Thanks to my random vision spawning, I struggled to control my emotions.

"I was leaving the bar when I heard someone crying. I just came to check it out and saw you crouched on the ground, comatose. It was obvious you were having a vision," Dean said, calmly.

"I don't need your help."

"Yeah, I know. Old habits die hard." He bowed his head, looking at the ground. "Look, about earlier in the bar…" He took a step toward me. I held out a hand to stop him.

"Don't." There was nowhere for me to escape. Luckily, he stopped.

"Come on, Shay. I'm sorry. I had every intention of giving you space, but I saw you and Thompson all cozy at the bar and I lost it. Last I saw, you were giving him the silent treatment, like you were with me. I got caught by surprise."

I blinked, feeling my hesitation. I kept silent, eyeing the door that led back into the bar.

"I've wanted you for so long. I know I didn't handle your rejection well. That's definitely not a strong suit of mine. Think of all the good times we've had over the years. Are you really going to throw it all away for one stupid fucked up mistake?"

Memories swirled in my mind. Late night movies. Board games. Studying for exams together. My icy exterior warmed a little. I crossed my arms, staring at him. The light from the streetlamp illuminated the haunted look he wore on his face.

"It was a really big mistake, Dean." I held my arms around my core, trying to warm my chilled body. Images of Harrison's evil deeds kept coming to the forefront.

"I know," he said, hanging his head. "I don't know what came over me."

I snorted, but made no move to get closer or say what he wanted to hear. His betrayal hurt and would always be a stain on whatever relationship I decided to have with him. He cleared his throat when I didn't say anything else.

"I have a bottle of water if you want it," he said, pulling one from his coat pocket. "I know how tough some of your bigger visions are on your body."

I eyed him and the bottle. His suggestion brought my attention to my parched throat. An icy air wrapped around me, raising the hair on my arms and neck.

"Shay…" A ghostly whisper sounded in my ears.

"Please, just take it," Dean said, holding the bottle of water out to me.

Shaking my head, I grabbed the water bottle from him and cracked it open. I drank greedy gulps of it, feeling the refreshing liquid quench my thirst.

"Thanks," I said as I capped the bottle. I pointed a thumb toward city hall. "I'm going to head back. See you around."

"Yeah," Dean said, watching me.

A tickle built in my throat. I coughed a few times, tasting a burning on my tongue.

"Weird. I forgot to swallow right or something," I

said, grimacing between coughs.

"It's probably a reaction to the chili flakes I put in there." Dean took a step toward me, his eyes burning into me.

I licked my lips, feeling a tingling sensation. I suppressed a shiver as the hot liquid warmed my belly. I took in a deep breath as a calm draped over my body. I struggled to process what he was saying.

He put chili flakes in the water. Why would he do that?

I was feverish despite the cool air. I ran my hands along my thighs, feeling my nerves firing in my fingers' wake. I only wanted one thing right now and that was Cade's hands all over my body. I turned my head toward Dean.

"Dean? What did you do?" I whimpered, finally piecing together what might be happening here.

Was I feeling more awake? Yes.

Was I starting to feel extremely turned on? Fuck yes.

"I think you know. Chili flakes mixed with a few other things can make a powerful aphrodisiac," he answered, stalking toward me. His hands rubbed down my arms, raising more goosebumps along my skin. I shivered. It felt amazing and wrong at the same time.

"You couldn't take no for an answer? What was all that before? More lies?" I placed both of my hands on his chest, giving him a little shove. He didn't even budge. My fingers flexed on his t-shirt. His strong chest muscles bunched under my touch.

Since when did he get so buff?

Dean brushed a piece of hair off my forehead. I leaned into his touch.

"What can I say? You make me want to explore the dark side of my family. Harrison's journal holds a lot of secrets. All very informative and productive."

I breathed through my nose, fighting against the arousal. My skin felt like it was on fire and only sensual touching would soothe it.

"Yes, I know him," I half growled, half moaned.

"It has some really good spells in there," he whispered, bringing us closer together. I tried to pull out of his embrace when his arms wrapped around my waist in a vice grip.

"Dean, let me go." My voice was breathy but firm. Having his strong arms wrapped around me fueled the erotism that burned at the top of my thighs. I curled my fingers into his chest, digging my nails into the fabric of his shirt.

There was no way I was going to give him anything, despite what I felt humming in my body. I pushed at him again, moving my head away from his as he leaned closer, trying to kiss me. My will was stronger than any dark spell he conjured to lure me in.

"I'm serious, Dean. Stop."

"Fuck. Shay," Dean snarled in my face. Spit flew out of his mouth, sprinkling my face. His cool façade finally shattered. "I waited so fucking long for you to give me a shot. And now that I've had a taste, I'm going to do everything I can to get more. We're destined to be together. Can't you see that? You are mine."

His words echoed in my head, wincing at the viciousness in his voice. I couldn't tell if I heard his voice or Harrison's. I swallowed past the panic threatening to overtake me.

"No, Dean. We aren't destined to be together. If anything, my visions have been showing me how rotten the Fellows family actually is."

"Rotten?" he snarled. "I can show you rotten, if you'd like. I can tell you like it a little dirty. I saw you practically fucking Thompson on the bar tonight. In front of all those people. But, you won't give a long-time friend the fucking time of day?"

He leaned forward again, closing the distance between us. His arms were in a strong grip around my waist. I couldn't lean back any further without breaking my back. His lips brushed against mine. Heat exploded on my lips, tingling and sparking. A loud bang sounded behind me.

"She said, 'No', asshole," a voice snarled, barely above a whisper.

Dean broke our kiss, gripping the back of my neck in a vice and turning toward the newcomer. Cade's head was dipped low and his stance was commanding as he stared at us. The ferocity in his bright eyes shined. Cade's fists clenched at the sides.

He looked fucking hot.

"Fuck off, Thompson," Dean said. "We're trying to have a private moment."

Fire erupted all over my body, inside and out. I leaned against Dean for support. I needed physical touch. I was going to explode if someone didn't give me some relief. Dean chuckled, running a hand down my hair, sending shivers everywhere.

"See, Shay wants to be in my arms. So, fuck off."

"Let her go, Fellows. Now," Cade said as he took a step forward.

Dean uncurled his arms, gave my neck a tight

squeeze before he shoved me away from him. I stumbled and fell on my knees, cracking them against the concrete sidewalk. A sudden coldness and pain doused my body, making me cry out.

Dean stepped toward Cade with a sinister grin on his lips. "I don't have time for this, Thompson. Shay needs me. Apparently, she was out here doing some nasty drugs."

"I highly doubt that," Cade growled. They circled each other.

"Do you know what happens when you assault a politician?"

"No. But I have spent some time in jail for beating up a cop. It's probably nothing as severe as a mayor attempting sexual assault. For a second time. I'm sure if I smash your face in right now, I'll get off with self-defense."

"Cade," I moaned, rubbing my hands all over my body. Each one of my nerve endings sparking at the contact. I pulled myself to sitting, letting my legs fall open.

If he could just touch...

"Cade," I said with more conviction. I stood on wobbly legs. "Stop."

"He was forcing himself on you," Cade growled. His voice was deadly.

I swallowed hard as his caveman presence sent zings of passion to my most sensitive spot. I squeezed my thighs together to stop the pressure building there.

"You saw her. She was melting in my arms," Dean quipped.

"Because you spelled me!" My blood beneath my skin boiled at his jaded viewpoint.

"He drugged you?" Cade asked, rounding on me. He grabbed my arms and pinned them to my sides, lifting me from the ground. His grip was firm, but not hurtful, just demanding and dominant. Seductive thoughts of role-play popped into my imagination as my eyes drifted along Cade's handsome face.

Dean moved back a step, but Cade glued him in place with a sneer.

"He drugged you? The fucking Mayor of Ipswich slipped you something?" Cade asked, bringing his intoxicating green eyes back on me.

I smiled up at him beneath my eyelashes. In the back of my mind, I scolded myself for my erratic behavior. But this whole knight in dark armor thing was turning me on hardcore. My control was shot. Cade's eyes darkened as his jaw ticked a few times. Confusion flashed on his face for a split second before returning to rage.

I glanced in Dean's direction. He tilted his head, warning me. Too bad for him, but Cade already knew my secret. Joke's on him.

"He gave me a tainted bottle of water and I seem to be having a sexual reaction to it," I said, breathy and sultry. Cade's face softened as he registered my words, but the anger wasn't pushed too far away from his eyes.

"You can't prove that," Dean said, smugly. "I saw her out here by herself. She could have ingested something. Plus, I think I have some prominent sway with the DA's office."

Cade's jaw flexed again as he wrapped an arm around my shoulders.

"You have to press charges, Shay," he said. "Who knows what this fucker is really capable of?"

I snuggled under Cade's arm. The warmth of his body kept the goosebumps at bay. For so long, I thought I knew Dean. His abuse of the community's power and potions have tainted his morality. All of it stemmed from my rejection. It was all my fault. I brought this on myself.

"I had just come out of a past vision with Lucia," I said. "Not tonight, Cade."

"Shay—" Cade started.

"Cade," I said, moving out of his embrace. "I'm serious. I'm not pressing any charges tonight. No one would believe me anyway. All of the people in charge are men. Men that are buddies with Dean. Please. I just want to go back to work and forget about all this."

"And give him a chance to flee?" Cade roared. The volume startled me, causing me to tense. Cade sighed when he felt my movements. He faced Dean, pointing a finger at him. "You better stay away from Shay or I'll knock your lights out."

Dean crossed his arms over his chest. His legs were still wide. Taunting. Pompous. "You said that last time, Thompson. But you have yet to do anything. You're probably just all talk," he jeered.

Cade made a move toward Dean when a large black hand gripped his shoulder.

"Let him go, bro," Aaron said. Brad was there, too, staring Dean down.

Dean's eyes flicked between the three men, calculating.

"Cade, please," I whimpered into his neck. I felt him nod, but he didn't take his eyes off Dean.

"You're lucky I care more about Shay than you, asshole," Cade said. A slithering smile pulled at Dean's lips. His dark eyes drifted up and down my body before snapping to the three men around me. He was out-numbered. He turned on his heel and exited the alley.

"What a dick," Brad said. "You okay, Shay?"

I nodded, nuzzling further into Cade's neck.

"I'll go fill in Harmony," he said, leaving.

"He drugged you?" Aaron asked. He bent down, and I saw his golden-brown eyes. With his expertly trimmed beard and creamy brown skin, he was just as handsome as Cade. I felt my lips smile and I batted my eyelashes at him.

"Oh, boy. Yes, he did." He laughed. "Seems like you're feeling a little aroused."

Cade growled and tightened his hold on me.

I pinched my fingers together. "A little bit."

Aaron squinted in my direction. "I think you'll be fine in a few hours. You'll either need sex or sleep," he said, winking. He slapped his hand on Cade's shoulder. "Let's go back inside. Drinks are on me." He left.

Cade tightened his arms around me. His heart raced under my ear. I felt him take a shuddering breath as I wrapped my arms around his trim waist, squeezing.

"Are you mad at me?" I asked him.

"I'm not mad at you, Shay."

My heart jumped into my chest as he pressed me against the side of a building. Spikes of arousal sky-rocketed in my belly. I moaned, leaning into him.

His green eyes sparkled against the dark streaks that ran along his face. His tousled dark hair begged to be tugged on. His jaw clenched as he racked his eyes along my body. My boobs jutted out as I arched against the side of the building and my breathing kicked up a few notches. I licked my lips in response to our position. For a few moments, the only sound around us was the puffs of our heavy breathing.

"I'm fucking pissed at Dean. How he had his hands on you. How close he came to just whisking you away, doing things to you that I couldn't save you from. It took every ounce of my control to not fucking knock him out," Cade said through his tight jaw.

"I'm okay, Cade. I promise. I only had a little sip before I realized what was happening."

"I'm also fucking pissed because apparently there's still so much I don't know or that you're keeping from me."

"I can explai–"

Cade took a step closer, pressing his hips into mine and stopping my words. I felt something erect dig into my most sensitive spot as he eliminated the space between us.

"Do you feel that?" he asked, leaning down to kiss my jaw.

I rolled my head to the side, giving him easier access. Fuck yes, I felt that. All my nerves were firing at the same time. *That* was exactly what I needed.

"That's how I feel when I'm around you. All the fucking time." His lips traveled up my jaw, kissing the skin below my ear. Shivers ran down my spine at his feather-light touches.

"Now, imagine how it felt to see that asshole's hands on the one person I can't fucking stop thinking about. Despite her controlling ass, her being a weirdo witch, and the secrets that she's still keeping."

My body melted at his words. My knees felt weak.

Cade pulled away, keeping his face close to mine. We were nose to nose. Our panting mixed together.

"I know." I swallowed. There were some things I wasn't ready to share with him. Images of Lucia's vision floated to the front of my mind. I shivered. "We can talk more about this later. Aaron and I have work to do. And I need to finish my shift without orgasming."

Cade's chest shook with laughter. Some of his anger receded. "I'll help you with that later, if you want."

I pulled out of his embrace, capturing his eyes in mine.

"Promise?"

Cade smiled wide enough for his dimples to show. "Promise."

Chapter 23

Getting back to work helped calm the chaos within me. Despite the arguments from Harmony that I should just go home. I didn't want to. I refused to stand her up on a weekend night. And as I told Cade, Aaron and I had work to do later.

The effects of the spell flowed through my veins, but I controlled some of my urges. Though, everytime I looked at Cade, wetness gathered in my underwear. I would need a new pair when I got home.

Aaron still sat next to Cade at the bar and had two empty Poisoned Apple Martini glasses beside him.

"So, I was doing some research," he said, talking a mile a minute. "You advertise a Lover's Reading. What the fuck is that and when can I have one?"

"Dude," Cade said, emptying his beer glass and shaking his head with a smile that caused heat to bloom on my cheeks. His presence was getting harder and harder to ignore, drugged or not. He was the light in a dark world.

"What, bro?" Aaron questioned, shaking his head. "I need some love in my life. My last boyfriend did not mesh well."

"It's just a special talent I have," I said. "After my shift, I can give you a Lovers Reading if you want."

Aaron's hazel eyes lit up and his mouth dropped open. "Are you shitting me right now? I want. I really want."

"You believe in all this psychic stuff, Aaron?" Cade asked.

I sighed as I washed the glasses in the attached sink. His question didn't offend me. It was just another example of the roadblocks we would have in our relationship.

Aaron slapped his hand over his chest as he feigned shock. "I can't believe you don't. You basically live in Wiccan central. How many fires have you put out due to candles?"

Cade shook his head. "Too many to count." He winked at me.

"Ipswich's history revolves around the psychic witches fleeing Salem during the witch trials," Aaron continued. Harmony and I shared a look and a smile. It was refreshing to hear someone else retell our history.

"We're sitting in a bar called, The Witch's Brew, for fucks sake, man. Wake up and smell the herbs," Aaron finished, giving me a blinding smile. He rubbed his hands together. "I can't wait to hear what you've got to tell me, Shay."

Cade's eyes lowered and his face scrunched up. He scratched his jaw, and then lifted his eyes, zeroing in on me. I gave him a smile. I told him these facts when he first sat at this bar, but he must not have registered them as important.

Now that he knew the truth, the proof would keep piling up.

****

"This town square is too cute," Aaron exclaimed as he walked through the grass, looking around the space. "It's so tiny and precious. It reminds me of a mother-

262

daughter drama I used to watch religiously."

I smiled, watching Aaron talk to himself, clearly feeling the effects of the Poisoned Apple Martinis. Cade and I walked side by side as we followed him. I liked Aaron the second we met. Although asking for help didn't come naturally to me, I felt confident in my planning partner. Aaron reminded me of Harmony: trustworthy, open-minded, and carefree. Qualities I needed with planning a town-wide event.

"Still feeling okay?" Cade asked. "We can do this tomorrow."

I laughed. "Why? Are you in a rush to go somewhere?"

Cade laced his fingers with me, sending shocks up my arm and down to my core. Should one touch be that powerful?

"Your face has been flushed since you got back to work. With the little sexy looks you've been giving me, I'm more than ready to get back to your apartment, babe." Cade cleared his throat and adjusted his pants. "But, I'm also worried about you."

I tucked my chin, smiling. "I still feel the heat in my blood. Like one kiss would throw me into a tizzy, but I got it under control...until later."

"The town seems excited to bring back this tradition," he said, changing the subject. "Why did it stop in the first place?"

"I'm not entirely sure. My ancestors have always been the local fortune tellers and healers. It was their festival. I'm sure there were religious conflicts with the Puritains."

"So, fortune-telling runs in the family?"

"You've seen the store, Cade."

"I know that your store sells all that New Age stuff."

I laughed. "New Age. Or Wiccan."

"Wiccan," he said as if he were testing the taste of it in his mouth. Cade gestured toward a bench. We sat down together. Aaron busied himself, making notes in his phone with a measuring tape in his hand.

Where did he get that?

"We can do this tomorrow if you want," I shouted to Aaron.

He swished his hand behind him. "I'm feeling inspired."

I laughed, wrapping my jacket closer to my body.

Cade stretched his arm out behind me. His body heat encased me, filling me with a comfortable warmth. We watched Aaron for a couple minutes longer, welcoming the calm. Aaron ran over and crouched down in front of us.

"I've got this whole vision in my head," he said. His hands waved animately. "It's going to be amazing. How do you feel about costumes?"

"Um, we were all just in costumes for the Halloween party, but I appreciate the enthusiasm," I teased, before getting more serious. I grabbed his massive hand in mine. "Thanks, Aaron. I am truly grateful for your help. I hope I can afford to pay you though."

Aaron smiled, making happy crinkles at the corners of his eyes. "Girl, don't worry about it. I'm doing this for Cade who's doing this for you. He's never let me plan anything for him before." He hopped up to his feet, pulling me with him. "Now for my Lover's Reading. That can call us even. Oh, and an invitation to the

264

Halloween party next year."

"Perfect," I said, smiling. "My store is just across the way. We can do it there."

Aaron clapped his hands as he bounced on his feet. We linked arms. His excitement was intoxicating. With all the shit that happened tonight with Dean, I was looking forward to giving Aaron his Lovers Reading. That was my normal, my safe place.

I snuck a peek behind me at Cade. He followed us with his hands in his hoodie pocket. He smiled at me, while his dimples poked his cheeks. The walk to the store was short. I unhooked my arm from Aaron's, unlocking the front door. With the lights flicked on, I lead the way into the Whitleys' sacred place. The wood and other earthly smells wafted in my nose, grounding me.

"Oh my Gawd," Aaron exclaimed. "This place is to die for. Look at all these tarot cards and crystals." He twisted toward the tall bookshelves. "And herbs. Oh, look at these..." he continued loudly to himself. I laughed as I lit a few purple candles, creating a soft flickering glow in the store.

"My Gram actually painted those tarot cards."

"She's very talented. I might have to buy a deck."

I watched Cade as he walked around the store's space. He looked at a few of the books and made faces at the statues, similar to how he reacted in my apartment. I pulled at my sleeves. The men were complete opposites. Aaron's face looked like a kid's in a candy store, and Cade's looked like a confused newbie.

"Okay," I said, "I usually conduct my readings in that little alcove, but we can do it here in these chairs."

I pointed to the vintage high-back chairs where the weekly gossip fest happens.

We all sat down. Aaron leaned forward, clasping his hands together over his knees, while Cade sat back, crossing one leg over the other. He looked sexy as fuck. Assessing. Observing.

I swallowed. The effects of the drugs ramped up to a thousand, swirling uncomfortably in my gut. I wanted to take him right now.

"So how does this work? Do you talk with the other side or something?" Aaron asked, distracting me.

I licked my lips, focusing on Aaron, not Cade. I felt Cade's smoldering, knowing gaze on me. My heart pounded in my ears. He knew what I was thinking.

"It's mostly through meditation," I explained. "I get visions of the future. More recently of the past, too." I suppressed a shiver. Lucia's vision wasn't far from my mind. When I was in the right state of mind, I would decipher that horrible vision.

Aaron leaned back with a grin on his face. "Aayyee. That's fucking awesome."

I smiled at his excitement, but my eyes flicked to Cade. He sat stoically in his chair. His inquisitive gaze caused swirls of emotion in my stomach. I squirmed knowing this would be the first time he got to see my actual powers up close and with the secrets he knew.

"Put out your hands," I said, refocusing. "Physical touch helps."

Aaron followed my directions instantly. I grabbed onto both of his hands, closed my eyes, drawing in Aaron's vibrant energy. Feeling a tug and hearing the air whoosh, my astral self activated. It traveled through the dimensions to a different time and place. Images flashed through my mind. I scrunched my eyebrows, interpreting what Fate was showing me.

"I see a lot of trees," I said. "A park. There's an old woman feeding the birds by the small lake." I heard Aaron gasp and I felt his hands twitch in my grasp.

"That's got to be the park by my apartment," Aaron said.

"It could be any park," Cade said.

"Bro…" Aaron scolded in a whisper.

Cade was right. It could be any park, but in my mind's eyes, I saw Aaron. His yellow and pink aura pulsed brightly.

"Uh-oh," I said, bringing their attention back to me. "You're chasing a small dog…Mr. Bananas does not listen well."

I heard clothes rustle and felt a stronger tug on my hands. I opened my eyes to see a dumbfounded look on both of their faces.

"Did you tell her about Mr. Bananas?" Aaron asked Cade. His mouth was slack. Cade shook his head. He was leaning forward in his chair now, watching me with intense attention.

"I just got Mr. Bananas from the local shelter like two months ago," Aaron said. "He's a little shit, but I love him."

I laughed. "His little sparkly bandana with his white fluff is so cute." I snuck a peek at Cade. His eyes blazed with shock. I supposed I was right about Mr. Bananas. I held onto Aaron's hands again, closing my eyes and resuming my reading.

"I see a guy holding Mr. Bananas. He's a light-skinned, glasses-wearing guy, with dark graying hair. He looks like a very hot dad. He takes the time to perfect his body."

Aaron whooped. "I love a hot daddy."

"Your auras match," I said, opening my eyes.

"What does that mean?" Aaron asked.

"From the years of my work, I have learned that people with matching auras are connected. Usually it's through love. Though sometimes it's only a deep connection."

Aaron pulled his hands from my grasp and sat back with a goofy grin on his face. "Looks like Mr. Bananas and I will need to take a lot more walks."

I laughed. "Good luck."

Aaron slapped Cade on his chest. "Dude. This is so exciting. What's this new daddy's name?"

I shook my head. "Sorry. I can't tell you that. I don't want to interfere with fate too much. You need to have the freedom to make your own decisions. I can tell you that his name starts with a 'J'."

Aaron nodded as if everything I said was the bible-truth.

"You'll know when you meet him," I said.

"How do we know you didn't make all that up?" Cade asked, looking from Aaron to me. "I mean, no offense, but you could have just bullshitted your way through that. How many men have a name that starts with J?"

I sat back, crossing my legs under my butt. Cade's eyes followed the movement. I expected his questions and was glad he was asking them.. I opened my mouth to respond when Aaron beat me to it. He was gathering all the proof he needed to truly believe.

"What the fuck, bro?" Aaron said with a roll of his eyes. "You gotta have faith. Plus, she knew things that neither of us told her. I mean, this is the first time I've even met her."

"I'm just asking questions," Cade huffed. "She didn't give you a name or a date. You could meet this guy tomorrow, next week, or even years from now."

"That's very Capricorn of you. You yearn for logic. I can only tell Aaron the things I see." I shrugged my shoulders. "It's up to him what he does with that information. Some people like to hear there's a chance that they're not destined to be alone. It gives them comfort. I like being a part of that. Most customers have gotten back to me saying I've been right and it feels like a lightning strike when they meet their person."

My face scrunched as the words left my mouth.

Like I felt with Cade...

"Well said, girl," Aaron said, breaking my thoughts. He turned to Cade, leveling him with a straight look. "Faith and hope, bro. Faith, hope, and daily walks at the park."

Chapter 24

"Where's Mildred?" Cade asked, toeing his boots off by the door and dropping my keys where they belong. He seemed so comfortable and natural performing those small tasks in my home, as if he'd been doing them for years.

"I don't know," I answered, sitting on one of the bar stools at the kitchen counter. "Probably off sleeping somewhere in my bed. Being a pillow hog."

I laid my head on my arms on top of the counter. Cade rummaged through my cabinets, looking for the glasses. Without lifting my head, I pointed to the correct one.

"Glasses are there." Cade followed my directions, pulled out two, and filled them with water.

"Here, drink this. All of it."

The spell's effects were wearing off, leaving me exhausted. A heaviness pulled at my limbs as I lifted my head. We drank our water, staring at each other. The air around us sparked with arousal, but my head screamed at me. The pain built behind my eyes. If I was going to get any sexual relief, I needed to ease this headache.

"Do you need medicine?" Cade asked.

"How'd you know I was in pain?"

"You winced and your eyebrows do this cute little scrunchy thing when your brain is working too hard."

I shook my head, smiling. "I don't want any medicine. I'll use a crystal instead."

Cade's head ticked to the side.

"Over there." I pointed to my shelf. "There's a silver box with a moon engraved on it."

Cade stepped around the counter and followed my directions. He searched the shelf, found the silver box, and opened it.

"In there should be a shiny silver stone, called hematite. It's about the size of a quarter and heavier to the touch than you would expect."

He sifted through the box, holding up the stone. "This one?"

"Yup."

He brought it over, setting it in my hand. I held the smooth stone to my forehead, invoking the crystal's healing powers to repeal the headache that throbbed behind my eyes. It sucked that this spell was making me feel horny with a headache at the same time.

"What are you doing?"

"I'm using this crystal to remedy my headache. The water should help, too."

"Do you ever use modern medicine?" I heard the unconvinced tone in Cade's voice. I shook my head. Modern medicine was the last thing I wanted to put in my body. "You use crystals a lot, I noticed. Based on your jewelry preferences and the sheer amount you have littered around your apartment."

"Yeah." I chuckled, keeping my eyes closed. "Crystals and stones have unique energies and functions for all sorts of things. They're very useful."

I imagined the hematite sucking the pain from my body into itself, crystalizing inside it, condensing it, crushing it into nothing.

"Huh. And different crystals have different purposes?"

The pain had immediately lessened. I opened my eyes to find Cade's curious green ones watching me.

"Some crystals have similar purposes and can be used together."

"And you use…potions?" Cade asked tentatively.

"Most covens use potions for all sorts of things. Even herbal tea can be perceived as a potion. My family are psychics, as you know. We use and invoke Fate and the Mother Goddess to guide us."

I set the stone down and stood up. I took a step closer to him. Now that my headache had lessened the only thing I felt was arousal. The curiousity Cade showed was just as attractive as his looks. He was making an effort to understand my world.

It was sexy as fuck.

His eyes darkened as he watched me stalk toward him. My clothes felt too tight and there was too much distance between us.

"You promised me something," I said, my voice husky. Cade lifted one side of his mouth as his eyes perused my body.

"I remember."

I closed the distance, raking my hands up and down his chest. He closed his eyes and sighed.

"You still want me after the things I showed you tonight?" I asked in a whisper. I leaned up and kissed under his jaw. He tilted his head to the side, giving me more access.

"I told you I didn't care that you were a witch. It's clear you have faith in what you do."

Disappointment stabbed my chest, but I pushed it aside. I was too turned on to dwell on it. I kissed along his jaw, skimming my hands down his tight abs. "But you still don't believe."

Cade's hands gripped my hips. My hands went to the waistband of his jeans. I popped open the button and pulled down the zipper. He shivered and shuddered under my touch. I dipped my hand into his pants, feeling his hardened dick. I sighed, reveling the effects my actions had over him.

"Fuck. Shay," he hissed.

"Cade. Do you believe me?" I asked him, dropping to my knees and pulling his pants down his muscular thighs.

His jaw ticked as he watched me. A haze of arousal swam in his eyes.

"The more I get to know you, the more I believe. There are things happening around you and in this town that are hard to ignore. I'm starting to believe," he growled.

Satisfaction filled my veins, mixed with a deep lust. I felt good to hear him say that. He was trying.

"I wonder what you taste like," I crooned, looking up at him through my eyelashes. I slid my fingers up and down his hard penis.

Cade brushed the hair out of my face and dug his fingers against my scalp. Tingles ran down my spine.

"You take the lead, I will follow," Cade groaned.

I stood, slid my hand into his, and led him into my bedroom.

****

A soft rumble of snores invaded my ears the next morning. A sharp pain pierced my head in contrast to the soft pillow beneath it. I forced one eye open, bringing my hand to rest against my forehead.

Hangovers...fucking...suck.

A heavy weight curled around my waist. Looking down, I saw long fingers and a tattooed arm. Swirls of excitement fluttered in my stomach, remembering the night that Cade and I enjoyed. Slowly, I rolled to the other side to face him. His mouth was parted as he slept. The corners of my mouth tipped up in a smile as I took in his facial features.

No worry lines were visible on his beautiful face. Watching him sleep qualified as creepy, but I didn't care. Last night, he asked questions about my powers with real interest and didn't run away.

I tucked my hand under my pillow, nuzzling closer to Cade's warmth. There wasn't anywhere else I wanted to be. Cade shifted, pulling me closer to his chest. He dipped his head to rest his chin on top of my head. I smiled before my eyes closed, hoping to get more sleep. Dare I say I felt content? All of this felt so right.

I felt protected, cherished, maybe even loved.

As my eyes drifted close, a familiar tug pulled at my stomach. Somewhere between being asleep and awake, I floated to another time and place.

A chilly gust whipped across my face as I focused past the outskirts of the festival square.

A dark shadow hid between two buildings. It felt sinister. Domineering. Angry.

"Everything okay, babe? You shivered," Cade commented.

I squinted, trying to get a better view of the shadow. I knew it was watching me and I wanted to get away from its scrutiny.

"Yeah," I said, turning back and planted a quick kiss on his lips. "I'm gonna put these things back in the store." I added the last few Wiccan things into a plastic tub.

"Need any help?"

I shook my head. "No." My instincts warned me to keep Cade away from the dark shadow. The hairs on the back of my neck stayed at attention while I headed toward The Wise Whitleys. The shadow felt closer, sensing it stalking me.

Rushing inside the shop, I exhaled a sigh of relief when the door closed behind me. My heart raced in my chest. I looked out the store's front windows, searching for the shadow.

Nothing.

I set the box on the counter before grabbing the cash bag. Walking fast, I headed to the backroom, where I placed the money in a locked safe. I smiled. That cash was going to save our store.

The bells on the door jingled.

"Cade," I called out. "I said I didn't need help."

Suddenly, the lights shut off. The blood in my veins froze. The shadow was here. I just knew it.

"It's not Cade," it growled. Its voice was a mix of familiar and demon. I stood straight, turning around slowly.

A blood-curtling scream escaped my throat.

I shot straight out of bed. I clutched my chest as my heart pushed against my ribcage. Beads of sweat gathered on my forehead, dripping down my face.

"Shay?" Cade leaned up on one elbow. "Are you okay?" His voice carried traces of worry.

"Yeah. I just had a really bad dream..." I said, puffing out rapid breaths. "Or maybe it was a vision."

"Do they feel different?"

I laid a hand on my stomach, feeling it push in and out as I worked to calm down.

"I can feel it here. It's like a tug inside my stomach. Usually I see images, but lately they've been more detailed. More movie-like. Clear and emotional. Like I'm physically there. "

"Maybe it was just a dream," Cade offered, kissing my shoulder. "Those can feel pretty real."

"No. They're visions."

"Of the future?"

I nodded.

"Want to tell me about it? I know I'm still new to all this stuff, but I'm a really good listener."

"Something bad is going to happen at the festival."

Chapter 25

"You've cleaned that crystal for at least thirty minutes now," my mother said from behind me.

"Ah!" I startled, gripping the crystal tighter in my hands. "You scared me." I waved the duster in her direction. "Sorry, Mom. My brain is not here." I placed the crystal back on its shelf, turning toward her.

"I can tell." She smirked, crinkling the wrinkles around her hazel eyes. "It's completely acceptable to be lost in your own head. You've been through a lot in the past couple of weeks. With Dean and the festival coming up, too."

"That's an understatement." I flopped down in one of the high-back chairs in the middle of the store. Mom sat beside me, tucking her ankles under her. Her bracelets jingled as she clasped her hands together.

"Have you heard from Dean?"

"No." I blanched. "Thank the Goddess."

"According to the coven, he's been avoiding all of us like the plague. Almost as if he can't get near us."

"Who spelled that?" I asked, lifting my eyebrow.

"Agnes. She might have placed spelled charms around the town, stopping Mayor Fellows from getting too close to us," Mom said.

"That trickster."

"Our coven takes care of each other, Shay." Mom studied me with a deep focus. "You're still reeling from the vision Lucia showed you."

"That. Plus the warning vision about the shadow. I can't figure out what the shadow means or why Lucia chose to show me her worst memory."

I dug my fingers into my hair. All of the coven was caught up on all my visions, eagerly waiting for the next one like a drama series episode.

"You said Harrison was chanting something while he...you know..."

I nodded and chewed on the inside of my lip. Unfortunately, Lucia's rape vision was branded in my brain. A tattoo on my memory. Permanent. I couldn't understand what she wanted me to see. Every time I tried to piece it together, I got stuck in the emotions of it all.

"I wonder if they're connected," Mom said, rubbing her fingers together.

"What's connected?"

"Well, Lucia showed you Harrison's deception and destruction right before his *ancestor* attempted the same with you."

"Fuck," I breathed out as if hit by a ton of bricks. My hands gripped the arms of the chair while leaning forward. "Harrison was chanting the curse and Dean was trying to do what? Finish it? I never heard him say spells." As silence filled the air, I flopped back in the chair. My thumbs traced an invisible path across my fingertips while I thought.

"If that's true," I started, "the curse is already intact, then why would Dean be trying to do it, too?"

"Maybe he's trying a different kind of dark love magic."

"But you can't spell someone to love you."

"It's forbidden and punishable. Not impossible."

"Oh my stars." My eyes widened as I searched my mom's face. "Mildred."

Mom's face mimicked mine, coming to the same conclusion. Mildred might have some insight on what we were missing. Dark magic was forbidden in our natural world. No love spells. No bringing back the dead. No world domination. Again, the entertainment business got it right.

"So, now you have a plan to go with the information you've received, yes?" Mom asked with a knowing smile. This was what I lived for—a plan.

"This fuels my soul."

Mom laughed, leaning forward to grip my knee. She tilted her head to the side. "Tell me what happened with Cade."

"That's what you really wanted to talk about, right?" I shook my head, laughing.

Mom shrugged her shoulders. Mischieviousness shone in her eyes. "You can't read me the same way I can read you."

I felt the blush creep up my cheeks as I thought about my night with Cade. And the next morning. Being with him felt easy. He was funny, caring, smart, and supportive. But, in the back of my mind, something told me this was too good to be true. One day it could crash, burn, and destroy my perfectly constructed world.

"For a Quaint, you sure have taken a liking to him."

"Can we go back to talking about Dean and Harrison?" I joked.

"No way, missy. You are aware that being with

279

Cade is satisfying the curse, right? For the first time in a while, I feel like we're actually going to save the store." Mom's eyes grew misty as she looked around. "That this," —she gestured to the store— "could finally be ours."

"Yeah," I said, swallowing. Nothing like laying the guilt and expectation on me to stay with Cade. I should be with Cade because I want to. Not because I need to. In my mind, that was a distinct difference. "Speaking of," I said, changing the subject. "Aaron is coming tomorrow to help set up for the festival. You're going to love him."

Mom blinked several times, clearing her tears away. We talked for the next few minutes about Aaron and the festival's details. There was a constant fluttering in my stomach anytime I thought about the festival. It wasn't easy to give Aaron the reins, but my confidence grew more each time he communicated about the details. Our inspirations matched.

It was the same with Cade, honestly.

A buzzing in my back pocket halted our conversation. I pulled out my phone, seeing a text from Cade.

"Ah, young love," Mom teased, reading my emotions. She stood from the chair and dropped a kiss to the top of my head.

Cade:—Guess who's at my apartment again?—

My lips pulled up at the same time that I rolled my eyes.

Shay:—Oh no! The She-Devil?—

Cade:—Yes. She's currently playing hide and seek in my sheets.—

Cade:—Are you free to get her? My shift starts in a

little bit and I don't want to take her to the station.—

Cade:—We ran out of bandaids the last time she was there. —

Shay:—LOL—

Shay:—I'll be there in ten.—

"Mom," I called out. "I—"

"You're leaving. I know," she said from behind the counter. "Be back to close."

I turned in the chair, giving her a look over my shoulder.

"The lust that just exploded inside of you was hard to ignore." She lifted her hands in surrender before winking at me.

****

My hand shook as I knocked on Cade's door. His apartment was one of the few in town, and it sat off of the town square, right in the middle of everything.

It's just an apartment, Shay...

I hadn't felt this nervous to see someone in, well, ever. Even after we spent the night, naked, the antsiness danced inside my bones. The door opened and all my emotions drifted away. Warmth flowed through my body. It felt like I was shimmering with recognition.

Cade smiled as he looked at me. "Hey. Thanks for coming."

My mouth salivated as I took in his appearance. He was dressed in his navy blue uniform. He was a sight I would never tire of, especially since I knew what he looked like underneath his clothes. The more I got to know him, the more my heart opened up to him.

"Sure. Mildred should know she doesn't live here."

"I feel like she's been over here more often lately."

"Like she's sneaking in and then leaving before

you get back?"

"My lips are sealed," I heard her say from inside the apartment.

"Something like that," Cade said, taking a step forward. "Do I need to buy cat food or something?" He reached out, his fingers trailing along my jaw, tucking a piece of my hair behind my ear. I shivered.

"What was the question?" I asked, leaning into his touch.

Cade closed the distance between us. His lips touched mine. It was a wisp of a kiss that held the same passion level as our other kisses. I felt like I could breathe again.

"Hot damn," Mildred said, meowing behind Cade. *"I think my fur got singed from that kiss. I miss men."*

I broke the kiss, laughing.

"Something funny?" Cade asked. "Was that a bad kiss?"

"Definitely not a bad kiss, just Mildred breaking up the moment." I pinned her with a look. "Like always."

Cade looked down behind him, scratching her head. "You have a strange relationship with your cat."

"That's only the half of it." I laughed.

"I have to be around when you finally tell him that I speak to you in your head."

I swiped some hair off my forehead, trying to ignore her.

"Do you want to come in for a few?" Cade asked, moving out of the way. I peeked around him. The place was tidy besides a few stray dishes and cups. His bed in the living room called to me. I bet it smelled like him.

"Um…" I shook my head. "I need to get back to the store. I haven't been the best employee. There are a few million things I need to finish up before Aaron gets here tomorrow."

"I suppose saving your business is a good excuse to not stay," Cade teased.

"Don't forget saving the entire Whitley bloodline," Mildred said. *"Especially if that includes making babies with Cade."*

I choked on a gasp.

"You all right?" Cade asked, giving me a strange look.

I cleared my throat, failing to ignore Mildred's snickers. I waved him off before slapping him on the chest, wiggling my fingers against his strong muscles.

"Is there something you aren't telling me?" His bright green eyes were calculating.

I shook my head. It was another lie, but telling him Mildred spoke in my head was beyond normal. I have no idea how to break that secret to him.

"Are you excited to see Aaron again?" I deflected.

"I'm always excited to see Aaron. He's like my brother. He was the one that bailed me out of jail. I owe him a lot." Cade's gaze pierced me. I was astute enough to know his wheels were still turning. "Ready for the festival tomorrow?"

"I hope so. I have to double and triple check my lists to make sure everything is set."

Cade gripped my hand and brought it to his lips. "Babe. You and Aaron are one crazy detail-oriented team. I'm confident things are going to be perfect."

A grim tickling in the back of my brain caused my face to fall. The dark shadow would be showing up tomorrow, too. And I had no idea what or who that meant. Was it literal or figurative?

"Are you sure you're okay? You're acting extra weird today."

"Thanks." I pasted a fake smile on my face. "Just thinking about things." I tapped a finger to my temple. "It's always weird up here."

"You are the worst liar in the world," Mildred added as she rubbed her furry body through his legs, meowing.

Cade gave me a lingering look before he crouched down to give Mildred love. She purred and rubbed her face against his.

"Okay, Millie. If you stay in your apartment, I'll come visit you."

"Yes, please," she mewed. *"Though we both know he's visiting you, not me."*

I pursed my lips, thinking. It was becoming apparent that Mildred had to have cast a forbidden love spell.

****

"You are in big trouble, kitty," I said, setting Mildred down on the counter.

She stretched her lithe body, arching her back. Then she plopped down on the counter. Her tail flicked back and forth.

"I think I'm in love."

"So, that means you have to stalk him?"

"Yes." She lifted her paw and began grooming herself.

"Mildred."

"What?" She snapped her jaw at me. *"What's the big deal?"*

"It's creepy. You're kind of obsessed with him."

"Well, I'm a fucking cat. So, there's not a whole lot

284

I can do with him besides cuddle. It's been decades since I've felt the touch of a man." Mildred stared at me with her neon green eyes. Her pupils dilated as she brought on a full pout.

"I understand that, kitty." I cupped her furry face. "But, like you said, you're a cat."

Mildred's pink tongue poked out of her mouth, licking my hand. *"I know."*

I nuzzled against her face. Her loud purrs echoed in the store. We stayed embraced for a few moments.

"Tell me about how you got turned into a cat."

Her purrs stopped and she stiffened. Her lips curled, showing off her teeth. *"Why?"*

I told her about the connection between Harrison and Dean.

"You did dark love magic, didn't you?" I asked.

"I think I have a dominant obsessive gene in my DNA and it got me in trouble," she said, bowing her head.

"Awe, kitty," I coaxed, picking her up in my arms, showing her love.

"It was a long time ago. I met this man and I became obsessed. Like...really obsessed. He was all I thought about. All the time. The problem was he was already married. I tried the usual tarot card and love boosting spells, but nothing seemed powerful enough. Nothing helped me achieve what I wanted. He kept saying that he would leave his wife for me. That never happened. One night, I had enough of his lies. So, I snuck into the Wiccan Library and tore a spell out of one of the ancient tomes. Since it was a dark magic spell, it required a sacrifice."

"Is that true for all dark magic spells?"

She rested her head in the crook of my neck.

"Yes. Something that takes a part of your soul. In Harrison's case, that was taking away someone's virtue. I sacrificed my familiar."

Her words in my head held so much grief and regret. My heart broke for my dearest companion. I could never sacrifice her. No matter how much she got on my nerves. But, there was something Mildred wanted. Someone she needed. Mildred was a persistent cat, I could only imagine how much worse it was when she was a complex human. I didn't judge her. She made her choices and has been suffering the consequences.

We sat together in silence. I squeezed her tight and her claws dug into my shirt. We held each other for a while, silently supporting each other. There was no other bond like witch and familiar. So, I knew that Mildred sacrificed a part of herself that day she chose the dark path.

Dean was on that same dark path. What was he trying to sacrifice?

"Is it the same sacrifice for every spell? Like all love spells need a blood sacrifice?"

"I think it's just whatever piece of your soul you could give to power the spell. In my case, that was killing something that Mother Earth had provided me."

"I wonder what it is for Dean."

"I've been thinking about that. I think he's trying to finish whatever Harrison started."

"You don't think Harrison's end goal was the curse?"

"I think he wanted to make Lucia his. Like a binding spell. And when that didn't work, he settled for a curse."

My head started to hurt. There was too much going on with the festival, navigating my feelings for Cade, saving the store and the Whitley legacy, now add Dean's eerie motives, which were connected to Harrison somehow.

"What does Dean want?" I sighed, speaking into Mildred's fur.

"He wants you and will stop at nothing until he has you."

"Sexually?" I stuttered. I was a smart person, but lately, I felt like I was drowning just below the surface.

"In every way possible."

Was Dean past the point of no return? Would he stop at nothing until he has me?

For the longest time he was the only man I trusted. I never knew my father, and being an only child surrounded by a coven of women, I didn't put a lot of faith into men.

Until Cade.

"What if he's just under the influence of something? Like a potion?"

"It's possible. Some witches and warlocks are more susceptible than others. Whatever is going on with him, it's going to explode soon. I feel it in my gut. I might not be an active witch anymore, but I can still sense things."

I felt that, too. My vision with the dark shadow confirmed some of the things Mildred eluded to. There had to be a chance to save him.

"Let's do a reading," I concluded, setting Mildred beside me. I gathered up my candles and tarot cards and lit a black candle for protection, silver for balance, and red for bravery. I set my intentions for this reading:

insight into Dean and his motives.

I shuffled the tarot cards three times, then cut the deck and turned over the top card.

The Five of Cups.

"Fuck," I breathed out. My voice was barely above a whisper.

"Holy Goddess. The Five of Cups. I think you have your answer."

My eyes were dry from staring at the card so intently, so I blinked several times. The Five of Cups featured a cloaked person with their head down among a five of fallen chalices. Some tarot masters called this card The Inheritance, symbolizing cross-generational tragedies. The problems of our ancestors fell on the generations below it. The Inheritance warned of fits of rage and tantrums within the mess of poor and detrimental decision making.

This card warned and confirmed that Dean was not in his right mind.

"Harrison might be influencing Dean," Mildred concluded.

"I think you're right, Millie." I scratched her belly. "He said he found some questionable spells in one of Harrison's journals the night he drugged me. I didn't make sense of it at the time. But now it's becoming clearer. Harrison is possessing Dean from beyond the grave."

"You need to stay away from him, Shay. This is dark and dangerous shit."

"If this we're true, then Dean needs help. The kind that only witches can give him."

Mildred snorted, crinkling her nose. *"You need to focus more on Cade, not Dean. Which one is more important? Cade needs to be warned."*

I knew the answer to that question right away. Cade was infinitely more important to me than Dean, but I wouldn't turn my back on someone. That wasn't who I was. If I could help, I would.

"Warn Cade? Why?"

"Who's standing between Dean and you?"

"Cade."

Chapter 26

Mildred snored from her sprawled out position on the moon carpet in the middle of the floor while I finished up inventory. The doors were locked and darkness blanketed the streets of our tiny town. Unease settled in my stomach like a large boulder from our conversation earlier.

Was Dean really out to destroy me in some sort of way? Was he really that blinded by his jealousy and rage that he would harm me?

A part of me refused to believe that. The old Dean was still in there some where. I just had to get it out of him.

Whatever secrets he held close to his chest, I needed to get them revealed.

My phone buzzed.

Harmony calling...

"Hey, Harm. What's up?" I held the phone to my ear with my shoulder.

"Hi. I feel like I haven't seen you in days. How are you doing? You know...after."

"I'm fine. Nothing bad really happened."

"Except for Dean drugging you so he could have his nasty way with you," she scoffed.

"It didn't get that far. I'm sorry I haven't been around lately," I said, shifting the convervsation.

"Girl, it's fine. The festival is tomorrow. I know

you've got a lot on your plate. I just miss my bestie."

"I miss you, too." I laughed. "You know I still live at the apartment that we share."

"Brad is just...so..." She moaned into the phone. "...amazing. I think I'm getting addicted to his tongue."

"This is the longest you've been with someone. Is it getting serious?"

"I think so," she said, her voice softening. "I still don't want you to do a Lovers Reading."

"I didn't offer. You don't have to listen to what I would tell you, though. You are free to make your own choices."

"I know. I know. What about you? When are you going to do yours?"

Blush heated my cheeks. Images of Cade swarmed my mind. "I don't think I can."

"Have you ever tried?"

"No. I'm not sure I'd want to..."

"Like what if you find that it's not Cade, you mean?" Harmony teased.

"You're insane," I deflected.

"That wasn't an answer."

A few seconds of silence passed. Both of us thought about the same thing. What if Brad and Cade were our soulmates? What if they weren't? Either way, that would be the biggest secret ever.

"I've got to finish closing up," I said, breaking the heavy silence. "Will you be home later?"

"No. Brad's taking me out and then you know where that will lead. So, the apartment will be empty." She hung up before I could respond, leaving me to interrupt her not so subtle meaning.

I placed my phone down on the desk and leaned

back in the computer chair. A loud crash sounded from the front room. I sprang from the chair, my heart pounded as I rushed out the back room. Mildred was awake, slunk down in a predatory crawl.

"What was that?" I asked, looking through the front windows, expecting to find something broken.

"I have no idea."

I pressed my hands against the cool window pane, peering outside. "Nothing looks out of the ordinary."

BANG!

I jumped back from the windows, landing on my ass. Mildred hissed.

BANG!

I screamed, scrambling backward along the floor.

"It's ravens!" Mildred screeched, howling toward the windows.

BANG!

"Are they running into the windows?" I asked, gaining my footing and standing up. "On purpose?"

BANG!

Each time a raven flew into the window, I startled. The sound of them crashing to their death grated on my nerves. Taking a step toward the window, another black feathered bird crashed into it. I covered my ears, cringing at the sound of their terrible screeches while their bodies crunched.

After thirteen ravens, the banging stopped.

"This is a clear warning," I said to Milred. We stood by the windows, staring at the lifeless bodies of the ravens scattered along the sidewalk.

"No shit."

"Warning for what, though? Lucia wouldn't be this cruel."

An icy breath whisked across my neck, bringing my shoulders up. I lifted my eyes from the sidewalk, zeroing on a dark shadow across the street. Violent chills ran down my arms, plastering my feet to their spot.

"There's a shadow," I said through chattering teeth.

"I don't see anything. Just dead birds." Mildred meowed.

I tried to point in the dark shadow's direction, but my arms were glued to my sides. Fear or something else had frozen me.

"Shaaay," a deep, dark voice called out. *"The time has come to fulfill your destiny."*

My chin quivered. The voice numbed me to my bones, making my body shake in fear.

"G-Get my ph-phone, Mildred. *Now!*"

Mildred peeked up at me, sensing my terror. Soon, she was back with my phone tucked in her mouth.

The shadow appeared to grow in size the longer it held my gaze. I knew it was using spell casting to keep me in place. I had to disrupt it somehow.

"C-Call Cad-de," I strained. My heart pounded in my ears.

Mildred worked the phone with her nose deftly. Ringing sounded through the store as my body tightened further. My brain felt like fog. I kept pushing against the spell, despite the terror I tasted on my tongue.

"Hi, babe," Cade greeted. His voice broke through the fear, but only slightly. "I just got off work. What's up?"

Mildred meowed into the phone.

I heard him laugh. "Hi, Millie."

Mildred yowled, panic lacing her tiny cat voice.

"C-Cade," I said, my voice quivering.

"Shay? What's wrong? Where are you?"

"Th-the store. Sp-spelled. H-hurry," I whimpered. The dark shadow rippled with power, morphing and moving as if it were a cloud moving through the sky.

"Come to me now, witch," the dark shadow said.

My body crumbled under it's suggestion. Sweat broke out on my head as I fought against the suggestion. I refused to go with that sinister blob. My will was stronger than its.

"Cade's running across the street, Shay. Don't give in to the spell."

Cade slammed his hands on the window of the door, zeroing on me. Confusion and determination pulled on his face. Mildred jumped up, using her paws to unlock the door for him. He ran inside, halting when he saw me frozen. My body was exhausted, but I refused to give in. Tears streamed down my face. I couldn't tell if it was from fear or relief.

Cade's hands were wide out in front of him, but he didn't touch me. "What's going on? You look like you're in a lot of pain."

Mildred paced back and forth.

"R-ravens. D-dark sh-shadow. Sp-spell." I hated that I sounded like a caveman. All of my energy was fighting the dark shadow.

"What do I do?"

"St-stand in front of me," I croaked.

Cade followed directions and stood in my line of sight, breaking the connection the dark shadow had.

I crumpled at the knees, falling forward as the tension from the spell released its hold. Cade's arms wrapped around me, stopping me from crashing to the floor. We slumped down to the ground together. My limbs felt like wet noodles. I breathed in Cade's scent as I buried my face in his chest. We sat on the floor, cuddled together for several moments.

Mildred laid by my legs, nuzzling her face against me.

"It's gone, Shay."

Cade's heart beat against his chest, filling me with relief and gratitude. He didn't hesitate to come to my aid. Again. It was becoming harder and harder to understand why I insisted on doing things myself.

"What the fuck just happened?" Cade asked, stroking his hand down my hair. The more he touched me, the more my body filled with energy, like he was recharging me.

"Honestly, I really don't know," I said, turning my head to look up at him.

His eyes blazed. "You said it was a spell."

I swallowed. The fierce expression on his face was distracting and arousing. "Some ravens flew into the window right before a dark shadow appeared across the street. It was holding me in an immobility spell. One I've never experienced."

"Then how did you know how to break it?"

"Intuition." I shrugged. "I was frozen in it's gaze. So, I figured I needed to break the connection somehow."

"What are you going to do about all those ravens on the sidewalk?"

"I'll take care of them."

I smiled, scratching her face. "Mildred's got it…" I brought my face to hers. "Thanks, kitty."

"I might have disappointed my familiar, but I've learned the importance of them to their witch. I'm always going to be here...bitch." She licked my face, rubbing her head along my jaw. She rubbed her body along Cade's chest before hopping off and slinking through the still open door.

"I have a feeling I'm missing something here. A lot of somethings, actually," Cade said, pulling me to standing. He gathered me in his arm. "More secrets."

My limbs felt tired and sore as if I did a heavy workout, but I was in control of them again.

"Take me home and I'll tell you whatever you want to know," I said against his chest. It was time for him to know the rest of my secrets.

****

The warm glow of my salt lamp illuminated my bedroom as Cade and I sat cross-legged across from each other on my bed. I cupped the warm mug of lemon balm and white tea to relieve the aches and pains in my muscles from being frozen. Cade ran a hand through his hair for the millionth time. He flopped back against my pillows.

"Okay, let me get this straight. You think Dean is possessed by his evil ancestor, Harrison, to finish what he started with your ancestor, Lucia."

I nodded as he continued talking to the ceiling.

"And the dark shadow that had you in a spell tonight is part of it because of a curse Harrison put on the Whitley bloodline."

I took a sip of my tea, its warmth soothing my throat. "Yeah. Basically."

Cade sat up, looking wild and puzzled. "You understand how crazy this all sounds, right?"

"I guess to a Quaint it would sound crazy. But, I'm used to it."

"You think Dean is going to harm me because I'm in the way of his spell?"

"Well, after tonight, I think it's more about me and less about you. Anything could happen, though." I took another gulp of tea and placed it on the nightstand. I lay down beside Cade on my pillows, placing my head on his shoulder.

"Doing okay over there?" I teased, after several minutes of silence.

"I'm getting there. Couldn't you just have a smelly ex-boyfriend that challenges me to a fistfight or something? How am I supposed to compete against an evil wizard?"

"It's warlock." I snorted, hiding my laughter. "Not wizard."

"You know what I mean," he chastised before tickling my side. I slapped him away in between laughs.

"I'm not sure he's even after you, especially after tonight. Honestly, Cade...Dean can't compete with you."

Cade stopped tickling me, leaning up on his forearms, pinning me below him. I wrapped my fingers around his arms, skimming them up and down. My legs spread open, giving him space. Seeing Cade above me filled me with warmth and security. My cheeks rose into a smile.

"Does that mean you actually like me?" Cade asked smugly.

I shook my head. "Nope. I don't."

"You're such a bad liar." Cade's eyes seared into mine. I tilted my head to the side, feeling lust build inside my body. It felt so right to be here with him. The first man I ever let into my life. Told my secrets to. Someone who I actually trusted.

My breath quickened as we stared at each other.

He smirked before licking my lips. His hair tickled my face as he drew his nose up the side of my jaw. I sighed, tightening my grip on his arms.

"Does this feel good?" he whispered in my ear, sending waves of arousal down my body.

I nodded.

"I need to hear your words, baby," he demanded. He placed a kiss right below my ear.

"Yes," I moaned.

He propped himself up on one hand as the other drifted along the side of my body. His mouth planted tiny searing kisses along my neck and collarbone. Hungrily, I arched my back, giving him all the access he needed.

"Good. You might get annoyed, but I'm going to be asking for permission every step of the way. So, you'll need to speak up. Do you understand?" he asked, facing me.

A mirad of emotions flooded my body at his attentiveness. I smiled and gripped the back of his neck, slamming my lips to his in a feverish kiss. Our lips danced to a silent tune made only for us. We were both breathless when I pulled back, laying back against the pillows.

"Does that answer your question?"

He smiled, blinding me with his genuine excitement. He brought his hand up, skimming his thumb along my jaw and down my neck. My skin erupted in goosebumps.

"You like my touch?" he asked, bringing his hand along my ribcage to slide his thumb under my boob. I pushed my chest into his touch.

"Yes," I breathed. "More."

Cade chuckled softly as his fingers found the hem of my old sweatshirt. I moved with him, allowing him to whisk it off my body, exposing my naked torso. His eyes darkened as he drank me in.

"Simply beautiful," was all he said before he leaned down, taking one nipple into his mouth.

The sensation of his tongue on me sent my body into a tizzy. I wanted his hands everywhere. I needed it. I wasn't going to stop until I had what I wanted. He pulled my boobs together, kissing, tasting, nipping at them.

My skin was on fire as I writhed under his muscular body. I tugged at his hair, moaning. His tongue slid over my pert nipples. Heat pooled at my core as my arousal heightened. I gripped his hair, pulling him up. Our lips collided in a scorching kiss that consumed us both, adding more fuel to the fire that burned deep in my belly.

He broke the kiss and pulled his shirt over his head. His chiseled chest was on full display. The perfect ridges and valleys of his muscles mesmerized me. My eyes drifted down his model-like body following the happy trail of hair to what lay beneath his boxer briefs.

Cade laughed. "We're taking this slow, babe."

I pouted, running my hands up and down his smooth chest. "Spoil sport."

"It'll be worth it, I promise." He leaned down, pressing his weight into my body. My skin blushed under his kisses as we laid skin to skin. Hip to hip.

Heart to heart.

I ran my fingers down his back, squeezing his ass. He groaned and pushed his hips into mine. His dick pressed against my clit, igniting sparks all the way to my toes.

I moaned.

"You like that?" he asked as he thrust forward again.

"Yesss."

Cade's hand ran down the side of my body, slipping under my pajama bottoms waistband.

"I knew it was a good idea to change into comfy clothes," I panted while his fingers worked their magic above my underwear. I squirmed under his touch, wanting more. Between his deft fingers and his kisses on my breasts, I was losing control and fast.

I ran my fingernails along the contours of his back, feeling the ripple of muscle beneath my touch as I arched into his hands. He groaned and goosebumps prickled against his skin. He worked me as if he were an artist and I was his clay. A surge of need flowed through my veins. I dipped my fingers under his boxers and gripped his strained cock.

Cade hissed through clenched teeth, dropping his forehead to my chest. "Jesus, Shay."

A triumphant smile tugged at my lips, knowing I can render him immobile with just a touch. My hand moved up and down around his velvety dick, feeling it grow harder with every stroke, fueling my need to control.

Cade panted against my chest, a tantalizing warmth that tickled my skin. He lifted his head, those intense green eyes locking onto mine with a fiery gaze that brought a cocky smirk to my face. He leaned back, gripped my wrist, and pulled it from his pants. I opened my mouth to complain when he popped the button of his pants. He discarded them on the floor.

I followed suit, lifting my hips to pull off my pajama bottoms, and throwing them to the floor next to his. I licked my lips slowly, my eyes sweeping over his sculpted body.

Cade climbed back on top of me. His dick poked against my dripping vulva. Shivers ran down my body in anticipation. He cupped the side of my face, and brushed a piece of hair out of the way.

"Do you want to keep going, babe?" he asked, eyes never wavering from mine.

I swallowed, feeling emotion clog my throat. I've had sex before, but what I was experiencing with Cade was so much more. Doing the most intimate act with another person was a sign of complete trust in the other person.

Is Cade someone I show the deepest parts of my soul to? Yes.

"Yes, Cade. Fuck me," I answered, staring into his eyes.

Cade smirked as he brought his hand between our bodies. His fingers skimmed across my heightened pussy. Wetness flooded between my thighs as his fingers explored me, teasing, wiggling, dipping, and diving in between my folds. At the same time, Cade leaned down to pull a condom from his wallet.

"I'm not going to just fuck you, Shay."

I opened my mouth to protest, struggling to form any words. He laughed, leaning back to roll on the condom.

"It's going to be so much more than just fucking, babe. Are you sure you can handle that?" His bright green eyes seared me with sincerity. Powerful feelings bombarded my chest. I sucked in a sharp breath as the pounding of my heart felt like it was going to burst.

"Let go, Shay," sounded in my head, remembering all the times the people in my life begged me to feel, not think. I pulled him down on me, pressing my lips to him like a woman ravished.

"Make love to me, Cade."

Chapter 27

Cade kept his eyes on me as he rested a hand on the side of my head. His fingers twirled around my hair. I leaned into his touch and inhaled, waiting for what would come next. His hair messed up from my exploits, flopped along his forehead. With the aroused glint in his eye, he looked like a sexual god hovering above me. His other hand grabbed his dick and he grazed it against my clit and vulva, tantalizing me. I closed my eyes, savoring the feeling.

"Keep your eyes on me, Shay," he commanded in a strained voice.

I opened my eyes at his demand.

"Ready?" he whispered.

I hung my arms around his neck, giving his lips a quick peck.

"Yes. More than ready."

A small smile graced his face. He pushed inside me, slowly.

"Ohh..." I breathed out, closing my eyes reflexively.

"Eyes. Open," Cade growled.

I opened my eyes again, finding his gaze strained for control. Cade kissed my nose as he pushed further in. When he was fully inside, we both sighed. I felt completely full in the best way. My internal energy hummed with satisfaction. I wouldn't be surprised if I was actually glowing. Witches have documented stranger things happening during sex.

He dipped his hand between our bodies and rubbed his thumb over my clit. Fresh wetness gathered at my core and my muscles clenched around his cock.

"Ah, fuck," he groaned.

"Start moving, Thompson," I commanded, feeling feverish and heady.

Cade grunted a laugh, causing his dick to jerk inside me, hitting my G-spot. "Yes, ma'am."

He moved his hips back and forth slowly, sliding in and out, finding a delicious rhythm. He gripped my hip with one hand and lifted me to meet him. My heart raced against my chest as I reveled in the pleasure that coursed through my body. Sweat sprinkled his skin. His muscles rippled with each plunge deep inside me.

With each movement, the fissure that he had created in the fortress around my heart spread wider and farther. Any doubts I felt about sharing my secrets with him floated away as we connected on the most primal level.

Cade groaned and sped up his thrusts. "You feel so good, Shay. I'm close."

"Keep going. I'm almost there," I puffed out between moans and satisfied sighs.

Cade let go of my hip and rested on his forearms on either side of me, capturing my lips in a feverish kiss. His hips pistoned faster as his hands gripped my hair. I hitched my hips in sync with his and wrapped my legs around his slim waist. I climbed higher and higher with each of his thrusts. I pulled my face away from his, not being able to handle the tantalizing ecstasy that sparked from each of my nerves.

I yelled his name out loud. Stars exploded around my eyes as an epic orgasm crashed over me. Weightlessness took control of my body, feeling like I was hovering on top of the bed.

"Great Goddess," I moaned into his shoulder, shuddering with each blissful aftershock.

Cade thrust his hips a couple more times before he groaned, adding more waves to my orgasm. His own orgasm took over, and he collapsed on me, his head nestled in the crook of my neck, kissing me softly. My chest heaved up and down as I caught my breath. For a moment, I had no clue where I was. Was I on Earth? In outer space? In another realm?

My eyes blinked several times while the details of my bedroom came back into focus. Cade pushed up onto his forearms, giving a smile that made my arousal flare up again.

"Fuck, Shay. That was…" He stopped at a loss for words.

I smiled, grabbing a hold of his face in both of my hands. "Yeah. That was…" I echoed, pressing my lips against his.

Cade's eyes were warm with lust as he slid out of me and stood up from the bed. He removed the condom and walked to the bathroom. I laid back against my bed, staring up at the ceiling with a goofy grin on my face. My bones felt like jelly and I felt completely sated.

He returned with a warm washcloth, laid down beside me, and propped up on his elbow, holding the washcloth out. Heat blossomed on my cheeks as I took the washcloth and cleaned up.

"You're embarrassed now?" Cade chuckled.

I shrugged my shoulders, tossing the washcloth

over his head in the general direction of the bathroom. Cade pulled me closer, letting my head rest on his chest. With his feet, he pulled up one of my fluffy blankets and wrapped it around us.

I sighed, replaying our romp in the sheets. My eyes drifted closed as I listened to Cade's steady heartbeat. His hand skimmed up and down my bare back. An overwhelming sensation bubbled in my gut. Cade was attentive and caring. Laying here with him, I couldn't remember why I fought against my feelings. Cade wasn't making my life more complicated. He helped calm it. He made it better.

"You're going to stay, right?" I asked, fighting against the sleep that was pulling at my consciousness. I knew we had had a rough night full of revelations and spells, but a tiny part of me still knew that Cade was a logical person. The shit that happened tonight should scare him away. I was used to this life, and it scared me.

"I'm not going anywhere, Shay," Cade said. His voice was thick with sleep.

"Even if Dean might be out to get you, us?"

"Especially because of Dean."

"Oh." I frowned. Cade's chest shook as he chuckled softly.

"More so because I like what we have here. I really like you, Shay. Everyone in town likes you and your family. You're intelligent, hard-working, motivated, and different from anyone I've ever known. Aaron is indebted to you because he says he found his soulmate."

"I'm excited to hear the story." I smiled against his chest.

"He said it's exactly as you saw. Which still blows my mind, but…" He paused, shifting so he can see my face. I looked up at him. "I know I've said this already, but I believe you, Shay. All of it."

I gulped down past the lump that had formed in my throat. A sudden giddiness bloomed inside my heart. He reaffirmed his sentiment he told me the other night. The more glimpses he was shown of my witch world, the more he continued to stay. I told myself I was never going to change who I was for a man. And with Cade, I don't have to.

With Cade's arms wrapped around me, I felt safe, content, happy.

Silence blanketed my bedroom. The orange and pink glow from my salt lamp flickered, casting moving shadows along the ceiling and hypnotizing me. My eyes didn't open for the rest of the night.

****

Deep satisfaction gripped my body as I stretched my legs and wiggled my toes. Soft sunlight shone through the windows in my bedroom as I cracked my eyes open. I breathed in, smiling. I turned my head, finding a peaceful, sleeping Cade laying on his stomach. His lips were slightly parted. With the sheet draped around his waist, I got an eyeful of his strong back that begged to be touched.

I turned my head back, staring at the ceiling. My heart thumped steadily against my chest, feeling completely at ease. Any worries I had last night about taking our relationship to the next level faded away. I smiled.

Aaron was coming today.

The festival was tomorrow.

We had a real shot of saving The Wise Whitleys.

I closed my eyes, sinking into the comfort of my bed. Cade had continued to show me the kind of man he was. The thought brought butterflies to my stomach. The prospect of a certain four-letter word rattled in my head. I wouldn't say it, yet, but now I knew the difference between that and lust.

A strong tug pulled at my stomach and air whipped past my ears. I gasped, causing Cade to stir. My astral self was knocking from the inside, begging to be let out. Fate wanted me to see something. I kept my eyes closed and let go of my astral body, feeling it leave my body to take me on a journey.

I stood on a dark sidewalk, surrounded by trees. The glow of the setting sun illuminated the area around me. I looked down, seeing myself.

Vroom. Vroom.

A man dressed in a leather jacket and a helmet pulled over and stopped beside me. His white sneakers stepped down on the ground as he straddled his motorcycle. I took a step back.

The man flipped up the visor of his helmet, revealing his eyes.

Bright green. An electric current zapped in the atmosphere, keeping my senses on edge. Around the man was a shimmering green and silver aura.

We spoke for several minutes. A few quips were tossed back and forth between me and him. He felt familiar. This had happened before, I thought to myself as I watched the scene play before me.

The man pushed up sleeves. My eyes spotted the dark ink design on his entire forearm. I recognized it immediately. It was a black and gray depiction of the

Capricorn symbol: a strong sea-goat.

My astral body swooshed as the scene dissipated, morphing into another one.

I stood in front of a building with big red doors, speaking to two men. "Aren't you the guy from last night?" I asked, trying to lighten the mood.

One of the men smiled, which blinded me, putting his hands in his jeans' pockets. "The guy you all but called an asshole? Yeah, that's me. I'm the new firefighter, Cade Thompson." His aura sparked brightly around him.

I pulled on the sleeves of my jacket, covering my hands. "Shay Whitley. I thought I recognized your tattoo."

My astral body flew forward, changing the scene again.

I stood on the grass in front of my apartment. The large tree shook beside the building. Meows sounded from the sky.

Cade, with his aura visible, grabbed the back of the ladder, mirroring the hold that another firefighter carried. Cade walked past me.

"Funny how the first non-candle call we get in the station is for a cat," Cade said.

"Not just any cat," I defended. I quickened my steps to walk beside him. "My cat. Even if she's annoying."

They set the ladder down. "We'll take good care of her, Miss," Cade teased with a smirk on his full, kissable lips.

More morphing and changing.

Cade spun me around to face him, holding me close. His dark eyeliner started to run as sweat peppered his face. The streaks of makeup gave his face an even more devilish look against the brightness of his eyes.

He gripped my chin, forcing me to look at him. The colored lights danced in his eyes. "I want you. So badly."

My astral body tugged at me again, sending me to another snapshot in time.

Cade's eyes shone as he gazed at me. "I know I said this before but, I believe you, Shay. All of it." His green and silver aura erupted from his body, encasing him in a glow. I looked down at our touching bodies.

My heart leapt in my throat when I saw that I had the exact green and gray aura outlining me.

We had matching auras.

Cade was my soulmate.

My body jerked against my pillow as my astral body flew back into my body. Sweat trickled down my forehead as my chest heaved up and down.

"Another vision?" Cade's calm voice said.

My head whipped to the side. My eyes widened in panic and it stole my voice. His eyes were open, staring at me.

Oh. My. Goddess.

Cade's my soulmate.

Chapter 28

I flung myself out of bed in full naked glory. My whole body shook uncontrollably.

Cade leaned up on his forearms. His arms and abs flexed.

"Shay. Seriously, what's wrong?"

I shoved my hands through my hair as I paced the floor beside the bed. Images of my vision circled through my brain. I had been so stupid not noticing it before. How could I have been so blind to all the signs?

Goddess. What should I do?

"Shay," Cade said again, moving to the edge of the bed. "You look a little crazy and panicked right now. Tell me what's wrong."

I whipped my head toward him. His eyes were wide and full of concern. I read his aura. Bright green and silver outlined him. I looked toward the mirror, seeing my aura. A perfect match. The colors symbolic of Capricorns and Virgos swirled together in a perfect dance.

Air rushed past my ears, creating a whooshing noise as if I were underwater. I was two seconds away from passing out.

Cade stood from the bed and gripped both of my hands. "Your hands are icy and clammy. There's sweat on your face and pulse is high. You're having a panic attack. Is this witch related?"

I blinked, trying to focus on him. "Um, y-yeah."

"Okay," Cade coaxed. His voice was even and in control. "So, you had a vision. You've had plenty in your life. You're used to them. What makes this one different? Was it a bad one?" He kept hold of my hands, dipping his head so we were eye-level.

"No," I said in a monotone.

"So…what was it about?"

I felt catatonic, like a leaf blowing aimlessly through the wind. Without blinking or thinking, I said the first thing that came to my mind.

"It was nothing."

"Are you fucking serious right now, Shay?" Cade asked, sitting back down on the edge of the bed. His eyes blazed as he stared at me.

"Yeah. It just shocked me, that's all." I licked my lips, doubling down on my lie.

"What shocked you about it?"

"I wasn't expecting to the see myself in the vision." My heartbeat ticked up again.

It wasn't just me.

It was him, too.

My soulmate.

Cade stood. His height towered over me. I felt the doubt and anger rolling off of him, but he looked magnificent standing before me. The glow of the sunlight outlined his body, creating an ethereal aire.

"I know you're lying," he said. "I thought we were past this."

I opened my mouth to counter his argument. Guilt swam in my stomach, creating an uproar of bile burning my throat. Here was my soulmate, standing before me, and I chose to lie. He said he believed me. He had accepted my witchness. What was wrong with me?

Cade walked around the side of the bed. He shoved his legs into his pants, pulling them up over his tight boxers. Panic settled in my chest. I didn't want him to leave like this. I didn't want him to leave at all. After our blissful night together, I wanted to keep pulling him closer, not push him away. I couldn't blame him, though.

I was the fucked up one.

Realizing I was still naked, I eyed his t-shirt on the floor. I dove for it and pulled it over my head. Instantly, my body melted as if I was in a Cade blanket. I lifted the collar to my nose, inhaling his scent as if I was burning incense. He looked at me, wearing his shirt. His eyes drifted up and down my body, hungrily. He shook his head.

"I don't know why you don't trust me yet." Cade took a step closer. "I can't handle it, Shay. My sister lied to me. And look how that turned out. If she would have just told me from the start, things would have ended differently."

My throat felt thick with emotions. Too many "what ifs" swirled in my brain, causing me to hesitate. I didn't want to take away his free-will. I didn't want him to be with me just because the Fates weaved it that way. I also didn't want to hurt him like his sister did.

"I-I can't tell you. Yet. It's big. Like life-altering big," I admitted, wrapping my arms around my body. My vision dropped a huge bomb on my and Cade's worlds. He had a right to know what I saw, but if I was struggling with the realization, how would he react? Even with all the signs, hints, and energies, I was in shock.

Cade shook his head, flopping his sexy hair over his forehead. He closed the distance between us.

"I can't be with someone who keeps secrets, especially the big ones. Haven't you kept enough from me?"

My gaze dropped to the floor. The guilt clawed at my throat and chest. I lifted my gaze, capturing his eyes.

"I get it but, Cade, I'm not ready to tell you. I will. I promise. I just need some time to decipher it. Please. I need to be one hundred percent with what I saw before I tell you." I set my hands on his chest, not pulling my eyes away from his. He needed to see the truth and the uncertainty in my eyes. He wasn't ready for this secret. I wasn't ready for it, either. Let alone reveal it.

He took in a deep breath through his nose. He nodded. "I'll give you some space on this. But, I don't like it."

I breathed out air I didn't know I was holding. Some of the tension in my body evaporated. I collapsed into his arms. He embraced me, setting his cheek on top of my head.

"I'm not giving up on this, Shay. If this vision was enough to wake you from sleep and throw you into a panic attack, you shouldn't handle it on your own."

"Astute as ever, Cade," I commented, trying to make light of the situation.

"Shay…"

I pulled back, tilting my head to look at him. "I hear you. Just give me a few days. Like I gave you before," I argued, shutting down anymore of his rebuttals. We stayed in our embrace for a few moments. Buzzing sounded from Cade's jeans.

"That's probably Aaron. I told him to text me when he got in."

"Okay," I said. "I can't believe tomorrow is the festival."

"Tomorrow is when everything changes for you. That's a lot of pressure," Cade said, dropping a kiss to my forehead.

He had no idea that today changed everything, too.

"Well, someone needed to take charge."

"That's true. Don't forget to ask for help. That's what we're here for."

I nodded, knowing everyone was willing to help, but a tightening in my chest caused me to pause. Saving The Wise Whitleys and its legacy was my responsibility. Now that Fate had thrown me another curve ball, I wondered if I had any real control over my life. Was I just a pawn in Fate's game?

"I need my shirt," Cade said, interrupting my thoughts while he pulled on his socks.

I looked down at his shirt I was wearing. "I'll be naked."

"I wouldn't be complaining," Cade flirted as he stood, keeping his eyes on me.

Heat exploded all over my body. I squeezed my thighs together. Cade wore nothing but his jeans. His hair was touseled and his muscles rippled as he walked toward me. My soulmate. Staring at me like he wanted to devour me.

Cade closed the distance between us and gripped my chin, tilting my head up. His eyes darkened. His other hand grabbed the front of his shirt I wore and tugged me toward him. He pressed his lips to mine, searing them. The fire in my stomach blazed. Behind my eyelids, I saw images of the two of us from my vision. I felt our energies intertwining, pulsing happily. I pulled back, panting. I couldn't listen to my heart right now. There was too much at stake to put my focus on my soulmate.

"Damn," Cade whispered. "I really need to go. Aaron is a sucker for punctuality."

I nodded, working to school my face. I wouldn't let Cade see that I was bothered.

"Keep the shirt. It looks better on you anyway."

"Wow. What a line," I deadpanned.

Cade laughed, shrugging his shoulders. "It's true, though." He grabbed his hoodie and headed for the door. I leaned against the doorframe of my room, watching him. My eyes drifted along his delicious body, soaking it in.

"Stop looking at me like that." He laughed, showcasing his dimples.

I shrugged a shoulder. On the outside, it looked like I was checking him out, and part of me was; but on the inside, I was panicking.

"See you," Cade said, still smiling as he went throught the front door.

With him gone, my apartment felt empty, cold. I ran my thumbs along my fingertips. Worry gnawed at my stomach. I was falling for him fast. Beyond head over heels.

In my bones, I knew Cade was meant for me. As much as I wanted the happy ending, there were too many conclusions. Too many unknowns. Too many chances for this secret to ruin every-last-fucking-thing.

****

With my matcha tea in my hand, I walked through

the town square toward The Wise Whitleys. The coven was waiting for me to finalize the last few details for the festival. That's what I needed to focus on. One problem at a time. So much rode on the line in the success of the festival. My whole world. My whole existence.

The bells on the store's door jingled as I walked in. Mom and Gram stood on either side of the counter talking.

"Sweetheart," Mom said in a serious tone. "What happened?"

"Nothing," I quipped, as I set my bag under the counter.

"Don't even try lying right now."

"Sweetie, you know better than to lie to an empath," Gram added. She leaned down, reaching into her bag. She wore her typical sweat jumpsuit, purple this time. When she stood, she blasted me with a purple-lipped smile. Gram set the bottle of tequila on the counter. "Shall we add a little tipple to this heavy conversation we're about to have?" she squeaked, opening it.

"Mom," my mom said, pinching the bridge of her nose. "It's the morning."

I eyed the bottle then my tea. Lydia's intentions were good, but there was nothing like the burn of alcohol to help you forget your troubles. Gram tipped the bottle back and held it out for me. I grabbed the bottle.

"I had Cade's soulmate reading this morning." I took a sip. "We're soulmates."

The dusty old grandfather clock ticked in the background, filling the deathly silence that hung in the store. I looked between Mom and Gram. Their mouths hung open and their eyes bulged. I pulled myself up to sit on the counter as they processed what I admitted.

"Are you sure?" Gram asked.

"She's positive," Mom answered for me.

Gram's purple lips smacked. "Well, hallelujah!" She hollered, slapping my knee. "Fate has given you one fine ass man to love."

I looked down at the floor, grinding my teeth together. Her words hit the nail on the head. Fate "gave" me Cade. That settled in my stomach like a boulder.

"Shay isn't exactly happy about this revelation," Mom said to Gram.

"Are you kidding me? They are perfect for each other. Both good-looking. Both care for this community. He's a smart, polite young man and he's helped our girl let go of some of her control issues. Plus, marrying him will probably break the curse. Fate's never wrong."

Marry him?

"Gram! Stop!" My loud voice echoed off the walls of the store. "Fate decided this. Not me!" I rubbed my temples, feeling pressure building. I hopped off the counter, needing to get out of here.

"Look, I didn't come here to talk about this. The festival is more important right now. I'm meeting with Aaron soon to go over the final details. I need to check in with the other businesses to make sure they know the schedules. There's too much to do."

"Shay," Mom said, grabbing my hand as I moved toward the door. "You've never gone against Fate before. You preach it to your costumers. Why the change now? Why are you doubting Fate?"

"Fate has controlled everything we do, from tarot cards to speaking to the dead to my visions. Have all of my decisions in my life been a façade?" I yelled, yanking my hand from hers. "Have I never had any real control? Why do you think I try to control other aspects of my life?" My heart pounded against my chest as panic rose in my chest. I closed my eyes, taking a couple of breaths. The walls of my beloved store were closing in. "I can not deal with this right now."

"Oh, Shay, honey," Mom said in a soothing voice. I held my hand up, stopping whatever she was going to say. "Be in the town square by noon tomorrow to set up our booth." I shoved through the door. I stood on the sidewalk, breathing heavily. My family didn't deserve my frustration, but I couldn't help it. I was drowning. Suffocating.

I eyed the fire station across the street. The big red doors were open and a couple of men were washing the engines. I ground my teeth, turned on my heels, and walked in the opposite direction. I tugged on the sleeves of my shirt over my hands while walking toward the Ipswich Cemetery. I needed peace, Mother Earth, and maybe some guidance from Lucia. The curse was still in the back of my mind, despite my constant focus on the festival.

I went through the gate and headed to my family's corner. The trees were mostly bare, most were dead and crumbled on the grass. The naked trees gave the cemetery a creepy feel, as if the branches were the fingers of the dead.

I slouched down on a bench, looking toward the sky and watching the clouds float by. Peeks of sun shone on my face, warming it. Crunching of the leaves sounded beside me. My head shot up, eyeing the dark form that walked up the path.

Dean.

"Don't come any closer," I warned him, feeling my body tense. My heart caught in my throat as I took in his appearance. He wore all black. His hair had grown past his normal buzz cut and he had stubble on his face. His skin was pale and his eyes looked sunken in. He looked like death in more than one way, reminding me of his costume from the Halloween party.

"Shay, please," he begged, coming closer.

"No, I think you've said and done enough."

"Something's happening to me."

I eyed him up and down. "What could possibly be happening to you that would cause you to hurt me the way that you did?" The conversation Mildred and I had about Dean possibly being possessed entered my mind.

"Shay, I need you." He took a step toward me, shrugging his slumped shoulders. His whole body was hauntingly gaunt.

My lip curled as I stood from the bench. I scanned my surroundings. I had clear paths to the exits of the cemetery and it was in the middle of the day. There's no way he would try something now.

I side-stepped toward the gate.

Dean got in my path, lunging for me. I yelped as he gripped my arms. He reeked of dirt and rot. His normally brown sugar eyes were dark, vacant.

"Dean. Let me go," I whispered. "Now."

"Shay. I need you so bad. I can't help it. I would do anything to have you love me the way I love you."

"Loving someone shouldn't hurt. And, I don't love

you like that, Dean. And I never will."

Dean narrowed his eyes in my direction. The sinister look sent shivers down my spine. Gone was the weakened Dean. He was replaced with something else. Something stronger.

"You don't know what you're saying. You're blinded by the firefighter. Like a bitch with a shiny new toy." His voice dropped to a low, gravelly octave as he spoke.

"Insulting me won't win me over, Dean," I spat. I tried to pull out of his grip, but he tightened his fingers.

Dean shook his head. "Shay, please," he said, his voice back to normal. He squeezed his eyes tight, struggling. When they opened, they were back to black.

"You will be mine," he growled. "After all these years, I will have a Whitley witch wholly–mind, body," His eyes drifted up and down my body, making me squirm. "And spirit. As it was always meant to be. As the gods promised me it would be."

This wasn't Dean.

"N-no you won't," I stuttered. I swallowed past the fear that choked me. I needed to get away from him. "The gods don't grant things like that."

A thought came to me. There was one thing I could admit to him that might break him free of this evil spell. I rolled my shoulders back, bringing my height closer to his.

"There will *never* be a me and you. Cade is my soulmate. I saw it this morning. You know my gift is never wrong."

Dean hissed in my face and threw me to the ground hard. Pain radiated up my arm. He gripped the side of his head and doubled over as if he was also in pain. He yelled. Standing, he seared me with a hateful look.

"That's not true!" His voice echoed through the trees, sending birds flying away.

I cradled my arm as I scooted away from him. Anger, pain, maliciousness rolled off him in a tidal wave.

"It is. Our auras match."

Dean's lips curled over his teeth. The skin of his face stretched. "You are meant to be with a powerful warlock, not a weak human. I'll show you." He pointed a finger at me, crouching to hover over me. "I'm not done with you yet." He looked me up and down before running away.

I sat on the cold ground for a few minutes after he left, holding my throbbing wrist close to my chest. My brain and body worked overtime to calm myself. I dug my fingers into the dirt, wiggling them. I called upon The Mother Earth Goddess. The moist, crumbly soil wrapped around my fingertips. I pulled on Her solid strength.

"Mother Earth, protect me. Show me what I need to know and do to help Dean. He's clearly not himself. I invoke your strength."

Despite my feelings with Fate right now, I wasn't going to turn my back on the very culture that brought me comfort in my times of need. Dean was physically fighting against himself. I shook my head as I breathed in the smells of nature.

There were a couple of things I knew now: Dean needed help and I had made him more upset by telling him Cade was my soulmate.

Once again, my actions continued to crumble my world around me.

Chapter 29

"Tents go up here. I want strings of lights connecting each of the tents and booths," I told the worker, pointing to where they needed to work. "Each tent gets purple, orange, or black table cloths and one of these pay machines."

I scrolled on my phone, studying the set-up plan that Aaron and I had finalized. I knew it by heart, but it was comforting to quadruple check. Preparations for the festival were coming along, even after my run-in with Dean in the cemetery.

One problem at a time.

I couldn't focus on Dean or Cade, whom I haven't spoken to since the morning of my vision. Today, I had to focus on my family's legacy.

Lydia was off to the side, setting up her menus. Chief Irons was directing his men where to put the EMT station and trash cans. Other townspeople milled around, helping where they could. I looked where Mom and Gram set up the larger main booth. The Wise Whitleys were offering tarot readings and medium readings. Mom turned her head in my direction. Her eyes crinkled at the corners while she frowned. I knew she felt my emotions, but knew better than to confront me again.

"Which booth is ours?" Wilma asked, coming up beside me. Agnes and she each carried boxes full of plants and jewlery made from crystals. I smiled seeing them.

"You're over there next to ours." I peeked into the box. "I just love your jewelry, Agnes."

"I'm glad someone does," she snarked. "Wilma keeps telling me how hideous they are. But they're beautiful compared to her crocheted plant pots."

"I heard that," Wilma sassed back.

"Agnes, you know I have plenty of your jewelry. They'll sell like hotcakes. And, Wilma, plants are just as important in witchcraft as crystals. Shouldn't you both know—"

Tingles erupted along my skin, causing my back to straighten and my words to die on my tongue.

"Here. Let me help with those boxes, ladies," Cade said, stretching his arms out.

Wilma and Agnes melted. Their gazes glossing over at his chivalry.

"Oh, what a gentleman," Agnes cooed, primping her hair and batting her eyelashes.

I cleared my throat, tightening my grip on my phone, causing pain to run up my arm. I winced. "We got it, Cade. Thanks, though."

He took the boxes from their arms as if they weighed nothing. "I'm here to help, Shay. I bet these lovely ladies want my help more than yours." His eyes flicked to me, taking me in from head to toe. I squirmed under his gaze, working to keep my face neutral. I needed to focus.

I nodded.

His smile widened, walking between Wilma and Agnes toward their booth. I breathed out and watched him. The way his jeans fit his hips. The way his biceps tightened as he set the boxes on the table. My heart sped up.

"Setup is going smoothly," Aaron said in my ear. "Ready for tonight?"

I startled, dropping my phone to the ground. "Aaron. You scared me." I bent to pick it up.

"You would've noticed me, but you were a little occupied." His eyes went to Cade before returning to me. His eyebrows high on his forehead.

"He's nice to look at," I admitted. No matter what I struggled with, I would always appreciate Cade's beauty. He was just as mesmorizing on the inside as he was on the outside.

"From what I hear, he's more than that."

Blush heated my cheeks, and I pulled on my sleeves. The motion made my wrist spike with pain. I winced again.

"Are you injured?" he asked, tone serious and brows furrowed.

"I fell in the cemetery this morning," I evaded. "It's no big deal. What did you hear about Cade and I?"

He looked at me for a second, assessing. "He said you guys had an amazing roll in the sheets, then you had a vision, and now you're avoiding him, because you won't tell him about the vision. Can I look at your wrist?"

The blush grew three times on my face. I held my wrist out. Aaron's fingers warmed my skin as he poked and prodded my wrist, making me bend and turn it. I winced when he bent it back.

"He told you about all that?"

Aaron nodded. "Why didn't you tell him about it? You're visions are accurate, babes. I mean, hello,

Jeffrey is amazing. I met him at the park. And he's trained Mr. Bananas so well," he said, his eyes shining.

"I'm happy for you, Aaron. I can't wait to meet him one day."

"I think your wrist is only bruised. Not broken or anything serious. Just take some meds and ice it." Aaron crossed his arms over his chest. "So about your vision?"

"It was just a vision that I don't have time to decipher. There are other things happening in my life right now. Fate didn't need to throw me another curveball," I snapped with more heat than intended.

"I hear you," Aaron said, engulfing me in a soul-soothing hug. "Life is never easy, Shay. As a witch with actual powers, yours is probably harder. Fate showed you something important for a reason. I'm here if you need a soundboard."

"Thanks." All my suppressed emotions pushed against the mental barrier I had built. All the words I wanted to say flooded my mouth. I wanted to spit out the truth, but I couldn't risk the dam breaking.

I had to save my family's store first.

"You need to figure it out, girl. Cade has been so pouty since I arrived and I can deduce it's because of you." Aaron tilted his head dramatically. "And whatever you saw in your vision."

"I can't think about Cade right now. I need to focus on my livelihood not love. Okay?"

"Love?" Aaron's eyes widened.

My face mirrored his. Did I really just say *that* four letter word out loud? Is that what I was feeling stressed about? That my feelings for Cade had wormed their way so far into my being, I couldn't bear the thought of losing him.

"Everything okay over here?" Cade asked as he joined the conversation. Aaron clapped him on the back.

"It's all good, bro. Shay hurt her wrist. So, she's going to need extra tender care." Aaron winked at me before turning away, helping some workers carry a table.

"How did you hurt your wrist?" Cade asked. His gaze swept down my body to my wrist.

"I fell in the cemetery." I peered down at my phone, going through my checklist.

"We haven't talked since yesterday morning," Cade started, dipping his head so we were eye-level. "You're avoiding me."

Yes.

"No, I'm not avoiding you. I'm busy. This is the biggest thing to ever happen to me. I need to make sure everything goes off without a hitch."

I certainly was not about to tell him that Dean cornered me again. He wouldn't understand why I didn't tell him.

"Try again," he said, his voice quiet and sultry.

The energy around us sparked. I rubbed my lips together, trying to ignore the Fate's call. It wanted me to embrace what was standing in front of me, even if he was mad at me for pushing him away. My perfect half.

I shook my head. My heartbeat pounded against my ribs as the world around me spun and blurred together. I needed to stay in control. I couldn't lose my head now. This festival was too important.

"I asked for space, didn't I?" I snapped.

"It's clear you're still bothered. You go to the

cemetery when you need space to think. I only want to help."

"Or is this just because you want to save me? Fix me?"

Cade grimaced.

"I don't want to give you space, Shay. You're hiding something. I know it's big," he said, ignoring my ill-formed attack. He took a step closer, running his hands up my arms, holding me where Dean did. I winced, sucking in a sharp breath. Cade looked at his hands.

"Are you hurt here, too?"

I looked away from him, feeling the emotion clog my throat. I couldn't relive that moment with Dean. I took a couple of deep breaths, savoring Cade's fresh pine sent and the aromas brewing from the festival.

"I'm fine. Okay? Please," I begged. "Let me focus on the festival."

"Trust me, for Christ's sake." I saw Cade's patience dwindle on his face, but stupidly I refused to concede.

"I can't...I have to go check on Harmony and the other booths. People are going to start showing up soon." I rushed into The Witch's Brew booth, collapsing on my elbows on the table.

"Holy shit, Shay," Harmony squealed. "You scared me."

"Sorry," I breathed out, holding my head in my hands. "I needed to escape."

"From Cade? Why? He's staring at you, by the way."

"I know. I can feel his eyes on me."

"That's new." Harmony snorted.

"Well, he's my fucking soulmate so it makes sense that I can feel him," I said under my breath.

"What the fuck?" she yelled. I lifted my head, grabbing her hands and pulling her down toward me.

"Shh."

"Sorry." Her heavily colored eyes were wide. "I didn't know it was a secret. Cade's your soulmate?"

"And I don't know what to do about it."

"Psh. That's easy. Sex him up, girl. Put a ring on it."

"Harmony."

"What?" She shrugged. "I don't see what the problem is. The man of your dreams is your soulmate. That's so much better than always wondering 'what if'."

"Fate decided that, not me."

Harmony pulled her hands from my grip to cup my face. Her eyes held mine. "Shay Moon Whitley. You've always made your own choices. If you don't want to listen to Fate, then don't."

"I thought I was making my own choices by at least entertaining the idea of a relationship with Cade. Now, I feel like it was all a façade orchestrated by the gods and goddesses."

"Isn't that the core belief of most religions? Yours isn't that different."

"You're not getting it," I said, yanking my head away from her hands and letting it drop with a thud to the tabletop.

"Babe, I can't even begin to understand what you're feeling. But having Cade as a soulmate isn't a bad thing. We've all seen what a great guy he is and how he treats you."

Steph Ziders

"Does he only like me because we're soulmates?" I sighed into the table.

"Maybe. You won't know unless you trust him enough to talk to him about it."

Harmony slapped my head. The force pushed my forehead harder into the table. I sat up, rubbing it.

"Stop this dumb pity party. You still hold all the power here. You can decide not to listen to Fate. But I think you're not going to like how you feel when you push him away for good. When has it ever let you down?" I frowned. Harmony flicked my nose. "Now get out of my booth. Your vibe is bringing me down."

"Do you have everything you need?" I asked, trying to get myself back into work-mode.

"Yes, boss. And if I didn't, I'd tell you."

What was next on my list?

****

The sun had set over the water on the coast. The clouds reflected purple, orange, and pink hues across the town square. I leaned against the post of our tent, taking in the scene. There were people everywhere. Locals, tourists, elders, and kids.

Aaron had set up a better social media account for The Wise Whitleys, using it for online orders and advertisements. I was shocked when I saw the number of followers we had.

"All of your adoring fans that have found their soulmates because of you," Aaron said to me. *"They want to share their experiences."*

A young woman with red hair walked across the square in my direction. She had a bright smile on her face as she walked hand in hand with a man. He had a fun-shaped mustache. Familiarity tickled the back of my neck.

"Shay?" the woman questioned when she stopped in front of me. "You probably don't remember me."

"Cynthia. Of course, I remember you." I smiled, and straightened from the pole. "The artist who hates camping." Red tinted her cheeks as she looked up at her partner.

"That's right. I had to come to your festival to support your business. I couldn't let you ladies go out of business. But also to introduce you to my fiancé."

I looked at her fiancé and held out my hand. "Hi, I'm Shay. You must be Henry."

Henry's eyes bugged as he looked from my hand to Cynthia. He shook my hand with a large smile on his face.

"I shouldn't be surprised that you know my name, but I am."

"Well, I did see you in Cynthia's Lovers Reading."

"Yeah." Henry ran a hand over his hair as Cynthia giggled. "I didn't really believe Thia until now," he said, gazing down at her.

"I'm a little sad that you cut the mullet, though," I joked. Henry looked much better without it. They laughed again.

"I made him cut it," Cynthia said. "The mustache looks better without it."

I nodded, laughing along with Cynthia. Cynthia reached out for my hands, gripping them both. Her face grew serious. Our laughing halted.

"I want to thank you. I've never been happier in my life. I'm so lucky to have found Henry."

I squeezed her hands. "It's my pleasure." It was the truth. I've always enjoyed my work and the joy I brought to so many people. It was a balm to my soul.

So, why couldn't I have that same joy?

She let go of my hands. She swung her teary eyes toward Henry and nodded. Henry reached into his back pocket and pulled out a piece of paper. He handed it to me.

"This is for you. For The Wise Whitleys," he said, draping his arm around Cynthia again.

My forehead scrunched as I unfolded the paper. *A check for $5,000.*

"Wh-what?" I croaked, lifting my eyes to them.

"Well, if it wasn't for you, we would have never found each other. I needed to repay you for the happiness that you've given us," Cynthia said. "And the future that we'll have together because of it."

"I-I can't accept this."

"Yes, you can," Cynthia said. Her eyes were bright with joy. "Your store is sacred and needs to keep doing what it's doing. I took what you told me about your vision and painted it. It was an instant masterpiece with a great story to go with it. When I put it up for sale, it sold in a matter of minutes. I knew I had to give you some compensation for the subject matter."

"Cynthia...I don't know what to say." My voice shook. Cynthia and Henry gathered me in their arms as tears slid down my cheeks.

"Don't say anything and just accept it. All of our dreams came true because of you. Now, it's time for your dreams to come true."

The three of us held each other for a few minutes longer. I wiped at the tears and pulled out of their embrace. Henry and Cynthia were teary, too. We laughed again.

"Thank you so much, Cynthia. Henry. Now please, go enjoy the festival," I said. "Before we all start crying again."

Henry kissed Cynthia on her temple, pulling her away.

"Expect a wedding invitation in the mail!" she called out.

I held the check in my hand, smiling. The atmosphere around me tingled. I looked up, finding Cade's eyes on mine from across the square. We held each other's gaze for a few moments. He was becoming as attuned to me as I was to him. I smiled softly. The money that Cynthia and Henry gave us tipped the scales in our favor. Cynthia's words rung in my head: time for my dreams to come true. Was that a life with Cade?

As if I were a siren singing her call, Cade walked toward me. The energy buzzed like a swarm of bees the closer he got. My body hummed and my heart fluttered.

"Shay?" Mom called to me.

I blinked my eyes, breaking the tether that pulled Cade toward me and looking at her.

"Who were those people, honey? I'm feeling flushed from their love for each other." She fanned her face for dramatics. I cleared my throat, turning my back on Cade.

"A former customer and her soulmate." I smiled. "They just gave us a five-thousand dollar check!"

Mom's hand dropped, slapping her leg. Gram whipped her head over toward me.

"What?" they both said, shocked.

I showed them the check and told them about my conversation.

"This is incredible," Mom said, holding the check.

"This, plus the money in our jar. We probably have enough to pay off the bank!"

Gram held her wrinkly hands over her mouth, shoulders shaking.

"I hope those are happy tears, Gram," I said.

She shot her hands in the air and yelled. Her yell brought a hush over the crowd. "WE DID IT, FOLKS! THE WISE WHITLEYS HAS BEEN SAVED!"

Chapter 30

Cheers exploded and echoed throughout the town square. Everyone embraced the closest person to them. Wilma, Agnes, and Gram jumped up and down in a hug circle. I smiled and laughed as I embraced my mom.

"You did it, Moonbeam," she whispered in my ear, between her tears. "You saved the Whitley legacy."

Aaron rushed over, grabbing both my mom and I into a big bear hug.

"We did it, ladies!"

"We couldn't have done it without your help, Aaron," Mom said, smiling wide when Aaron set us back down. He knocked his shoulder into mine.

"I'm glad Shay let me help."

"I know how to ask for help when I really need it," I grumbled with little inflection.

Mom and Aaron gave me a look before laughing.

Movement to the side caught my attention. Chief Irons blushed as he stepped up to my mom. She tucked her hair behind her ear, grinning at Chief Irons. He shuffled on his feet, reaching his arms out. Mom embraced him, her smile not leaving her face. An itch in my mind's eye grabbed my attention. I zeroed in on Chief Irons and Mom. An aqua-blue sparkle with yellow ribbons fired around them like a bubble. My eyes widened in surprise. Their auras matched.

I turned my head, scanning the crowd for Cade.

Despite being in a sticky spot, I needed to celebrate this success with him, too. He had supported me with this idea from start to finish. I found him weaving through the crowd in my direction. A large grin was on his face. He nodded and spoke to people as he made his way through the townspeople.

I took a step in his direction on instinct when a shiver ran down my spine, halting me. I looked up. A dark cloud hung in the sky, standing out from the rest of the cotton-candy backdrop.

A raven streaked across the cloud.

"You know," I said to Mom and Aaron, keeping my eyes on Cade. He saw my expression change and picked up his pace to get to me. "I should get this money into the safe first." I heard the monotone in my voice.

"I can take care of that, honey. Go celebrate," she said, pausing for a split second. "What's wrong?"

I took my eyes off of Cade, seeing the raven fly overhead again. My pulse ticked up. A sudden coldness seeped into my bones.

"I just want to make sure this money is secure. It's our lifeline right now. Then, I'll be able to celebrate."

"You're scared," Mom said in that serious tone. "And lying."

"I'm fine. I'll be right back." I scurried away toward the store after grabbing the money jar and check. The energy shifted as I broke away from the crowd. The hair on the back of my neck stood, sending constant shivers down my spine with each step I took. My breathing increased. I knew I was being followed. I unlocked the front door and slammed it shut behind me.

My heart beat against my chest, feeling like it

would break through.

Calm the fuck down, Shay.

I straightened from the door, flicking the lock and walking into the back room. An eerie quiet pulsed throughout the store. The sounds of the festival sounded miles away.

I crouched down next to the safe, entering its code. When it opened, I placed the money and check inside, shutting the heavy door with a loud thud. I lowered my head, exhaling. Knowing the money was tucked away safe eased some of my fear.

I ran my thumbs across my fingertips. My emotions were all over the place. I kept seeing omens and felt dread. I lifted my head as realization dawned on me. I had a vision of this moment. Something was coming for me.

Scritch, scratch.

"Who's there?" I called out. A furry body lept down from the window, causing me to scream. "Mildred. What the fuck?" I clutched my hand to my chest.

"Shut up, Shay. Something's happening," Mildred said. She slithered her body between me and the backroom door.

"How do you know?"

Thump, thump, thump.

"Footsteps?" I asked in hushed tones.

"I came to warn you. Someone's coming."

As Mildred said those words, the backdoor burst open, crashing loudly into the wall. I screamed, falling back on my ass. A large, looming, dark cloud stood in the doorway.

"Finally, I have you alone!" The voice was

gravelly, low, but familiar. "Or at least somewhat alone." A dirt-stained hand reached out, gripping Mildred by the scruff. She hissed and yowled, showing her teeth.

"Mildred!"

The hand shoved Mildred behind him, tossing her out of the backroom. The door slammed shut at the same moment Mildred landed on her feet in the middle of the store.

"Shay!" She screeched in my head. The tiny backroom filled with the dark smokey figure. My eyes burned and my throat clogged.

"Wh-what do you want?" I asked, scooching back, despite the frozen nature of my limbs.

"You," it growled.

"You can't have me!"

The dark cloud morphed, growing bigger, before dissipating. Dean stood before me, larger than I've ever seen him. His head hung low and his eyes were completely black. His skin was scorched with bits of ash and soot.

"D-Dean?" I asked, looking around for an escape. The window that Mildred jumped through was too high and too small. Dean blocked the door.

It's probably spelled closed anyway.

I was trapped.

"Shay! Don't do anything he says!" Mildred commanded in my head. *"I'll go get help."*

"I told you earlier in the graveyard that I would stop at nothing to have you. It's our destiny," Dean said, stalking toward me. "And sorry, poor child, but Dean isn't here anymore."

I crawled back more, running into shelves. Pain

338

radiated up my spine.

"Harrison."

"She's smart and beautiful. We're going to be a match made in hell." Harrison smiled.

"I told you it was never going to happen," I argued. "Cade's my soulmate. *We're* destined."

Harrison laughed. Inky black spit flew from his mouth as he dropped his head back. "You stupid bitch. You haven't even accepted Cade as your soulmate yet. The bond is not complete. Plenty of space for me."

What is he talking about? I have to accept Cade for the connection to be solidified?

"There will never be you and me," I said, standing on shaky legs and staring him down. "Why can't you accept that?"

"Lucia said the same thing," he growled. "I ended up having her anyway."

Fury ran through my veins, remembering how Harrison took advantage of Lucia. My hands tightened into fists. My nails broke the skin in my palms.

"Lucia showed me how you raped her," I hissed. "You're a diabolical coward."

Harrison laughed again. The erratic cackles sent shivers through my body.

"Yes, I am evil. Probably born that way, but once I found Mammon, the demon of —"

"Greed," I interrupted. All hope vanished. His lips curled.

"See. You are smart. I've been waiting centuries for you."

"What is it you want exactly?" I asked, stalling him to give Mildred enough to find help. Harrison clapped Dean's hands.

"This is the best part. Where the bad guy explains his plan, right? I won't disappoint you. Mammon showed me power I never thought could be possible." He held his hands out, scanning his fingers. "The only thing that was missing from my plan was the love of my life, Lucia Whitley. Mammon promised if I followed his instructions, Lucia would fall at my feet and be mine forever. Where a woman should be. You see, Mammon gave me a tiny taste of his power, but I needed to conceive an heir with another powerful bloodline, the Whitleys, in order to gain his full power."

I bit down on my tongue, holding my words. He raped Lucia to conceive a child for Mammon, the Demon of Greed.

"You didn't succeed, obviously. There's no Fellows in my blood," I said.

"Exactly," Harrison said and lowered his head, narrowing his dark eyes at me. "I misinterpreted Mammon's instructions. Lucia had evaded me somehow, but not before I could spread my seed to another, knowing I wouldn't give up."

I blanched.

"Once my weak body failed, all I had to do was bide my time until someone in the Fellows family showed powers in necromancy. Luckily, Dean and I had a common goal: procure a Whitley. It was as easy as pie once he found the clues I left."

Sweat dripped down my back as Harrison took a daunting step toward me. Darkness and evil swirled around him in a toxic cloud, choking me of my senses. The only thing I heard was him. The only thing I saw was him.

My body quaked as he closed the distance.

Keep him talking.

"Stay away from me. I've fought off Dean once. I'll do it again," I said through clenched teeth. Harrison laughed again. His face much closer to me. I squeezed my eyes tightly as I felt his hot rank breath on my face.

"You are no match for me, little witch."

Icy fingers skimmed down the side of my face. My chest hurt while I tried to suck in a breath of fresh air. All around me was smoke, sulfur, and death. I didn't know what he wanted from me, whether it was a child, my blood, or my life. None of those things I would give willingly.

I gagged on a sob when his hand gripped my neck, squeezing and lifting me from the ground. I felt his other hand drift down my body toward the waistband of my jeans. I felt my mind short-circuiting as it prepared for preservation. I turned my head to the side, opening my eyes for a brief second. Through my watery vision, the stars were starting to peek through the night sky. The moon was full and bright as it rose in the sky.

I zeroed in on the moon. Mother Goddess.

Harrison's hand tightened on my neck, cutting off more blood and oxygen from my head as my jeans were ripped off.

My vision began to tunnel.

Mother Goddess, I invoke thee, I prayed as I drifted further from consciousness. *I call on the Crone, the Maiden, the Mother, the women of the Whitley bloodline to protect me. Save me from this horrible fate and I promise to live my life in your debt. I will do your work. Mother Goddess, I invoke thee. Save me.*

Chapter 31

My eyes shot open as a blinding light lit the backroom. Harrison flew backward into the wall. I slumped to the floor, landing hard on my bare ass.

Harrison growled, covering his face with his hands.

I blinked as a misty shape formed between me and Harrison. Long dark hair blew in a ghostly wind–Lucia.

Another misty figure appeared beside Lucia. Followed by several more. All women dressed in different outfits, indicating different time-periods. I gripped the shelves behind me to stand, but I couldn't muster up enough strength. My legs felt wobbly and my brain was foggy. Lucia turned around. Her blue eyes searing into me.

"Give me your hand," she said, holding out a delicate hand.

The witches in the room held their hands out toward Harrison, keeping him back with light emanating from their opaque bodies.

"Shay Moon Whitley," Lucia said, pulling my attention with her command. "Stand with your ancestors. It's time we sent these demons back to hell."

I swallowed, looking between her, her hand, and Harrison. Mother Goddess heard me. I placed my hand in Lucia's. Her cool skin contrasted against mine. Energy zapped up my arm, giving me strength. She pulled me to stand and we walked hand-in-hand to the front of the semi-cirlce of Whitley witches. I felt a surge of power run through my veins as the witches joined hands.

"Mammon, Demon of Greed, we banish you. May you never return," Lucia said, holding her head high. She looked between the coven of witchy ghosts and nodded.

"Mammon, Demon of Greed, we banish you. May you never return," my ancestors chanted in unison.

Harrison let out a guttural yell. The power of his scream hit us, but we didn't waiver. A dark mist appeared around him.

"Mammon, Demon of Greed, we banish you."

The dark cloud expanded and swirled behind Dean's body. Dean's body crumpled to the ground, separating from Harrison and Mammon. Harrison's clean-cut image melted away, morphing and transforming. A large, red-tinged body filled the space. Char and ash splotched his skin. His fingers were bony with black nails.

"Mammon, Demon of Greed, we banish you."

"YOU CANNOT BANISH ME!" Mammon roared, clutching his head and doubling over in pain. He held steadfast in his stance in the room, growing with each growl. Massive waves of energy slammed into us, forcing us back a few paces. My chest ached from the impact of his power. Some of the chanted diminished.

"Keep chanting, Whitleys," Lucia urged. "We are stronger together! With the blessing of Mother Goddess, Mammon, Demon of Greed, we banish you. Say it with me."

Collectively, we straightened our backs and stood

tall as we repeated her words. Suddenly, a burst of shimmery green mist popped in the room. The green mist grew, transforming into a three women, connected at the waist and beyond beautiful.

Mother Goddess.

My eyes widened, taking in her appearance. She was otherworldly. Warmth encircled my body as Mother Goddess stood between the coven and Mammon. Mother Goddess was a sight to see. The three versions of her, The Maiden, The Mother, and The Crone were beyond beautiful and their magic circled them in an ethereal wind.

"Mammon, Demon of Greed, we banish you," the coven said. Mother Goddess formed her hands together, creating an energy orb. The green orb shot forward, slamming into Mammon.

He yelled in pain, curling into himself. He fell to the floor on his knees in front of us and Mother Goddess. Black soot and sludge escaped his mouth as he yelled. His body cracked and crumbled at disturbing angles.

"Mammon, Demon of Greed, we banish you."

Mammon looked up, staring at Mother Goddess. His red eyes flashed with pain and anger. Mother Goddess snapped her fingers. Mammon poofed out of existence, disappearing from sight. Silence filled the room as the smoke dispersed and the moonlight shone through the tiny window, creating a silvery glow.

Mother Goddess turned toward me. The Crone, The Mother, The Maiden. They were the same woman but at the three most important stages of their life.

"My child," they spoke in unison. "We heard your prayers. You are not in our debt, for you do much good in the world. We urge you to listen to your heart and our guidance. Life is not meant to be alone."

I swallowed and bowed my head. "Thank you, Mother." Tears streamed down my face as I basked in her awesome presence.

Mother Goddess smiled, looking between all the Whitley witches. "My sisters," they said. They morphed into a green mist and dissipated. The Whitley witches misted away, each giving me a smile.

My heart rate slowed, feeling content and triumphant.

Lucia gripped my hand, bringing my attention to her. She cupped my face and smiled. We would forever be kindred spirits. She nodded and disappeared, too.

"Shay!" Cade yelled from the other side of the door while he banged. "Shay! Back away from the door. I'm going to knock it down."

My lip quivered as I scanned where the witches and Mother Goddess stood, where Dean laid, and the door. The adrenaline that coursed through my veins began to wane. The skin around my neck felt raw and welted. Swallowing hurt. Loud thumps sounded against the door, crashing it open after a couple of attempts. Tears continued to roll down my cheeks as Cade, Aaron, and my mother appeared on the other side.

"Shay! Oh my gosh, what happened?" Mom asked, looking down at Dean and at me. Tears formed in her eyes. "Are you okay?"

Cade ripped off his shirt as he stepped over an unconscious Dean. I shivered, realizing I was practically naked from the waist down. Cade pulled his shirt over me, encasing me with warmth and comfort. He pulled me to him and I breathed a sigh of relief.

"Shay," Mom said.

I shook in Cade's arms. He tightened them around me. His fingers dug into my hair, pinning me to his chest. He laid his head on top of mine, his breathing strained.

"Dean...Harrison...Mammon," I tried to say. The words burned in my throat.

"Mammon?" She gasped. "How did you defeat him?"

"I had help," I coughed.

Cade tipped my head back, assessing my neck. He peered over to Aaron, who was checking Dean. Aaron came over and looked at my neck, touching it gently with his big fingers.

"Seems like her larynx and skin on her neck are only bruised. She just needs to rest," he said. He swallowed. His face filled with concern. "Do you need...checked anywhere else?"

Mom gasped again and Cade stiffened.

I shook my head. Harrison wasn't able to get that far.

A collect sigh resounded through the space. Mom came over, cupping my face in her hands.

"I felt your fear and your pain, but I couldn't do anything about it. We were stuck in the town square. A spell was keeping us from getting to you."

"Mammon." I frowned.

"A bright green light pierced through the veil that surrounded the town square, freeing us," she continued. "Poor Mildred was just scratching and scratching at the barrier to no success."

Mildred.

I looked behind all of them out toward the store.

"Your devil-cat is fine," Cade said. "She's being coddled by Dotty, Wilma, and Agnes."

I exhaled. More relief flooded my body. A moan sounded behind us. Dean stirred on the ground. He sat up, lifting a hand to his head.

"What happened?" he asked. His voice was back to normal. He looked like death and was bruised all over. The toll of being possessed was steep. Cade released me so fast, I stumbled backward. He snatched Dean's body up by his shirt.

"Stay the fuck on the ground," Cade growled, raising his white-knuckled fist.

"Cade!" I whisper-yelled.

"Fuck…" Dean said, scanning his surroundings and coming to the realization of what happened. "Do it. Hit me. I deserve it."

Cade's jaw tightened. His arm shook as he fought against his better judgement.

"Aaron. Call the police." Cade threw Dean back on the floor roughly but stepped away from him. "This maniac needs to be locked up for his *repeated* attempts on Shay's life," Cade commanded. Everything about him was stiff and rigid.

"Cade," I squeaked, placing a hand on his shoulder. "No."

"No?" Cade whipped his head toward me. "Why the fuck not, Shay? How many more times are you going to let him push you around? How many more times are you going to side with him? I don't know exactly what happened here, but he's involved. He's gone too far."

I cleared my throat and swallowed.

"I'm not siding with him. There's more to this than

what you see on the outside. Cops won't be able to help him."

Cade gripped his hair before tossing his hands in the air. "Are you kidding me right now?"

I shook my head. Mom stepped up beside me, wrapping an arm around my shoulders. She understood the magnitude of this situation. Dean had been possessed. Did that excuse his actions? No. But, at some point it stopped being Dean and became someone more evil, controlling, and demonic. He needed a Wiccan intervention, which the police wouldn't be able to provide. Our police department was small and they would probably pass this up to the county level. There would be even less Wiccan people there.

"Cade, I know how you're feeling right now," Mom started. "But, maybe this isn't the time to talk about it." Cade puffed out a large breath. He gestured toward me.

"Shay needs to press charges."

Mom opened her mouth to reply. I spoke first, coughing. "That's my choice to make, Cade, and I'm not making it tonight."

Cade fisted his hands again and stormed out of the backroom.

"What do we do with him now?" Aaron asked, looking at Dean.

"Let's take him to the hospital for now, Aaron. I'll speak to Sheriff Probst," Mom said.

Aaron nodded as he tucked Dean under his arm and pulled him up. Dean groaned in pain as he teetered the line of consciousness. Mom turned to me, staring me in the eyes.

"Are you sure you're okay?"

Tears formed in my eyes. I couldn't even begin to sort out all the emotions that I felt. I got to spellcast with Mother Goddess and dead Whitley witches.

"Yeah. I had help from the whole Whitley family tree."

She nodded with a watery smile. "Go home. Get some rest. We'll talk tomorrow." She gathered me in her arms and kissed my forehead. She pulled away and followed Aaron out of the store.

I stepped through the backroom door, finding Cade pacing the store's main room.

"Cade," I whispered.

He stopped and looked at me. "He needs to be in fucking jail, Shay."

I licked my lips. "Dean needs help."

Cade slammed his fist down on a table, shaking the statues and charms that lay on it. I jumped at the sudden noise.

"It's so simple. Do bad things, get punished."

"No, it's not. Not in my world."

"Why not?" He took a step toward me. "Because of you being a witch? That's such bullshit. He tried to rape you. Twice! What if he would have killed you? Would he not have gone to prison then?"

I shook my head, feeling my own anger rise at the same rate as Cade's. I crossed my arms over my chest.

"It didn't get that far. So, there's no point to your 'what ifs'."

Cade pulled at his hair, growling in frustration. "I don't get you. You are taking that dipshit's side. Just like Leyla all over again."

"Do not compare me to Leyla," I said through gritted teeth. "I'm not a Quaint. I'm a witch. We live by different rules."

Cade narrowed his eyes. "Wow. Sticking to your guns, even when you're wrong."

"I'm not wrong."

We stood in The Wise Whitleys staring at each other. The anger in the room was so thick I could barely see straight.

"I'm trying to help you here, Shay." Cade said. His voice barely above a whisper. "I can't keep standing by on the sidelines watching you make the same stupid decisions over and over because you're too stubborn to listen. You don't trust me."

All of the air whooshed out of the room. I heard my heartbeat in my ears, but I didn't know if it was from fury or devastation.

"That's not true," I argued. I did trust him, more than I've trusted anyone else. Didn't I?

"Yes, it is," Cade said with a humorless laugh. "You would have told me how you got hurt. How Dean's actions were getting worse." He paused. Pain etched on his beautiful face. "You would have told me about your visions." I wrapped my arms around myself and hung my head. I rubbed my thumbs along my fingertips, not feeling any calmer. His words hurt.

"My world isn't so black and white, Cade! Being a psychic witch, my world is messy and unpredictable. That's why I try to control most of things around me. I didn't predict this happening with my former best friend. But I'm going to do everything in my power to make sure he gets the help that he needs so he doesn't do it again."

Cade shook his head as he turned his back on me. His shoulders were tense.

"If you can't see that my world is gray, then I don't think whatever we have can work," I said after a few silent minutes. "It's going to be something we constantly argue over. A constant stain on the feelings that I have for you. Are we worth it? Am I even worth it?"

The words tasted like bile on my tongue and my throat felt like sandpaper. If he wasn't willing to bend, then neither was I. This was the perfect prelude to how he would react if I told him we were soulmates.

No matter how much letting him go killed me on the inside, he was right. I didn't trust him. At this point, I'm not even sure I trust myself. To be honest, I had no clue how to handle this situation that was thrust upon me.

Cade's leafy green eyes drifted up and down my body, as if he were committing me to memory. With a sharp inhale, he nodded, turned, and stalked out of the store. The door slammed shut behind him at the same time the door shut on my heart.

Chapter 32

I held Mildred close to my chest as Harmony unlocked our apartment door. The three of us entered in silence. My body fought against all of my movements. Mildred jumped from my arms, but stuck to my side as I shuffled into my bedroom.

"I'm going to get you some water and pain meds," Harmony said.

I sat on my bed. Mildred used her teeth to pull off my shoes and nudged me with her head to lie down. I did.

My bed surrounded me in comfort and warmth. I felt none of it. I was numb. My brain had officially stopped voluntarily functioning. Harmony came back into the room.

"Here. Take these." She placed pills in my hand and a glass of water.

I swallowed them down, wincing at the pain. No crystal was powerful enough for how I felt. Mildred hopped up on my bed, curling around me on the side. Harmony sat down on the edge, pulling one of my blankets up over me. She gripped my hand, toying with my fingers.

"I'm so sorry all of this happened to you, Shay."

I rolled my head to the side to look at her. "It's fine."

"No, it's not. Dean attacked you again and you

broke up with your soulmate."

"It wasn't Dean. It was Harrison and the demon Mammon."

"That's bullshit, Shay, and you know it," Mildred said in my head.

"How is that bullshit, Mildred?"

"Because Dean had to invoke Harrison and open himself up to that type of possession. He's not completely innocent."

"I agree with whatever Mildred's saying," Harmony added. "For the record."

I mulled what Mildred said over in my head. Dean was at fault to a point. But, I doubt he would have wanted it to go as far as it did. Or was I a complete moron?

"What are you going to do about Cade?" Harmony asked.

"Nothing."

Mildred snorted and Harmony shook her head.

"What?" I asked. "He doesn't want to see my side of things. He won't let me handle things. He's a Quaint. He thinks I don't trust him."

"He's your partner, though. He's your soulmate, Shay. Does that not mean anything? Shouldn't his opinion matter?" Harmony said. "And, you don't trust him. If you did, you would have told him about your vision right away."

I swallowed, lifting my eyes to the ceiling.

"You didn't see how he reacted when he heard you scream but couldn't get there to help," Mildred added. I shook my head, feeling tears well up in my eyes. Tonight was hard on him.

"It doesn't matter now, does it, Mildred? We both

decided this wasn't going to work." My voice cracked. A tear slipped out and rolled down the side of my cheek. Harmony leaned down, wrapping her arms around me. Mildred followed suit, tucking her body into my side even more. Sobs racked through my body. I might have defeated Harrison and Mammon but at the cost of my soulmate. What was stopping me from letting him in?

"It's not too late, Shay. To trust him. Tell him everything. Hear him out when you're both in better head spaces," Harmony spoke into my neck.

I shook my head. Harmony rolled over to the other side of me, keeping her arms around me. I don't know how long we laid together in my bed, but we must have fallen asleep because by the time I woke up, it was deep into the night.

Cold. Devoid. Dark. Hopeless.

****

A week had passed since the Cade-ocalypse. Everything around me was colorless and bland. I moved through this past week in slow-motion, barely eating or showering. I stuck my nose in my armpit and sighed in relief. I did shower today, but I know I didn't wash my hair.

I've been keeping myself occupied since the festival. We paid off our store from the bank. The Wise Whitleys was officially ours. The success of the festival had helped our business in store and online tremendously. For the first time in decades, we didn't have to worry about finances. The Wise Whitleys' legacy was secure.

Retelling my coven about the Whitley witches and Mother Goddess was a high note to my week. Gram said that getting that type of help from past witches was extremely rare and I should feel privileged. And I did. Every day, I thanked Mother Goddess and my ancestors. But, the dark cloud that hung over my head dimmed the brightness from that blessing.

The aftermath with Dean was a different story. I still hadn't pressed charges, but he's been in cuffs at the hospital. He had to have emergency surgery and was still dealing with the physical effects of his long-term possession. Sheriff Probst said I had until the end of the week to make a decision.

Mildred and Harmony asked me every day what I was going to do. Each time I said the same thing: Whatever I choose.

I leaned on my elbow at the counter of The Wise Whitleys. The jingling of the curtain to the backroom sounded through the store.

"Let's do some tarot together," Mom said, standing beside me.

"No thanks. I don't really feel like it."

"I wasn't asking," she scolded. She wrapped her arm around me, pulling me into her side. I moved into her embrace effortlessly, laying my head on her shoulder as she wrapped both arms around my body. I breathed in her lavender scent, feeling a calm wash over me.

"I wish there was something more I could do for your emotions, like absorb them," she whispered next to my ear.

"I'm fine, Mom." It was the same lie I've been telling all week. "I made this choice."

She pulled back from the embrace, keeping her hands clutched on my arms. Her face filled with sorrow as her hazel eyes roamed my face. Her long gray hair rested in two braids on her shoulders. Her make-up was sparse but accentuated her natural bohemian beauty. She gave me a sad smile.

"Don't you think your choices should make you happy and not sad?"

"Who says I'm not happy? The festival was a success. Business is good. I'm no longer being targeted by a demon. Those are all good things."

Her eyes squinted as she searched my face.

"Tarot. Now." She grabbed my hand and let me to the palm-reading table. I shuffled behind her.

Mom opened a cabinet tucked away on one of the bookshelves. Her bracelets clanked together like the singing bowls in Yoga. She pulled out a worn velvet bag. One that I had never seen. She set the bag on the table and smoothed out her hands beside it. Something misty swam in her eyes as she looked at the faded mandala stitched into the bag.

"I haven't used this deck since I met your father. This was the deck that your grandmother painted for me when I turned sixteen," she said softly. Mom lifted her head and looked at me. "Tradition, you know."

"Oookay…" I said, watching her closely.

Mom took in a deep breath. Her eyes closed in sync with her breath.

"This deck foretold my future. A different future than this one. I was in love with someone else before your father. He would sit with me while I practiced tarot, letting me use him as a guinea pig." A small trickle of tears dripped down her cheek. She brushed them away before searing me with a determined look.

"One night, I indulged too much of something

herbal and earthly. Your father and I ended up getting pregnant with you. When I told this other man, whom I loved, the pain and betrayal he felt absolutely wrecked me. He loved me, but I hadn't listened to my gift or my skill with tarot. I didn't tell him how I felt and I lost him. Every time we're together, now, I get punished by the pain he still feels." Her breath hitched as she gathered her emotions.

I reached across the table and grabbed her hand. "Is that why you never wanted me to give you a soulmate reading?" She looked up at me with watery eyes.

"Yes. I already know who it is and it's probably too late for me." She covered my hand with both of hers. "But, it's not too late for you. Listen to the Fates. Trust it."

"Fate controls everything in my life," I said, pulling back from her. "I'm trying to hold on to some assemblance of free-will."

"I understand that, Shay. I do. You are allowed to make your own choices. I just don't want you to make the same mistake I did." Mom slid the deck across the table in silence. Her face was hard and unbudging. "Fate wants you to live your best life. You are lucky enough to have a gift that grants that to you."

"Fine," I conceded, slamming my hand over the cards and pulling them out of the bag. They were beautifully painted with a mix of blue shades, but minimal and traditional. Much like my mother. With the cards in my hand, I imagined my energy powering them, like a battery. I shuffled, cut, and set them on the table. Breathing deeply, I turned over the top card.

The Chariot: reversed.

"The Chariot," I read. "Symbolized by a warrior in

his chariot behind black and white sphinxes. Usually, The Chariot indicates triumph in some big achievement. But, it's reversed, telling me that although I am resisting change for a good reason, nothing is actually being imposed on me. I can choose another option. Re-evaluation is needed."

I slumped back in my chair. A whoosh of air left my lips. Mom watched me as I pieced the information together. Fate was once again telling me what I needed to hear. I needed to reflect and re-evaluate my choices.

We sat in silence for a few moments.

"I think you need to ask yourself one important question, Shay Moon."

I crossed my arms in front of my body and ducked my chin down like a deviant child. "And what's that, Mother?"

She stood and came around the table to where I sat. She dropped a kiss on my forehead as she whispered in my ear.

"Is Cade worth trusting as your equal?"

My answer was instantaneous: Yes.

A loud *clunk* fell against the floor near one of the shelves.

"What was that?" my mother questioned, clutching a hand to her chest. Her gaze darted around the space looking for the source of the falling sound. My footsteps clomped on the hardwood floor, walking in the direction of our statues' shelf as if something mystical drew me in their direction. Looking around the shelf, nothing was out of the ordinary, except for the metal figurine that sat on the ground.

"A Triple Goddess statue fell," I said.

I bent down, picking up the figurine. A curvy

outline of a woman was in the middle of the statue with two crescent moons on either side, symbolizing The Maiden, The Mother, and The Crone. Sparks tingled my skin as I focused on The Mother in the middle of the statue. The Mother of The Triple Goddess symbolized responsibility, maturity, nurturing, and fulfillment of life. Memories of seeing the Mother Goddess in real life sprang to my mind.

"Listen," a hushed, ethereal voice whispered in my head.

I gasped. The voice was the same as the Mother Goddess's.

"Trust your gift," the same hushed voice spoke again. *"And your heart."*

My throat constricted. A green glow illuminated from The Mother, causing me to exhale audibly.

As if struck by a bolt of lightning, I quaked. All the signs were there: the tarot, the voices, my visions. I ground my teeth together as I clutched the figurine in my hands, cradling it next to my heart. My heart warmed as I thought about Cade, but my brain fought against it.

It didn't matter that Fate decided Cade was my soulmate. I hadn't yet. We are fundamentally too different. He's too logical. And, I clearly don't trust him. No relationship could last without that solid foundation. I heard what everyone was telling me, but something blocked me from moving forward.

"Can I have this statue?" I asked Mom. Her hazel eyes smiled as she looked at the figurine in my hands.

"Of course you can have it. It's clear you have a connection to it."

I walked over to the counter, setting the statue

down. My eyes flicked over to the backroom. The door was removed and my mother put up a curtain of iridescent blue beads.

Memories of that night flooded my brain. Cade's reactions were the clearest. The hurt, pain, and relief that flashed on his face. My throat tightened. I promised myself to be done crying, but my body had other plans.

I felt the same things he did. My lack of care in my appearance and short fuse was evidence of that. I couldn't go back on my decision, could I? Would he even be willing to accept anything I said?

I rolled my neck, feeling the tension. My body has been tense all week.

"You're coming over for the New Moon Ritual tonight, right?" Mom asked, breaking my thoughts.

"Yup. Mildred and I will be there."

"Good," she said, smiling. "It'll be good to set your intentions for the month. Clear slate and all that."

I nodded, looking back down at the Mother Goddess statue.

Clear slate meant clear thinking.

Chapter 33

The night sky was dark and misty. The new moon was just a shadow, reflecting zero light onto the world around it, kind of how I felt. The air had finally turned from crisp to chilly in a matter of nights. The Winter Yule approached quickly as the trees were fully bare.

"Can you walk faster? I'm freezing," Mildred snarked.

"I'm sorry, the sky and stars are just so beautiful. We're almost there. And you have fur. If anyone's cold, it's me."

Mildred snorted from her carrier that was strapped across my body.

I have been on a wash, rinse, repeat cycle as I moved through my depressing life. I still didn't know what I wanted to do about Dean and just thinking about Cade brought tears to my eyes. Mildred had to convince me to leave my bed and shed my dirty pajamas, promising to behave for a whole week. She does not grovel or negotiate.

After a few short minutes of listening to Mildred's complaining, my mother's house came into view. The Cape-Cod style house had been in the Whitley family for as long as I could remember. All the women in my family grew up in this house and passed it down through the generations. One day it would be mine, too.

I looked up at the house, a smile forming on my

face. I breathed in deeply as I let the familiarity and comfort fill my warring brain. My mother kept up with its appearance over the years, keeping the old-time original feel. The only thing that clearly wasn't from colonial times, were the colors she had painted it.

Mom was a Pisces, a water sign. The front door was painted bright aqua color, the perfect mix of blue and green, symbolizing healing and emotional clarity. The porch was cluttered with typical Wiccan charms, hanging baskets with assorted herbs for spells, and gaudy wicker furniture that my grandmother used to spy on the neighbors.

I climbed the steps of my family's house, seeing moving shadows in the front windows. It appeared we were the last to arrive. I opened the door, feeling the rush of warm air cocoon my body. Mildred pawed at the mesh of her carrier.

"I smell Gram's special kitty food. Let me out."

I closed the door behind me, toed off my shoes, and bent down to unzip Mildred's bag. She bounded out, running straight for the kitchen. Mildred was motivated by two things: food and men. Since Cade wasn't coming around anymore, she had been beyond unbearable and getting a little fatter.

Though, I did put an extra lock on the windows to stop her from visiting him at night. I wasn't in the right mind to see him during the day, let alone if he came to drop her off in the middle of the night.

"Shay? Is that you?" Mom asked from the side parlor, even though she already knew.

"Yeah," I called, as if she didn't know it was me. I hung up my knit poncho on the coat rack and shuffled into the side parlor.

"You look like shit," Harmony commented as she wrapped her arms around me from behind.

"Thanks a bunch, bestie," I deadpanned. She took a step back, giving me a snarky smile.

"That's what best friends are for. Laying it all out on the line."

I stared blankly at her.

"Everything's going to work out, girl." Her face softened.

"Doubtful. I've made my bed, now I have to lie in it."

She ticked her head back and forth as she grabbed onto my hand. I was tired of having this conversation with everyone since I pulled the cord on Cade and my relationship.

"Come on, you stubborn ass-witch, let's set our monthly intentions," Harmony said.

"You're not even a witch, Harm."

She led me forward toward the protective circle that Agnes and Wilma were setting up with crystals and plants.

"Now, you're just being mean," she teased. "This is the first one I've had off in a few months."

My lips tipped up in a smile that felt foreign to my facial muscles. "I'm glad you were able to be here. This one feels more important than the others."

Harmony's black lips spread wide on her face. "I'm always going to be here for you, babes. Even when I move out."

"You're moving out!?"

Harmony nodded. Her smile grew. "I think Brad and I are going to move in together. But nothing is set in stone. I just wanted to test the waters with you, you know?"

"I think that's great, Harmony. You and Brad clearly have a connection. You shouldn't let that slip through your fingers."

Harmony's brown eyes bounced between my blue ones. She raised an eyebrow, sending me a silent message. I swallowed, choosing to ignore her insinuations.

I pulled her along with me as we passed through the sitting room and into the side parlor. This was one of my favorite spaces in all of the house. It had large windows around the room and a few Wiccan-themed stained-glass skylights. The space was covered with plants, candles, and crystals. It had a calming energy about it.

I breathed in the parlor's energy, feeling the tickling sensation across my skin. We didn't have an altar, per se, but this was where we did our coven gatherings because of the closeness to nature.

"Why are you using the Blue Kyanite crystals, Agnes? We're in the Sagitarrius New Moon, you should be using Black Obsidian," Wilma complained as she shook her tiny brass watering can at Agnes.

"Who's the crystal witch here?" Agnes shot back, propping her hand on her hip and cradling the shiny blue crystals in the other.

"We all use crystals," Wilma said with a roll of her eyes. She pointed with her watering can again. "Those aren't in a pentagram."

"Oh my Goddess, leave me alone! After how many years of New Moon rituals? Don't you think I know what I'm doing?"

"Why *are* you using Blue Kyanite?" Harmony

asked in a soft voice, standing next to Agnes.

"Oh, not you, too." Agnes narrowed her eyes at Harmony. Harmony took a step back with her hands up.

"I'm actually curious."

Agnes blew out a calming breath, looking in my direction. She pointed her hand at me. Harmony looked my way. I flopped down in a chair, resting my head in my hand.

"It's for me," I said. "Blue Kyanite is used for emotional and mental healing. Apparently, this New Moon Ritual is going to be focused on me." I shook my fists in the air in a very lackluster cheer. Gram and Mom came into the room.

"All right, witches, let's get started. The New Moon is high in the sky," Mom announced. She walked further into the room, giving me a kiss on my head, and taking her point at the top of the pentagram. Her white dress floated around her like clouds. Dotty hobbled over to me in her blue tracksuit, blue nails, and blue lipstick. She grabbed onto my hands and pulled me to standing.

"Let's go, missy. You've got some healing to do and we're here to help you," she whispered.

I held onto Gram's hand and stood next to her in our pentagram shape. Wilma and Agnes still bickered in their spots while Harmony watched with a smile on her face. My mother cleared her throat, bringing everyone's attention to her.

"Let's open the circle. Everyone, close your eyes and breathe in deeply. 'May the Circle be open.'"

"May the Circle be open," we chanted together as one voice.

I breathed in deeply. Cinnamon, passionflower, and

myrrh wafted in my nose. The heady, warm, spicy scents helped me focus on my New Moon intentions.

"We're all gathered here tonight to set our intentions for the month. In your head, state your intention for the month. May it be for yourself or someone else, be truthful," Mom said in an authoritative voice.

I rolled my shoulders down my back and widened my stance into something more comfortable. I let my eyelids drop closed.

"I want to heal and find confidence in my decisions," I spoke into my mind.

It was the truth. I wanted my heart to heal its gaping wound from falling for Cade. No matter how hard I tried to push him away in the beginning, he wormed his way in. Images of us sprung in my mind. The smile on his face that showed his dimples when he looked at me would be a permanent painting in my mind. All the times he came to my rescue, whether I needed him or not, were memories I would cherish.

Even our amazing sexual attraction would be difficult to duplicate with anyone else. Cade was my soulmate after all. He was my perfect half. The light to my darkness.

I frowned.

I felt incomplete without Cade. Everything around me was dulled, gray, and uninspiring. But, something still held me back from moving forward. Internally, I rolled my eyes at myself. I was a walking cliché right now in the middle of the New Moon Ritual.

A chime sounded throughout the parlor as my mother brought everyone's attention back to the ritual. I opened my eyes, finding several pairs on me. I blinked my eyes a few times, taken aback by everyone's warm smiles. My heart swelled as I concluded that everyone had set their intentions for me. I hung my head, playing with the ends of my blonde ponytail.

"Sisters," my mother started after a few seconds, "lift your arms in the air and feel the energy of Mother Earth and Lady Luna swirl within you, granting your intentions. Smell the cinnamon for harmonious relationships, myrrh for healing, and passionflower for calmness. Aids for giving you a peaceful month."

I raised my arms in the air, feeling the energy of the coven wrapping itself around me in a warm security blanket. After a few more chants and a song, we closed the circle. While my coven moved to the kitchen for tea and other drinks, I escaped the attention and headed upstairs.

My feet moved on their own accord as I walked down the familiar hallway to the last door on the right. The door to my childhood room stood before me. Taking a deep breath, I pushed open the door. The door jamb squealed from years of being unused. A puff of dust wafted up in the air as I stepped through the threshold.

I flicked the light on, immediately being transported to a younger, easier time of my life. The room's walls were a faded green, with wrinkled band posters and strings of star-shaped lights.

My bed sat in the same spot with its leafy comforter. I laughed. I was obsessed with nature when I was younger and even more so when I turned sixteen. There were leaf rubbings and earthy paintings strewn around the room.

I walked over to my desk. Several lists and notes

were still pinned to the corkboard. My old aspirations and goals. I ran a finger around one of them, before plucking it off the board. In scratchy but flourishing handwriting, a younger me wrote: find my soulmate.

The paper shook in my fingers as I sat down on my bed. How could I forget that one of my goals was to find my own soulmate?

A tiny drop of water fell onto the note. I had found him and pushed him away like a stubborn asshole. My chin quivered as I struggled to breathe and control the tears welling in my eyes.

What had I done? Why couldn't I trust Cade? He was the key to my eternal happiness and I chose Dean over him. I made a horrible, horrible mistake.

"I'm such an idiot," I said out loud.

A chilly blast of air swirled around me, flickering the note in my hand and bringing goosebumps on my skin. I lifted my head, looking around my room. Papers and book pages fluttered in the breeze.

"You aren't an idiot," Gram said, appearing in the doorway. I whipped my head to the side.

"Gram, you scared the shit out of me," I told her, swiping away my tears.

Gram walked further into the room and sat beside me on the bed. "I'm not Gram," she said. Her wrinkled face turned toward mine.

My eyes widened. She had a faraway look in her eyes. She was channeling someone from the other side. Gram's face smiled, but it looked oddly familiar from her normal grin.

"Lucia? Why are you speaking through Gram instead of appearing?"

"Because I can do more this way."

"At the store, you held my hand and performed a spell."

Gram reached out and gripped my hand. Tingles of energy singed my fingertips.

"I had the power of the entire Whitley bloodline and of Mother Goddess. There are limitations. Now, stop with the questions and listen."

I gulped and looked down at our joined hands.

"I don't have a lot of time," she started. "Your grandmother isn't as strong as she used to be."

"You could have channeled through her."

Gram shook her head. "This is about *our* connection, Shay. You and me."

I nodded, turning my body to give Lucia my full attention. Despite it being Gram sitting beside me, Lucia's spirit was shining through her eyes.

"I made a mistake a long time ago and it's haunted me ever since," she said. She looked down at our joined hands. "I was the one who made the curse, not Harrison."

"Wh-what?" My eyes widened while staring at her.

"Yes. It was me. After his attack, instead of turning him in, I chose to create a spell that would protect the women of the Whitley bloodline. I knew Harrison was after our power, not so much me." My body tensed.

"You're the reason why our legacy weakens, the store included, unless there's a man in our lives." I felt the fury behind my words. If it wasn't for her stupid curse then...

"It was a mistake," she repeated with a stern voice. "I tried to do a protection spell, but I did it wrong and ended up cursing the family. I thought what I did was best for our family and its future witches. Things were very different back then. Women were seen as property. Something to be owned. And I wanted to make sure that no one else in our family *ever* experienced what I went through. That no one could get close enough to take our power."

I felt the determination in her voice as I processed her words. I shuddered, remembering the vision she showed me with Harrison. The anger I felt in my body cooled. She was desperate.

"But I made another mistake," Lucia said.

"Oh, there's more?" I deadpanned.

"I made the wrong choice by not holding Harrison responsible for what he did." She lowered her head again. "I was too afraid of him. Turning him over to the police would have fueled his need for revenge even more. He was too powerful and too influential in our town. I convinced myself he wouldn't get punished anyway. It was a mistake. Because I didn't turn him in, he got to run free, planting his evil seed in another woman. Giving his bloodline life."

"He never tried to go after you again?"

She shook her head as she lifted her eyes to mine. "I got married right away to another powerful man who had higher connections that Harrison did. My darling husband was able to provide the protection I needed to feel safe again physically. The curse kept him away, too."

I breathed out, absorbing her story.

"Why are you telling me all this? Harrison and Mammon are defeated."

Lucia cupped my face. Her eyes full of concern, love, and affection.

"You and I are connected in more ways than one,

Shay. We share the same gift, the same determination, and the same stubbornness. It's how I was able to communicate with you. I see you following the same path I did."

"I think some things are a little different for me."

"True, although, you aren't listening to the signs that are around you. Are you certain you've made the right choice of not holding Dean responsible for his actions? By not trusting your soulmate?"

"People deserve a second chance. And Cade..." I choked on his name before continuing. "He doesn't understand our world."

"Child, Dean's had more than two chances to do right. Instead, he opened himself up to demon possession the same way Harrison did. As far as Cade, he's proven that he's willing to listen if only you let him."

My lips curled into a frown as I got lost in thought.

"You're a very intelligent woman," she continued. "I believe you can find a solution that satisfies both you and your soulmate–if that's what you want."

My chin quivered as I held back tears. I wanted Cade, more than anything. I hoped it wasn't too late.

"My darling sister witch," Lucia said, gaining my attention again. "You are blessed with an amazing heart and brain. Use them together. Listen to them. There is much happiness in your future, if only you accept it."

My voice caught in my throat as spoke, "Thank you. For everything, Lucia."

"There's one more thing you need to know."

My shoulders slumped, slanting my head. "There's more?"

"It wasn't until years later that I realized in order

for the curse to be broken, a Whitley witch needed their soulmate."

What. The. Fuck?

"All you have to do is accept them."

I blinked at her, stunned by her words. With a smile, she brought my hands to her lips, kissing them.

"I'll always look out for the Whitley witches. We're family. Farewell, my child. My sister."

Gram's head dropped and her gripped loosened on my hands. After a few beats, Gram lifted her head, looking around.

"Oh, my dear, Lucia finally channeled through me. I knew I hadn't lost my touch," she cackled. "Did you hear the things that you needed to hear?"

"Yes. Did you hear them, too?"

"I'm never too far from the surface when I channel a spirit that deeply. I heard. Are you mad at her for creating the curse?"

"No, I don't think so. She was just trying to protect us. Protect herself. I get her motivations."

Gram nodded, patting the tops of my hands. Lucia was trying to protect us in her own way. She admitted it was wrong. It would have been easier to just turn Harrison over to the authorities. My eyes flicked to the door before returning to Gram. I knew what I had to do. I stood from the bed, moving to the door.

"Will you fill everyone in on what Lucia said?" I asked. She nodded.

"It's about damn time, Shay." Her blue lips smiled.

Chapter 34

I was a woman on a mission.

Tiny dots of snowflakes fell from the sky and my sneakers crunched along the sidewalk. It was deathly dark outside, thanks to the changing seasons. I didn't care. I needed to find Cade. I was ready to tell him my biggest secret.

The snow added to the refreshing effects of the New Moon as it added a clean layer of white dust on top of the rotting leaves, hiding the decay. Away with the old and in with the new.

I pulled my phone from my back pocket. My fingers protested against the falling temperatures. I opened the message thread with Cade.

Shay:—Hi. I need to talk to you. Are you working or at home?—

Whether he was at work or at home, I hurried to my apartment to take a real shower. After slipping on the slick sidewalks a few times and rushing up my apartment steps, I flung myself into the bathroom, and took the fastest shower of my life.

For the first time in a week, my clean wavy hair fell in long tendrils down my back and matched the perfection of my minimal make-up.

My heart beat against my chest as I checked my phone. There were still no responses from Cade. I rushed through the apartment and shoved my feet back into boots. I was going to find him, listing the places he could be in my mind. My first stop: the fire station.

I flung the door open and screeched in surprise.

Cade.

My eyes soaked him up. Dark circles were under his eyes, his hair was messy, and still looked beautiful. His green eyes burned into mine.

"I was coming to find you," I said when I finally found my voice. "You didn't respond."

"Found me." He licked his lips.

"Do you want to come in? I need to talk to you."

He nodded, stepping through the threshold. I was instantly warmed by his body heat as he walked past me. He was toeing off his shoes when I shut the door. That was a good sign.

Silence echoed throughout my apartment as we stood in the living room. There was so much I wanted to tell him, but I didn't know where to start. I was so focused on finding him that I didn't even practice a speech, like I normally would've.

Now that he stood in my apartment, I had forgotten what I wanted to tell him.

"You look like crap," I said instead.

"Thanks for your honesty, but the past week has been pretty rough."

"Same."

"You still look gorgeous."

Heat bloomed on my cheeks as I pulled on the sleeves of my faded purple hoodie.

"Cade."

"Shay."

We said at the same time.

"Wow, what a clićhe," I said.

"We're just a regular rom-com movie," Cade added with a laugh.

"I want to go first," I said, gesturing to the couch. We sat down, facing each other. "I'm sorry for not hearing your opinion."

Cade opened his mouth to respond, but I held up a hand, stopping him.

"I've decided what I wanted to do with Dean."

"Okay, what's that?"

"I'm going to press charges."

Cade's head ticked back.

"That's not all," I said. "The coven is going to bind his powers until he learns reconciliation. My mom spoke with Sheriff Probst and they were already planning on keeping him in a minimum security facility with mental health practitioners. So, he'll be able to rehabilitate successfully. He needs to be held responsible for attacking and drugging me, but he needs Wiccan help, too. He was possessed, after all."

Cade blew a breath out from his lips as he leaned back. He toyed with his fingers as he thought.

"What made you change your mind?"

I smiled. "You...and a ghost."

"A ghost?"

"One of my ancestors, Lucia, has been kind of like a guardian angel these past few months. She helped me see some things more clearly." I filled him in on Lucia's visit through Gram. Cade straightened, gathering my hand in his. Instant sparks zapped up my arm, settling comfortably in my body.

"I thought about what you said about your world not being black and white," he said. "And honestly, I don't care if you press charges on Dean or not. I realized that *my* world is much more colorful with you in it. I don't care that you're a witch or always smell like fresh herbs. Or that your apartment is decorated like a Halloween store and you're cat is strangely human. I was wrong for asserting my less-informed opinion on you."

My chin quivered and tears welled in my eyes. Not from sadness this time. Cade's face softened as he cupped my face. His thumb swiped under my eye, wiping away a tear.

"A tiny part of me is happy that you're pressing charges, though."

"I didn't want to make the same mistakes Lucia made," I swallowed. "I want to trust you. You've proven to me that you are more than a Quaint."

"Are you going to start sharing more?"

I fidgeted with the sleeves of my shirt. There was one more thing he needed to know.

"Um, yeah. There is something else you need to know." Cade draped an arm around me and pulled me to him. This final secret had been haunting me, but being cradled by him soothed my nerves.

"Is it about your vision you had after we had sex?" he asked.

"Yeah…"

"Ready whenever you are, baby. You can tell me if you want. I get that there are a lot of things I don't understand about witchcraft, but I'm not letting you push me away again."

I took in a deep breath. I don't want any secrets between us. If I was going to share my world with him, I needed to share it one hundred percent.

"So, my vision that morning was of my soulmate."

"Okay…," he said, keeping his eyes on me.

"It's you…" I confessed. My voice was barely above a whisper. "You are my soulmate, Cade Thompson."

Chapter 35

Cade blinked. His chest rose and fell a few times. He pinned me motionless in his stare. His silence hung in the air like a thick uncomfortable wool blanket.

"What if I don't believe in soulmates?" he asked.

And there it was. The real moment of truth. Surprisingly, I felt calm inside. I had admitted what I wanted to him, but more importantly, to myself.

"Then you don't have to be with me. I'm not going to corner you into a relationship." The corners of his mouth lifted. "I accept you as my soulmate."

"How do you know we're soulmates?" he asked. His fingers drew lazy circles on my shoulder. His eyes tracked mine as he searched my face. Heat singed my cheeks and neck.

"It was the most intense vision I've ever had. Snippets of memories of the two of us. In my vision, we had matching auras of green and gray. No two auras match and dance in tandem except for soulmates."

Cade ran a hand through his hair. "Why didn't you tell me?"

I sighed, resting my head back on his arm. "I was scared. I didn't want you to be in a relationship with me because Fate said it. I didn't trust you or the Fates; and it was a mistake. I realized that no matter our differences or how annoying your hero-complex is, my gray world was just gray. My life is just better with you in it."

Cade smiled. His strong fingers gripped my chin. He pulled my face toward his. I let him. His lips touched mine and light exploded behind my eyes. I melted into our kiss as all the pieces of our puzzle were finally fitting together. When we were breathless, I pulled away and cleared my throat.

"There's one more secret I need to tell you."

Cade's eyes widened. "There's more? What's bigger than us being soulmates?"

I gave him a sheepish smile. "Only if you want to know more, I guess."

"Lay it on me."

I swallowed roughly and took a deep breath through my nose. I held his eyes with mine. "I've never said this to anyone, but I think—"

"I love you, too, weirdo," Cade cut me off, finishing my sentence.

I scoffed as he took the words right out of my mouth. I straightened from the couch, slapping him on his chest. "Cade!"

He laughed. He gripped my hips and put me on his lap.

He stared at me and tucked a piece of hair behind my ear, ignoring my protests. I leaned into his touch.

"I knew you were the woman for me when you gave me your sass on the side of the street," he said. "There was something intoxicating about your presence. I couldn't stay away. Like magnets." He smiled, keeping my hair between his fingers. "Then you told me you were a witch. And meant it. My whole world shifted. I didn't believe in any of that stuff. Logically, you were either fucking crazy or telling the truth."

I frowned.

"But, I saw how you were with the townspeople, loyal and kind to a fault. I saw how you worked your ass off, giving to others without complaints. How motivated you were to save your store. How you handled Dean and gave Aaron hope. At some point, the fact that you identified as a witch didn't matter anymore. You were just an amazing woman with a little added mystery. I'm fucking over the moon that we're soulmates. That's my secret."

I choked out a laugh through the swelling emotion in my throat. His eyes held mine in a heated stare.

"I fell in love with you long before your vision. And I have no way of Fate telling me that."

Tears fell down my cheek. Cade caught them with his thumbs.

"I fell in love with you, too, despite my stubbornness," I confessed in a whisper.

Cade pulled me down to him. His lips found mine in a tender kiss. I poured all the love I felt for him into that kiss. My hands gripped his hair, pulling him even closer. Heat seared my skin as the kiss turned desperate. Any fear or anxiety I felt about what the future held slipped away as we moved our lips and bodies against each other.

The air around us swirled as if someone blew a fan on us. My hair tickled my face. I pulled back from Cade, looking around the room for the source of the air.

My mind's eyes sparked as a bright, shimmering light glowed around us.

Cade peered up at me, questioning.

"Where is that green and silver light coming

from?" He asked.

"Those are our auras shining." My hands flew to my mouth as I gaped at Cade. "You can see our auras?" I asked, stunned.

Cade looked around. "Huh...yeah. I guess so. Am I becoming a witch by association?"

I laughed at his genuine excitement. I had no idea what him seeing our auras meant. After a few seconds, the greenish gray shimmer faded away, but the sparking electricity of our connection still tingled.

"Well, I guess I need to get used to weird stuff happening more often now."

"You will."

"Joy," he teased. "Are we officially a couple now?"

"Only if you want to be."

Cade wrapped his arms around me and stretched his face forward to kiss me on the nose.

"I want nothing more. Except maybe to hear more about this curse business and Dean being possessed."

"We've got time," I teased as I got off his lap, sitting under his arm on the couch again.

Cade's chest rose and fell at a steady pace. My eyes drifted closed. Although I was a witch who had premonitions, I had no idea what the future held. At this moment, this was where I wanted to be. My heart felt full. Its fortress was now in ruins. A smile on my face grew as I snuggled closer to Cade.

"I love you, Shay," Cade whispered. His voice was steady.

"I love you, too...soulmate."

"Life will never be a dull moment with you and Mildred, will it?" He gave me a cheeky grin, showcasing his dimples. I hit his chest, rising up.

"Oh, my Goddess! Mildred is going to be so excited."

"Why?"

"She's in love with you, too. And will be so happy to have you around more."

"How do you know that?" he asked, stroking my hair with his hand.

"I forgot about another secret. Mildred is my familiar and can speak to me in my mind."

Silence stretched across the apartment.

"I'm not even going to touch that one right now."

I snorted a small laugh. "Welcome to my witchy world, Cade."

A word about the author...

Steph Ziders has been dreaming up stories for a long time. She graduated from West Virginia University with a Master's in Elementary and Early Childhood Education. After teaching for 11 years, she found a new way to share her stories by writing them. Steph lives in New York with her husband and three children. When she isn't writing, you can find her playing video games, binge-watching, and "out-coloring" her children.

http://stephzidersbooks.com

Thank you for purchasing
this publication of The Wild Rose Press, Inc.

For questions or more information
contact us at
info@thewildrosepress.com.

The Wild Rose Press, Inc.
www.thewildrosepress.com